SWALLOWING the SUN

Sally Bennett Boyington

Tales of the Watermasters
Volume 1

Wordsmith Pages

Published by Wordsmith Pages
Edited by Nancy Basmajian
Cover design by Kara Hudgens Photography Co.
Original cover art © Kara Hudgens Photography Co.,
used under exclusive license

ISBN: 978-1-951303-02-0 first paperback edition

⋀

For more information about the Hohokam culture on which this book is based, go to www.wordsmithpages.com. Walk with the Watermasters!

To

Matt, for his steadfast support and encouragement
Marcia, my dear friend, who didn't get to read this version
and my mother, on her last adventure

Also by Author

Homegrown Muse
(as Sally P. Bennett)

Coming Soon:
Rainbow Knife
Blows a Bitter Wind
(#2 and #3 of Tales of the Watermasters)

Short Fiction:
The Witch Ho'ok
The Making of the Ta'atchul

Find out more at www.wordsmithpages.com

Contents

Prologue   1
Starflower   5
Rush   61
Deerchaser   119
Spadefoot   173
Voices   225
Epilogue   287

Glossary   298
Author's Note   302
Acknowledgments   304
About the Author 305

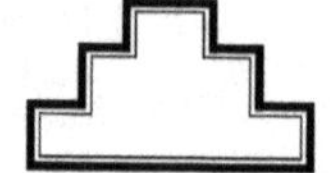

Prologue

Swift come the clouds to the Rainsinger's call as the spadefoots start their singing.
At the rim of the world the storm awaits, with thunder and lightning beginning.

—FROM THE SONG MAGIC OF THE STORMBRINGERS

The woman's cries trailed off into a moan, then died away into nothing.

The pale-haired man who paced to and fro outside the birthing hut paid little heed. Her wails had risen and fallen too many times for him to believe this was truly the end.

In the heat-baked courtyard, the rasping of the kuhtpul—insect harbinger of the summer storms—replaced her cries. The man halted and lifted his painted face toward the sky. He sniffed the breeze, which bore the scent of shegoi leaves, fresh and sharp like rain. His gaze skimmed past the rounded roof of the stick-and-mud hut, past the plastered adobe wall that enclosed the Smokemothers' compound in which the birthing hut and courtyard lay, past the priests' temple that stood taller than the distant mountains, and up to the stormclouds sweeping toward him across the desert valley.

A movement at the low entrance to the birthing hut caught his attention. The gray-tinged braids of a woman emerged first, then the rest of her, stooped over. The man could not see what she carried. Slowly, slowly she straightened, one hand at the small of her back. In the crook of her other arm, she held a mewling bundle.

"Is it a boy?" the man demanded.

Her head jerked up and she frowned. In the deep furrows beside her mouth, her coppery skin was as dark as mesquite sap.

The man moved forward to take the babe from her, but she blocked him with an upraised hand, wet with blood. He averted his rain-colored eyes from the sight and stared at the newborn in its wrappings.

Her wrinkled lips quirked in a contemptuous half smile. She challenged him: "You dare speak so, to me?" Each word, slow and gravelly, puffed out tinged with tobacco. Each phrase required its own breath.

"*Is* it a boy . . . ?" He paused a little too long before adding, ". . . Revered Grandmother?"

Though not much older than he, she was one of the four high priestesses of Mother Ge. Even those such as himself, a priest of the temple who served the Ta'atchul rather than the goddess, could not leave off the required words of respect.

Her dark eyes shifted from him to the swaddled infant, then back. "You have no claim on this child. No right to be here making demands. Go back to your stolen rituals and leave the business of children to us women."

"That child is mine."

"This child," she said, lifting the bundle, "as with all the children born to Mother Ge's maidens, belongs to the village."

"He belongs to me. The moisture of my body made him."

"So *you* say."

"Unless a man is no longer needed to get a woman with child," the priest snarled, "I *am* the father of this one. For I am the only Stormbringer who bedded this one's mother. And she vowed to you, when she entered the goddess's service, that she lay with no man before me, did she not?"

The priestess made no reply, merely lifted one eyebrow. Flames tattooed above it disappeared into the wrinkles on her forehead.

For the third time he asked, "Is it a boy? Do not lie. Those for whom I speak are more powerful than any half-forgotten goddess. If you cross me, the sky shall rain down fire and death upon you and yours—"

"Threats, is it?" She uttered a bark of laughter. "Morning Green, you cannot be such a fool as to think any man can control such magic. Your kind may praise yourselves for calling the rains, but in truth they come at the bidding of she whom I serve. She has opened the belly of the clouds since time out of mind, long before you priests brought your blasphemous ways to the valley."

"Yet it was *we,* not your goddess, who ended the Long Thirst and brought back the rains."

She fixed him with a level stare and warned, "You play with forces you do not understand. Persist, and Mother Ge will destroy you."

He shook his head. "If what you held was a girl, you would simply tell me. Your silence reveals this is a son. *My* son. The one whose coming has been so long foretold: son of outlander and old blood."

"The one of prophecy, you think? Barely born, and already you would inflict greatness on him," she muttered. "Step aside, priest, if you want this child to be welcomed into the village. The birth-blessing must be spoken lest he be cursed . . . and where will your grand plans be then?"

Morning Green scowled but made no protest.

She turned her back on him, then peeled the cloth away from one end of the bundle to reveal a purplish, lumpy face.

She held out the newborn to the east, where swollen, fast-moving clouds blocked the sun. "O giver of life," she intoned, "send now the sun to light this heart with love." She turned to the south. "O bringer of water, send now the fog to fill this blood with strength." Thunder grumbled, long and loud, drowning out the next words of the birth-blessing.

Seven times she offered the baby to the world: to the four directions, to the sky, to the ground, and to the center where she stood. Seven was the number favored by Mother Ge, and her people had long arranged their lives by it.

The air chilled as rain began to fall. A breeze scented with shegoi and saltbush dispersed the odor of tobacco lingering around the priestess. Fat drops breaking on the newborn's face made him howl, but a flash of lightning through the growing darkness silenced him for a few breaths. Then he renewed his squalling, stronger, with more determination.

Again Morning Green stepped forward and reached for the baby he claimed as his son. The priestess warded him off with an outstretched arm.

"He is *mine!*" the priest snapped.

Through long days of song and prayers to the Ta'atchul, Morning Green and his fellow Stormbringers had bent the sky to their will. They had barely completed the midsummer liturgy when word came to him about the impending birth.

Immediately he had set aside his ceremonial robes and trappings: the brilliantly hued macaw-feather headdress, the netted tunic strung with white shell beads, the ocelot-skin apron, the spiral-painted staff to pull down the clouds, the double rattle that coaxed the rain into existence. Even after stripping off the regalia, standing there in a simple white shirt and turquoise-dyed kilt, the priest was a fearsome sight. Black stripes wound around his pale arms, and the top half of his face bore a stairstepped cloud-mountain in black paint, with streaks of gray cascading down white cheeks.

But he and the priestess had known each other since his entrance into the valley with the small party of priests nearly forty turnings earlier—in those long-ago days, a boy just turning into a man. An outlander.

She did not flinch from his vehemence, merely stood there in stubborn resistance.

The tiny mouth paused momentarily in its noisemaking to root against her unhelpful chest. A stain of color on the downy-soft brown cheek had practically the same shape as the tattooed lightning bolt underlying the white and gray paint on Morning Green's cheek—a tattoo that marked him as a priest.

Her face grew thoughtful. She broke the silence by asking, "Tell me, man, how do you plan to feed him?"

"His mother—" Morning Green began.

Flinging up her hand, the priestess ordered, "Speak not her name, for she did not survive the birthing. She had not the strength to bring the babe into the world and remain in it herself."

"No matter." His voice held no emotion. "The prophecy says nothing of her, only the child."

The priestess cocked her head to one side, birdlike. "Does it not trouble you that she died because of your selfishness, your desire for more and more, always more?"

"Say, rather, my desire to save us all! As for her, even the followers of the goddess must recognize there is sometimes a need for sacrifice."

"Pah! You men, you bring only death. Men bleed, and it is an injury. Women bleed, in our moontime, and we take no harm from it. It proves our gift for life."

"This one took harm—and not only her! How many women have you tended at childbirth who have died, of late?" he accused.

Her hands tightened on the bundled infant, who protested. But she said only, "He will have to be fostered."

"No! I forbid it!" The priest sliced his painted arms through the air, fingers stiff and raking.

"Is not a living son better than a dead one?"

He did not want to agree with this woman, who had so many times opposed him. But if the child lived, people would forever say *There goes the son of Morning Green, the man who saved the People of Two Rivers.*

In the distance, spadefoot toads bleated as they dug their way up to meet the rain, the first in nearly a hundred days. They would enjoy only a momentary pleasure aboveground, in their mating frenzy, during this time of the male rains of summer. Then they would vanish once again into the sands where they waited out the dry moons and the female rains of winter.

Morning Green at last said, "This child is the one of prophecy, the one born to old blood and outlander, with the destiny of remaking the world. He is my gift to the future." The priest swept a hand toward the village. "Take him. Place him with a family. When he is weaned, then will I come for him. His name it shall be Spadefoot, in honor of his birth at the coming of the rains. And everyone will know of him."

Starflower

Thirsty, the people they waited and hoped. Hungry, they cried out.
Cloud flew over and found Yucca Woman; alone and in beauty she slept.
Cloud drew near and for her wept a single, salty tear.
This droplet on her belly fell and there a baby grew.
When Corn Man he became, the people they rejoiced anew.

—FROM THE STORY-SONG OF YUCCA WOMAN

All that Starflower saw in the pondweed at first was a pile of rags. Curious, she reached out with her long-handled corn knife. It encountered something solid underneath. As she lifted the stone blade, some of the cloth came away too. There was a man's body, face down in the stagnant water, limbs splayed unnaturally, black hair loose and floating, strung with tiny green beads of pondweed.

She gasped, then clapped her hands over her mouth to keep from making another sound. Never disturb a body, said the stories from the First Days.

The corpse stirred. It pushed itself up. Its head turned slowly to stare at her out of empty eyes. The skull was engulfed by a ball of lightning, which shrank and then filled the rotting belly with the brightness of a tiny sun. An owl perched on its shoulder shrieked once and flew at her. . .

Though in some corner of her mind she knew it was only a vision, she turned and ran. She hardly felt the branches that whipped at her face and the tangles of undergrowth that caught at her feet as she pushed her way out of the willows and tall reeds that edged the river. Away from the water and the horror it held, her panic took her into the mesquite bosque.

As she plunged onward, the dark, twisted trunks rose one after another to block her escape. Thorny twigs caught at her hair, tugging it from its neat coils. Time and again the branches pulled her to a stop and she had to untangle herself to run again.

On and on through the trees she staggered, limping now, with a tenderness in the ball of one foot. Her breath came raggedly.

At last her legs and lungs betrayed her. She stumbled against a tree, then sagged down into the gritty leaf litter at its base. She lacked the strength to rise.

There she crouched, cold with sweat and dizzy, each breath an effort.

The pounding of her heart shook her whole body. After a while she became aware of footsteps approaching, soft and almost unheard in the layer of leaves, yet heavy enough to vibrate through her bones. The fine hairs on her neck rose.

She looked up through tear-filled eyes—a shadowy form loomed before her. She cried out in protest and shrank back against the rough bark of the mesquite tree.

Hands closed around her wrists and drew her upright. She kicked, tried to get free to claw at her captor. He ignored her resistance, simply pulled her against himself and wrapped his arms around her.

The heartbeat under the cheek plastered to his warm chest told her this was no formless floating spirit. But to be seized and held so, trapped, was more than she could bear. She screamed—or tried to. So tight was his embrace, she couldn't drag enough air into her lungs to utter more than a whimper.

"Don't be afraid," he told her as she strained to get away. "I won't hurt you."

She struggled until there was no fight left in her. Then, sobbing, she slumped against him.

His grasp loosened a little.

She wriggled her arms between them and braced her fists against his ribs. Pressing back as far as he would allow, she gasped for breath and strained to catch a glimpse of his face through eyes wet and hazy.

This was no stranger, she realized as her heart battered against her ribs.

Though she'd never before been so close to him, she recognized Spadefoot, son of the Rainsinger. The blot on his cheek was unmistakable. Outlining that birthmark was the lightning-bolt tattoo borne by all those initiated into the priesthood. Two other tattoos also marred his face: a spiraling wind maze on his other cheek and the stepped line of a cloud-mountain on his forehead. Together they marked him as a high-ranking priest, though he had lived only a few turnings more than she had.

Which was worse, she wondered dizzily—to be caught by a spectre or by a priest? She shuddered.

"I won't let you do anything to me!" she cried. "I'll kill myself first!"

His grip tightened for a moment, but then, to her amazement, he let her go.

Hastily she shoved away to put more space between them. She went to brandish the sharp knife she'd brought up to the river, but her hands were empty. Starflower retreated another step and wiped her eyes with the back of her hand. The dirt and sap and sweat from her terrified run made her eyes sting and water fiercely.

Spadefoot opened his arms wide but stayed where he was. His undyed cotton tunic glowed in the dimness under the mesquites. "I am not going to hurt you. Stormbringer am I, vow bound to protect all the people of the valley." His voice, soothing and measured, echoed in her head, the words sounding like something from a song. His eyes, as deep and dark as the legendary bottomless waters of Blackpool, seemed to expand as she gazed into them.

She forced herself to look away and focused on his hair. In the priestly fashion, it was shaved on the sides and at the front, with the remainder pulled back and wrapped with a ribbon into a fist-sized club standing up at the back of his head.

She took another tiny step away.

"You can trust me," he said.

She wanted to. But . . . trust one of the priests—those who used women as mere vessels?

Everyone said bearing children would make the fields fertile and produce ample crops. If women giving birth was a good thing for the village, women giving birth to the children of the priests was supposed to be even better.

Trust a priest? Only a very stupid girl would do that.

Yet the alternative would be to start off again—alone and lost, with death stalking her.

She chewed on her lower lip and resisted the urge to take another step backward. If he moved, of course, she would be off like a runnerbird. "How can I trust you?"

"Because I'm a priest, you mean?" His eyebrows arched. "Is that why you're staring at me like you're worried I'm going to eat you? Or is it just my pretty face?"

Her gaze flashed to his birthmark, then dropped. "I don't mean to cause offense."

He shrugged. "One born as I am can't afford to take offense."

She couldn't think of any reply that wouldn't sound bad. What could she tell him—that he hardly looked as ugly or scary up close as rumor said?

He smiled, as innocent as a child. "Let's try this again. My name is Spadefoot. What's yours?"

"It's better if you don't know." Starflower folded her arms.

He might take her refusal to give him her name as petty. Childish, even. But names, real names, adult names such as hers—chosen after a naming quest—could tell a stranger much about a person. Hers was also the name of a basketry pattern. A basket built on a framework of willow, willow she'd come to the river to cut.

"Now that I take a closer look," he said, "I do recognize you. You're that girl whose father is putting the land at the end of the canal back into fields. You're a far piece from home."

Her cheeks warmed. "Those fields aren't my home. I'm of Cloud-Leaf Clan!"

The clanholdings of her mother's family were ancient, the furthest thing from her father's crazy attempt to claw drylands back from the desert. She'd spent all but the past few moons of her life in the midst of the clan's well-irrigated fields. In her heart, home would always be there. A few days ago she'd decided to do whatever it took to get herself and her brother back there.

"Cloud-Leaf Clan or no, you're still a long way from home." He reached out and tucked a strand of hair behind her ear.

She took another quick step away. Ever since her father had uprooted her and dragged her to the priests' end of the village, in the shadow of the temple, she'd heard too much about them to accept Spadefoot's flirtation.

Still, as a priest he had the power to protect her from the spirit she'd unwittingly disturbed. And he didn't *feel* wrong, or dangerous.

"You told me I could trust you," she said haltingly. "Is that the truth?"

"Of course."

"Not that I have another choice." She spoke to herself, but he responded:

"There are always choices. So why did you choose to come here, to this particular spot?"

She blinked and considered telling him the truth—that she'd followed the big canals up to the river to cut willows to make a granary, because the willows here grew longer branches than the ones downcanal, closer to the village, especially after such a dry summer. She could tell him that as a maker of useful baskets, she would be valuable to her clan and she could take her half brother and escape her father's house and be independent of any other man as well.

And then she wouldn't die in childbirth, as her mother had done, and her older sister, and the mother of her half brother, and Spadefoot's own mother.

Yes, she could tell him all that. But . . . the less he knew about her, the better. Besides, laid out like that it sounded pathetic, even stupid, a plan that was sure to fail.

"I came to be alone," she told him finally.

"Alone can be frightening."

She supposed he'd never been frightened in his life, though she didn't dare say that aloud.

"What were you running from?"

His voice filled her head. Soft and soothing, strangely compelling, that priest-trained voice made her feel like leaning in to it, to him. A moment passed, and another, before she understood what he asked. "How do you know that?" she demanded. "Were you following me?"

"No, I heard you crashing through the brush. And the mesquites made a mess of you. It's obvious you were running without paying attention to where you were going. Running away. But from what, I wonder."

Starflower looked down. Her legs were scratched and muddy. One of her sandals was gone, which explained the raw places she suddenly felt on the sole of her foot. Cuts from the mesquite thorns began to sting on her face and arms. She put up a hand to her hair, which had been ripped out of its ribbon wrappers and hung ragged on her neck.

Her face heated. No wonder he hadn't recognized her right off. She muttered, "Show me the way to the village. Then you won't have to look at me anymore."

"Oh, I don't mind the view. It's not often I see girls who aren't presenting themselves to please me." He winked.

She strongly wanted to kick him. Barring that, she wished she dared turn her back on him and stalk off. But she had no idea which way would lead her out of the mesquites, and she would be better off in his company if a spirit was pursuing her. Fear rolled back over her, dousing her flare of temper. She bit her lower lip.

He moved away and leaned against a tree but kept watching her—for what, she didn't know.

"I take it you're lost," he said.

"I got off the path, yes. If you call that lost," she added. "And then . . ." She paused to steady her voice as she recalled the vision of the owl-spirit swooping toward her. "Then I must've dropped my father's tools. He'll be so angry . . ."

"What happened?" Spadefoot asked. "Did a heron fly up and frighten you?"

She flushed but reminded herself he didn't know about the owl. She very well could have been startled by nothing.

"Did you see a snake?" he went on. "I wouldn't think less of you for admitting to it. My vow-brothers call me one who leaps at shadows." He grinned.

She quelled the memory of what she'd encountered at the river's edge. "Just point me in the right direction, if you really want to be helpful." Her voice rose and sharpened, she knew, betraying her frayed nerves, but she couldn't help it.

"Did you meet up with one of the Wilders? No matter what the Rainsinger says, they're nothing to be afraid of."

"I doubt the Wilders spend time around here. I would never have come if there was any chance of encountering one of them."

That was true enough—though she hadn't actually given the Wilders a thought earlier. Fortunately they lived a long way downriver. They were said to be the most debauched of the Watermasters—the men who kept the canals running—and so unruly that even their own kind had cast them out, to live wild on sandbars in the river, clanless and landless.

But alive. Maybe she had run across one . . . who was no longer.

Her whole body tensed like a drawn bow as the image of the horror she'd seen rose again before her eyes. She put out a hand to steady herself on a low-hanging branch.

"That's it, isn't it? You saw someone?"

"Not just any someone," she told him through stiff lips. Needing to share what had happened, she rushed on: "There's a body back there, by the river. Under the willows."

He straightened. "A dead body? A person?"

"Yes, yes. A man. Or, it was a man, before he . . . He was . . ." She found no words to describe how the body looked, face down in the dark water, hair floating around the head. With her free hand she gestured weakly. "Dead."

"Who is it?" he demanded.

She stared at him. "How would I know?"

"Didn't you look?"

"No! Disturb the body? Only a fool would do that!"

"I think you'd better show me."

"I will not!" She took two strides away from him. The dignity of her retreat was marred by the squeak she made when she stepped down on her sore foot.

He caught her by the hand and spun her around. "Show me."

"I'm not going back there!" She tugged against his grasp but couldn't free herself.

"You would rather stay here, all alone?"

"I would rather you take me home," she cried. Scarcely had the demand left her mouth than she realized if her father saw her in the company of one of the rain priests, he would be furious. "No, no, just show me how to get back to the canals. Just get me started!"

"Not until I've found out what's going on." His voice sounded grim. "Stay put. I'll be back."

Spadefoot released her and walked away but paused after a few steps and turned to face her. "There's probably nothing to be afraid of. I doubt some Wilder hit him over the head and dumped him in the river."

She gaped at him as her heart began to thud against her ribs again. "You think he was *killed?*"

Her people, the People of Two Rivers, didn't kill each other. Of course, they hardly ever drowned, either. And something—whether evil intent or unlikely accident—had made that man no longer alive. She hadn't stopped to wonder at the cause.

"Are you coming?"

Go back to the corpse? "No!"

But then she would have to stay here. Her gaze darted from one tree to another that could hide a madman or conceal a free-floating spirit, a spectre ready to wreak revenge on the girl who'd disturbed its earthly remains. She swallowed hard.

"All right, then." Without another word, he started off.

She stared at his back. "You can't leave me!"

But that was exactly what he did. She'd left behind a trail of scuffed leaves and broken twigs, and he was following it back toward the river.

He'd left Starflower with only two alternatives. Stay here, alone, to deal with a killer or a phantom by herself—maybe even both. Or tag along after a priest who showed no signs of wanting to ravish her and surely could protect her from either of the more-dangerous options.

Before he was quite out of sight, she sighed and limped after him. He would eventually have to go back to the temple. She could go with him as far as the canal crossing.

She was resolved, though, that nothing he could do would make her look at that gruesome body again.

Rather than rush to catch up, she stayed a few steps behind him. That way she wouldn't have to talk. It seemed safer.

The ground became spongy underfoot. Cottonwoods and willows eventually replaced the mesquites. Gooseflesh rose along her arms. She tried to convince herself it was from the chilly breeze that blew off the river. But she knew perfectly well it came from inside, as she wondered what she was doing, following the young priest.

The first time she'd ever seen him, across the canal that separated her father's farmstead from the priests' temple, she'd imagined Spadefoot to be lonely, for he seemed apart from the other priests. Now that Starflower's father had upended her life, separating her from her clan-sisters and aunties, she knew how it felt to not fit in. Then she'd learned that Spadefoot's mother had died bringing him into the world and he'd been forced to leave his foster mothers to join the temple.

She'd thought, in those early days, that she had much in common with Spadefoot.

But lately . . . lately she'd heard more rumors about him, and still more, a never-ending stream of gossip. He was weather-wise, some said, and felt water in his bones. Others claimed he was the one of prophecy, destined to save their people from a terrible cataclysm. Still others said that the

Cornmaidens, required to lie with the priests, fell in love with him one and all despite his ruined face. And she'd heard, too, that he was arrogant and overproud.

People said he could charm any woman with merely a curve of his lips. But Starflower refused to be charmed. He didn't care about her or her feelings at all. Arrogant, yes. He had to get his own way, no matter the consequences to her.

She was cold and frightened and lost and her foot hurt more with every step. And he didn't care.

As she counted up her grievances, she fell farther behind.

In a while he stopped, bent over, and pried a sandal from the muck. He turned back toward her. "Here." He held out her sandal. "This should make the going easier for you."

"Thank you," she muttered. She took the braided sandal and knelt. She kept her face averted so he couldn't see her blush at thinking ill of him. After putting her big toe in the loop, she laced the cords around her ankle and tightened them into place. When she had regained her composure, she rose.

He asked, "We must be getting close, don't you think?"

She feared it was true, as he grasped her hand in his warm one and drew her forward. They'd come a long distance together, it seemed to her. Her heart beat faster as she waited for the owl to appear again.

She closed her eyes and worked to convince herself she was safe in Spadefoot's presence. As a distraction, she tried to envision the granary she'd planned to make from the willow trees she now walked through. Their branches trailed like bony fingers across her shoulders. She shoved that disturbing sensation away and concentrated on her project.

But the granary wouldn't take shape in her mind now. Earlier, she'd felt it like a real thing under her hands, felt the split shoots pliable to her touch, bending up into graceful curves bound by coils of beargrass. It would be a huge basket, almost large enough to stand up in. Which was why she needed long willow branches.

As her chest tightened, tears threatened to start flowing again. She squeezed her eyelids ever more tightly shut to hold them back. She hadn't managed to cut any willows, and she'd lost the knife and carry net she'd taken without her father's permission. Worst of all, the image of her creation had been erased from her mind and replaced with that horrible thing she could never unsee.

Spadefoot's hand clenched into a fist and ground her knuckles together.

She gasped in pain. Her eyelids flew open as he brought her to a stumbling halt. Before her watering eyes could focus on what lay before, she cast her gaze straight down. There, at least, she saw nothing more ominous than fallen limbs and leaves and underbrush.

"Sorry. I didn't mean to hurt you." He released her. "Did you see anyone when you were here before? Other than the dead man?"

"No, of course not. Nobody ever comes all the way out here."

"We did, today," he reminded her unhelpfully before moving away.

She rubbed her abused hand and watched him shift sideways, step down, down again. His lower legs disappeared. She turned her head and stared blindly at a clump of willows in the other direction.

A light splash told her he'd waded into the water. Then came a nauseating sucking sound that made her think he'd pulled the body out of the mud. Maybe rolled it over to see the face, to put a name to it.

She wished he hadn't suggested a violent death for the corpse.

Her imagination conjured up a terrible possibility, even worse than the scene it had created earlier. Spadefoot had a reputation for strength, with his compact, muscular body, the same that had held her so tightly she couldn't move. He was powerful enough to hold a man's head underwater until the struggle to survive ended.

Her nerves crackled as she wondered whether she would be the next to die. Had she allowed fear of a disembodied, pursuing spirit to push her right into the arms of a killer?

No, a priest would never do something like that, she told herself. But herself replied, *Just why did he come out to the river, so far from the temple? And what, exactly, is he doing now?* She barely allowed herself to breathe while she listened in vain for any sound, any hint that he was sneaking up behind her.

Finally she could no longer just stand there. "What is it? One of those Wilders?" She kept her unseeing eyes fixed in the opposite direction.

"He's my brother."

"You mean—" she puzzled out what he must have meant, for the Rainsinger had only the one son—"a priest?"

Eventually he answered. "A vow-brother, yes. And my friend."

The heavy sorrow in his voice convinced her that he hadn't killed the other man. But the relief she felt lasted for only a heartbeat, as a ghastly squelching sound followed. She spun about and saw him stooped over the body, lifting it.

The hair wasn't tied up like a rain priest's should be but hung free, hiding the face. She shivered. "What are you doing?"

"He deserves to be sent on his last journey with respect."

"Can't you leave him, have the Lifeweaver come later, to sing his spirit to rest right here? If he's your friend, you can't want to disturb his—"

Her protest caught in her throat as he heaved the corpse onto his shoulder. He grunted as he worked it into position, taking forever. Then he stood. Water and mud and pondweed dripped off, streaking his tunic and leggings as he staggered, then clumsily turned.

Her gorge rose. She couldn't go with him if he bore that grotesque burden. She swallowed hard and cried, "But what if the killer comes back looking for his victim? You won't be able to defend yourself!" *And what about me?* she wanted to say. *Who's going to defend me . . . against that?*

"There's no killer out there."

"You can't be certain of that! How can you know such a thing?"

"There's no blood. He just drowned."

Her skeptical response poured out before she even knew she was thinking the words. "You think he just fell in and *died?*" That was ridiculous: everyone knew how to swim. In a world filled with canals that provided the only relief from the desperate heat of summertime, even the youngest of children learned to keep themselves afloat. No one drowned.

Spadefoot readjusted the body. The bloated face shifted to look right at her with open eyes, priestly tattoos stark against skin gone slack in death. She felt herself choking, unable to breathe, dying of it: not the cold and wet of drowning, but burning hot and dry. Her hands went to her throat, trying to dislodge whatever blocked her breath.

She had no idea what Spadefoot said; his words didn't penetrate the ringing in her ears. Maybe a prayer to send the restive spirit winging into the land of clouds. Maybe no more than a lullaby as one might sing to soothe a child. Whatever it was, his eyes held hers, replacing that dead stare in her mind, as his resonant voice drew her out of the engulfing darkness.

She fought free of the corpse. With a gasp, she drew welcome air into her lungs.

"Don't be afraid," Spadefoot soothed her. "That angry-spirit nonsense is just a story, the kind old women tell children to make them afraid of death, to keep the curious from getting underfoot. There's no harm to you from a drowned man."

"He burned! Not drowned, burned!"

"What are you going on about? What did you see?"

A spark of caution made her lie. "I saw nothing! Just leave it, leave it here, put it back, and take me home!"

He shook his head. The motion turned the corpse's face away from her, far enough that she could no longer see its staring eyes.

"My brother here was a good man. One of the very best—even if you find that hard to believe of a priest. He would never have hurt anyone during life, and he certainly won't in death. If you can't find it in your heart to believe that, just stay here. I'm sure you can find your own way home." He started off, heavy-footed and ungraceful.

Trying not to look at the thing he had slung over his shoulder, she called after him, "You aren't going to be able to carry it all the way back to the temple."

"Probably not."

"Then why bother?" She got no answer as he walked away.

Knowing Spadefoot was her best chance to get herself unlost, she followed, keeping him in sight. "The body won't be going anywhere."

"Animals could get at it," he answered.

The distance between them meant they had to talk in loud voices that broke the silence, which helped relieve her nerves.

Spadefoot went on: "Or someone else could find it. There could be all kinds of rumors about where he was found and how he died. Look at you, saying he burned instead of drowned, when he was right there in the water."

"You think there'll be less talk if people see you carrying a body through the clanlands?"

His back stiffened. Starflower lamented her quick tongue: what was she to do if he decided to stay near the river with the body and not help her get home at all?

He remained silent for a few steps, then suggested, "Let's make a pact. I'll get you back to the path. In return, you forget what you saw here today. Do you think you can manage that? Can I rely on you not to tell anyone about where the body was found, or about my being here? No matter what?"

"As if I have a choice!"

"I told you before, there are always choices. Who you let into your life. Who you shut out. The trick lies in making the right choice."

"I don't understand!" she wailed.

"I wouldn't expect you to. I'm just starting to grasp the idea, myself."

"You talk in circles and say nothing. But then, what else should I expect? You're a priest, and I, I'm nothing but a—"

Abruptly he swung about, but all he said was, "Do we have an agreement?"

"Yes!"

"Don't be mad. You get all wrinkly when your face puckers up like that. Smooth out that pucker with a smile, and go back to being beautiful."

Her hands flew to her cheeks before she realized he was teasing her.

"Go through the trees there." With his free hand he pointed at a break in the assemblage of trunks. "See the path?"

"Yes." She did, now.

"Keep your head about you, and you'll be out in the open soon. From there you can see the temple."

∧∧

She soon passed under the last branches of the mesquites. Thin, patchy clouds masked the sun, but they made no promise of rain, only held back the sun's warmth. Her muscles felt stiff, every step an effort.

Before her lay the vast wildness of the desert, marked by small mounds of cactuses and some dusty saltbushes among widely spaced shegoi plants.

A line of trees in the middle distance marked the route of the big canals she would have to cross. To her right they flowed, into patchy fields and scattered huts of isolated farmsteads before the clanlands proper began. Before her, away in the distance, rose the massive temple, marking her direction.

As she trudged along, she thought about how her panic had started to dissipate as soon as she heard Spadefoot's voice. Even her fear of the corpse had eased once he'd picked it up and just walked off with it. She no longer feared the spirit would pursue her.

What sort of magic did he have? she wondered. How had he changed her dread into embarrassment and her distrust into trust with just his voice and manner?

She hadn't even thought to look for the corn knife and carry net when he led her back to where she must have lost them. She'd just stood there, as obedient as a puppy.

Then she'd argued with him, squabbling as she would with her brother! Yet it had worked out all right. They'd made a bargain. He'd shown her the way home, just as she'd asked.

And he thought her beautiful.

She tried to hold onto that inner glow of satisfaction, wrapping herself in it like the rabbit-fur mantle she'd recently pulled out of the storage basket for the oncoming winter. But with every footsore step, her sense of triumph diminished.

The day likewise ebbed. A chilling breeze nipped at her skin as she walked through the lonesome wildland.

The Moon of Small Rains had been dry so far; the dirt she kicked up soon covered her scratched legs with a dusting several shades lighter than her skin. Every footfall had to be carefully placed to avoid the raking teeth that lined the edges of the agave leaves and the tiny fishhooks hidden within the cottony-tufted, ankle-high cactuses.

After a while she paused to catch her breath. She shaded her eyes from the sun and gazed off at the scrubland that stretched out before her, flat and seemingly featureless until, still too far away for her liking, the Temple of the Mist rose up.

She'd set off this morning prepared to try something out of the ordinary. But her plan had been utterly ruined, from disturbing the dead body to being disturbed by Spadefoot. Becoming lost and terrified, losing her father's tools, getting dirty and scratched and disheveled—all that misery with nothing to show for it!

She sucked in her lower lip and began to worry at it. She hadn't asked her father for permission—either to leave or to take his tools—when the notion of gathering willows came to her that morning.

As she stood there, she became aware of an emptiness at her neck and lifted her hand to where her shell necklace should be. Her fingers encountered nothing but skin. Her necklace—the one she'd spent so long collecting matched shells for, polishing and piercing them, preparing the yucca fibers and braiding them into a cord, stringing the shells—was gone!

The loss of the necklace struck at her heart, and tears threatened again.

She turned back toward the mesquite bosque, no more than a thin dark line now. The river seemed too far away, with sunset coming on, to go back and look for her necklace. It would certainly be broken, the shells scattered, impossible to find.

Still, she was tempted to at least try. And did she really dare go back to her father without the corn knife and carry net?

Starflower crossed her goose-pimply arms tightly against her chest and rubbed her hands up and down to warm them as she tried to decide what to do.

She could make another necklace. A better one, she tried to convince herself, now that basket making had taught her fingers to be more nimble. As for her father's tools . . . with the harvest over, he might not notice their absence right away. He would certainly notice hers if he finished the day's work and she didn't have supper ready.

She had no choice but to return to her father's hut before the sun sank any lower toward the horizon. Tears ran down her cheeks as she started toward the temple again.

With loss and failure and fear of her father's mood running through her mind, the return trip felt twice as long as her journey to the river even after her tears dried. Time and again she gasped and shuddered at what turned out to be nothing more than the rustling of small creatures in the brush.

But she kept going, heading toward the Temple of the Mist, until it was no longer the only sign that people lived in the desert land. Around it, like children seated before a talespinner, the plaster walls of the house compounds of the village gleamed in the sun's setting light. Their shadows stretched out spindly and black.

As she got closer to her father's house, she began to consider what special supper she could prepare for him that might soothe his temper.

With not all of the canals repaired after the unexpectedly heavy spring floods, the first harvest had been sparse, the second not much better. Even those fields that had been irrigated lay empty. They bore only a tracery of dusky green from potherbs not yet large enough to be picked and stewed up to flavor meat. But she had saltbush and some rabbit jerky put by.

She'd traded a few of her practice baskets for corn, and there were still some beans, speckled and tepary, as well as a few jars of the tiny seeds that made good filler for stew. Starflower had been making the stored food stretch as well as she could, but she feared she wouldn't be able to continue that for much longer. Eventually, she'd have to talk to her father about what they would eat over the winter.

Or get herself and her brother back to the clanlands, where food wasn't so hard to come by.

But for tonight . . . tonight she could pretend there was plenty.

Starflower felt a tug at the hem of her skirt, then the sting of another scratch on her leg. As she disentangled her skirt from the hooked spine of the agave, she told herself to pay more attention to where she was going.

She had to make her clothing last for another full turning, at least. The thirsty cotton plants had not yielded many bolls this past summer, and most farmers expected to plant food crops come spring, not cotton.

Straightening, she noticed off to her left a small gaggle of boys. In their midst stood a woman with two long black braids—one streaked with white—and wearing a deerskin tunic over skin leggings. Starflower recognized her as a clan-sister named Deerchaser and envied the warm, protective clothing the other woman wore.

Deerchaser held up a bow and slowly fitted an arrow to the string. After she repeated the movement a few times, the boys mimicked her with their own small bows. They spread out into a long line, with a black and white dog bounding around behind them. Arrows raggedly arced out over the desert.

Starflower knew what the clan-aunties said—that a woman had no business even possessing such skills, let alone teaching them. The only good thing about the move to the other end of the village, Starflower had once thought, was that it had taken her brother away from Deerchaser's influence.

Presumably not interested in farming, Deerchaser had joined the hunters, her father's people. Instead of giving life, she now took it. Unwomanly, she was called. But she was helping the boys keep their families fed in these lean days.

Someone tapped Starflower on the shoulder. She cried out in surprise and spun about. She winced as agave teeth raked across her shin again.

"Oh, it's you," she said, upon seeing her brother. She set a hand on her hip and waggled the forefinger of her other hand at him. "Don't sneak up on me like that."

"It wouldn't be sneaking if you paid attention." He smirked.

Vineslayer's face was longer than hers, more like their father's, even though he hadn't lost all the baby fat in his cheeks. The twist of his mouth made him look even more like the father they shared.

She opened her mouth to say *You* were *sneaking* but instead asked, "What are you doing here?"

"Father is looking for you."

Her heart began to thud behind her breastbone. "Oh? Do you know what for?"

"Maybe so, maybe no. What'd you sneak off for?"

"I was harvesting willows."

He eyed her. "What were you doing, really?" he asked.

"I told you. Cutting willows."

"Wha' d'you want willows for? And why up to the river?"

"How do you know that's where I went?" she demanded. "Did you follow me?"

"You went to meet a Wilder, didn't you?" His mouth twisted as though he'd sucked on a coyote-gourd.

"Certainly not."

"So, some other man, then. You must be the stupidest sister alive. Morning Green says—"

"But of course, *Morning Green* says . . ." An image of the pale-skinned, creepy-eyed Rainsinger flashed into her head. Just the thought of him made her skin crawl. Hard to imagine *he* could be Spadefoot's father.

Vineslayer kept talking over her rejoinder. Once she started paying attention again, she heard: "—the Watermasters are a moral blight. Seducers and debauchers!"

She couldn't help it; she laughed, which made his face darken. "You're too young to be listening to such things," she said. "Much less saying them yourself. It makes you sound weird." She pointed toward the boys with Deerchaser, still at their archery practice. "Why aren't you off playing, like them? Or even with them?"

"You used to tell me to keep away from her." He sneered. The curled lip looked odd on his youthful face. "She's one of those women Morning Green talks about. A stupid woman ruined by a Watermaster's lust. Is that going to be you?"

"Of course not." Starflower held out her right hand and shook it at him for emphasis. "You'll never see the mark of any man on me." Not for her the braided-hair bracelet of a temporary handfast, much less the tattoo of a heartfast. There would be no mating at all for her. On that she was resolved.

"You're already marked," he pointed out.

She drew back her arm and looked at the deep scratch on her wrist. This one she hadn't even felt.

Vineslayer shook his head. "You don't know, do you!"

"Know what?" she asked as she considered whether to get supper started first or set herself in order before her father saw her.

"You should've picked one of those boys always hanging around."

"What are you babbling about?"

"They all took off today, when they saw you weren't here. It made Father mad."

It wasn't her fault the boys liked spending time around her or that, in exchange for the privilege of her company, her father put them to work. If they'd left him to do everything by himself, he really would be angry. No wonder Vineslayer was here waiting for her. "Is that when he asked where I'd gone?"

"No . . ." He rubbed the back of his neck and shifted from foot to foot. His mouth twitched as though he wanted to say something but didn't quite dare.

"Out with it, brother."

He dropped his chin and muttered, "Father wants you to seduce the new Canalmaster."

For a moment, she didn't think she'd heard him right. Then she laughed and started walking again. The Canalmaster. The Watermaster in charge of every canal that served the village.

"I'm not making this up!" her brother insisted.

"Now you're just being silly," she tossed over her shoulder at him. "I don't know where you got this notion from, but—"

"Father told me. Well, as good as." Vineslayer pattered after her. "The Canalmaster came by today."

She slowed down and listened as he rambled on.

"But you were gone, and then Father couldn't find you. After the Canalmaster left, Father started shouting at me when I said you went up to the river."

Starflower spun around. "Did he hit you?" She looked at her brother's face and arms for any new bruises but saw none. Their father generally used his fists on Vineslayer and his words on her.

Getting away from him seemed more important every day, as long as she could do it in a way that would let her—and her brother—eat regularly and have shelter from the winter's cold and rain. Going back to the clan had to be better than living way out here, away from everyone she knew and at her father's mercy.

Vineslayer said, "No, not this time. It's you that's in trouble, not me."

Shaking her head, she turned and started for the fieldhouse again.

"You should pick one of your boys!" he called.

She couldn't do that. Lying with a man, getting with child . . . that way lay certain death. But she wasn't going to talk to her brother about that.

"Wait up." Vineslayer's steps drew near as he hurried forward. "You can't go along with this!"

She quickened her own pace. "There is no 'this.' I don't know what you heard—"

"Just listen, will you!"

Struck by his intensity, she stopped and studied him, though she knew their father would make her regret every moment of delay.

"Father needs water from the canal. He's already been turned down once."

Starflower didn't understand why her brother seemed so upset. "Isn't that good news?"

Only the Canalmaster would decide where an irrigation ditch should run. What their father wanted wouldn't matter, for without the Canalmaster's support, there would be no water directed into the new fields he was carving out. That the Canalmaster had refused him meant her little family would get to go back to the clanlands. Didn't it?

"If you don't change the Canalmaster's mind, Father will have to turn to the Ta'atchul!"

He sounded as though he would be glad of it. She tried to interrupt as she realized where Vineslayer was taking his argument, but he wouldn't be stopped.

"Our father sees nothing wrong with trading you to a lecherous, wicked Watermaster, corrupted by foul desires. Even though such a thing would taint you forever! And me along with you. The priests would never accept me as a Seeker—"

She grabbed him by the shoulders. "Stop with this crazy talk! You're just repeating what the Rainsinger says. Why must you listen to that addled old man!"

"Morning Green knows what the Watermasters really are!"

"He does, does he? He looks into their hearts and . . ." She forgot what she was about to say as she considered how easily Spadefoot had gotten her to trust him. Maybe the priests really could see into people's hearts.

"You can't bed a Watermaster! You can't go along with this plan!" her brother wailed, sounding more his age.

Exasperated, she told him, "There is no plan! Father is not trying to get rid of me, and he certainly can't force me to go to any man's bed, Canalmaster or not."

She released her grip on him and began to pick her way through the desert scrub as quickly as she could. This time her brother didn't follow her.

What Vineslayer had suggested would go a fair way toward explaining why her father had been teaching her about what men and women did together. He'd said it was so she could recognize when a man desired her—and use that desire to her own ends without letting it go too far.

But her flirtations had been aimed, up to now, at the young sons of farmers, coaxing them to work in her father's fields rather than in their own family's. Flirting was one thing; seduction, something else entirely. Starflower couldn't accept that part of Vineslayer's argument.

Her father might not be kind, but she couldn't believe him cruel enough to give her to any man—not when he knew how much she feared having a child planted in her belly. Plus, she would become practically useless to him at that point, for a woman who carried another man's child wasn't to be flirted with, and certainly not bedded.

As she neared her father's new field, she rammed her big toe into something hard and heavy, making her cry out in pain. She looked down and found she'd stumbled into a rock, which didn't belong here, so far from the boulder-strewn slopes that rose beyond the southern edge of the village. The encounter had loosened the rock from the ground but did it no other harm, while her toenail was cracked down to the quick.

A tiny string of red droplets beaded up along the edge of her broken nail. She knelt and wiped them off. They left a bright stain on her thumb. Absently she wiped the blood onto her sash, but it welled up again, and she used her thumb a second time.

The rock bore signs of long use as a metate for grinding corn, but it had been broken in half across the deep-worn trough. No corn fragments remained after all its time in the field. It was a boundary marker, she realized, though she could no longer see the dark stains from the generations of women who would have left their moontime blood on the pitted surface, gifting it to the goddess in return for ample crops, healthy children, long life.

Slowly, trying to remember the daily prayer to the Allmother that her clan-aunties had taught her, Starflower swiped her thumb across the rock to leave her own mark. Her own sacrifice.

Where this broken relic of the past rested was now only desert, but she knew what its presence here meant: once, before the Long Thirst, this field had been part of somebody's clanlands. This stone had marked one corner. Prayer flags planted around the boundaries would once have drifted in the breezes, displaying the clan symbols for all to see. Briefly the land appeared to her as she supposed it did in her father's dreams, lush and green with crops. But only if he could get water to it.

She rose and headed toward the fieldhouse. Beyond it lay the banks of the old canal, which coiled around the priests' temple like a snake.

Vineslayer was probably wrong about the Canalmaster turning down their father anyway, she thought. Watermasters were tasked with only one thing: putting water in farmers' fields. For one of them to refuse—that seemed unimaginable. Unless the Canalmaster held out for something more, some kind of personal reward. Something like . . . her?

When she saw her father storming across the field toward her, she could tell that her brother had been right about one thing: he was in a mood.

As he neared, she studied his face. His nostrils flared with fast breaths and the muscles in his neck were tense. She prepared for the worst.

"Where have you been?"

Starflower stopped herself from flinching. Her father disliked it when she showed any fear of him. "Vineslayer said you sent for me. I'm sorry I wasn't here."

Her father passed his angry gaze over her. "Just as well, the way you look right now." He flicked a finger at the juncture between her neck and her shoulder, where her necklace used to rest. It hurt, and she couldn't help but wince.

Hoping he hadn't noticed, she dropped her chin so he couldn't see her eyes. "I'll go get cleaned up."

But he grabbed her arm before she could turn toward the fieldhouse. The low hut made of mud-plastered sticks woven into a framework wasn't much protection, a far cry from the adobe-walled compound in which she'd grown up, with neighbors nearby. But still it would serve as a haven if she could just get inside and be alone until he calmed down.

"You look like you've been rolling in a cactus patch," he snapped.

"I went out to gather willows, but then I saw . . ." She pulled away by burying her face in her hands. This time, she didn't have to pretend to be upset, as she sometimes did to distract him. "It's too awful. I can't even talk about it. I was so scared! And I fell—"

"Never mind that," he told her. "I convinced the new Canalmaster to come back tomorrow, but we'll need to have you ready."

She pulled her hands away, gazed up out of tear-filled eyes, and sniffled before asking, "Ready for what?"

"Don't be a fool! At least pretend you've got some sense."

"You mean for me to . . . to seduce him into giving you the water?" Her mouth suddenly felt dry, and her voice shook so much, she could hardly get the words out.

"Certainly not."

Her budding relief died as he went on, "This Watermaster earned a reputation in his younger days, for leaving as soon as he has his satisfaction. All you have to do is let him *think* you'll be receptive. Make him work for it. Make him crave you all the way to his bones. Make him need you like his next breath."

"I can't do this! You know I can't!"

"Why not?"

Her skin felt too tight. Trembling and disoriented, her heart pounding, she tried to put her thoughts together. "The Canalmaster isn't just the son of a farmer, like the boys my own age, the ones you've been pushing me at. It's one thing to flirt and play with them. But this?" Her heart beat so hard, she thought he must hear it. "This is different. I can't take on a Watermaster!"

"I've told you, you don't have to actually lie with him."

"How can I stop him?" she wailed. "You've told me a man's desire for a woman is as strong as hunger or thirst!"

Her father's fingers flexed as though he wanted to hit her, and his chest puffed out. "I've told you it *can* be. And I've taught you how to make it strong. I can show you how to keep his fire burning hot without ever quenching it, too. What you're saying is, you don't trust me in this. No, it's worse than that. You would put your own wishes above mine."

"That's not it at all!" she rushed to say. The lie came so fast, she thought her tongue might trip over it. "I would never refuse you. But you've said you don't want me to show any favoritism, to pick any one over another."

"This is different." The tone of his voice brought her eyes back to his face.

The pulsing of a vein at his temple warned her to be quiet; he was too deep in his rage to put up with any argument. She swallowed the next words. Mind racing, she took a deep breath and shifted her gaze to the laces at the neck of his tunic.

"This is for me." He struck his chest and she flinched. "That mud-grubber warned me the ditch to this field can't be remade. He told me to try dry-farming instead. Agaves! Cactus pads!" He hawked up a gob and spat it on the ground.

Could the Canalmaster be right? She managed to hold back the ill-advised words and pretended to listen as he ranted.

For the whole night, Starflower lay awake on her sleep pallet, unable to close her eyes. With relief she at last saw the dim light of morning filtering down from the smoke hole centered in the roof of the brush-walled fieldhouse. Dust motes floated in the gray shafts of light: now a tree, now a face, now a body. She shuddered and turned her head away.

Vineslayer's whuffling and her father's snoring reassured her that they slept. In the middle of the night, her brother had crept in. Sensibly, he'd avoided all of their father's shouting about her ingratitude and stupidity and betrayal, as well as the Canalmaster's interference and incompetence.

After silently speaking the usual prayer for safekeeping to Mother Ge—though she wondered how much good it had done her the previous day—Starflower pushed away the deerskin bed cover and rose. In the brisk air, the skin on her arms and legs puckered, making the previous day's wounds ache. Her neck felt bare. After she patted it a few times, she remembered she'd lost her necklace.

The night had been long and sleepless. Every time she'd closed her eyes, she'd seen that corpse or heard her father's ranting, sometimes both together. She repeated the prayer and swiped her hand down her front as a gesture of cleansing to keep malevolent spirits away. She hadn't had time the previous day to perform any purification rituals. No opportunity this morning either, unless she wanted to wake her father.

For a moment she wavered, but then her resolve stiffened. The plan that had come to her in the night might not be any good, but it was something!

She grabbed her rabbit-fur mantle from the storage net nearest the door. After she settled it over her dress and tied it shut in the front, she freed her night braid from under the fur. She then slipped her bag of personal items off the mesquite pole, one of two that held up the arched roof, and fastened its cord around her waist. With the necessities collected, she picked up her boots and tiptoed toward the door.

She tried to, anyway. Her legs felt so stiff that she staggered at first, barely able to hobble.

Throughout the night, she'd considered ways to get her father the irrigation water he needed. She could aim at the Canalmaster's sense of fairness and convince him to give her father this chance to produce some badly needed food. Or she could let the Canalmaster know the field had once been watered and could be so again; the challenge of bringing land back under cultivation might be all he needed. Or it might be vanity that would sway him, the notion that a lesser man might not be able to restore water to what had once been ditch-fed clanlands, but he surely could.

Or maybe the Canalmaster, who rumor said had all the women he wanted, would consider something else more valuable than coupling with a woman, if only for the novelty of it.

Unfortunately, she hadn't spent much time listening to what people said when this new Canalmaster took the place of the doddery old one a few moons back, so she had no idea what that "something else" could be. But others might—and she knew exactly where to go for that kind of gossip.

Starflower felt for the bone locking pin in the inner door, then remembered she'd left the door unsecured for Vineslayer. Like the sleep pallets, the door was woven of reeds on a wooden frame. With the approach of cold weather, a deerskin covered it, making it heavy enough that she couldn't open it with just one hand.

To free her other hand, she slipped her feet into the boots without lacing them up. She opened the door, careful not to drag it on the stone threshold and wake the sleepers. She passed through and silently pulled it closed from the other side, while stooped over in the low entry tunnel.

The outer door, a single layer of reed matting, was easier to manage. She closed the door behind her, turned, and tried to step forward, but her feet caught on something. She cried out and fell to her hands and knees.

At first she was too concerned about having woken her father to do anything more than listen. Her heart pounded so hard, she worried she wouldn't be able to hear if he stirred. But then she realized her fingers were tangled in a carry net, her nose not far from a long-handled corn knife made of the finest chert. In confusion she stared at the net and the corn knife for a moment. Had Vineslayer followed her after all and brought back the tools she'd lost?

She shook her head. If he'd known about her trip to the river and her encounter with Spadefoot, much less the dead priest, he wouldn't have kept it to himself.

No, it had to have been Spadefoot who'd returned the tools. She rose and looked for him. There was nowhere for a man to hide; the whole area around the fieldhouse had been cleared of brush. Evidently as she'd lain awake all night, he'd come and gone in secret.

Though the return of the tools should have eased her mind, she felt no relief, just a dark weight settling on her shoulders. With this gesture, he'd put her in his debt. Helping her find the path back to the village had been no inconvenience for him. But this? How was she supposed to repay this kindness? If kindness it was intended to be, rather than some young man's daring exploit, like climbing up the side of a mountain after eagle eggs.

She shook her head, determined to put this latest Spadefoot puzzle out of her mind.

Carefully she freed herself from the netting. She crisscrossed the laces over the leather tops of her boots and tied them under each knee, then gathered up the carry net and the knife. The carry net was soaking wet, with bits of pondweed on it. She knew putting it away without first letting it dry was a bad idea, but she would have to take care of it later.

At least the net was here, and her father would never have to know what she'd planned the previous day. He'd spent so much time berating her that he hadn't thought to ask where she'd been or what she'd been doing. He hadn't even let her prepare supper for them, just grabbed a mesquite journeycake and munched on it. She could have had some, too, she supposed, but she hadn't felt like eating anything.

She carried the tools to the crude stick-walled storage bin and stowed them. Then she walked over to the vatto, the shade structure that was the first thing her father had built at the field. She wrestled the red clay olla from the crook of the mesquite limb that held up one corner of the vatto's arrowweed roof.

Starflower knelt and dumped the remaining water from the olla into an empty stew pot. She poured the last few frigid drops over her hands and rubbed them together to rinse off the grit from this most recent fall. Though the first touch made her gasp, she stroked her wet fingers over her cheeks, forehead, and chin. Then she wiped them on her dress, the cleanest thing she had handy.

She reached into the bag that hung from her waist. Her fingers brushed against the cloth she'd secreted in there, but she wasn't ready for that yet.

Groping deeper, she found a set of long cords and her bone comb and hairpins and took them all out of the bag. With deft movements, she separated the three strands of her long braid, combed out each one, and smoothed her obsidian-black hair into a single fall down her back. This she split into two. She took each section and coiled it above her ear, using the cords to bind the thick part of the coil as close to her head as she could reach and securing the loops with a few well-placed bone pins. As she put herself in order, tension eased out of her shoulders.

At last she rose with the sense of being somewhat prepared for what was to come. She took the dipping-gourd and a woven grass ring from where they hung on the mesquite post. She hung the gourd from her waist and placed the ring on her head between the thick coils of hair. Then she set the empty olla onto the ring, centered it, and, balancing the jar with her body, started down the uneven path that led toward the dipping-pool.

When she got there, she dragged the olla off her head. But she'd forgotten about the grass ring on which the olla rested. The ring tumbled to the ground. She had to quickly pin it under one foot before it rolled down into the water. Off-balance, she clutched at the olla and managed to trap it against her body so it didn't fall too—and shatter.

Hands shaking, she set the olla on the ground and looked down into the pool.

It was deep, even deeper than either of the main canals, both unused, that curved around the Temple of the Mist nearby. Some people said Spadefoot was the one who somehow knew water was there and had the pool dug. In any case, it was too deep for her to haul the filled olla up out of. She made sure she had the loop of the gourd's twisted yucca-fiber cord around her wrist and then descended the steps carved into the plastered side of the pool.

She eased out on the flat-topped log placed across the pool, just above the water that seeped up from below. She rested on her haunches and let the gourd settle into the water. Once it was full, she pulled it out, then made her way back along the log and up the steps.

Often, she had the feeling while at the pool of being watched. This morning especially, after knowing that Spadefoot had come and gone just outside the walls of the fieldhouse, she felt exposed. But there was nowhere nearby for anyone to hide, nothing but knee-high brush except for a young mesquite scarcely taller than her shoulder.

She told herself she was being foolish.

But just as she stepped out onto the bank, there came the call of an owl. She flinched and spilled some of the water. Hearing an owl so close to the village wasn't uncommon. In daylight and when she already felt jumpy, though, it seemed ominous, for sometimes a restless spirit took the form of an owl. Even though she had no reason to think the dead priest was haunting her, the fine hairs lifted on the back of her neck and she felt a little dizzy, rooted in place, heart racing.

She forced herself to move and quickly poured the remaining water from the gourd into the olla. Her hands shook a little, and she spilled more of the water.

Retreating to the depths of the pool, she held her breath and listened closely for any movement overhead. When she heard nothing except birdsong, her nerves started to settle. She took a few deep breaths and tried to believe this was a morning like any other. After all, she wasn't planning to do anything that would hurt anyone else.

She dropped the gourd into the pool again to fill. This time she looped the cord around her ankle so she had both hands free. She reached into the bag at her waist and drew out a cloth wrapped around cotton padding—what women used during their moontime.

She didn't need a lot, she told herself. Just a little. One smear of brilliant red.

Slowly she drew her mottled tan-and-white chert utility knife from its sheath. Just a few days before, she'd reflaked the stone edge, making it thinner and sharper, in preparation for her granary project. Without giving herself time to change her mind, she hiked up the hem of her dress, then sliced across the curve of her inner thigh. She was careful to keep the knife above the fleshy part where her legs rubbed together, and she tried not to go too deep.

As blood started to flow along the cut, she stowed the knife in its sheath and clapped the padding directly over this latest wound. Her moontime was the one excuse her father would accept for her to be away from him for a few days.

Unfortunately her woman's blood had not yet become regular enough to count on. To show him proof, she had to take matters into her own hands.

3

Starflower followed the Cornmaiden through the rooms of the Smoke-mothers' apartment. Though not even half the size of the temple, this was the largest building she'd ever been in, and she was all too aware that above her head lay another set of rooms. A draft heavy with the odors of tobacco and mystery invaded her nose.

She tried not to feel nervous. The expressions of the Cornmaidens in the courtyard when she'd asked for an audience with the Truthspeaker had made her think no one ever came in asking for the head priestess. Still, one of the girls had jumped up and gone to see whether such a thing could be arranged. The sidelong glances of the remaining girls stung like the cut she'd inflicted on herself earlier that morning.

This stop was an afterthought, not part of her initial plan. She intended to ask the Truthspeaker if Mother Ge ever made a different path for women, one that didn't involve getting with child. Not all women could have children, after all—that was what a handfast mating was about, a full turning to try to get with child. A test of a woman's fertility.

The first girl had come back quickly and gestured for Starflower to go with her. The rest seemed eager to be rid of her. She heard their whispers behind as she stepped into the open doorway. The walls were so thick, her full stride took her barely into the first room, and her eyes had trouble adjusting to the dimness within. She stumbled a few times. Each called forth a hiss of amusement or impatience—Starflower couldn't tell which—from the Cornmaiden. Her clumsiness and a foolish fear that the roof might come down upon her combined to make her wish she'd never thought to come here.

Her guide soon waved her into a much darker room. There was a rustle of cloth in the corner.

"Who is this come before me?" came a voice sweet and melodic. Not that of the Truthspeaker, whose strong tones were familiar to everyone in the village. Not the ancient Seedkeeper, either, she who had been the midwife for so long; she had a rough voice punctuated by coughing. One of the other two high priestesses, Starflower realized: the current midwife or the seer.

A hand came out and sprinkled something pungent on a brazier in which the dull gleam of coals offered only enough light to see forms and shadows.

"Starflower, Revered Grandmother. I'm Starflower, of Cloud-Leaf Clan. I wanted to see the Truthspeaker?" She made it a question, for she couldn't very well come right out and say *Why was I brought to you instead of her?*

"She is occupied with matters of more import. Now, then, tell me, Starflower of Cloud-Leaf Clan, for what purpose have you come? Have you changed your mind about vowing your service to Mother Ge?"

She knew then which of the high priestesses she'd been brought to—the Dreamwalker. The priestess who had sprinkled corn pollen on her in the ceremony in which girls experiencing their first moontime were recognized as women grown. The priestess who had picked her out from the others, gazed at her with piercing eyes, and told her that Mother Ge had chosen Starflower to be one of her handmaidens—an honor Starflower had rejected. The seer, known only as the Dreamwalker, for her name (as with all the high priestesses) had long been forgotten.

"No, that's not . . ." Starflower bit down on her lower lip. She didn't want to ask her question of the Dreamwalker. This one didn't deal with the village council and reputations and the like, as the Truthspeaker did. This one might be able to tell her whether she was in danger from touching the corpse of the priest—but she couldn't ask about that without breaking her promise to Spadefoot.

"I've always seen something of myself in you, Starflower. Find the courage within yourself and speak."

She laced her fingers together to keep them from twitching. "I want to know about . . . about men. You know men, Revered Grandmother." And, so people said of all the senior priestesses, somehow managed to get their way with men long after Cornmaiden prettiness sagged into wrinkles. "Far better than I do. Or wish to. You know what they want."

Silence radiated from the lightless corner.

But Starflower knew what wasn't being said. "Not that! Not bedplay! That can't be what drives them *all*. My father—he's had no woman for many turnings. What he wants most in the world is these fields of his own."

"Not many men are like your father. Perhaps none."

Starflower shifted uncomfortably. "I . . . didn't come to talk about him,

Revered Grandmother. What I want to know is, what can a woman offer a man other than bedplay and babies?"

Again the hand came out. A heavy, bitter smell rose off the brazier. It made her head swim.

"A strange question from one who turned down the chance to become more than simply a woman," the priestess said. "To answer it, I will need to understand more than you are saying."

Starflower's tongue felt stuck to the roof of her mouth. She felt a compulsion to speak of her certainty that she would die in trying to birth a baby. She resisted; the seer must not know of her visions.

Cloth rustled. A puff of tobacco-laden breath suggested the Dream-walker had leaned forward. "Where does this question of yours come from?"

With an effort, Starflower kept herself from backing up. In the fog that crept into her mind with the stink from the brazier, she found herself saying, "I don't want a child. Or to be bedded, as if all I am is a face and a body. I want to be something else to a man."

Another silence settled in, like ice in a footstep.

The Dreamwalker broke it this time, her voice hardening. "I cannot help you in this. A woman's highest purpose is to bring babies into the world. To create life, like Mother Ge herself. Anything else, deliberately holding yourself empty, as you propose to do . . . such a thing violates the will of the Mother-of-All-Creation and shall not go unpunished."

A dull throb rose behind Starflower's eyes. She put the heels of her hands to her temple and pressed. It didn't help. The room was too close, her thoughts too chaotic. She took her hands away. What came to her tongue was a question she hadn't even known was in her:

"So, the women who die in childbirth, are they being punished by Mother Ge?" She heard her voice rise but couldn't help it. Anger at the emptiness she felt—in her head, her chest, her gut—made her keep talking. "My mother, my young brother's mother, my older sister? Because women die all the time trying to birth babies."

"And babies die, in the womb or once born" was the response. "Men die, and women, too, from accidents or when made sick or cursed by envious witches. But they are the unlucky. Why should you believe you will be one of them?"

Starflower couldn't answer that without revealing the dream-visions haunting her. But if they could indeed be the result of a curse, and weren't sent by Mother Ge . . .

"Witches?" she asked. "Have you known of any witches in truth? Or do they exist only in stories?"

"You're too young to remember the lean times that follow floods. When food is plentiful and there is little sickness, no one talks of witches. If someone has the ability to harm his neighbor, why risk doing so when he can get what he needs without being accused as a witch? But still, sometimes, bad luck collects around them. So I ask: Know you any reason why all these women around your father have died?"

Was the high priestess implying that Starflower's father could be a witch, a wielder of magic to harm others? She realized with a leap of her pulse that she could accuse him and be rid of him that way—but no. For all his faults, her father was no witch. And things could go very badly for her and Vineslayer if people thought him one.

As heat rose in her cheeks, her thoughts seemed less muddled. She fanned the embers of anger, made the flame grow, revelled in the sudden sense of clarity it gave her.

The Dreamwalker had no right to try to split Starflower off from her family. She was here because she had no mother. She wanted advice from a more experienced woman because she had *no mother!* Whose fault was that? Not her father's!

Her hands balled into fists. She felt like ants were crawling on her skin. But she also felt free to say what was in her mind.

"No more reason than any other woman," she said through tight lips. "Spadefoot's mother didn't survive birthing him, either. What they all had in common isn't my father, it's the priestess who stood between their legs, waiting to catch the babies when they fell out!"

The Dreamwalker's voice roughened. "You dare say that all the time she was the Childcatcher, a midwife armed with all the wisdom of Mother Ge and entrusted with bringing forth new life, she simply let the mothers die?"

"You said yourself, a woman's highest purpose is to make children. Once they've done so, what more use are they?"

"As mothers, as mates, as those you come to for advice."

"But you won't give me the advice I wanted. You just tell me I'm wrong to even ask! That Mother Ge is going to punish me—"

"Not content to speak against she who was the Childcatcher, you would now criticize the Allmother herself?"

Starflower's breath caught as she realized that was exactly what she'd done. Maybe she did indeed deserve to be punished. Maybe Mother Ge had realized what an ungrateful girl she was and, to punish her, had led her to a dead body and sent its spirit to haunt her. The owl that morning. Had that been a warning?

"You go too far, girl! Get out! Out!"

She tried to apologize, to tell what had happened to her, to ask what it all meant, but the Dreamwalker would have none of it. "Argue with me," the priestess said, "and I'll tell the Seedkeeper what you accuse her of!

Moonbright!"

The Cornmaiden popped into the doorway so quickly, she had to have been standing right outside, where she could hear all that had been said. She led Starflower away by the hand like a disobedient child.

Days later, Starflower sat crosslegged on a double-thickness reed mat and worked on a basket. Before her, a fence made of ocotillo limbs stood between her and the clanlands. She deliberately worked there, near the fence. It was a reminder that her father wanted her to put down roots just like the ocotillos did in such a dry, undesirable place.

The moontime hut lay close by the trash midden, near enough that she could smell the nightsoil deposited since the most recent burning. She could hear dogs squabbling over offal. Despite all that—the stink, the barking and snarling, the ache of her cut—she felt suffused by a new courage.

The old Starflower, the one she'd been before encountering the body and meeting Spadefoot, had often felt overwhelmed by the boisterous, bawdy stories, songs, and conversations of the moontime hut. She'd dreaded seeing her childhood friends there, for they'd been a few turnings behind her in stepping into womanhood and seemed jealous of her early blossoming. She'd also stung under the hostility of the older girls who had been inducted into womanhood at the same time as she had, for they resented the attention boys paid her.

But this new Starflower, she didn't care about any of that. She had her tools and supplies, everything she needed. She sat in the shade of the vatto at her clan's moontime hut and lost herself in her task.

"She's here."

"Hmm?" Starflower pulled up the slack in the black witch's-claw strip and tightened it around the lengthening beargrass coil with a tug. Only then, satisfied that it was secure, did she take her attention away from her work.

Before her were two dusty sandaled feet and above them a red moontime skirt. She lifted her gaze farther and shaded her eyes with her hand against the hazy backdrop of sky. The girl's expression seemed sly.

"Who's here?" Starflower asked.

"Deerchaser, of course."

"Oh. Yes. Yes, of course." But she didn't get up right away.

"Aren't you going to go talk to her?"

Starflower glanced back to the skeletal base of her basket and wished she could just keep working on it. She didn't expect to get much out of

Deerchaser, probably no more than the clan-aunties had told her: "His name is Rush," one of the matrons had said. "They say he got the name when he was a ditchrunner, because he was a fast runner." She'd winked and added, "There's some who think he's fast in other ways, too." She fluttered her hand in a crude gesture. Another had said only, "These days he keeps to himself."

Eventually, as Starflower persisted in asking about the Canalmaster, the older women had looked at each other and suggested that if she really wanted to know something about him, the one to ask was Deerchaser, who would be coming later.

So it was later, and Deerchaser had finally arrived.

Starflower set the base of her basket on the cloth she'd put down to keep her supplies clean. When she tried to rise from the mat on which she'd been working, dark stars swam before her eyes and her legs wobbled. She had to place both hands on the ground for balance.

The wooziness lasted for only a few moments. Other women sometimes complained of such weakness during their bleeding. She wondered whether her moontime was indeed upon her, if she could have brought it on simply by telling her father it was so. Or perhaps her own body felt the effects of being surrounded by women draining off their fertility, isolated from men who might otherwise take harm from so much woman's power.

As she straightened, the cut on her thigh pulled and hurt. With two fingers she wiped a trace of sweat from her upper lip. She'd been unaccountably warm this day.

The gate in the ocotillo fence lay on the other side of the hut. When Starflower limped around the hut, the first thing she saw, on a bench by the gate, was a tray of deer liver—presumably brought by Deerchaser—which served to strengthen the blood of women in their moontime. One glance at the glistening chunks made Starflower's stomach lurch. She put her hand to her mouth and quickly took a step back.

The deer lifted its head, long ears twitching in alarm, and looked directly at her. Though Starflower knew it was just in her imagination, she couldn't stop seeing it, a dream-fogged scene. *An arrow of lightning streaked out of the sky. Before it could pierce the deer in the side, a hand grasped it. Beyond the hand, mantled in darkness and smoke, was a face with wide, staring eyes.*

"Don't ask me to cry over a dead priest," Deerchaser said, out of sight around the hut.

The waking vision mercifully shattered, freeing Starflower from its grip. She leaned against the mud-plastered wall of the hut and closed her eyes. She felt hot all over, yet chills ran through her.

"But what if the rumors are right—and it's the Wilders that killed him?"

asked another woman.

"Why would they do such a thing, take such a risk? Anyway, I heard there was no caliche pick in the corpse when it came out of the canal."

"Then why would so many people say there was?"

"A lie started by the Rainsinger would be my guess. Where else would such talk of violence come from, if not that two-tongued poisonous snake? I told you what he has in mind for the sun-festival. Should we all stay silent and let the priests do as they please?"

Starflower, listening, bit her lip. She wanted to get it over with, ask Deerchaser everything about Rush. But her clan-sister seemed just as frightening as the high priestess, the way she was talking.

"It's just deer hearts," said the other woman.

"For now," Deerchaser shot back. "What makes you think they won't go beyond that for the next sun-festival, even sacrificing a living creature, willing or not?"

"I say more power to the priests if it means we eat well. It's fine for you—you hunters don't need rain. But with the canals only half fixed, we farmers surely do. Besides, if what the priests are planning is wrong, surely it's for Mother Ge to punish them, not us!"

"Maybe she did. Who's to say that priest wasn't struck down by Mother Ge herself?"

"You're just being difficult. Everyone knows the Wilders killed him."

"I don't know that. Anyway, one could just as well argue Spadefoot killed his own vow-brother. I saw them both heading up to the river that morning—the day he must have died."

Starflower clapped her hands to her ears but couldn't unhear Deerchaser's words. She stumbled backward. With her first step, her heel caught on one of the work mats. Unbalanced, she fell and hit her head. She cried out, then felt nothing as darkness took her.

"So the cactus ball inside her clung

Upon his manly parts,

And he, he learnt a lesson dear—

Don't play with women's hearts."

Starflower heard the final lines of the rowdy story-song of Handsome Man and the Makai's Daughter as consciousness crept back. Muzzily she wished her father was like the makai, that he cared for his daughter and didn't want to foist her off on another man, one who took advantage of all the women he met.

Raucous laughter pelted her ears. Women shrieked as though they'd never before heard the familiar story of Handsome Man getting a well-deserved comeuppance.

She realized she lay on one of the deerhide-padded benches in the moontime hut. Besides being far too warm, the air held a stink that made her queasy, a mixture of poultices and potions and smudging bundles and too many bodies . . . and blood.

Her ears still rang with what Deerchaser had said about Spadefoot and the other priest going up to the river together that fateful morning. Starflower remembered her initial suspicion that Spadefoot had killed him. If that was true, she'd walked about, hand in hand, with a madman, for so he would have to be, to take the life of another. Her stomach clenched and her head started to throb.

He didn't kill you, she reminded herself. *You survived.* That didn't make her feel any better.

Carefully she raised herself to lean on one elbow. With the other hand she explored the back of her head, which hurt worse than her leg now. She found a lump there, though when she took her hand away she saw no blood on her fingers.

Her clan-sisters' voices slurred into the familiar words of the next song in the cycle, the birth of the witch Ho'ok. She guessed they'd been indulging in the agave liquor she'd refused earlier.

"What happened?" she asked groggily.

One of the clan-aunties waggled a rootlike forefinger. "You must've fainted. Added a bit of excitement to our day."

"We figured you're with child," said a younger matron.

"No!" Starflower exclaimed. The uneven singing lurched to a halt.

She sat upright, then wished she hadn't, as the movement made her head pound. She moaned and clutched at it with both hands.

"No? You mean, no, you aren't with child? Are you sure?" Deerchaser, seated on the adjacent bench, looked at her with eyebrows arched. Above one brow was a flame marking the birth of her boy; below the eye, a teardrop marking his death.

Not for her the red skirt worn by the rest of the women in the hut, some of whom were even bare on top; Deerchaser sat there in leather leggings and a tunic. Starflower fleetingly thought she had to be roasting in the overwarm hut.

Then she remembered seeing Deerchaser while coming back from the river that same morning the priests had gone up. Anxiously she searched Deerchaser's face for a sign that her clan-sister had observed her, too.

But Deerchaser didn't seem sly or knowing. Starflower cast her mind back to the question she'd asked. "Of course I'm sure. I've never been with a man *that* way!"

"How long has it been since your last bleeding?" Deerchaser's gaze sharpened.

"I'm in my moontime now." No one contradicted Starflower. Women never paid much attention to what others did in the moontime hut. "That's why I'm here."

One of the clan-aunties urged, "At least have something to eat. Did you breakfast this morning?"

"No. I forgot."

"Your carry sack is there beside you," said another of the aunties.

Starflower rose and found it placed next to the bench. She picked it up and walked outside, still woozy, though the fresh air helped revive her.

Only then did she remember there was no point in looking in her carry sack for food, because when she'd made this plan she hadn't thought to pack any. She hadn't expected to be here so long. And in the days spent waiting for Deerchaser, she hadn't felt particularly hungry.

"I didn't bring anything to eat," she confessed to one of the clan-sisters who had followed her out.

"Here," said the other woman, a young mother from the outer clanlands. "I brought some squash leather." She dug in her own carry sack.

Though Starflower didn't think dried squash would sit well in her stomach, she decided not to argue. Her clan-sister's willingness to share her food was generous—especially considering that some of those fields had needed to be watered with ollas hauled from canals several fields away.

Starflower took the yellowish strips handed to her. As she bit into one, saliva burst into her mouth. She nearly cried from the intensity of it.

She'd gnawed her way through the first piece when she became aware that several clanwomen had come out of the hut and were watching her. "Why are you all looking at me?"

"Are you sure you can't be carrying a child?" Deerchaser asked. "You said you hadn't been with a man *that* way." A hand gesture made her meaning clear. "Have you been . . . together . . . with a man in any way?"

A bite of squash lodged in Starflower's throat as she inhaled. Coughing, she thumped on her chest until she felt the lump slide down to rest heavy in her stomach.

"I'm only asking," said Deerchaser, "because there are boys—and men, too—who will say a lot of things are safe, when they really aren't."

"I am absolutely not with child. And I know how babies are made, that they come when a man puts his—" She searched for a word that wasn't too crude. "His dangly bits in you." The others laughed. "My father explained it all to me."

"Your father!" exclaimed Deerchaser.

One of the older clan-aunties snorted. "As if men know anything about baby-making."

"They know all about the fun parts," said another woman.

Starflower recognized the voice as the one she'd heard earlier, talking to Deerchaser. Laughingbird, her name was.

The clan-auntie chuckled in turn. "They *have* the fun parts."

Ignoring them, Deerchaser folded her arms and advised Starflower, "You certainly can't trust them to tell the truth."

"My father wouldn't lie to me!" Starflower replied, though she knew he would have no qualms about lying if it meant he would get what he wanted—water in his new fields.

"All men lie," Deerchaser told her.

Starflower shook her head.

"You always see the worst side of men," said the clan-auntie to Deerchaser.

"I've been right more times than not, haven't I?"

Laughingbird said, "She *was* right about that one who was beating his bedmate."

Unnerved by such casual talk of women being beaten, Starflower drew in a sharp breath. Her father's face flashed into her mind, then Rush's.

"The thing about fathers is, they're undependable," Deerchaser went on. "There when they feel like it, gone when they don't."

Starflower, feeling small and vulnerable, asked, "And how are mothers any different?"

Laughingbird, who had several children, grinned. "Mothers have no choice. We're in our children's lives forever."

"Unless they die!" Starflower's head hurt, and the squash wasn't agreeing with her. Until she heard her own words and saw Deerchaser's face go grim, she didn't realize they might be taken the wrong way, that Deerchaser might think she meant the children died, rather than the mothers.

Deerchaser asked her, "You think your father is on your side? You trust him to take care of you?"

"Why wouldn't I?" Starflower exclaimed defensively.

"Like he did your mother? And your brother's mother?" Deerchaser continued. "Your father has a bad reputation among the clan-sisters. Some even wonder where he finds his satisfaction these days, so far from the village, with only one female—you—within reach. Especially since no one admitted to being your sister's bedwarmer, and her carrying a baby."

Starflower stared at the ring of faces around her, all watching her, judging.

"Now you're all alone with him, with just your brother," Deerchaser said. "It's unnatural, the three of you with nobody else around—"

"You would know all about that!" Starflower exclaimed. "Your only friends are those young boys. What do you get up to with them, hmm? Tell me that. Tell us all!" Shocked by what she'd said, she put a hand up to her mouth, too late to stop the terrible words.

Deerchaser's nostrils flared as she stared at Starflower. She turned without a word and started for the gate.

Starflower limped after her clan-sister. "I'm sorry! I didn't mean—" She grabbed Deerchaser's arm.

Deerchaser spun about, breaking her hold, and shoved her.

Unable to regain her balance, Starflower staggered back and fell on her rump. Her teeth closed on her tongue as the shock went from her tailbone to her head in an instant.

The pain of it flashed into anger and then humiliation, as she slumped there and told herself she deserved to be punished for repeating cruel gossip.

Deerchaser strode over and knelt by her. "Are you all right? Me and my temper. I never meant to push you so hard." Her face was knife-edged and as pale as the Rainsinger's.

Starflower clutched at Deerchaser's arm, desperate to make her understand. "It was my fault. I should never have said such a thing!"

She'd changed her mind about wanting to talk with Deerchaser, for what if the other woman remembered seeing Starflower and put her together with the priests? But she couldn't let her clan-sister just leave, not with that vile slur between them.

"Deerchaser. Her mat is behind the hut," one of the clan-aunties said gently, "where she was working. She might be more comfortable there."

As a few of the other women helped Starflower up, Deerchaser seemed to be having an argument with herself. The kinder side evidently won. She took Starflower's arm and began to walk slowly back the way they'd come, then past the door and around the hut.

As they came to the work area where woven reed mats lay scattered about, Starflower glanced sidelong at Deerchaser. Though considerate in her movements, the woman still had a set look on her face. The insult obviously had struck home.

Laughingbird told Deerchaser, "She wanted to talk to you anyway. Maybe you should sit with her for a while."

Deerchaser's mouth compressed into a pale, thin line. She closed her eyes and took a deep breath, then another. She shook her head after a few more moments and sat. She gestured for Starflower to do the same.

Once they were both seated, Deerchaser said, "You were spying on me, before, when you fainted. Why?"

I didn't faint, I fell, Starflower wanted to say. "I just wanted to talk to you. I wasn't trying to overhear." To distract Deerchaser from asking what she'd hoped to talk about, she asked, "Why did Laughingbird say that priest was killed by the Wilders? Wasn't he found near the temple?"

Deerchaser eyed her. "Where did you hear that?"

"I heard he drowned," Starflower persisted. "So what could the Wilders have to do with it?"

Giving a one-shouldered shrug, Deerchaser said, "Laughingbird said there was a caliche pick thrust into his chest and he was holding part of a shell net like the Wilders wear in their hair. Why so curious about this priest?"

"She's just stalling, I imagine," said the clan-auntie who had known where Starflower's mat was. "She's been saying for days that she wants to know about the Canalmaster."

Starflower sighed and briefly closed her eyes. So. It was out now.

"Is this true?" Deerchaser demanded. As Starflower admitted it was, Deerchaser said, "I don't talk about him. Ever."

With her intention revealed, Starflower decided to press forward. "Everyone says you're the one to ask about this new Canalmaster. So why won't you talk about him?"

She remembered Vineslayer's comment about Deerchaser being ruined by a Watermaster. But she didn't see how Rush, new to the village and from away up north, could have been that Watermaster. "Has he done something to you?" she asked, hoping the answer was no.

A thin clan-auntie said maliciously, "Tell us, Deerchaser, has he?"

In answer, she turned on the older woman. "I'm not saying anything, yea or nay, with you vultures flapping around!"

"Just go, would you!" Starflower exclaimed. "The rest of you couldn't—or wouldn't—answer my questions and insisted I ask Deerchaser. Well, I have, and she won't answer with you all standing here. So go away!"

Eventually they allowed themselves to be shooed back to whatever each had been doing before.

Once the two of them were alone, Deerchaser jabbed a forefinger at Starflower. "You've gotten away with way too much in your short life, just because you're pretty and pretend to be sweet and not overly bright. You may fool the men, which doesn't take much when they're so happy to be led around by what you call their 'dangly bits,' but you don't fool me, not for an instant. We aren't friends, Starflower. Never will be."

"I don't need a friend."

"Of course not. You're too good to take any notice of me, except when you need something."

"That's not what I meant." Starflower sought the words that would explain how important this was to her. "I *have* to know about the Canalmaster. What he's like, what he wants, what he likes—"

"What will make him do your bidding?" the other woman interrupted, sarcastically. "What will make him fall all over you like the boys who follow you about like puppies?"

Starflower flushed. "That's not it."

"Must you have every man at your feet?"

"*I* don't want him!" she found herself saying. "It's my father's idea—"

"Oh, I see. Your father needs the water for his fields, and Rush is holding out for you. You think you can control him?"

Starflower wondered what would happen if she told her clan-sister what she actually had planned. But she couldn't risk it. She sighed. "I would just like to understand him a little. With your help."

Deerchaser gave a bitter laugh. "Maybe it's not such a favor as all that, for me to tell you what I know. I'm inclined to do it. Yes, I believe I will," she said with a nod. But for a long moment she said nothing. Then: "He got me with child. And then left."

Starflower stared at her. *With child.* Deerchaser must have meant her son, who had died several turnings earlier. But then the Canalmaster must have been here before, a long time ago. As a ditchrunner? How old had Deerchaser been? Not much older than Starflower herself?

"What, you have nothing to say?" Deerchaser linked her hands over her belly. "I know I'm not pretty, the way you are. I wasn't back then, either. So why would he pick me?"

"He must have . . ." The word *loved* died on her tongue. "He must have cared for you."

"Evidently not, or he would have stayed."

Starflower blinked; she couldn't argue against that. "Were you willing? Did you lie with him because you loved him?"

"There's no love in seduction."

The flatness of Deerchaser's voice made Starflower think that answer was a lie. "All right, let's not call it love on either side. Was it a seduction or . . . or worse?"

"He didn't have to force me. I was willing. Let that be a lesson to you, about making stupid decisions when you're young, believing what people tell you. Especially believing what men say when their rattles-and-flute are in charge. Their 'dangly bits,' as you put it, so nicely."

"Not all men are driven by their desires! My father isn't!"

"Keep telling yourself that, if it makes you feel better. But tell me this, do you trust him the way a daughter should? Or do you wonder why he's taken you away from your clan, away down to the other end of the village? Gotten you all alone, except for your brother?"

"It's because the most important thing to him is carving these fields out of the desert. Not me, not my happiness, not my life!"

A strained silence fell.

Finally Deerchaser stirred. "Just be careful. Rush doesn't want the responsibility of being a father, so if you're thinking of holding him by claiming that child in your belly is his, that won't work."

"I am not—"

"And don't plan on him staying for any length of time, either with you or in the village. He loses interest quickly. In everything except his precious canals."

"Then tell me how to keep his interest. Without bedplay."

"If I knew—" Deerchaser closed her eyes. Her face sagged into lines that Starflower hadn't noticed before. After a moment she took a deep breath and looked right at Starflower. "If you really want to appeal to his better side, be interesting. Be smart. Be curious."

She laid a hand on Starflower's shoulder, bent close, and whispered, "But be careful. In his mind, rules were made for lesser people." She pulled back and gave a decisive nod. "Don't expect him to do what anyone else thinks is right. He'll go his own way, that one. Just like a Wilder. Which, in truth, he is. They all are, those Watermasters. You can't count on them for a single thing—except maybe to upset all your plans."

Starflower listened intently as Deerchaser went on: "You say your father is obsessed with his fields? Rush is the same way with his canals. There's no room for anything else. Don't expect that to change. It makes him very good at what he does. The village needs him. So. Don't break his heart—if you manage to find it."

Deerchaser rose nimbly. Raising her voice, she called out, "See you at the games." She waved to the others, who watched them from beyond the moontime hut. Then she strode away, leaving Starflower to sort through all that she'd said.

4

Starflower had returned from the moontime hut confident that she could strike a bargain with the Canalmaster and prepared to face her father.

Once Deerchaser left, the other women became chatty. From them she had learned that Rush was attentive to his duties. Unlike the old Canalmaster, he walked the canals every day. He knew all the problem spots in even the smallest cross-canals—though no one seemed confident that he could get them fixed by the next growing season. Everyone claimed to like him better than the old Canalmaster.

But as far as they knew he paid no particular attention to any woman. They found that peculiar for a Watermaster, especially given his history with Deerchaser. Starflower thought it a promising sign that he seemed more interested in canals than dallying with women.

She hadn't paid much attention to those who complained that he'd messed them about or decided a dispute wrongly . . . farmers always complained about others getting more water than they had any right to. She had gone back to working on her basket once the complaints descended into a bitter argument between two neighboring clan-sisters.

Starflower made no protest when her father came to her on the morning of the next trade day and told her to fix herself up. She felt as ready to take on the Canalmaster as she ever would be. Covert applications of poultices had finally begun to heal the cut on her thigh, and the ache of it had eased, along with the dizziness and fever that had plagued her at the moontime hut.

Yet as she stood with her father on the trade ground between the temple and the mound where the Canalmaster lived, her heart beat faster and her palms were sweaty. She felt conspicuous as people jostled by.

Unlike nearly all the other women, she wasn't wearing a deerhide dress on this chilly fall morning. Her father had insisted she wear her one-shouldered summer dress, of thin and drapey cotton, caught at the waist with a broad woven sash. He'd given her a multistrand turquoise necklace that he said had belonged to her mother—she remembered her older sister wearing it—along with some shell bracelets she didn't know he had. They all felt cold on her skin.

"What if this doesn't work?" she asked. "What if he isn't so easy to . . . ?" Unable to come up with the right word, she waved a hand erratically.

Her father laughed and touched her bare shoulder. His hand felt warm but still she shivered.

His hand tightened. "He's a man, isn't he? And you're very pretty."

She smiled because he seemed to expect it. Her insides went even colder.

"If only you'd been here the other day," he said, "you would have brought him right around with that smile."

"I couldn't help that my moontime came upon me."

His eyes narrowed. He squeezed her shoulder, not quite hard enough to bruise.

She dropped her gaze from his and held very still. Could he know she'd lied to him about her moontime? "And it wasn't a waste of time," she murmured. "From the clan women I learned quite a lot about what kind of man he is."

"He's the kind of man to run back to his rathole and hide, that's the kind he is. It's on you, daughter"—he shook her slightly—"to draw him out, convince him to give me my water."

"What if he says it can't be done?"

Her father's jaw tightened. "Our future depends on how persuasive you can be. You'd better be prepared to do a bit of flirting."

"I don't think he'll want to stop at that."

"I know what you're worried about," he assured her. "But I've taught you how to please a man without it going too far. You won't get with child if you do as I say."

"It's a narrow path to walk." She pulled away, trying to look obedient rather than rebellious, and faced him.

Her father shrugged. "He won't dare do anything you don't let him. He needs the good opinion of the clans, or he'll be done here. You may not be the brightest girl in the village, but surely even you can see that. Now, go."

As she moved slowly through the crowd, her skin prickled as though someone's watchful gaze followed her. She glanced back but saw only her father looking at her. Everyone else focused on their own enjoyment. Boys and girls shrieked and darted in and out among the buildings, young men shouted in blustery pleasure, and young women laughed in high-pitched voices, while matrons and their men sauntered along in pairs and small groups.

With harvest over and the fields resting for winter, the villagers seemed almost lighthearted. Starflower envied their ease. She hadn't felt that way in a long time.

The sense of being observed stayed with her. She looked back at her father again, but he was gone, lost among the many people out to find entertainment in the day.

Something drew her gaze to the top of the Temple of the Mist, where a lone man stood, immobile, robes billowing around him. She wondered whether it was Spadefoot. She bit her lower lip as she remembered what Deerchaser had said about two priests together that fateful morning. Could Spadefoot have killed his vow-brother and then pretended so well that he hadn't? She shivered again.

Cheers came from up ahead and someone bumped into her from behind. She forced herself to pay more attention to where she was going, though in the back of her mind she kept thinking about Spadefoot and his vow-brother.

The flow of movement halted as the crowd bunched together. Spectators for the chich'wipedho game filled the space between the temple precinct's high adobe wall and the old ballcourt, where the Far-Traders usually set up. The play of the game ranged from the edge of the village to the canal bank, but most of the spectators stayed near the temple and the traders.

From where she stood, she could just see the wall atop the great mound, the Masterholding, shared by Watermasters, healers, and hunters. Starflower worked her way toward it through the crush of people. In the mound's shadow, she finally lost the oppressive sense of being watched—and was able to set aside the fear that hadn't left her since her father had told her what he expected her to do.

Because it was a trade day, the Watermasters' ward was open to all comers. But there was no gate in this wall. Anyone wanting to speak with the Canalmaster had to climb a thin-runged ladder to get over the outer wall, then another to get up to the Watermasters' plaza.

Her dress being only down to her knees made climbing the ladders more manageable. And with the ballgame occupying everyone's attention, she set aside the self-consciousness she felt at going somewhere she'd never been and, some would say, didn't belong.

Once in the half-walled plaza, high above the old ballcourt and the traders' stalls, she eased down onto a long adobe bench along the wall, in the midst of a dozen or so men and women, entirely strangers to her and mostly of an age with her clan-aunties and uncles. From there she watched the Canalmaster.

His strong white teeth flashed often as he spoke to the farmers a few at a time. Every time one small group left, and before the next was brought to him, he rolled his shoulders and cracked his neck as though his body was stiff from inactivity.

He sat on a mesquite branch that had grown in such a way as to form a narrow seat with three legs. At his feet was a plastered floor into which had been carved a pattern of lines, which curved and separated and connected in a way that reminded her of veins in a leaf. Sometimes he would kneel and use a long saguaro rib to indicate a single point on a line or would sweep it along a larger section as he looked at the farmer who stood nearby and more often than not nodded.

When his ditchrunners, not much older than Vineslayer, came to ask Starflower what problem she brought to him, she told them she didn't have fields, she'd just come to meet him. They threw her suspicious glances but didn't tell her to go away.

This was one of those heart-brightening days of fall when it seemed nothing could go wrong. The petitioners made their arguments and complaints and requests and demands, one after another; their faces shifted from discontent to at least thoughtfulness, if not outright happiness, before each farmer disappeared down the ladder. She had time to study the Canalmaster, to watch his expressions and interactions with the others.

His patient manner, whether talking or gesturing or pointing at the lines, seemed to soothe and calm those people who were agitated. It reminded her of how Spadefoot had eased her terror that day when she'd gone up to the river, though the two men weren't alike in any other way.

The Canalmaster was lanky and tall in comparison to most of the other men she knew, certainly in contrast to the solidly built Spadefoot. Also, he had a nice face, pleasant and honest. Beyond that, he looked exotic, completely unlike the farmers of the village. His hair was braided into thin snaky ropes with shells and beads woven in. His mud-colored cotton tunic and leggings streamed with blue ribbons at the seams. On the breast of the tunic were sewn beads and shells in bright patterns that included herons and turtles and fish, symbols of the Watermasters.

Oddly, his face had no tattoos, not even the wavy line signifying the river-serpent, which appeared on the forehead of most of the Watermasters she'd seen. She wondered if the lack of tattoos was common for his people up at Sky River.

From his mesquite-limb bench, he looked at her inquiringly. She realized there was no one left waiting with her to vie for his attention.

Rush, she reminded herself. He had a name, he was a man.

She stood up and smiled. Not in the way her father had taught her to do—arching her back and tossing her head. Instead, she smiled as though he was already a friend, someone she liked and respected.

He rose and sauntered over to her.

"Hello," she murmured.

"Hello to you." His grin flashed.

She felt it all the way to her toes—and realized this man could be dangerous to her. She was surprised and not altogether pleased. But she delivered her compliment with a quiet smile: "That was impressive. You worked everything out so people went away happy."

"Most people, not all. There's nothing I could do that would satisfy some. Take your father, for example. You are Earth Holder's daughter, aren't you?"

"Yes, that's me." She took a breath and summoned her courage. This was the moment of decision: her father's plan or her own? "I'm Starflower. Of Cloud-Leaf Clan."

"Yet your father doesn't have use-right to any clanlands up there."

"He did before," she explained. "Because of the problems getting water to the outer clanlands this season, he decided to try something different."

"Ah. So it was his idea to restore those old fields?"

She shook her head. "I don't know anything about that." All she knew was that he'd come home one day and said they were leaving. But some sense of loyalty—more to the village than to her father—made her ask, "*Could* you get water to those fields of his, if you tried?"

Rush laughed. "No, not even if we worked for a hundred turnings."

"Why not?" She'd noticed earlier that his eyes lit up and his face became more mobile when he talked about watering fields. That fit with what Deerchaser had said about his work being the way to get closer to him.

"Something changed down by the temple," he explained, "at the dogleg where the canals split, curved around, and bent back on themselves."

"Something?"

He grinned again. "I could talk washouts and waterstones until your head spun. But somehow I don't think that's what you've come for today, Starflower of Cloud-Leaf Clan. It's an interesting name."

"Do you know what it means?"

He said he didn't.

"It's a basket pattern. I make baskets."

"Do you, now?"

"Yes, and I understand how to start with just a few sticks, weave colors in and out, and make something complicated and lovely in the end."

"So . . ." he prompted.

"So, I was looking at these lines you've drawn here." She pointed at the plastered area.

"What do you think of them?"

"They're the canals, aren't they?" Though they were just deeply incised lines, with no fields or buildings marked, she could see the network of canals of varying sizes—from the large mains all the way down to the ditches that spilled into the fields. "Where's Cloud-Leaf Clan?"

He pointed with the saguaro rib. She could see it then: the clanlands of her mother's people were at the north end of the village; the sharp curves of what he called the dogleg were far to the south, beyond the desert flats where the women were currently playing their chich'wipedho game.

"I may not know the details of how you keep them running, but I can see the pattern. It's like a basket, the way all the little parts fit together."

Her comment seemed to surprise him. Cocking his head to one side, he studied the lines. After a bit, he shrugged and said, "I don't see it. I see plunge pools that need to be filled with rocks. I see headgates in need of repair, walls and beds that have to be replastered. Neighbors who hate each other yet can't imagine not having the other around to fight with. But it's interesting to hear that someone else can view it in a whole different way."

"Do all Canalmasters have these lines? Drawings? What do you call them?"

"Maps," he said. "And yes, you'll find one on the top of each of the Watermasters' mounds."

"Maps." She tested the word. Farmers didn't need such things. They knew their own fields, and even the clanlands, as well as they knew their own face. But if you were the man who had to tell them there wasn't enough water to spread out over all the fields, maybe it was necessary to show them where it would go.

"So are you here for yourself or on behalf of your father or your clan?" he asked. "I've met a lot of farmers who say they want to talk about what I do but really want to talk about getting me to do something for them."

He gave her the opening, but she couldn't bring herself to take it. "Why can't I just be curious?"

"Let's say you are. Did you find out what you came for?"

"Yes, I think I did." She clasped her hands, took a breath, and said, "I don't want anything from you. I have something *for* you."

"I've heard that before."

She flushed at his knowing gaze. "I'm not offering"—she felt awkward even saying the word but forced it out—"bedplay."

"What, then?" he asked.

"A mating in name only. No lovemaking, no children. You can have all the other women you want!"

He snorted in disbelief.

"I swear—"

"Listen to me." He placed a gentle hand on her shoulder. "The farmers hereabouts are already at each other's throats imagining favoritism everywhere. This . . . connection you suggest would just set them on me." He removed his hand and folded his arms across his chest; she missed the warmth of his touch on her chilled skin. "Oh, and tell your father he won't get any water in his ditches by sending you to me."

"I told you already, he didn't send me. Truly." Seeing Rush's too-evident doubt, she hurried to explain what she meant, before she lost her nerve. "What if I told you I could ease your way, make the farmers accept you as one of us?"

"I'm a Watermaster. Nothing you can do to change that."

"A lifemating. Heartfast." Her reckless statement to Vineslayer about never wearing a man's mark on her wrist had given her the idea.

He shook his head.

"Kin by blood bond to Cloud-Leaf Clan. Tell me that wouldn't change how they treat you," she challenged him.

Expressionless now, he said, "No clan woman concerned about her reputation would take a Watermaster as a mate."

"But I'm not concerned about my reputation." She put her hands on his folded arms. "I know what I'm saying. Think on this: as a basket maker I don't have to have fields of my own. There would be no issue of you playing favorites."

He glanced at her hands, so small compared to his. Then he raised his gaze back to hers. "We Watermasters are already tied to the clans by blood. Why do you think the farmers mistrust us so? It's because there's no way of knowing who a baby's father is—blood-bound or not. Women don't always claim the true father of their child."

He shook off her touch and pointed toward the throng below. "*He* could have been fathered by a Watermaster. Or her." His finger stabbed toward someone else. "Or that one there. Taking me as your mate is not going to earn me acceptance by your clan."

"You're wrong! Let me prove it to you. Come to our clan-feast. You'll be welcome, as my guest." Surely he would see that it was a heartfelt invitation, not to be turned down lightly.

Rush hesitated. "Will your father be there?"

There was a chance he would come looking for her, but Starflower hoped he wouldn't. She shook her head. "He isn't of the clan."

"Why are you doing this? And granted that you are, why choose me?"

She sidestepped his first question. "You're new here. You seem—" No, he didn't seem lonely, she thought, stopping the words on her tongue. "Alone. Maybe by choice. But if not, I can fix that."

"I was assigned to Crookstaff Village before. I know people."

"Yes, so I've heard. But that was long ago. Things change." That was as close as she wanted to come to bringing up Deerchaser.

They descended the ladder and wandered over to the old sunken ballcourt, to see what the Far-Traders had brought for this moon's gathering. Winter offerings sometimes included the heavy, curly-coated skin of the great humped beast of the eastward plains, copper bells or cocoa beans or bright macaw feathers from the southlands, large flat shells from the seacoast with all the colors of the dawn sky reflected in their inner surface, even carved pipes or animal figures of blood-red or tawny stone from the vast country away to the north.

Rush made her laugh at his way of looking at the village she'd spent her life in and the people she'd grown up among. He didn't set out to charm her, she realized; he was just good company. While she might not understand what he'd seen in Deerchaser in his younger days, she had a notion of what Deerchaser had seen in him.

The offerings at the trade ground this time included nothing of particular interest for Starflower, although Rush, who seemed fascinated by sharp things, spent some time looking at crystals and various other stones and tools. She stayed close by him but had little interest in what he picked up and poked at.

When her uneasy sense of being watched returned, she looked around. Spadefoot stared at her from a space left open in the crowd. Her heart started to pound, and she wrested her gaze from his.

Only then did she understand why no one wanted to stand just there.

Beside Spadefoot was a wizened man—his father, the Rainsinger of the Temple of the Mist. Wrapped in a gray cloak, he leaned on a hook-topped staff. His face and hands, all that was visible under his wrappings, were pale as shell except where tattooed. His white hair, shaved at the sides, was bound up into a knot with leather cords. His unblinking eyes were the color of fog instead of the normal brown; he looked right at her.

His age should have kept him from posing a threat. Yet she stood frozen as her heart thudded against her ribs. She felt menace flowing off him.

Spadefoot seemed indifferent now and no longer looked her way. She started to nibble on her lower lip.

He'd sworn her to secrecy but hadn't promised the same to her. Would he have told his father about meeting her by the river? Perhaps something had gone wrong with his plan to move his brother-priest's body to the temple. Unless Spadefoot had lied to her about that—maybe to hide the fact that he had killed his vow-brother himself.

"I'm boring you," Rush said.

Starflower jerked. She'd forgotten he was there. She turned away from the priests and summoned a smile. "No, not at all. But I am hungry."

"So that's what it is. I was beginning to think it was thunder, and all along it was just your stomach rumbling."

She couldn't help but laugh. "Nonsense." With unfortunate timing, the tantalizing smell of roasting meat wafted to her nose just then and caused her stomach to growl.

He grinned, then took her hand to guide her through the crowd as he placed himself a little ahead to clear the way. She glanced back at Spadefoot. Now he was watching her again, but his father appeared to have found another target for his baleful gaze. Could it be Rush who'd been under the Rainsinger's earlier scrutiny, not her? As for Spadefoot . . . she couldn't let him into her head. Not now.

Rush would have taken her nearer the temple, maybe planning to escort her all the way to her father's fieldhouse. She tugged him to a halt. With her free hand, she waggled her forefinger at him. "Are you forgetting something? I promised you a feast and a welcome in the clan."

"Ah, yes, this unlikely promise of yours." But he didn't argue, just smiled down at her and turned aside to take them out of the trade ground to the west instead of the south.

An unfamiliar emotion sparked to life in her. She rather thought it was happiness.

"Why aren't you out there with your clan-sisters?" he asked a little later, as they followed the canal toward the Cloud-Leaf clanholdings.

"Out . . ." she repeated, momentarily confused.

"Back there. At the games."

"Oh." They'd left the field well behind them, but the occasional shout could still be heard.

"Cloud-Leaf Clan isn't playing until later," she said. "I don't play, myself. I don't care for the running."

Her generous breasts made it uncomfortable, even with the wrappings the players wore across their chests. But she would be too embarrassed to say that to him. "Still, I do my part for the clan. I make baskets for the games." She didn't mention this was the first time she'd made one to give away as part of the stakes for the winners.

He asked how long she'd been a basket maker.

She told him and then, prompted by another question, began to describe the baskets she'd made. She mentioned that she had in mind a granary for her next project. Hoping flattery might make him more agreeable, she said, "I'm sure under your care, the next harvest will be so bountiful, we'll need lots more granaries to store it all."

He smiled but said nothing.

They soon neared the gleaming adobe walls of the clan's compounds, where the odor of rich stews and squash soup joined that of the meat, a most pleasurable welcome.

Most of the clan elders sat on blankets in the sun as they soaked up warmth into their old bones. They looked at her and called out greetings but only eyed Rush. Clan-sisters tended the cookfires without glancing up. He didn't seem to notice them.

The responses on both sides disappointed her. Her plan would work only if he was welcomed by the clan—and also satisfied his male urges with other women. Though perhaps not women of Cloud-Leaf Clan, she decided. That could be awkward, too close to home and hard to ignore.

Toddlers sat in laps. Other young ones ran around in what looked like a game of tag, being shooed away from the fires and the most crowded areas by anyone who happened to see them.

Some of the older boys had settled down to a kintsu game; they leaned against the rough-plastered wall of the nearest compound and awaited their turn with the four sticks. She couldn't see what the stakes were but supposed it was some dare. That was the most common thing for boys, who had few possessions to wager.

Starflower assessed Rush's reaction out of the corner of her eye. If he wished for a child of his own like the ones swarming around the clanholdings, he gave no sign. He seemed more interested in pots full of stew and in the deer meat being uncovered from the roasting pits and handed out in woven-grass envelopes.

They found a relatively quiet space between two compounds to eat. They had finished their bowls of stew, and Starflower was just mustering the courage to ask Rush what he thought of her proposition, when others joined them. The clan's talespinner was there, finishing her meal. People began to clamor for a story.

"Let's go," Starflower suggested as she saw the opportunity for conversation vanishing.

But the gray-haired woman seemed happy to start her tale, and Rush, heavy-eyed and comfortable, said he was happy to lean back on his elbows and listen, so Starflower subsided.

"Back in the days of the First People, when all things began, there was a small village. It was a quiet place, where kin ties had become so tangled that everyone could call all others clan-brother and clan-sister. Time brought no changes, and nothing ever happened that had not happened a thousand times before. Then came to womanhood the prettiest girl the village had ever known."

Starflower narrowed her eyes. Although the talespinner hadn't glanced her way before sitting down, the decision to tell this particular tale didn't seem accidental. She was used to people calling her vain—and tried not to let it upset her.

"She would choose no man as bondmate," the wrinkly old woman went on, "for she said she liked all equally well. Cloud sailed through the skies, saw her beauty, and wept in sympathy for the men of the village. Unseen by any but her, a single tear from Cloud fell full upon her belly. And it pleased her to be so honored by the son of the Allmother."

Though she knew such a thing could no longer come to pass, Starflower found herself rubbing a hand over her own belly as if she'd taken this other girl's place. Of late, these old stories played out in her head as though she were there as a witness instead of just listening to a story. And was it any less unlikely to have a baby made from a raindrop than one whose soul came from a vengeful spirit as had plagued her sleep, even while in the moontime hut in the protective company of her clan-sisters?

"As she grew in size, her lovers quarreled over who had lain with her and broken their pact to court her openly. Finally, after seven months, twin sons were born. All the men claimed to be the father. She called the people together, with the men surrounding her, and placed the babies in the center of the circle. Whoever they crawled to, she said, was their father. But the babes, as she knew they would, chose no one, and so no man of the village could claim to be her mate."

When the tale moved away from the mother to focus on the twins as they grew older, Starflower felt herself released from the vision. Not from the story, though; she found herself drawn in by the twins' cleverness and daring. She cheered along with the entire audience as the narrative came to an end with the younger twin turning himself into a heron out of loyalty to his brother, who had sacrificed himself to save the world.

Rush opened his eyes and smiled at nothing before turning his head toward Starflower. "Good story," he said.

His response startled her. She would've thought a tale about fatherless children would strike too close to home for his liking. But the Watermasters were said to have descended from the heron brother, so maybe that was the part Rush liked.

He pushed to his feet, walked over to the talespinner, knelt beside her, and said something that made her cackle and swat him on the shoulder.

The old woman's rheumy eyes shifted toward Starflower. At her necklace, she realized. Suddenly self-conscious, she laid her hand over it.

"Eh, no need to hide it from me, girl," the talespinner said. "I remember your mother wearing it. You have something of her face."

"I'm like my mother, you think?" Hearing that pleased Starflower. No one had been given her mother's name, so it was never spoken. Starflower sometimes wondered whether she was the only one who ever thought about her mother now.

The talespinner's gaze pinned her in place. "In looks, yes. In your choice of men, let's hope not." She cast a sidelong glance at Rush, then returned her focus to Starflower. "Three women from the clan we gave your father—"

"Three?" Starflower asked with a frown.

"The mother of your sister, then your own mother, then your brother's."

She inhaled sharply and clutched at the necklace. She and her sister didn't share the same mother? No one had ever told her that, not even her father.

"Three was more than enough." The talespinner's face took on a grim cast. "That's why we pushed him off onto the worst of the clanlands. Just as well he left. But you should come back, girl. Without him. Mate yourself to a boy of the clan."

She felt Rush's I-told-you-so stare and flushed.

"As for you, young Canalmaster," the elderly woman said, "what are you doing to protect us from the Wilders?"

"I don't believe the Wilders are any more of a problem now than they ever have been," he answered gravely.

"No? What is, then?"

"Food enough to last the winter. Repairing the canals so next fall we don't have the same worries. Those matters won't be helped by stoked-up fears of the Wilders."

"Perhaps, perhaps," the old woman allowed.

As they made their goodbyes to the talespinner, Starflower had no idea what to say to Rush.

Everything had gone so well up until that last exchange with the old woman. Although there hadn't been a warm welcome, no one had said or done anything to jeopardize her plan. Not until *Stick with your own kind,* as the elderly woman might just as well have said. *The rabbit doesn't lie down with the rattlesnake.*

And then that business about the Wilders. Starflower didn't know what to think about that.

"She told a good story," Rush said, as they wandered along the canal branch that led back toward the heart of the village. "I enjoyed it. And the food."

Starflower realized she'd been silent since leaving the talespinner. "She didn't really mean it. About"—*sticking with your own kind*—"about just leaving my father's household." She struggled to come up with a truth that would explain why she couldn't just leave. "He doesn't want me to choose one of my admirers, not yet. Then he wouldn't have help in the fields."

"You said it was your father's decision to leave. It sounded like he was forced to."

"He's no worse off now than he was." She shrugged. "It's still hauling water, only from the dipping-pool now instead of a canal. And he can be his own man, not bound by the clan."

"He could always grow agaves, nopal cactus, even yuccas."

"They all take time to establish, don't they?"

"True enough."

And by then, she figured, the canals would be running again. She opened her mouth to ask whether her father would ever have water in the ditches for his fields, but she remembered what Rush had said at the outset: not for a hundred turnings. "Don't let's talk about my father," she said.

"All right. What should we talk about?"

She cast around for something completely different from her father and water. "Do you want any more children?"

"More? As far as I know, I don't have any."

"But—" She broke off. Maybe he really hadn't known about Deerchaser bearing his son. Or maybe Deerchaser had lied about who the father was, after letting everyone assume it was Rush through all those turnings. In any case, Starflower had no reason to try to get at the truth; it made no difference to her.

He explained, "There haven't been as many women for me as some might think. Oh, as a ditchrunner, I had my share of flirtations. Most went no further."

"But your reputation . . . ?" she prompted. According to one of her clan-aunties, his pursuit of the females of Sky River was the stuff of legend, like Handsome Man all over again.

"I enjoyed the reputation. Though I can't say I earned it."

"So, *do* you want children?"

"You're persistent, aren't you? Why all these questions about children?"

She shrugged. "The talespinner's story got me thinking, that's all. Do you?"

"Not now. For one thing, I'm getting too old to chase around after youngsters and keep them out of trouble. My bones are weary."

"Weary bones, no heart? Those sound like excuses." But she was glad to hear them. Convincing him to leave her alone after they were mated might be easier than she'd expected.

"What about you? Isn't that what you've been dreaming about ever since you were a little girl?"

"Babies?" *If he only knew.* "Hardly. I have a younger brother. If I ever *did* have a desire for motherhood, he ruined it. I don't want children. Ever."

"Then what is it you plan to do with the rest of your days? No bedplay and no children seems a dull life for a woman."

She held up and let him pause, then turn to face her. The ball game wasn't far off now, with whooping spectators and players calling to each other. She wanted to get this settled while he could still hear what she was saying. "Making baskets and granaries and reed matting and the like. All I would need you for is a reason to have no other man."

His eyes searched hers. "I've told you no already."

"Because you think it would be unwise for me? I've shown you what Cloud-Leaf Clan would do. They would accept you."

"They accepted me for a short time, fed me and entertained me and then gave me a warning. A lifemate, as you're talking about? That's something very different. Besides, I'm not drawn to you in that way. You're young enough to be my daughter."

She refused to take offense. "That's exactly why this would work. You wouldn't be trying to get me to change my mind and lie with you. We wouldn't have to even live together." The words tumbled out.

She drew a breath, remembered what was at stake, and kept going. "You could seek out female companionship, and I . . . well, I've already told you how I would benefit."

She knew she'd finished too abruptly and her voice had sharpened, but her control was slipping. What if he ever told anyone of her offer? The humiliation would be too much to bear. Everyone knew everyone else's business here.

"You would share me with other women?" His disbelief was obvious.

"Yes! That's exactly what I want!"

Silence fell between them, drowning out the calls and hoots and jeers of the running women and their audience.

"What do you think?" she asked at last, nerves strained. She didn't know what else to say to convince him.

"I think this is some trick of your father's."

She twisted her hands together. "If you promise not to demand any intimacy from me, I'll promise never to see my father again. I don't care if his new field does go back to desert."

Rush didn't seem to hear. His eyes were on the game.

She continued, trying desperately to find the one thing that would make him agree. "There are great advantages to you in this. My clan is one of the oldest, and it's influential among farming folk. You would be one of us, not an outsider. You saw that today, with the clan-feast."

No response.

"Just think how glad the farmers will be to have their sons back, no longer mooning over me," she said, trying to lighten the mood, make him smile, startle him into a laugh like the ones they'd shared just a little while earlier.

She saw that his gaze was fixed on one of the several darting and running figures. They all sported pads and guards on their joints and vulnerable parts, making them nearly indistinguishable.

Starflower tried to pick out who he was watching. The woman was thin, with two braids falling down her back, one having a twist of white in it.

"Deerchaser," Rush muttered, so faintly that Starflower didn't think he even realized he'd said it. He walked down the canal bank and started toward the game with not so much as a backward glance at her.

Confused at first, she stared after him. Then realization struck. He was hot on the track of Deerchaser.

A storm of fear and despair blew through her. She shivered as she saw her hoped-for future torn from her grasp.

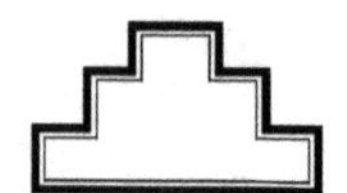

At last they came to the house of Cloud, their father, and they called to him through his door, but he denied them.

—FROM THE SONS OF CLOUD STORY

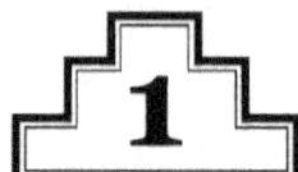

"Deerchaser." He whispered her name again. He felt as if . . . if he took his gaze off her, she would disappear.

Upon his return he'd asked after her, the girl who had once been everything to him. One of his ditchrunners, of the same clan, had told him she was still here—but no more than that. Rush hadn't let himself press further.

As several moons passed without him seeing her around the Cloud-Leaf clanholdings or elsewhere in the village, he had supposed she still felt angry over his leaving, so angry as to deliberately avoid him. Until now, he had thought himself unconcerned by her absence. Now the pounding of his heart proved he had been lying to himself.

That she would hold a grudge after all this time had seemed unreasonable. She *had* deserved better, yes, but so had the rest of those he'd so abruptly left behind, from the other ditchrunners, who'd had to cover his territory, to the old Canalmaster, who had treated Rush like a son.

When she heard of his return, she should have come to him to make peace. They'd been friends, hadn't they?

At that, he lost the brief flare of righteous indignation and fell into memory. They had been more than friends. She had been his first lover, and he hers. That flavored his recollections of her with poignancy. He had no way of knowing how she remembered him.

He watched the women of one clan slapping at the chich'wipedho balls—a pair of rounded mesquite roots tethered to each other with a rawhide strap—with their long bent sticks as they raced down the field toward the goal. They were good enough to keep the rolling ball always slightly out of reach of the sticks of their opponents.

Deerchaser had no reason to think fondly of him, he had to admit. He had, after all, deserted her without saying goodbye.

Only then did he remember Starflower. He glanced over his shoulder and found she was gone.

He knew better than to walk away like that from a woman he wanted to keep on his good side. Was Starflower, with her bizarre proposal, one of those or one he would count himself well rid of? He rather thought the latter. Her father certainly was one to avoid whenever possible.

Rush's feet had led him to the edge of the chich'wipedho field, where the cheering was deafening. This late in the day, it would be the final game. The winners would split the accumulated prizes from the previous matches, and their clan would host the Far-Traders during the upcoming New Fire trade gatherings.

Hosting was a strain at the best of times. This winter, with food shortages likely, promised to be an especial challenge. But the honor was too great to pass up. Crookstaff Village, one of only four villages in the entire valley with a temple in its midst, drew celebrants from all along Earth River for the midwinter festivities. During the Long Thirst, all the clans had shared what they had for the sun-festivals. Rush hoped they could come together and do the same again if the traditional generosity would otherwise be jeopardized.

He scanned the field for Deerchaser. When he failed to pick her out among the others, he wondered whether he had been mistaken, fooled by some trick of the light or the distance. But the woman he had seen moved just the way Deerchaser used to, quick and sinuous. Perhaps it wasn't her, of course: these many turnings later, she would likely have taken a lifemate, borne children, thickened and coarsened . . .

Still, he remained there on the edge of the chich'wipedho field and looked for her. He recalled the many times in the past he had waited for her just so, admiring her grace, her boldness, her strength. The many times he had left once the game ended, to meet up with her later, somewhere no one would discover them together.

For their growing affection wouldn't have been allowed. Even then, when relations between farmers and Watermasters were less strained, the farmers had tried to keep the Watermasters—or, as too many called them in disgust, those worthless fish-eaters—from their daughters. There certainly would have been no chance of an alliance between a clan-daughter and a Watermaster like that proposed by Starflower. Perhaps things had indeed changed here at Crookstaff Village, if Starflower thought there was a chance for a life-mating between them.

With a shake of his head at that optimistic notion, he turned away from the chich'wipedho field—and saw Deerchaser.

She crouched at the edge of the field, hands on her knees. Divided into two tight braids behind her ears, her hair dangled past her elbows. Around her bounced a black dog marked with bands of white that reminded Rush of the stripes on the women's gambling sticks, the kamas. Then she moved, and he forgot the dog.

Carefully she straightened, as though stiff. She draped a long cotton cloak over her sweat-soaked body, which bore thick padding on the knees and shins, in the shadowy join of her legs, crisscrossed over her breasts and ribs. She was turned partly away from him as she watched the players with a burning intensity. After a while, she lifted one fist high and joined the rest of her clan in jubilant cheers of victory.

Rush stood back and watched as several boys swarmed her and had their hair ruffled in teasing response while the dog wove through their legs in a careful dance. When the well-wishers faded away, she stood alone. No man claimed her.

He told himself it didn't, couldn't, matter. He had returned to Crookstaff not to rekindle a youthful indiscretion but to restore the canals. He needed to prove himself worthy of the trust placed in him by the River Council, the elder Canalmasters of Sky River and Earth River, who met a few times every turning. That meant the farmers here would have to consider him a skilled Canalmaster, not the feckless ditchrunner he had been before.

That respect seemed painfully slow in coming. But during his tenure in the north, on the long, complicated canals of Sky River, Rush had learned patience. Given time, he would change the villagers' perception of him.

Could he do the same with Deerchaser? Five strides would bring him to her side, let him begin to replace the flawed image she had of him with a better one.

But he couldn't move. Nerves kept him in place. His mouth felt as dry as it had been the first time he'd set eyes on her—naked and splashing in the river with her friends. Beautiful she had seemed to him then, only a little less so now.

She picked up the rest of her things and packed them in a carry sack. Slowly she moved as though exhausted by her exertions on the field. Sweat streaked and grimy, she should have been anything but erotic, yet he found himself wishing he had the right once again to touch her.

Then there was no need to move. She came right toward him, muttering under her breath as though speaking to the dog that trotted along with her.

". . . too old for this," he heard. Without lifting her gaze, she drew nearer.

He put out a hand and caught her shoulder. "Deerchaser."

Her quick spin away left him with only her cloak in his grasp. Her eyes locked with his. Something flickered over her face. It disappeared before he could identify it. Pleasure? Guilt? Perhaps even fear?

The dog barked at him, once, sharply.

"Give me that!" She reached for the cloak.

As he handed it to her, he noticed changes in the way she looked.

Woven into one of her long black braids was an odd white streak. Above her eyebrow on the same side as that unusual marking, a flame tattoo could faintly be seen. That and a teardrop under her eye signaled the birth and death of a child. But her wrist showed no mark. The child was born of a handfast, then, with a man who hadn't suited her well enough for a more permanent mating. The thought pleased him, though he knew it shouldn't.

Her face was thinner, older, sharper than before. As he should have expected, after—how long had it been since he had seen her last? Twelve turnings, more? Fifteen? He'd lost count.

"You played brilliantly," he said with a smile. "As always."

She put on the cloak again and stalked away. The cloth swirled around her ankles, revealing fine bones framed by the lacing of her sandals. The dog eyed him with suspicion, tail down and no longer wagging.

Rush sidled around it to catch up with her, then fell into step at her side. Shortening his stride to match hers startled a sidelong glance from her. That she noticed both amused and saddened him. In the old days, he probably would have expected her to adjust her pace to his.

But in that, too, he had changed. He had learned to watch what others did in response to his own actions. He had learned to plan and coax others to come around to his way of thinking. That approach had served him well at Sky River. The River Council counted on it doing the same at Crookstaff Village.

One of the secrets to making it work was keeping emotion out of it. He was having some difficulty with that where Deerchaser was concerned—though he wasn't sure what sentiment the sight of her had brought on.

Besides the streak of white in her hair, her face bore lines he would expect to see in a much older woman. There weren't many laugh crinkles around her eyes; instead, grooves of sadness ran alongside her mouth.

"Does this usually work?" She kept her gaze straight ahead.

"Does what usually work?"

"The flattery, the fake smile. The attention."

"There's nothing false—" he began.

"Don't waste your attempts at charm on me. Go find someone who actually wants your company."

"Anyone in particular?" Perhaps, he thought, she had been watching him with Starflower. Perhaps she was jealous. Though there was no reason for her to be—unless she still had feelings for him. He grinned at that thought.

She only shook her head.

They reached the vatto where the stakes for the chich'wipedho game had been placed. Deerchaser poked through blankets and pots and grinding stones and mats, everything imaginable that a newly mated girl setting up a household could want upon leaving her mother's home.

Rush wondered what she could be looking for. When she uncovered a storage basket, she smiled and lightly stroked her forefinger over the coils, tracing the graceful black lines. With the softening of her expression, he realized he wanted her to look at him in that way again, as something she would take home with her and treasure.

He thought he might get her to reveal whether she still had feelings for him. Just out of curiosity, of course. "Starflower said she made one of the baskets."

"Yes. This one. I saw her working on it." Deerchaser started down the path that led away from the village center, not toward the clanholdings but more in the direction of where Starflower's father, Earth Holder, had begun to carve fields out of the unforgiving desert.

Rush sauntered along beside her. He wondered how to break through the dam of apparent indifference she had built around herself. He decided to take a direct approach. "If you're wondering why I didn't come to say goodbye, I can explain."

"Don't bother. I had no hold on you." Her gaze remained fixed straight ahead.

He recalled the difficulty he'd had back then in trying to get through the first day without her, then a sevenday, a moon, a season, the whole first turning. "You're wrong about that. It took me a long time to get you out of my mind."

She glared at him, then returned her gaze to the path. "Don't pretend what we had mattered. It only makes you look the fool."

His stomach tightened. "Is it foolish to tell you how I felt?"

"I doubt you felt anything. The whole village knows you went from one woman to another after you left here."

"There weren't that many." Not that she would believe the denial. He knew what rumor said. "Are you still angry that I left so abruptly? The Canalmasters didn't give me time to come to you. What else could I do? When my parents died, I was called home to take care of my young brother and sister."

She shot him a piercing glance. "You?"

"I was all they had."

"And how, as a lowly ditchrunner, did you manage being their father and mother? You could barely manage your own self."

Her mockery stung. "I did turn them over to the care of one of the

Watermaster families, yes. But I had a posting nearby. I saw them practically every day."

At first. Later, once they were comfortable and happy with their foster family, he had left them to work on a different canal system. Heat climbed up his neck. "I had responsibilities, as a Watermaster."

"It doesn't seem like too much of a sacrifice," she observed. "You've done well for yourself."

Once, long ago, he could have told her what an impossible situation he now found himself in, with canals that mysteriously wouldn't work as they were supposed to. Once, he could have shared his hopes and his doubts. No longer.

He knew he should just say goodbye and let her go—but he couldn't bring himself to do so. "My brother and sister both have families of their own now." He cleared his throat. "I see the tattoo—you had a child?"

"Very perceptive."

"What happened to him?"

She looked straight ahead. "What makes you think it was a boy?"

He couldn't see her with a girl. "Just a guess."

"He's dead. Drowned." Her knuckles went white on the strap of her carry sack.

He didn't know what he had expected, but it wasn't that. Illness, perhaps, the kind that carried off babies and young children at the age of weaning. "How old was he?"

She hesitated for so long that he thought she wouldn't answer. Then, "Six," she said.

"I'm sorry." What a tragic end, to have her son survive the difficult first turnings only to die by water, which normally brought life rather than taking it. With another woman, he might have offered the comfort of a man's embrace. With Deerchaser, he was not at all sure she would accept even a few words of sympathy from him.

They walked along in silence for a while. Her dog got distracted by a bush that needed to be thoroughly sniffed, then marked.

"And the father?" Rush reached out and tapped a finger against her arm to regain her attention.

"What about him?"

"The father of your child. I see by your wrist it was no heartfast. Did he—"

She shook her head. "You have no right to pry into my history with men."

"No, I don't." He heard what she refrained from saying: *Given yours with women.* Rumors, always rumors. "So, were there many?"

"Many men?" She sounded incredulous at the notion but quickly added, "I didn't sit around grieving after you left, if that's what you want to hear."

It wasn't. He was ashamed to admit it, but she should have been as miserable without him as he had been without her.

"I was busy building myself a life." She lifted her chin in a stubborn gesture so familiar it made his throat hurt.

"Who with?" he shot back.

As she whipped up her hand to slap him, he grabbed her. The thinness of her wrist startled him so much that when her other hand came around, balled into a fist, it connected, glancing off his temple with enough force to snap his head around.

"Ouch!" they said together.

She snatched back her captive hand to cradle the one she had hit him with.

"Here, let me see." He reached out to massage her hand.

She pulled away as her dog rushed up, barking at him.

He shoved his thumbs into the sash of his tunic. "You're as prickly as a jumping-cactus!" he said in exasperation.

"Then why don't you go away and leave me alone!"

He might have done just that, except . . . he couldn't. "It seems to me you've been left alone more than enough. No bondmate, no child."

She stood with bowed head, but at least she was listening rather than running away. She shushed the dog and patted its head after it quieted.

Rush said, "It must have been difficult for you, managing without a bondmate, and with such a young child."

"My son was the best thing that ever happened to me."

"That's good, then," he said awkwardly.

"He wasn't something to 'manage.'"

She was distancing herself, he realized, even though her shoulder was but a hand's-breadth from his chest. "Let's go get something to eat," he suggested.

Her lip curled. "I don't think so."

"Why not?"

"You've already eaten."

"How can you be so sure?"

She flicked the front of his tunic. He looked down to discover a greasy stain, still bearing particles of squash and obviously fresh.

As he laughed, and Deerchaser even smiled a bit, he heard his name called. One of his ditchrunners, Tumbler, the one from her clan, raced toward them.

After a quick exchange of greetings with the boy, she said to Rush, "You seem to be much in demand. Watermaster affairs never quite leave you alone, do they?" She walked away without a backward look. Her cloak swirled around those shapely ankles.

Anxiously Tumbler asked, "Did I mess things up?" He shifted his weight from one bare, dusty foot to another. "Didn't mean to."

Rush thought back to the time when the soles of his own feet were callused enough to run unprotected over the village paths and canal banks. Then, it had been a mark of pride; now, it struck him as rather silly.

The skinny boy seemed impossibly young and earnest. Rush had trouble believing he had ever been like that. But he couldn't have been much older when he met Deerchaser. *If this is how she remembers me*, he thought, *changing her opinion will be quite the challenge*. And then he reminded himself that he couldn't afford the distraction of a woman.

"No harm done," he told Tumbler. "What did you find out?"

Hoping to understand where the rumors had started about rampaging Wilders, Rush had sent the boy to ask whether anyone had seen the rain priest the night of his death. The body had been found before dawn, face-down in a canal where the water was deep enough to drown a man. It was the last point on that canal with that much water; below, the repairs were still in progress. It seemed too far from the river for the Wilders to come, too far from the temple for a priest to go.

Rush had thought maybe the young priest had set off to visit family. But no one who lived near where he was found admitted to knowing him.

Granted, it was hard to find someone's family when you didn't know his name—and even if you knew, couldn't speak it aloud, for fear of tempting the unbound spirit to take over your body in place of the one it had lost. Though Rush considered that to be nonsense, he didn't expect the villagers to risk speaking a dead man's name.

It was particularly difficult because no one could be certain that the Stormbringers had sung the young priest's spirit to rest. They conducted only a few ceremonies in the open; all others were kept secret behind the walls of the temple precinct. What was certain was that the Lifeweaver, the healer tasked with freeing the soul from a body and sending it safely out of the world, had not been called in by the priests.

"No one upcanal seems to know him," Tumbler said. "I went all the way up to The Wing."

Rush decided he would have to give up on finding the dead priest's kin. He had run out of ideas. And there was nothing he could do to quell the rumors anyway. He had his own concerns that, at the moment, were more pressing.

He patted Tumbler on one bony shoulder. "You did your best, I'm sure. Go on up to the mound. Your gran probably saved back some stew."

The boy ran off, leaving Rush to stride along behind.

Unlike most of the other ditchrunners, who came from villages nearer the river, Tumbler had family at Crookstaff Village. His clan-grannie —sister to his grandmother—kept the Canalmaster and his many assistants well provisioned.

She also scrubbed their clothes. Rush reminded himself to ask her to clean the stain off his tunic.

"All you Watermasters," Deerchaser used to tease, in those days long past, "you assume you never need to wash your clothes, because you're always in the water."

Rush shook his head ruefully. That was no longer true in his case. As Canalmaster, he seldom got into the canal. The actual work was for others to do. He missed it.

He turned toward the Masterholding, the mound precinct of Crookstaff Village, which consisted of four wards inside a high wall. Two of the wards, approximately the same size, housed the Watermasters and hunters. Each of those groups had a flat-topped mound with plazas and work areas and living quarters. In the third ward, at the same elevation as the rest of the village, the healers had their rooms; the remaining space was where messengers and Far-Traders stayed.

Before the construction of the priests' temple a few generations earlier, the Watermasters' upper rooms atop the mound must have been the tallest structures in the village. Sometimes Rush thought that said a lot about the problems the Watermasters had with the farmers—always being measured against the priests and falling short.

He was nearly to the Masterholding when Plastercrack, another of his ditchrunners, trotted into view. "The Rainsinger's son, he's looking for you!" Crack called out.

The way tongues ran on, half the village would hear of this unexpected turn of affairs before morning. "Keep your voice down," he advised as the boy neared.

Rush had never met Spadefoot, the Rainsinger's son, but had heard more than enough about the young priest's exploits: that green shoots sprouted in his footsteps, that he was a master dowser who could find water no matter how far below the surface, that he could compel obedience in the unwary with just his gaze. Above all, that he was the one of whom an ancient prophecy spoke, the one who would prove the savior of the People of Two Rivers.

All foolishness, of course. Rush had no time for it.

On the morrow, he would head upcanal to meet with the other Canalmasters of this stretch of Earth River. He would have to figure out how to explain to them that relations with the farmers of his territory were not easing but becoming more strained. This death and the rumors swirling around it had stirred up the farmers. They didn't want the Wilders anywhere near, even on work crews. But without the Wilders, the repairs would progress even more slowly.

Rush thought Spadefoot's timing could hardly be worse. He decided whatever the priest wanted would have to wait.

The round-faced ditchrunner got close enough to whisper, "He's . . ." He jerked a thumb toward the top of the mound.

"Surely not alone!"

"Can't do no harm . . ." Crack began.

Rush didn't let him finish. He headed for the ladder that allowed access to his living quarters, his foodstocks and water supply, his tools, the canal map. There was no telling what the priest might do out of sheer, willful opposition—if he was as unscrupulous as his father, the Rainsinger.

"What d'you think he wants?" Tumbler asked from his perch at the base of the ladder.

"Nothing good."

"Will you beat him up for coming where he don't belong?"

Rush waved the boy off the ladder and started up himself. He had climbed only a few rungs before he remembered being that age. He looked down at the two ditchrunners and said, "Don't you think a fight would only make things worse?"

Silence.

He then asked, "Are you much of a fighter, Tumbler?" The boy was gangly and a little uncoordinated, his muscles ropy; Rush thought him unlikely to win any fight, though he was gutsy enough to make a good attempt. "Or would you be better off talking your way out of trouble?"

They both looked at him with no expression at all. Given the soreness on the side of his face, Rush figured the impact of Deerchaser's fist showed up as a telltale red mark on his skin. He wasn't about to explain how he had come by it.

And this wasn't the time to lecture the boys on proper conduct for a Watermaster, on the importance of a man's reputation, on being smart rather than brash. The only way to defeat the Rainsinger was to get the canals working as soon as possible. Rush would lose a physical fight—maybe not actually but strategically—if he let himself be goaded into trading blows with the Rainsinger's famous son. He knew that. He wished things were different. It would be so much simpler.

⋀

When Rush discovered Spadefoot crouched beside the plaster canal map, the situation wasn't as bad as he had feared. Tumbler's clan-grannie sat on the bench under the vatto where Starflower had waited for Rush to finish earlier that day. She stood up and inclined her gray-haired head in dignified reassurance, then went away, leaving the two men alone.

Rush approached the map enclosure. "What are you doing here?" He stifled the flare of anger over the intrusion, deliberately kept his voice level and reasonable.

The priest rose. The dark blotch on his face, outlined by the lightning tattoo, made him instantly recognizable. He was even younger than Rush would have expected. Twenty turnings or less, at a guess.

Spadefoot gestured toward the incised lines at his feet. "These are the canals you oversee? I never realized there were so many." He seemed genuinely interested.

"There's enough."

Rush didn't have to look down to see what the young priest saw. There were between eight and ten main canal branches, depending on how you counted them, each with two or three ditchrunners, plus a ditch boss in charge. His was a small system compared to some along Sky River but still the largest and most complicated in this part of the valley.

"It must be quite a responsibility," Spadefoot said, "having all the people of the village depending on you."

Rush didn't know how to take that. It sounded like praise, but who could tell with a priest? They were good at saying one thing and meaning another.

The younger man asked, "These connected squares, like fishnets—are these fields?"

"That's right. Clanholdings, most of them."

Spadefoot nodded. His keen gaze returned to the map. "The pattern does more than show me the land your canals bring water to. The shape of it is pleasant to look at, too."

Rush narrowed his eyes. Now the priest sounded like Starflower. But admiring the map of the canal system couldn't be what he had come for. "Why did you wish to see me?"

Spadefoot's attention returned to Rush. The dark splotch on the young priest's cheek puckered and shifted as muscles worked underneath, while Rush felt himself seized and caught, his very thoughts laid bare by a penetrating stare. Then the priest released him, a little shaken.

"You have heard about the passing of my vow-brother," Spadefoot said.

"Yes, of course."

"And the rest of it—that the Wilders killed him."

"If you've come to accuse—"

Spadefoot raised one hand. "I know this to be untrue. As you must, too." He let his hand fall and leaned forward. "We both saw the body," he stated with intensity. He shook his head. "There was no caliche pick, no Wilder shell net as I've heard some people claim."

Rush rubbed the back of his neck. "Yes, he looked to have drowned. So? Why come to me with this?"

"He said you could be trusted."

"Who said?"

"My vow-brother."

Startled, Rush asked, "Why would he tell you such a thing? I never even met him."

Spadefoot shrugged. "This is what he told me."

"All right, let's say I believe you. What is it you want from me?"

The young priest folded his arms. He bent a severe look on Rush. "First you have to understand why the Wilders could never have been involved in his death."

"And why is that?"

After a brief hesitation and a twitch of his mouth, Spadefoot said, "He was one of them."

Rush heard it with disbelief, snorted, and shook his head. A Wilder as a priest? Maybe when the sun came up in the west or snow fell in the heat of summer.

"Why would his own kind kill him!" Spadefoot continued—it wasn't a question.

The way those words were casually tossed out made Rush's skin go tight. The air seemed to draw close around him. "His own kind? It seems his own kind would be your kind. The priests." This revelation, as unexpected as Starflower's proposal but far more disturbing—if true. "Why do you say your vow-brother was a Wilder?"

"He told me so."

"And you believed him."

"Yes." The young priest gave one quick nod.

"But Morning Green despises the Wilders."

Rush didn't realize he had said that aloud until Spadefoot replied soberly, "The Rainsinger didn't know. I'm the only one who did, I think."

"Why would he reveal such a dangerous secret to you?"

"The one who has departed this world . . ." Spadefoot seemed gripped by some strong emotion. In a voice that sounded hoarse, he went on, "He was more than a vow-brother. He was my brother by blood."

That could mean a lot of things among the People of Two Rivers, anything from sharing the same mother to being of the same clan. "Let's say all this is true," Rush allowed. "I ask again, why do you tell me this?"

Spadefoot's mouth twisted. "The divisions among our people grow stronger every day. Farmers resent Watermasters, clan elders complain of the young, the priests of the Ta'atchul envy the influence of the priestesses . . . We are in danger of splitting into groups, each eyeing the others with suspicion. And now, with the Wilders being blamed for my brother's death, the distance will become all the greater."

The young priest put his finger on it, Rush thought grimly.

The River Council saw much the same thing. That was why they had sent him to Crookstaff Village. Rush was a new face but nevertheless had a history in this place. They had hoped the farmers might accept him as they wouldn't one of the local Watermasters, the ones Morning Green had been maligning for their inability to fix the canals. But more important as far as the council was concerned, Rush had spent time around the three temples of Sky River and knew well what the priests were capable of.

The Watermasters and Wilders couldn't afford to let the priests of the Temple of the Mist sow even more division. And that, rather than anything else Spadefoot had said, was what made the death of the other priest yet another problem for Rush to deal with.

He folded his arms. "You claim the Wilders' innocence, but the rumors have a life of their own now. What do you expect me to do about them?"

"I don't expect you to put an end to the rumors," Spadefoot said. "That isn't why I came."

"Then why did you?"

Spadefoot stooped and picked up a jar Rush hadn't noticed before, a flat-bottomed red ceramic vessel capped with a wooden plug. "I bring his ashes for delivery to his family, so his name can be given to another. His mother is of the old blood."

Rush knew that some of the families of Earth River still clung to the oldest of the old ways, burying their dead under the floor to mingle their ashes with the dust of their ancestors, to guide the life-path of a new generation. Spadefoot, as a priest, could hardly admit to sympathizing with such an ancient tradition. He would need someone to act as a go-between.

Again, yet again, why Rush?

He didn't reach for the red bone-jar. "Why not send word to his kin through one of the Wilders who come to the trade ground?"

"He told me his mother came from The Wing. That is why I brought this to you today." Spadefoot freed a hand and gestured toward the jar. "I know you head upcanal soon for a meeting of the Canalmasters. On the way, you could go to The Wing and find his kin and deliver him to them."

The Wing lay outside Crookstaff Village, far up the main line of the canal. Hardly more than a collection of fields where the canal meandered across irrigable land, The Wing had long ago reminded some fanciful Watermaster of the trailing edge of a bird's wing. The name had stuck for untold generations.

The people who farmed that stretch of canal kept to themselves. Living between two larger villages, they didn't think of themselves as belonging to either. And they didn't talk to outsiders.

Although The Wing was part of the territory assigned to Rush, he had never been called on to negotiate a dispute between neighbors there. The farmfolk of The Wing handled repairs and washouts on their own and accepted their water allocations without argument. In short, they were no bother, and nobody bothered with them.

"It's safe," Spadefoot told him. "His spirit was sung to rest."

"You do realize the Wilders live in the opposite direction from The Wing, downstream on Earth River? If his mother was a Wilder, he wouldn't have come from The Wing."

"His mother's people are from The Wing. So are mine. Sisters, they were. But his father, I think, was a Wilder."

It made a crazy kind of sense. If some lovestruck Wilder had messed with a young woman of The Wing, that might have made the whole lot of them, and perhaps all the Watermasters, unwelcome there ever since.

Interrupting Rush's churning thoughts, Spadefoot held out the bone-jar.

"All you want is for me to take his remains to The Wing?" Rush asked.

"Yes, if that's where his mother is."

"And if not?"

For the first time, the young priest looked uncertain. He pulled his arms back toward his chest, hugging the jar. "You might have to go to the Wilders to find her. Or if she isn't to be found there, you could discover who his father is and give the ashes to him."

Rush frowned. "You don't know his father's name?"

Spadefoot glanced away. In a few moments he muttered, "I don't know his mother's name either."

"So I'm supposed to take the remains of a priest whose name can no longer be spoken," Rush said, almost amused by the sheer ridiculousness of it, "to a place where Watermasters are almost as unpopular as priests, to find his mother, whose name I don't know. Why should I do this?"

"It could help silence the rumors about the Wilders. And it's hardly even out of your way."

Rush considered the slim chance that Spadefoot was right.

Lately the Wilders hadn't endeared themselves to the farmers of Crookstaff Village. In return for their sporadic labor when it was needed to repair washouts and rebuild canals, they demanded an ever-larger share of corn and squash and beans at harvest as their numbers grew. That commitment sometimes made for a lean winter among the farming clans. This winter, after the poor harvest, it could be catastrophic.

In olden times, the Watermasters had been all that stood between complete disaster and having any crop at the end of the season. But now that the rain priests had come with their promises, many of the farmers begrudged having to give over their hard-earned foodstuffs to both priests and Watermasters.

They particularly resented the "wild" folk for their lives of ease—as the farmers imagined the Wilders' existence along the river to be, with no fields to sow or weeds to pull. The Wilders' day-to-day reliance on fish netted from the river and plants gathered from the marshes, desert, and foothills seemed more like play than work to the farmers.

Farmfolk knew nothing of the uncertainty that plagued those who didn't have use-rights to the rich fields of the farming clans. Nor could they be expected to understand how eagerly the Wilders looked forward to their occasional meals made from the bounty of the fields.

To make matters worse, the Wilders went out of their way to look and act different from everyone else. They had that in common with the people of The Wing. Both groups held themselves apart from their closest kin: the Wilders from the Watermasters, and the farmers of The Wing from the farmers of the lower canal branches.

And then there were the occasional love affairs with the pretty daughters of the clans, who seemed fascinated by either the exotic look or the air of danger around the Wilder men. It made for fertile ground in which to grow rumors about the Wilders killing a priest.

Spadefoot held out the bone-jar again.

This time Rush reached out and took the ashes. It was a weighty charge, to deliver the remains into the keeping of the dead man's people so far away, in inclination if not distance. But if there was even the slightest possibility of laying to rest this latest rumor about the Wilders, how could he refuse?

As Rush trotted along the canal path, he wished he had never met
Spadefoot. He hadn't been able to hand off the dead priest's ashes at The
Wing; the bone-jar still bumped and jostled against his chest as he moved,
slowing him down and making him embarrassingly late for the council
meeting. He knew Twistedtrack, who hosted the meeting, would punish
him for that.

Rush usually took a more direct route from the end of the Crookstaff
clanlands to the mound at Coyote-Willow Village, where the main canal
drank from the river. The canal at The Wing wound back and forth like the
track of a snake, and he had to follow it absolutely; the farmfolk of The
Wing didn't tolerate cutting across fields even when they lay empty after
harvest. But this morning The Wing itself had been his destination, and so
he had to take the long way along the canal.

Another time he might have lingered at The Wing for a closer look at
the irrigation ditches, to figure out whether his suspicions about the upper
canal were true. This morning, though, he couldn't justify a longer delay,
even if it might give him a line of attack against Twistedtrack. What he
could do was try to improve his frame of mind so that when he got to the
meeting, he could deal with the predictable punishment without
overreacting.

To that end, Rush tried to think about his failed errand in a different
way. The bone-jar, all that remained of what had once been another life,
was secured to him with sashes woven out of cotton that had drunk deep
from water delivered to the fields—by Watermasters. Moving as he moved,
rising and falling with the flexing of his muscles, the remains of the dead
mimicked the ebb and flow of life.

Around him were reminders that he could still appreciate the living
world in a way the dead priest couldn't. Scudding clouds laid down

shadows in patches on the plastered walls and granary-topped roofs of Coyote-Willow Village. It was a beautiful day, as were most during the Moon of Small Rains. Cool enough that he wore a light poncho against the chill, warm enough that he sweated a little as he jogged along. The sun's high angle showed how late the day had become.

As he noticed that, his mood soured again. A restless night had prevented him from starting on his journey upcanal as early as he should have done. The thoughts keeping him awake should have focused on the future: getting the canals flowing again, quelling the rumors about the Wilders, building strong relationships with the farmers who relied on him. Unfortunately, no productive brainwork had caused his wakefulness. For that, he had memories to blame.

He had been unable to close his eyes without seeing Deerchaser's face lit up by laughter, her mobile mouth ready for a kiss, her lithe body rising over him. His own body had responded as though there truly were a woman in his sleeping quarters.

It was an uncomfortable way in which to endure the darkness. And then there was the strange offer from Starflower to absorb. And the stranger conversation with Spadefoot.

His mind had leaped from Starflower to Deerchaser to Spadefoot in a whirlwind of thoughts that continued until dawn. When he started on his journey upcanal, he had found it a relief to simply move.

He would have been done with his grisly errand by now if the people of The Wing had cooperated, but he had found no one there willing to take the ashes, no one who claimed to know anything about one of their sons who had become a rain priest, no one willing to admit that a woman of The Wing might have joined with a Wilder to make a baby. There had been cold, flat, hostile stares and one denial after another.

So he had left, still with the bone-jar lashed to his chest. His patience had worn thin after a sleepless night and a detour that had proved a waste of time.

But now he was nearly at his destination. He veered off the main canal path and up the narrow trail that led to the mound, winding through thick, green stands of the arrow-straight rushes that were his namesake.

As long as he kept moving, he didn't have to think.

The problem with trying to run away from his thoughts was that eventually the trail had to end. This day, it was at the gate in the wall that surrounded the mound.

The gate was only woven matting on a frame, nothing that would keep him out even if it had been closed. Today it stood open. Blocking the opening was a young Watermaster who stood bare-chested, with nothing but crossed arms to ward off the morning chill that lingered in the shadows.

Rush didn't know why there was a guard today, when there had never been one before. He assumed Twistedtrack was making a point about his lateness.

Twistedtrack, the Canalmaster here, had made his disapproval of Rush's installation clear. There was a ditch boss in the old Canalmaster's service that Twistedtrack wanted to see elevated to manage the canal system downcanal from his own—install his own man rather than some interloper at Crookstaff Village. But the River Council had decided otherwise and sent Rush.

Rush went to swing around the youth, as tall as himself but more heavily built. The young Watermaster shifted to again bar his way. Rush stopped.

His temper began to rise, but he tamped it down. "Were you told to keep me out or just delay me more?" he asked in a deliberately neutral voice.

The other gazed at him without expression or a reply.

"Step aside," Rush ordered.

"Go back where you come from. You ain't getting past me."

"Are you refusing me?"

The youth set his jaw and glared.

Rush, almost glad for the younger man's resistance, stepped back. He took off his poncho, then said, "One more chance. Move. You're wasting my time. The time of all those waiting for me above."

The youth didn't move, just squared his shoulders in an unspoken challenge for Rush to make him move. Rush had made similar dares in the past—but never to a higher-level Watermaster, someone he was expected to obey. Such a rebellion had to have been ordered by someone higher, and it could not go unopposed. Rush had to prove that he was not a man to be trifled with.

He smiled, then undid the knot in the binding and unwrapped the long cloth, supporting the jar as he did so. To have it fall and shatter would be most unfortunate. His smile broadened as he caught the youth goggling at the bone-jar. Carefully Rush placed the jar on the hard-packed ground against the wall.

Though his opponent had the advantages of size and youth, there was much to be said for craftiness, which improved with age. The fact that the young Watermaster would stand as guard shirtless in this breezy fall weather suggested he valued his image more than reality, appearance more than practicality. Rush counted on that.

Without warning Rush charged him, drove one shoulder into the younger man's belly just below his ribcage. All the air went out of the fellow and he landed on his back inside the wall enclosing the mound. Like a turtle unable to turn itself over, he lay there immobile.

This wasn't the first time an opponent had underestimated Rush. That had happened a long time ago, marked in his memory as the occasion on which he had first spoken with Deerchaser. Outmatched in skills, size, and intention, he'd been ready to give in to the inevitable when he saw her, one disapproving female face in a crowd of men wagering on youth versus experience. With her watching, he refused to allow exhaustion to beat him, and he battled on, until at last one lucky leg sweep got through and Rush twisted the older man's arm until he gave in.

Several moons after that, Rush had still been trying to convince her that such informal contests of skill and strength were not stupid time-wasters but as worthwhile as the chich'wipedho game she excelled at. This day, it seemed just a waste of time.

Rush knew he could have taken up the jar of ashes and gone to the mound while his opponent figured out what had happened, but he wanted to send a message to Twistedtrack so the other Canalmaster didn't try anything like this again.

The younger man got his feet under himself and stood, though he still gasped for breath. "No man tricks me and gets away with it."

"Tell you what," Rush said. "I'll give you a fair chance to take me down. No tricks. But if I put you on the ground again, you let me pass."

The other eyed him closely and then, with all the misplaced confidence of youth, agreed.

The two circled each other. Rush waited for his opponent to signal his approach with a flex of the chest wall. The younger man made a feint to the left before grasping at Rush's shoulders. Rush drove his arms up and broke the tentative hold. A step and pivot and push sent the youth flying over Rush's hip to land precariously balanced on one knee in the dirt and his other leg at a painful angle.

Face contorted by rage, he rose—and charged forward just as Rush had done. Rush crouched at the last moment and drove his shoulder into his opponent's midsection for the second time. The air left the younger Watermaster's lungs with a whoosh. He rolled sideways down Rush's back before falling on his elbows and knees, desperate for breath.

Rush set his foot on the other's backside and pushed him over.

He picked up the bone-jar, wrapped it in the long cloth he had used to carry it securely up the canal path, and passed the ends of the cloth around his neck to tie it in place. Then he put on his poncho and arranged the folds to hide the jar as best he could. The youth sat, knees up and arms braced on them, and glared at him.

Rush said, "I promise I won't tell your Canalmaster or anyone else about your defeat at my hands. You can tell them or not—as you please." He counted on the young guard's pride to keep him silent. Then he strode through the gap in the wall.

Climbing the ladder to the top of the mound was tricky, with his balance off because of the jar. He supposed a woman heavy with child would have felt much the same awkwardness, though a woman experienced tiny day-to-day changes as her baby grew in her belly, rather than having it show up all at once. He imagined Deerchaser, round with child, but firmly put the image out of his mind.

The other Canalmasters sat beside the incised map of the riverward section of the canal system. Rush made mental notes each time he came for a meeting and then, when he returned to his quarters, transferred what he recalled to thin rabbit-skin vellum, using a charcoal stick sharpened for the purpose. Between the plaster map, his sketches, and walking the canals himself all the way from the river to the temple, he had a good sense now of what the main canals needed to be fully restored.

Making it happen . . . that was proving more difficult.

His fellow Canalmasters sat in a row under the vatto that shielded the canal map. One empty reed mat waited for him—inconveniently, at the other end of the line of seated men so he would have to disturb them all to get past.

That would be Twistedtrack's doing, to make his late arrival obvious.

He stood there and listened to them talk about ditch rechanneling and headgates that needed replacing. The problems remained the same from one moon to another. The precise locations changed, but he failed to see why such predictable difficulties deserved the combined attention of these seven Canalmasters over and over again.

Meetings of the Canalmasters of Sky River were quite different, consisting of discussions about matters affecting the entire community: what the rain priests were doing, what the mood of the clans was, whether the Skywatchers predicted a dry winter or a risk of big floods. According to the Sky River Canalmasters, there was more to what the Watermasters did than just coaxing water to run through the canals.

Under Twistedtrack's influence, the Canalmasters of Earth River seemed oblivious to all that. But then, Twistedtrack had no temple nearby, no priests to contend with. Only Rush, out of this entire group, had that. And the enmity of Twistedtrack.

Twistedtrack sat closest to where Rush stood. The older Canalmaster blocked the narrow space between the map basin and the half wall at the edge of the mound. Between his bulging belly and the balding, broadmouthed head that seemed to rest directly on his sloping shoulders, he resembled a frog.

Injured in a fall soon after being elevated to his post, he was the only one of the present company who didn't personally inspect the canals he was responsible for. And instead of the meetings rotating from one observation mound to another as they did up at Sky River, the meetings were all held here, at Coyote-Willow, to accommodate Twistedtrack's infirmity.

Next to Twistedtrack sat the oldest of the Canalmasters, Sevenshells, the one who spoke for Earth River on the River Council and bore the responsibility for the shortest canal, the one farthest downriver. It drew from Earth River near the spearpoint-shaped island where the Wilders lived, between the two channels of the river where it split.

Sevenshells had a multitude of thin braids hanging straight down like the snake-spit rains of early summer. Rush knew, because he had counted them during spells of boredom at earlier meetings, that each braid had seven white, thumbnail-sized shells woven in.

Beside Sevenshells was Mudpack, in charge of the northern portion of the canal that split off from the main channel at The Wing. The southern portion divided again into the many canals of Crookstaff Village, Rush's responsibility. Beside Mudpack were the three Canalmasters from the canals that headed on the opposite side of the river: Upper Blackpool, Lower Blackpool, and Stonewood. In the meetings, they went not by their names but by their canal designations.

Other than placing Twistedtrack above Sevenshells, the seating order seemed to reflect their relative status—with Rush at the bottom. He supposed, with a wry twist of his mouth, that at least Twistedtrack allowed him to sit under the vatto rather than at the other end of the mound, out of earshot, as he was pretty sure his host would have liked to do.

"Sorry I'm late," he inserted into a lull in their discussion. "Yesterday's trade day held a few too many surprises."

"Trade day, yes." Twistedtrack's thin lips flattened. His protruding eyes above and lack of a chin below made his face all the more froglike. "And plenty of female company, I'll be bound. Too much to ask that you rise early enough to join us."

Rush forced a smile. "Always glad to be here."

He stooped under the vatto's roof and stepped past his fellow Canalmasters, placing his feet carefully between theirs and the low rim surrounding the canal map. He sat crosslegged on the reed mat at the end farthest from Twistedtrack and pulled his poncho around himself to ward off the chill in the vatto's shade—and hide the bone-jar from view.

The others continued sharing what they had accomplished since the last council meeting. Rush placed his left elbow on his knee and leaned his chin on his hand.

He thought about his own situation—work crews who forgot to show up, wasted time quarreling or messing about, ignored his instructions.

Repairs that seemed solid but failed as soon as they were tested. A lack of water coming downcanal.

On previous trips to Coyote-Willow, he had seen plenty of water in the fields close to the river. The ditches at The Wing seemed in good shape too. Farther from the river, in the ditches that fed the fields of Crookstaff Village, the water levels were much lower than they should have been. He wondered if Mudpack had noticed the same thing.

Twistedtrack glared at him and interrupted the droning on of Lower Blackpool to demand, "Do these details bore you? Or did your night of debauchery make you too tired to stay awake?"

Bored, yes. Tired, yes. But not because of any pleasuring. Rush usually kept his tongue at these council meetings. Today he lacked the patience for it. "You say we all need to know each others' canals as well as our own. Isn't that what the ditch bosses are for?"

Senior among the ditchrunners and just below Canalmaster in rank, the ditch bosses knew the path, the grade, the shape of every canal and ditch segment in their assigned area. Rush had inherited nine of them from the old Canalmaster. Their number included Holdsbreath, who seemed more loyal to Twistedtrack than to either Rush or the people of Crookstaff Village.

"You've been here for the blink of an eye!" Twistedtrack snapped. "You think you know how things should be done? This is just what we feared when you arrived."

"Who is this we?" Rush asked, looking at the other Canalmasters.

Twistedtrack didn't give any of them time to say whether they agreed with his low opinion. He rushed on, practically spitting: "Inexperience. Lack of respect for how we do things here on Earth River. Inability to accept guidance from those who really know what needs doing. Shirking any real responsibility."

Rush glanced from face to face. None of the other Canalmasters would meet his gaze. Not even Mudpack, who Rush had hoped might be counted as a friend. The Stonewood Canalmaster had his eyes on the plaster map and seemed distant from the budding argument.

Still polite, though it took considerable willpower, Rush commented, "It's true that things are done differently on Sky River. The Canalmasters there have a distinct notion of what is important for us to discuss among ourselves."

Stonewood asked, "What is it you think important?"

Rush hesitated. If he had any proof, he would accuse Twistedtrack of deliberately dropping the level of the canal head at the river, to deprive the Crookstaff fields of water. He knew what the excuse would be: the floods of the previous winter had caused downcutting of the river channel. But even during the late summer heat there had still been plenty of water in the broad river.

In addition, there was his growing suspicion that someone was sabotaging the canal and ditch repairs as soon as they were made. Holdsbreath seemed the most likely, on Twistedtrack's direct orders. Without something to back up such grave accusations, though, Rush was all too aware that his position would be weaker than if he kept his mouth shut and looked for incontrovertible evidence. And then presented it privately to each Canalmaster, to persuade them individually before confronting Twistedtrack.

"It's you who is to learn from us, not the other way round!"

Rush ignored Twistedtrack's outburst. "It's not the proper depth or curve of a channel or what task your work parties next set to. It's what the farmers think about what's happening. What they're starting to say among themselves."

"What farmers think!" Twistedtrack sneered. "Are you some kind of seer now, able to divine the thoughts of others?"

"It doesn't take magic to do that." Rush directed his words to the other five Canalmasters, who might be capable of being swayed away from Twistedtrack's way of doing things. "I just keep my ears open to grumblings. What will happen if work parties refuse to take our orders or to work side by side with the Wilders? What if the farmers decide they no longer need the canals, now that the priests promise ample water for their crops? What if they decide they no longer need us?"

Twistedtrack snapped, "We won't run from shadows! *You* may have lost the faith of your farmers. The rest of us need fear no such thing! *I* have served my people for more than thirty turnings. They'll prove loyal—they wouldn't dare do otherwise."

"The priests take credit for ending the Long Thirst," Rush argued. "Against that, what do your many turnings signify? They claim to be able to magic water out of the very sky—"

"You think the farmers so gullible as to believe in claims of magic?" scoffed Twistedtrack. "And if the priests are so powerful, how did one of them get himself killed?"

"Killed?" Sevenshells repeated, eyes widening.

"By Wilders, as some would have it," Twistedtrack said. His mouth puckered, as if he'd been chewing on hackberries.

Sevenshells asked Rush, "Why is this the first I've heard about such a thing?"

Rush felt the weight of the jar and the knowledge he carried. Sevenshells, living so close to the Wilders, should have heard before Twistedtrack. But Rush hadn't thought to send a message. Hadn't thought it necessary. "I—"

Giving a dismissive wave of one hand, Twistedtrack interrupted. "One doesn't meddle in another's business."

Stonewood, seated next to Rush, said, "Enough arguing. Speak, Rush. No, Twistedtrack—" He held up his hand when their host would have interrupted. "I will hear him out."

Twistedtrack angled a searing look at the older Watermaster. "It's time to admit I was right, that he's the worst possible choice for this position. One of the old Canalmaster's ditch bosses would be far better. Someone with strong ties to the village and a less wild reputation."

"I served the old Canalmaster," Rush reminded him. "And I do have ties to the village."

"Fathering a child and running off can hardly be described as a tie," said Twistedtrack. "The people of Crookstaff know you can't be counted on to stand up to your responsibilities."

Rush frowned. "What are you talking about?"

Silence fell as the others looked at each other. He knew he wasn't going to like this. After a few moments, the one named Mudpack stirred. "Deerchaser and her child," he said.

Rush wasn't sure he'd heard that right. "What?"

Lower Blackpool explained, "Everyone assumes her son was yours. Is that wrong?"

"Yes!" But then Rush considered the timing. He had no idea when Deerchaser's son had been born. The boy was six, wasn't he? Too young to have been his. Only, how long ago did the boy die? He hadn't thought to ask. A cold knot lodged in the pit of his stomach.

A child might have resulted from their bedplay. But surely someone would have informed him if he had a child. The old Canalmaster, for one. Or one of the other ditchrunners. Or her. *Someone.*

The awkward expressions of the others told him they all believed he'd known about this child when he left Earth River all those turnings ago. His chest tightened, and he felt disoriented. "She never told me."

Slyly, Twistedtrack said, "Everyone believes it to be so. That's all that matters."

Sevenshells frowned. "Even if she didn't tell you, didn't the old Canalmaster get word to you?"

"No." Rush found his hands clenched into fists. He tried to open them, relax his shoulders, his neck, tried to breathe. "He must have known I would come back, if ever I found out."

He could tell they didn't believe his denial. "I don't run away from my responsibilities." His brother, his sister, they had been his responsibility too. He hadn't run away from them. But they weren't the issue. "I swear I never knew."

"You see the man they sent us," Twistedtrack told the others. "A liar, a coward, a man lacking in honor."

"You lie!" Rush was on his feet and ready to launch himself at the crippled man's throat before he even knew he was moving. He shook with the effort to hold back. The bone-jar pulled him off balance, and he sat abruptly to keep from toppling over.

Twistedtrack went on, "It's time to elevate Holdsbreath to Canalmaster, as we should've done straight off."

"No!" Rush exclaimed. But no one paid him any mind. He wanted to pace, to run, to leap over the side of the mound, to pound his chest and tear out his hair. He did none of those things, just forced himself to be still and figure out how to convince them that he was the right man in the right position.

"We cannot go against the River Council in this," Sevenshells said.

"We must!" snarled Twistedtrack. "Before it's too late. You've heard him whining about the priests. We need someone strong, who will stand up to them."

Mudpack looked doubtful. In his musical voice, lively and keen, he said, "The farmfolk of Crookstaff Village have gotten used to Rush. Through my own people I've heard they like him and believe his decisions to be fair. What reason would we give for replacing him?"

"Remind them that Holdsbreath is bloodmated," Twistedtrack said. "There would be no fear of him seducing and abandoning one of their clan-daughters."

Mudpack frowned. "Nothing against Holdsbreath, but as Sevenshells says, this isn't our decision alone. I wouldn't want to go against the River Council's recommendations."

"Rush could get himself a mate," suggested one of the Blackpool Canalmasters.

"Wait . . . what? No!" The suggestion made Rush's head spin. Solemn vows and matching tattoos and living together with the same woman for turning after turning? That wasn't a Watermaster's life. The wrappings around his chest, holding the jar in place, seemed to tighten, squeezing him so that he couldn't catch his breath.

Mudpack pursed his lips in consideration. "It isn't unreasonable to ask for proof that you're ready to settle down. That you've set aside the mistakes of your youth." A couple of the other Canalmasters nodded.

Rush went cold to the bottom of his feet. He still reeled from the news about having a son—a son!—with Deerchaser. A son he had never known about, would never know, for the boy had died, had lived and died without him ever knowing.

"The right woman can rebuild the worst reputation," Sevenshells allowed.

Feeling cornered, Rush pointed out, "Any farmer with a Canalmaster mated to his daughter is going to demand favors."

"But of course," came the reply from one of the Blackpool Canalmasters.

Sevenshells nodded. "Everyone expects it."

"How can my decisions be respected if I show favoritism to one family?" Rush argued. "All the other farmers would have to wonder whether I'm saying something because it's right or because I want to give someone an advantage."

"A good Canalmaster who proves himself evenhanded in all other judgments can stand a little resentment where his family is concerned," said Twistedtrack.

Rush looked down the row of Canalmasters at the ugly little man, sitting there puffed up with self-importance and unconcerned with doing the right thing. "I'll wait to choose a bondmate," Rush said viciously, "until I'm certain we'll be happy together, like Sevenshells and his mate. *I* don't need to promise water to get a woman in my bed."

Twistedtrack's frog-face darkened. "Are you implying that I had to make such promises?"

Sevenshells waved him into silence and asked Rush outright, "Do you have a woman in mind?"

Starflower's offer popped into Rush's head. Followed right away by a vehement *no*.

Before he could speak, Mudpack mused, "I wonder if Rush has a point." Twistedtrack scoffed, but Mudpack gestured him to silence and went on, "No, hear me out. Maybe our bondmates *should* come from outside the farmfolk."

"Healers? Hunters?" Upper Blackpool snorted. "It would take a braver man than I to link himself with the mamakai, with who-knows-what potions to drop in your stew. Much less a woman who can cleave you from nose to navel with her butchering knife if you say one wrong thing around her."

Twistedtrack glared at Rush as if he had been the one, rather than Mudpack, to make the suggestion. "Hunters? How would you get past their notion that the canals are evil, being built by men rather than made by the goddess?"

Rush listened as his fellow Canalmasters raised suspicions about the other groups that shared the Masterholding with him. The ridiculousness of this whole conversation struck him, though it all seemed tragic rather than funny. If the canals failed, then the crops failed. The hunters might be all that stood between the farmers and starvation.

Going into winter, the people of Crookstaff Village were fighting for their survival. To think the farmers would judge him on what he had done all those turnings ago was absurd.

Yet he couldn't help but think about the slowness of the repairs, the question of whether someone could want him to fail. He had suspected sabotage a few times, even considered whether Holdsbreath could be delaying the repairs, under orders from Twistedtrack. But perhaps someone from Cloud-Leaf Clan was upset over what he had done—was thought to have done—to Deerchaser.

Someone like Tumbler, perhaps. Rush knew he was being irrational, and he wanted to throw his suspicion away from him like a rattlesnake. But at this point, he didn't know if he could trust anyone.

Mudpack snorted. "They aren't so different from anyone else. They live in houses that are built; they hunt with weapons that are made."

But Twistedtrack didn't give up his argument. "They pray to the goddess before they go to the hunt," he sneered. "And after, they thank her for her help. That's not our way. We build with wood and rock and plaster, not prayer."

Mudpack pointed out, "The hunters are of the People of Two Rivers, just as we are, since the First Days. Their blood mingles with that of the clans, as does ours. Who among us cannot count a few deerfolk as kin?"

Stonewood spoke then. "We're all of the same people: Wilders and Watermasters, farmers and healers and hunters, even rain priests and the Allmother's priestesses. Just as the waters from all the hills and mountains come together to form Earth River and Sky River, which meet and mingle and flow in one mighty river out of the valley, so too do we all need to be as one. Rush will remain in his position. It would be best if I do not hear of any of you speaking against him in this council. Or outside, to anyone else—Watermaster, Wilder, or farmer."

That quiet statement put an end to not only the discussion but also, as he of Stonewood Canal rose to his feet and pushed past the others, the entire meeting.

3

The other Canalmasters followed Stonewood. All but Rush said goodbye to Twistedtrack and thanked him for his hospitality.

Rush couldn't pretend to be grateful. Even simple good manners were beyond him as he set off alone on the broad path atop the canal bank; he didn't wait for Mudpack as was his usual habit.

He felt caught in a whirlpool, fighting the undertow. Round and round his thoughts flew while he loped along under the midday sun. He wanted to think about what else had been said during the meeting but kept coming back to this:

I had a son.

The truth of it tore at his heart, made his stomach churn. He would never know his own child. The boy he'd made with Deerchaser had died. No one had told him, either of the birth or of the death. She hadn't told him. Not even when he'd seen her the day before and talked to her about her son. Their son.

He wanted to get back to the village, hunt her down, force her to tell him why she had kept it secret from him, and only him. The Canalmasters all seemed to know. Did everyone in the village know, too?

Rush had struggled to become a good man, a careful man, one who had, with great effort, put behind him his youthful weaknesses and foolishness. And now! All of a sudden, lies and rumors and assumptions threatened everything he had spent so many turnings trying to build.

He had thought all he would have to do was coax the water of the canals to where it was most needed. He had imagined his worth would be measured by fertile green fields, by granaries filled with corn and beans, by long garlands of dried squash rounds, by baskets full of tangled cotton bolls ready to be cleaned and carded and spun. By a system in balance, capable of both harmlessly bleeding off torrential floodwaters and urging precious rivulets into every thirsty field.

When the River Council had sent him back to Earth River, he'd had no doubt he could accomplish all that. But now the attentions he had paid to one woman—barely more than a girl, when he was barely more than a boy— could unravel it all.

Even Starflower must have known, clan-sister that she was to Deerchaser, for hadn't she asked him if he wanted any more children? *More?* he'd answered, in happy ignorance. *I don't have any.*

He passed right through The Wing but hardly realized it, so caught up in his brooding was he. Soon Rush came to the split in the canals and headed south, toward Crookstaff Village. After a bit, the jar bumping against his chest reminded him that he could not yet go home.

His steps slowed, halted. In the middle of the canal path he closed his eyes and took several deep breaths. He wrestled with his better self. A responsible man would master his temper, set aside his sense of betrayal, and do what needed to be done.

With the folk of The Wing having denied all knowledge of the priest found dead in the canal, Rush would have to look for the dead priest's kin among the Wilders—assuming Spadefoot had told the truth and wasn't just wasting Rush's time. Maybe the jar was filled with dust and not a man's remains after all.

But he believed the young priest genuinely mourned his vow-brother's death and wouldn't lie about the importance of getting the remains to his family. Not that it mattered, Rush's better self reminded him. He had made a promise; he had to at least try to fulfill it. If nothing else, he could warn the Wilders of the rumors so they wouldn't be caught off guard.

He jogged back along the canal path toward the river. From where he was, Coyote-Willow Village was about as far east as the Wilders' island was west. If he found the young priest's mother without too much trouble, he could dispose of the jar of ashes and still get home well before sunset.

His footfalls landed in cadence with words that drifted through his head. Rain priest, Wilder. Mother, brother. But over and over a thought inserted itself: *I had a son. And now he's gone.*

Being of the heronfolk meant Rush didn't always understand how other people felt about their kin, for the Watermasters weren't like the farmfolk, divided into clans and keeping track of use-rights to fields based on the mother's lineage.

Both his parents had been born heronfolk. That made him different from most Watermasters, who were born to one of the farming clans but decided young that they didn't want to be farmers.

That was partly why Rush had been so shocked when the Canalmasters said he should find a bondmate. The Watermasters of Sky River, where he'd been born and raised, saw little point in making a woman choose between her clan and her lover. If she was born to a farming clan, her children would have use-right to the clanlands when they grew up. Until then, they would be cared for by the entire clan.

There was no need for a formal declaration. A man and a woman would sleep together until they no longer wanted to, and then each would find someone else. Evidently things were different down here at Earth River.

Rush didn't know how the Wilders felt about kin ties and raising children. He wondered whether part of the reason the Wilders had split off was because the Watermasters didn't really have a place for young children, no home. A Watermaster slept and ate on the mound but spent the rest of his time traveling across the landscape.

What would happen to a woman from The Wing if she fell in love with a man her kinfolk didn't approve of—someone who wasn't one of them, such as a Wilder? Would she be sent away, forced to live among the Wilders to raise her children clanless and landless?

He pondered the unanswerable questions as he made his way downcanal. In his distraction, he failed to hear the footsteps coming up from behind until it was too late.

A blow to the back of his head felled him. He heard a shout but didn't think it came from him. For a time he was aware of nothing.

Hammering on the inside of his skull roused him. He realized his body was being jolted about. He put his hands up to his head, trying to hold it on as someone settled him with his back against something hard.

"Awake?" asked an unfamiliar man's voice, gravelly and deep.

Almost sympathetic, Rush thought. He was having trouble opening his eyes. "Were you the one who tried to kill me?" he asked muzzily.

"Kill you? No. If it'd been me hit you, you wouldn't've woke up."

"I heard a shout. Was that you?"

"Scared him off."

Rush tried to nod his head, but that made the pounding worse. He gasped in pain.

The man asked, "D'ya see who it was?"

"No. Did you?"

The other man started to reply. The words faded and rose, lapping at Rush like windblown wavelets in backwater.

Rush forced his eyes open. Beside him knelt a Wilder, a big man. Instead of numerous matted braids entangled in a shell net and covered with mud, as was typical of his kind, his hair was cut short in mourning for a recent death.

On the ground at the man's feet lay a heavy staff, pointed on one end and nearly black, made of stonewood, sturdy enough to hack out the rock-hard caliche that underlay the desert soil. Those caliche picks made fearsome weapons on the rare occasions when tempers flared.

Whether one could be driven through a man's chest, Rush had no idea. But he knew it wasn't a caliche pick that had killed the young priest; the body was unscathed when Rush had it delivered into the care of the priests.

Rush passed a hand over his ribs and took a deep breath to test whether they were still in one piece. They were, but he found only a shirt under his hand. No poncho, no cloth ties, no jar of ashes. "What happened to the bone-jar?"

"'s fine. Safe."

Rush introduced himself.

The other man didn't name himself in return. He said, "We've naught to do with any death, if that worries you."

"It worries some people down in the village. But I didn't come to accuse you of anything."

"Why're ya here, then? We don't get many Canalmasters come to us. Ditchrunners, yes, t' bring us word when strong backs 're needed."

Rush didn't have his wits about him. Even if he did, he wasn't prepared to deal with the strained relations between the Watermasters and the Wilders. He had his hands full with the farmers and the priests—and now, evidently, the other Canalmasters. "Some people say the young priest who joined the Ancestors was the son of a Wilder and a woman from The Wing. Would you know anything about that?"

The Wilder looked at him but said nothing. From the wild grief in his eyes, Rush saw there was a great deal of emotion pent up, as if behind a brush dam. He thought he wouldn't want to be downstream when the dam finally let go.

"Are you his father?" Rush asked.

That prompted a shake of the Wilder's head. "No, not I."

"But you know who is?"

The man gave a short nod.

"Then do you know who I should deliver his remains to?"

"It's I who'll take Nighthawk home."

"That's his name?" Rush asked. "You have no fear of saying it aloud?"

"'s been a baby born. He's been called Nighthawk. To keep the name alive."

"Will you take N—" Rush found himself reluctant to repeat the dead priest's name so soon after his passing, even though another soul now bore it. "Take the remains to his mother?"

The Wilder shifted his weight, and a dark look came over his face. "No, not his mother. I must be, I s'pose, the nearest thing to kin now."

Rush heard the sorrow in that and put it together with the signs of mourning. "His mother passed away too?"

"Few days back."

Had the young priest known? Was that why he had left the temple to come up toward the river—to mourn his mother's death? If so, what a tragic end for him, for the whole family. "There's no father?"

The Wilder's eyes narrowed. His nostrils flared. "His father! You wish to know who his father is? His blood father's one o' yours—Twistedtrack!"

Rush's first response was doubt; he might dislike Twistedtrack, but surely the other Canalmaster could never have been so monstrous as to force himself on a woman. Yet the anger in the Wilder's voice, on his face, in every taut muscle was convincing.

"He weren't crippled in body back then." The Wilder's face bore a terrible expression. "But in mind, yes, always. He took her against her will, got her with child, scared her with threats of what he'd do 'f ever she told."

"And did she?" Rush asked, seeing a way to confirm this story—if he dared go back to The Wing and challenge those who had disclaimed all knowledge of the dead priest. Of Nighthawk. "Did she tell her people?"

"Them!" The Wilder spat on the ground. "They wouldn't fight for her. She came to us 'cause she liked my brother. We offered her a home. And the baby too."

He continued, "We came upon Twistedtrack one night and broke him, so never would he be able to force a woman again. But we were too late." He pressed his lips together and smacked the sharp end of the caliche pick into the ground a few times.

The news about how Twistedtrack came to be crippled both shocked Rush . . . and didn't. If the Wilders had inflicted rough justice on him, then Twistedtrack was lucky to still be alive. But what did the Wilder mean by *too late?*

"She was already with child," Rush guessed.

The big man muttered, "Twistedtrack got to her sister, too. She chose to become a Cornmaiden." The Wilder stared levelly at Rush. "And bore a child."

"Who?" Rush didn't need to hear the answer.

He thought about Spadefoot's interest in the one called Nighthawk, referring to him as a brother. Not just a vow-brother, but a brother by blood. And Spadefoot had said their mothers were sisters. Did Spadefoot too believe that the Rainsinger wasn't his father?

Rush tried to remember exactly what the young priest had said when he asked Rush to take the bone-jar.

"You see why we kept this quiet," the Wilder said.

Rush thought he did . . . but he realized he was running down a different track when the man told him, "Anyone who crosses the Rainsinger comes to a bad end."

"You mean N—" Again Rush couldn't speak the name. "Your young kinsman? You don't think Morning Green had one of his own priests killed!"

"He might've done."

"And blamed it on the Wilders?" Rush went to shake his head but winced as the pounding started up again. He stilled the movement. "But the body was found so far from the river."

"That was Spadefoot's doing. He was to meet Nighthawk that morning up by the river. When he found the body instead, he waited for nightfall—moved it to the village, as close to the temple as he could and still leave it in water."

"How do you know all this? How do you know what Spadefoot and your boy intended?"

Instead of answering, the Wilder reminded him, "It's not only Nighthawk who's been killed; it's his mother too. Right before she could meet Spadefoot. As I said, anyone who gets crosswise of the Rainsinger . . ."

Rush, appalled by the charges of killing and brutality, closed his eyes and his ears to the Wilder's claims. For a moment he sorted through the pieces. Spadefoot was to meet his mother's sister, she would tell him about his fathering by Twistedtrack, and . . . and what? What had the Wilders expected the young priest would do then? Avenge the assault on his mother? Or was this an even more dangerous situation?

Rush felt as if he was picking apart a very complicated knot, like the ones he tied in the fringes of his sash to calculate distances and drops. "But you don't think Spadefoot was the one who killed either of them?"

"No. Weren't him. We watch."

"You watch Spadefoot," Rush said, to clarify.

"When he leaves the village, we watch. We been waiting for him to come to us."

Rush saw the caliche pick punching into the dirt again and wondered what sort of welcome Spadefoot would find if he ever did come to the Wilders. As blood kin to a well-loved woman or as the son of the despised Twistedtrack?

Suddenly Rush needed to breathe more deeply than the rock behind him would allow. He pushed himself to his feet. His head spun, so he closed his eyes and took some deep breaths until the dizziness lessened. When he was sure he wouldn't fall over, he asked, "Does he know the Rainsinger isn't really his father?"

"Nighthawk was going to tell him, but whether he did already . . ." The Wilder shrugged one shoulder as if it didn't really matter. "It's for you to tell him now."

"That he isn't really the one spoken of in prophecy? That he isn't even the Rainsinger's son?" Rush barked out a harsh laugh as he foresaw the effect that would likely have on Spadefoot, on the Rainsinger, on the whole village. Assuming this story about Spadefoot's parentage was even true. It could just as well be an elaborate lie, a way of getting back at the priests, revenge for blaming the Wilders for the death of their kinsman. How could Spadefoot be the one whose coming was prophesied if his father wasn't an outlander?

The Wilder didn't answer. He turned away, picked up the red jar from a depression between the gnarled roots of a nearby tree stump, and left without another word. He walked into the band of cottonwood trees and willow thickets along the river and disappeared from view.

Rush realized his teeth were clenched so hard, his jaw ached. His hands were fisted, his head throbbed, and his gut had more knots than his sash. *Breathe,* he told himself. *Feel each breath. Feel nothing but each breath.*

That sage advice, given to him by an old Watermaster up on Sky River, had in the past helped relieve the urge to hit, kick, or break something. It failed him now.

He was being drawn into plots and plans he had little control over. And his easygoing nature, the patience for the whims of others that he had acquired through conscious effort, his desire to persuade others to his opinion rather than knocking them on the head with their foolishness, all seemed to be slipping from his grasp, leaving him shaken.

The rest of the homeward journey took longer than it should have. Rush could only walk, slowly; his head wouldn't let him proceed at his usual pace. That gave him far too much time to mull over what he had been told.

Nighthawk's mother might have been lying when she accused Twistedtrack of brutalizing her, and she could have included Spadefoot's mother in that lie for reasons no one would ever know. Both were dead now. Neither could ever testify to what had happened—and maybe Nighthawk's mother hadn't done so even back when it happened, when her own kin had cast her off.

Instead of lodging a formal accusation against Twistedtrack, the people of The Wing had sent her away, perhaps in hopes of not offending the Watermasters. Rush had always assumed the people of The Wing had rejected the Watermasters, had gone their own way like the Wilders. But maybe it was the other way round, that Twistedtrack had pulled all the Watermasters out of The Wing or even threatened the farmers there into silence.

Maybe Spadefoot's mother had joined the Cornmaidens for the same reason Nighthawk's had gone to the Wilders: because neither woman had anywhere else to go. It was an appalling thought. Clans weren't supposed to betray their own.

Rush knew it was all just speculation on his part. He couldn't be sure the dead priest's mother had told her story truthfully, much less that the Wilder had told him the truth. Or even Spadefoot. All he could be certain of was that someone claiming to know the young priest had taken his ashes.

Regardless of whether any or all of it was true, there could be no proving it, now that the priest and his mother were both dead—unless Twistedtrack were to confess. The unknown Wilder certainly seemed to believe the story he had told Rush. But part or all of it could still be a lie. It could well be a ploy to get Spadefoot to go to the Wilders. To draw him out, get him alone, vulnerable, off guard.

The priest's death could have been an accident, a slip of the foot on wet rocks, an actual drowning. Maybe it happened up by the river, as the Wilder said, but maybe it happened where the body was found.

The priest hadn't been killed with a caliche pick—Rush knew that for a fact. But some people were certain he had been.

What gave rumors strength? A bit of truth.

Anyone at the temple could have shoved a caliche pick into the priest's chest to suggest that he had met his end through violence. Then the body, after being defiled, could have been shown to a few influential people to cast blame on the Wilders.

Such a plan would require Spadefoot's cooperation, of course. Perhaps he was a loyal son, acting on the Rainsinger's orders. Or perhaps he got rid of his vow-brother to protect his secret—that he wasn't actually the Rainsinger's son.

But then why tell Rush that the Wilders were innocent? Why send Rush out looking for his vow-brother's kin? Why risk having Rush learn so much about Spadefoot's origins?

There were too many questions and no answers.

By the time Rush neared the Masterholding, lit by the last rays of the setting sun, he was footsore, chilled through, and stumbling tired. Every jolt in his knees sent a stab of pain up his spine to the top of his head.

If he had a woman who belonged to him, he thought dimly, she would be waiting for him with a hot meal and open arms, warm coverings on the bed, and soothing words of comfort. The idea of a lifemate didn't seem as absurd in that moment.

He strode as quickly as he could manage to the base of the ladder that leaned against the wall. His hands were so cold, he could hardly grasp the rungs of the ladder. When he was halfway up, the sole of his sandal slipped. He rapped his cheekbone and temple on the nub where the rung was lashed to the upright. The impact was right where Deerchaser had hit him earlier. The front of his head started pounding again. It joined with the throbbing at the back to make a circle of agony.

But he bit back the foul words that sprang to his tongue. He was nearly home, and this trying day was nearly done. He told himself there was no use in giving in to ill temper.

Then he rounded the corner of the ditchrunners' quarters and saw Spadefoot seated cross-legged under the vatto. "Fuck," he said.

A bowl sat on one of the flat stones that encircled the fire. Rush's nose told him it held rabbit stew. Tumbler's clan-grannie had put his supper to warm. Normally he would have felt grateful.

But not this time. With his quarters left unguarded, there was no one to watch the rain priest. The rest of the Watermasters weren't back from their daily assignments yet.

"You look like you're about to keel over," Spadefoot told him with a lift of his brows that rippled the lines tattooed on his forehead. "Did you have some trouble at The Wing?"

Rush put up a hand and felt a lump starting on his face. His touch redoubled the storm at the back of his head. "I tripped," he said. He walked over and slid the pin out of the door latch, then pulled the reed door open.

The firelight showed a light haze of dust on the floor of his sleeping quarters. There were no footsteps in it. Evidently Spadefoot hadn't made himself at home.

"I didn't go in," Spadefoot assured him.

"What are you doing here? Don't you have duties at the temple?"

"They can spare me for a little while."

"Then they'll have to get by without you a while longer." Wondering whether he had the strength to manage the upcoming exchange, Rush entered his quarters and pulled the door closed after him. He supposed if he took too long, especially if he collapsed on the sleep pallet as he wished, Spadefoot would come in and roust him out.

And then there was the stew, calling his name. Bitterly he told himself he should be happy Spadefoot hadn't eaten it.

He took off his poncho and hung it on one of the mesquite posts, then unwrapped the cloths he had worn to hold the jar. He used one to rub the dried sweat and travel grime off his arms and legs. Sitting on the fur-covered bench just inside the doorway, he unlaced his sandals, though he couldn't lean over very far without his head going from throbbing to pounding.

He fumbled to release the knot of his sash and pulled off his clothes. Only after he had dried himself off all the way up to his blood-crusted hair did he pull on a fresh cotton shirt and breechcloth. He added deerskin leggings and a tunic. Over the leggings, he cross-gartered the high boots he generally saved for winter wearing.

Without a judicious application of soaproot and warm water, there was nothing he could do to clean off the dried blood. That would have to wait.

When he stepped out of his sleeping quarters, he felt a little more capable of dealing with Spadefoot. Rush seated himself on a mat beside the fire. He took up the bowl and breathed in the luscious, thick odor. The heat of the curved surface seeped into his hands. His hunger sharpened, causing his stomach to rumble, as exhaustion and cold eased their grasp on him.

"Were you successful? Did you find my brother's kin?" the young priest asked from where he sat, across the firepit from Rush. It wasn't the same place he had been just a few moments ago. That was where Rush sat, on a nicely warmed mat.

Rush looked down at the wooden spoon that rested against the side of the bowl. He grasped the carved handle and took his first mouthful of food since the journeycakes he had consumed on the way to the meeting at Coyote-Willow Village. Twistedtrack wasn't a generous host, and at The Wing they hadn't offered any sort of breakfast. Then there was the Wilder, whose horrifying tale had spoiled Rush's appetite.

Saliva, almost painful in its release, burst into his mouth as he chewed. He swallowed the stew and sighed with pleasure. Ignoring Spadefoot's obvious impatience, he ate until the gnawing of hunger eased. "I did as I promised," he said at last, hoping that would satisfy the younger man, make him go away and stop staring expectantly at Rush.

"My brother is back with his people, then?"

"He is. So you can go back to your father with a clean conscience." Rush watched for a reaction to *your father*, referring to the Rainsinger.

Spadefoot threw him a sidelong look, but Rush didn't know what it meant. It might mean Spadefoot knew he and Nighthawk shared the same father—who wasn't the Rainsinger. Or it might indicate a suspicion that the Rainsinger had gotten rid of his vow-brother or at least started the rumors that blamed the Wilders for it. Or maybe Spadefoot was sick of being under the Rainsinger's thumb, like any son trying to declare his independence. Or it could mean nothing at all.

Too tired to work it out, Rush placed the empty bowl back on the fire ring. He hoped Tumbler's clan-grannie would scour it clean with sand when she came back with supper for everyone else.

Spadefoot asked, "Did you find out anything about his father?" Not *our father*.

Rush studied the younger man's face for any resemblance to Twistedtrack. The tattoos on cheeks and forehead, the birthmark, the shaved-off hair at the sides instead of braids hanging down, all hid any similarities there might have been. "Nothing certain."

"I had thought . . ." Spadefoot waved off the words rather than completing whatever he had intended to say. "No matter. Did you find out a name?"

"*His* name, yes, your brother. They've named a baby after him already, so they now feel free to speak of him." Yet Rush didn't feel comfortable even thinking the dead priest's name.

Spadefoot's mouth tightened. "Was it his mother you met?"

Rush shook his head. "I gave the ashes to the brother of her mate."

The young priest frowned. "Not to her? You gave them to some Wilder, just because he claimed to be kin?"

"Would you feel better if I'd given them to a woman who claimed to be his mother?"

Spadefoot eyed him but made no answer.

Rush wanted to confirm something, just one thing, from the confusing welter of information. "Or did you know his mother was dead?"

"What?" Spadefoot stiffened, then leaned forward, hands opening and closing on his knees. "When did that happen?"

His surprise seemed genuine to Rush. "Around the same time as his own passing, I would guess. Within a few days."

"The father. Did you learn his name?" Spadefoot asked.

Rush toyed with the idea of telling him that Twistedtrack was his real father and had been accused of violating his mother. Regardless of whether it was true, it would cause a spot of trouble for Twistedtrack. That might even be a way of ending his interference—through his man Holdsbreath—in Crookstaff Village. But then Rush would be no better than whoever started the rumor that the Wilders had killed Spadefoot's brother.

Rush said, "He has no living blood kin among the Wilders, is what I was told."

Spadefoot bowed his head and just sat there quietly.

Laughter and what sounded like Tumbler's light young voice came from below. Rush felt old and discouraged and desirous of solitude as he again became aware of the aching in his head. "Everybody is coming back for their supper and their beds," he told Spadefoot. "It's time for you to go."

"You didn't answer my question." Spadefoot brought his head up sharply and searched Rush's face. "'No kin among the Wilders,' you said. But you didn't say yes or no, that you found out our father's name."

"*Our* father?"

"You knew that. I can see it in your face."

"So, you believe your vow-brother is actually your brother by blood, through a shared father as well as sister-mothers. But you don't know who that shared father is." Rush almost wished Spadefoot would argue that the Rainsinger, his father, must have had two sons, not just one. That would simplify things.

But he didn't. Instead he said quietly, almost too low for Rush to hear, "Then I'll never know."

"Why was he going to meet you up at the river?" Rush hoped to startle Spadefoot into revealing a truth.

"You know about that?"

"The Wilders."

Spadefoot nodded as if that was enough explanation. "Nighthawk's mother was going to show me our father."

Show. Rush's pulse quickened. An interesting word, he thought. Twistedtrack never, as far as he knew, left the Watermasters' compound at Coyote-Willow.

So had the mother intended to show Spadefoot the mound and explain about the boys' father? Or was someone else responsible, not Twistedtrack at all?

"You moved your brother's corpse. You told me you found the body by the temple, but that wasn't the truth, was it?"

Spadefoot hesitated, then said, "No."

"You found him by the river. And you moved him. Alone." Rush let doubt creep into his voice.

"That's right. I floated him down the canal, mostly. The water was shallow enough for me to wade in it."

It still would have been hard going in the cold water, with places under repair where Spadefoot would have had to haul the body out and carry it up the steep bank and along the canal path to the next spot where the level was high enough to float the body. It would have been easier if he'd had help. Rush didn't know why he was pursuing the issue, but it seemed important to find out how alone and isolated Spadefoot felt.

"Why did you do such a thing?"

"Partly I didn't want anyone to wonder why he was up by the river."

"And the other part?"

"I wanted to make sure he was found. I wanted his soul sung to rest. I wanted . . ." Spadefoot waved his hand and fell silent. This time he didn't restart the conversation. But he also didn't rise to leave.

Rush wondered what Spadefoot was waiting for. An answer, perhaps, to the question of who he really was.

Both of them seemed to be flailing in the dark, unable to discover the truth. Finding only shadows that hinted at maddening undercurrents.

To look at another and see some aspect of himself was unsettling, making Rush again think, *I had a son.* Would that boy, like Spadefoot and the dead priest, have sought out his absent father? Or would he have counted himself well rid of someone he had no need of?

In resistance to that thought, to convince at least himself that he wasn't as rotten a father as Twistedtrack, he added, "It might be better to leave this matter of your father as it is. There are some things it's better not to know."

Spadefoot stared hard at Rush. The birthmark on his cheek rippled under his tattoo. "They may not have told you my father's name, but they told you enough to guess, didn't they?" His voice rose, and he leaped to his feet. "You know who it is!"

Rush eyed the young man an arm's-length away, hands fisted and face flushed. Spadefoot was so much like the gate guard at Coyote-Willow, prideful and impatient and . . . just young. Even watching youth in the throes of emotion was exhausting, Rush thought, feeling himself very old and tired.

And battered. The lump on his cheek twinged, and he had trouble seeing out of that eye. The back of his head ached steadily. "I went to The Wing as a favor for you and because it was the right thing to do, consigning your vow-brother's remains to his kin. And I went beyond, to the Wilders, for the same reason, when the people of The Wing proved unhelpful."

"Give me his name!" Spadefoot demanded.

"To what end? You have a life here, as the Rainsinger's son. As the one whose future is laid out in prophecy. What point is there in pursuing something different?"

"I need to know!"

The flaring shadows cast upward by the small fire twisted Spadefoot's blotched and tattooed face into something inhuman, almost animal in its markings.

Rush said, "I can't tell you."

"You can, but you won't! Why do you shield him? What are you afraid to have me find out?"

"There are others involved. This isn't only your story."

"Who else? My mother? Nighthawk? They're all beyond caring! It's only me and my father now."

In the younger man's sneer, Rush did see a trace of Twistedtrack. "Go back to your own life," he advised. "The Cornmaidens, the rituals, whatever it is you do in the temple. Your vow-brothers. Aren't they all the family you need?"

Spadefoot placed his fists on his hips and puffed out his chest. "You talk of Cornmaidens? At least they know where they stand with us. I don't need to lure a woman with false promises and then leave her crying! We priests are not like you Watermasters."

Spadefoot turned on his heel and strode off, pushing past the boys.

Rush saw Crack and Tumbler staring at him from beyond the young priest. He wondered how long they had been there, how much they had heard. The young priest had been far too free with his words.

Rush heard whispering on the other side of the reed door.

He eased up on one elbow, moving slowly to let the pain in his head subside—from intolerable drumbeats to a steady ache. His scalp felt tight, itchy. Lightly he touched the back of his head and hissed in a breath as his exploring fingers found the knot where he had been struck the previous day. Above it was a clump of hair thick with hard, dried blood. His cheek felt swollen and hot.

After he got his bare feet under him, he staggered to the door. There he paused and waited for the swimming sensation behind his eyes and the lurching of his stomach to ebb. He dragged the door open.

He stayed there for a moment. Tumbler and Crack stopped talking when they saw him. Their eyes widened and their mouths fell open. He guessed he looked even worse than he had the previous night.

"You told me not t' fight," Tumbler accused. "And then you did!"

"Not really. I didn't get a chance to hit back."

Neither of the boys staring at him seemed impressed by his attempt at a joke.

Before he went to confront Deerchaser, he decided, he needed to get cleaned up. He hadn't known until that moment that he was going to demand an explanation from her. Now it seemed the only thing to do.

"But the Rainsinger's son . . . !" Crack breathed.

"It wasn't Spadefoot, and there was no fight. I fell on my way home last night. Hit a rock." He gestured toward his head.

The boys glanced at each other. "You fell on the canal path?" Tumbler asked, his doubt obvious. "And hit a rock? With your face?"

Rush decided he didn't blame them for questioning him; he wouldn't have believed it himself. "Never mind."

The boys seemed relieved when he sat down and gave them things to do. Crack brought Rush a cloth soaked in water to take off the top crust of blood in his hair and on his scalp and cheek, while Tumbler built up the fire to heat water. "My gran says warm water cleans better," the boy explained to Crack.

Rush didn't wait for the water to get warm. He propped a shoulder against the wall of his quarters and applied the cloth to the back of his head. With a gasp he wondered how cold water could burn so. When he took it off and rinsed it in the bowl, the water darkened to a brownish color.

Tumbler said, "That looks bad."

"Go to the bonemenders," Crack told the other boy. "Get something t' put on that."

"I don't need fussing over," Rush told them. They ignored him.

Tumbler went off toward the ladder while Crack took over the task of cleaning the wound and rinsing the blood out of Rush's braids. Rush had to admit that being tended to was better than trying to take care of the back of his own head. He closed his eyes and tried not to flinch at the touch of the cloth.

Tumbler returned shortly with a small cactus pad. He burned off the spines, then sliced it open before laying the greenish oozing flesh onto the cut and binding it in place on Rush's head with a clean, dry strip of cloth.

"It's all right. I'm as good as I'll ever be." The queasy feeling whenever he moved too abruptly had subsided. He thanked the boys and tried to send them away, but they turned stubborn.

Tumbler told him, "My gran said to stay with you while your head hurts."

"My head is fine." As long as he kept perfectly still, it only felt like bone awls jabbing into his skull. "Why are you still here this morning, anyway? Don't you have work to do?"

Normally he would have gone out to inspect the canals already. But when he had something else to do—like a hearing or a council meeting or confronting a woman over her betrayal—they were supposed to make the rounds of the ditch bosses and work crews and bring back any problems to him.

They exchanged glances.

"What is it?" He struggled to his feet, though to manage it he had to ignore the battering of his pulse at the top of his head.

He became aware of the buzz of a crowd, not quite as loud as on a trade day but coming from the direction of the old ballcourt—or the temple beyond. "What's happening?"

Tumbler folded his arms and stayed silent, but Crack weakened and answered. "The Rainsinger says the Ta'atchul have a message for him to deliver. A procla— something."

"Proclamation," Tumbler finished for him. "Only, my gran says you shouldn't go out there. She says everybody'll know about the fight."

Rush's first thought was a rebellious one: *Who cares what people think?* His second was what the bandage around his head and bruise on his face would say about him. Not *The Canalmaster is reliable and all grown up. We can trust him. He doesn't need to settle down and take a mate.*

He sighed. "You know Spadefoot didn't do this to me."

"You argued with him," Tumbler said.

"Over a woman," said Crack.

Tumbler finished, "If we heard, others might've too."

Rush closed his eyes briefly as he strove for patience. He wanted to snap at the boys, but of course it wasn't their fault. "Whatever you think you heard, it wasn't an argument over a woman." Though at the end, Spadefoot had accused him of leaving a woman crying. Deerchaser, he supposed. Everyone but him seemed to know what had happened between the two of them.

He needed to understand why he was the last to know—but that would have to wait. If what the Rainsinger planned to say was so important that the whole village was invited as witnesses, Rush had to be there.

He explained, "I have to hear for myself what the Rainsinger has to say, rather than getting it secondhand. I'm not saying your gran is wrong, Tumbler; she's a smart woman. Tell her I'll be careful."

Rush stood in the gather ground outside the temple precinct with what seemed half the village, awaiting Morning Green's appearance. He had taken a long cloth, one of those he had used to support the jar the previous day, and wrapped it around his head, as some of the Far-Traders did. He hoped the odd head-covering would draw attention away from his face.

Now that he had been up for a while, he felt stronger. He had pressed a cold rock against his cheek to reduce the swelling. The bruises were mostly just aches now, and his head no longer pounded. He shifted his weight from one foot to another as he, along with many others, waited for Morning Green to appear.

Rush prided himself on being a man who believed in things that could be seen, touched, measured—exactly the opposite of the priests' claim to power. That was why he had to be here; he needed to hear the Rainsinger for himself. Otherwise, it would be all rumor, gossip: *they say* . . . and *did you hear* . . . But he was impatient for this spectacle to be over.

Out of the corner of one eye Rush caught a flicker of movement in the guard tower that topped the wall, high above the heads of even the tallest in the crowd. The blast of a shell trumpet echoed off the walls of the nearby house compounds, silencing everyone watching from below.

A steady hiss, as of rain falling, began almost imperceptibly. As it became louder, it was joined by the slow, deep beat of a big cottonwood drum and then a hum that surrounded the crowd and made Rush's teeth ache.

The Rainsinger strode onto the tower platform. His robe, the smoky gray worn by all the priests of the Temple of the Mist, blended into the cloud-streaked sky so that he seemed a shadow rather than a man.

He stopped at the edge of the platform and flung his arms into the air. The wide sleeves of his robe slid down toward his shoulders to reveal arms thin and bone-white. His hands were blackened, and the fingers he held toward the sky might have been a pair of unleafed mesquite trees, so bent and gnarled were they.

On his arms were painted dark swirls and dots that confused Rush's eyes. As though in response to Morning Green's presence, the sun blazed out around him through a gap in the clouds, and a gasp went up from the crowd. Rush lifted a hand to shield his eyes from the glare.

"Is it the sun-festival, Papa?" came a small voice nearby.

"Not yet, little one."

"What, then?"

Several people shushed the child in unison. Rush felt sorry for it. The adult world was intimidating enough without having strangers join forces against you.

He felt like saying something in the child's defense, but that was for the father to do. A harsh voice in his head wondered who had done that for his own son.

Rush's eyes recovered quickly from the sun's brilliance. He could see that strings of shell beads cascaded from the shoulders of the Rainsinger's robe. Morning Green's face was painted like his arms. Stiff raven feathers as flat as a comal stuck straight out from his head.

Again the shell trumpet sounded. The Rainsinger lowered his arms and opened them as if to embrace all those who had come to hear him speak.

"Oh, my people." Sorrow tinged his voice. "Many days have I spent in fasting and prayer, many nights walking the white starpath, begging the Ta'atchul for answers." His hands came around to the front. "Why, oh why, are the granaries empty? Why, oh why, are the children hungry?"

A rough-voiced man on the other side of the plaza shouted, "Tell us, Rainsinger, what do they say?"

"Yes, Rainsinger, tell us!" said someone near Rush. A chant of "Tell us! Tell us! Tell us!" started. It was ragged at first but tightened into a rhythm that matched the beat of the drum. Someone began to stamp his feet; others soon did the same. Around them all, still more people clapped. The plaza started to pulse with the beat, until the entire group seemed to become a single heart pounding.

Rush had never felt so much a part of anything. It was exhilarating and terrifying all at once.

"They have sent me the most terrible vision!" At the first sound of the Rainsinger's voice, the crowd stilled and fell silent to listen. Only the drum and the hum and the rain-hiss continued. "A cataclysm comes that will forever transform the People of Two Rivers. To survive, you must turn from the old ways. The Ta'atchul will not save you . . . only you can do that! You must be strong!"

"We are strong!" roared the rough-voiced man.

"You must be determined!" the Rainsinger called out.

"We are determined!" This time, several others responded along with the rough-voiced man.

"You must be ready!"

"We are ready!" Everyone answered that time, even Rush. The words leaped from his mouth before he knew he was going to say them. Startled, he clamped his jaw shut.

"Repent now, repent, and cast off the wicked! For the harsh days of judgment draw nigh!" The Rainsinger threw off his robe and stood naked to the waist in the sunshine, shocking the crowd into utter silence.

Rush had never heard of Morning Green being out in the day without being covered from head to toe; his pale skin, some said, would burst into flame. But here he was, painted all over with the same black markings that writhed along his arms and on his face. The curves reminded Rush of the shadow-dancers who risked rattlesnake bites during the spring sun-festival.

"After dark dreaming, remade by the Ta'atchul," the Rainsinger went on, his ribs shifting bewilderingly under his painted skin, "my knowledge it spreads no less wide than the ocean. It was the hot dizziness made by the sun; I ground it to powder and painted my face. It was the cold drunkenness left by the rain; I shaped it as feathers to place on my head. Weep now, my people, for all thee shall hear."

The incantation reached out to Rush, weaving around him, in and out, over and through. He fought against its draw by paying attention to the background noises. The eerie, inhuman hum he identified as the sound of a roarer, a flat paddle on a rawhide cord that the bearer spun above his head in a circle. There was the drum, made from sections of ancient cottonwood trunks hollowed out with fire. The hiss of rain from some kind of rattle gradually died away, though Rush listened closely for it.

"It's as thy made-father they send me, in anger—"

A sound like thunder made everyone jump. Rush knew how that noise was made in priestly rituals: it was a pottery vessel being smashed. One of the priests of the Sky River temples had let the secret out, and the Corn Maiden he'd been with had spread it widely.

"—now to the flat land I come. Down from above, the whirlwind they follow; below, the waters they drink. Alone I stand, alone, sorrowing over our young brother's passing. First he was to die—" another pot crashed "—but woe, he shall not be the last. His death it serves as a warning, repentance and sorrow to bring."

The rain-hiss began again, joined this time by the light melodic line of a flute, while the drum and the roarer's hum faded. The cloying scent of burning herbs drifted to Rush's nose, numbing his thoughts and faculties; he had the sensation of swimming, as water closed over his head.

"From my right hand, a white fire comes burning, and from my left hand a black fire." The Rainsinger clasped his hands together. "Both sides then together the fire keep burning; in the smoke I search out the faithless. The women, the children, the old ones, the men—all those who doubt, they shall fall."

"Save us, Rainsinger!" the rough-voiced man shouted. "Save us!"

Rush suspected he was another priest, perhaps one of the big guards who accompanied Morning Green when he walked through the village.

Again the crowd joined in with "Save us!" This time, without the drum to unify them, the chorus remained ragged and quickly died away. The flute and rain-hiss could no longer be heard, but the smell of the herbs intensified.

"The faithful, the grateful, the loyal, the true," the Rainsinger said as he separated his hands and gestured to the enthralled listeners, "all these shall be guarded from harm. How shall thee discover thine enemy? Thus shall he be: holding thy child and lying with thy woman. . ."

His pale eyes seemed to focus on Rush alone, startling him. Rush's mouth went dry, and he wet his lips. *Does Morning Green know Spadefoot isn't really his son?* In the next instant, the Rainsinger's gaze moved away and released him.

". . . eating thy food and demanding to be clothed; stealing thy name and bragging of wickedness. Then hither I come, from this, mine own temple. I stand here to tell thee the truth—if you want it."

"We will hear the truth! We will hear it!" several people shouted to him. "Save us! Save us all!"

The Rainsinger beamed his approval at them, and the cry of "Save us!" swept through the crowd. They began to tighten up, shift forward, to get closer to Morning Green. Out of step with everyone else, witnessing them all merging together, Rush felt the force of their unity. He tried to hold back, to slide past people to get to the edge of the plaza, but in the attempt to move apart, he took an elbow to his tender ribs. While he focused on the pain, balling it up small and pushing it aside, he gave in and drifted forward with the current.

Four priests—the liturgists—identical with their black hair drawn up into topknots, stepped onto the platform. The crowd once again quieted expectantly. Rush glanced around for an escape through the dam of closely packed bodies, but in vain. All eyes rested on the tower platform.

The top half of each liturgist's face was painted black, the bottom half white. Each of them wore gray leggings and a netted shirt with shell cylinder beads between the knots. Each held a staff bearing a white cloud-mountain, its stepped edges outlined in black; shell strands hung down from the flat bottom of the cloud-mountain nearly to the ground.

Dressed and painted all in black, white, and gray, with none of the brightly colored feathers and skins worn during the public ceremonies of the sun-festivals, the priests seemed more ominous than usual. Two of the four liturgists stepped forward to stand just behind Morning Green, on either side.

The roarer's hum started again, this time accompanied by the rasp of a scraper-stick, unseen but clearly audible in the plaza where all but Rush stood openmouthed and dazzled.

The two forwardmost liturgists intoned the first line of the priests' standard incantation, the one the outlanders were reputed to have said upon first arriving in the Valley of Two Rivers, during the last days of the Long Thirst: "The land is burning, the people are ill."

Rush knew it was intended as reassurance, a reminder that the priests had saved the People of Two Rivers from the hard times just a few generations earlier that had transformed his people and the world they had made; the effects of the Long Thirst still echoed in people's minds. And still showed in the walls of the canals.

The Rainsinger said, "Forth I go and look about: before, behind, to either side, above, below, within."

People around Rush began to say the familiar words quietly, as though taking comfort from them, though they were not pleasant.

The two priests at the back stepped forward, in line with the others, and said, "Scars of green have marred the earth."

"Forth I go and listen close," said the Rainsinger. "Plaints of the ungrateful break on the cliffs, and the cold sky turns away."

"The clouds they bring the rain no more," said all four.

"Forth I go and loudly call: no answer comes from the ash-parched air. You cry, you cry, my people, but all that is left is the dust of your bones."

For a time, nothing broke the silence that followed the last word, not even a cough or the shifting of a foot.

The Rainsinger looked out somberly over his audience. He placed an open hand over his heart. "This have I spoken, true words all. Those who reject them shall perish. For this is the vow of the Ta'atchul, to save the ones who are worthy."

He let his hands fall and bowed his head.

"How do we prove ourselves worthy?" someone shouted from the outskirts of the gather ground.

The Rainsinger said, "That will be up to the Ta'atchul. I am merely their humble servant."

Rush snorted, but if those around him heard, they made no sign. Everyone's attention remained fixed on the gray-robed priest who stood above them.

"We can't endure another drought!" called out the frantic crackly voice of some elder who might have endured the desperate turnings of the Long Thirst. "The last one nearly killed us!"

As though he had opened the floodgates, everyone started speaking at once. Close to him, Rush heard, "It's the heronfolk who are to blame—" But away in the crowd, that rough-voiced man called, "If we're looking to root out wickedness, it's the Wilders we should start with!"

The Rainsinger lifted his spindly arms again and gestured for silence. "I have heard accusations that the Wilders killed the young vow-brother from the Temple of the Mist. If any man among you knows this to be so, come you forth now!"

No one moved.

Then someone roared, "We'll make them tell us!"

The Rainsinger shook his head. "Do not be overhasty in seeking vengeance," he warned. "If anyone, Wilder or not, can be identified as the one who harmed the young vow-brother, he must be brought to the temple. Through his blood, the Ta'atchul will determine his guilt."

A chill went down Rush's spine. The People of Two Rivers had many ways of determining guilt or innocence. Not one relied on blood.

"How can you tell one Wilder from another, under all that mud and matted hair?" a woman asked, prompting laughter and jeers from the rest of the crowd.

Ignoring her comment and the responses, the Rainsinger said, "The Ta'atchul, the Beloved, they sent us, the Stormbringers, here to the Valley of Two Rivers to save every one of the faithful. Save you not just from the Long Thirst, the many turnings of the sun when the rains did not come, when the crops failed for season after season, when the canals turned to dust. Now we will save you from the perils of ignorance. The old ways failed you, but the Ta'atchul will not—not so long as you believe. This is the time for unbelievers to cleanse themselves. To disavow everything that would hold us back as we step into a new world, a world without difference and fear and strife. To renounce those who would hold us back."

Most of the people around Rush nodded and murmured their agreement. But he heard in the words a criticism of the Watermasters, who could easily be portrayed as the ultimate unbelievers—never mind that the canals had been the lifeblood of generation after generation as far back as the story of the People of Two Rivers stretched. *What do these people think they're agreeing to?*

"Go now," the Rainsinger told them. "Go, and tell others of the truth you have heard this day. Go, and consider how to live a righteous life. Go, and imagine what you can make of this world, if you hold the Ta'atchul in your heart."

The throng began to disperse, some speaking low-voiced to others, some solitary with head bowed. Rush saw an opportunity to retreat with the latter. At the edge of the plaza, before he could reach a quiet place and put his thoughts together, Earth Holder confronted him.

The farmer lost no time in coming to the point. He had somehow heard about Rush's argument with Spadefoot the previous night—but as a real fight in which the young priest had taken away Rush's survey rod and beat him with it.

"It was over Starflower, wasn't it?" her father demanded.

"For the last time, there was no fight!"

"Then how do you explain that bruise?"

"It was an accident in the dark. I slipped, that's all."

Starflower had sworn that her father hadn't sent her to make that shifty proposal, but Rush had been suspicious. Rightly so, he saw now.

"Why would I fight over any female?" He kept his tone light, flippant. "They're much the same to me." That was what everyone seemed to think, anyway.

Earth Holder's expression hardened. "My daughter isn't like all the others you've trifled with."

"There haven't been that many."

"Starflower would be a prize for any man!"

"She does seem quite superior," Rush agreed.

"Ha! If you believed that, you wouldn't have shamed her in front of her clan! Deserting her for that . . . that *hunter*."

Rush blinked, uncertain of who the man meant.

"What will everyone think," Earth Holder went on, "but that you seduced a foolish girl, stole her natural affections, and broke her heart? How many times do you think you can get away with that kind of wickedness?"

Backing away from the wild-eyed man, Rush put up his hands, palm out, in a placating gesture. "I did nothing to shame her. I didn't fight with the Rainsinger's son. Just ask him. What reason would he have for fighting over your daughter . . . with anybody, let alone me?"

Earth Holder glared. "He has nothing to do with her! He isn't like you, a bounder and a seducer! He's a decent man. Like his father, unwilling to look away any longer while the Watermasters lay ruin to us all!"

"You can't be such a fool as to believe that," Rush told him tightly. "The Watermasters aren't trying to ruin anyone. We're just trying to keep water flowing in the canals and ditches!"

"Soon I won't need your pathetic scratches in the earth—no one will. We won't need to go begging to your kind any more."

"You believe the rains will come at the bidding of the priests? If it was so easy, why hasn't it worked already? The summer rains were light, and the fields showed it."

Earth Holder's eyes glittered. "All must believe, or all will suffer," he declared with burning certainty. "The Watermasters do not believe."

He turned and strode away—toward his new fields.

Rush looked at that broad, receding back. *All must believe.*

What Rush believed was that without the Watermasters, the weirs in the river would be torn out by floodwaters every time there was a heavy rain. What he believed was that without the Watermasters tending to the canals, the seasonal floods would utterly destroy them.

The Rainsinger might claim that his Ta'atchul would send just the right amount of rain right when the crops needed it. But summer rain fell in patches. One field might get a downpour while the next one over remained dry. Without the canals and the feeder ditches, how would that rainwater be distributed evenly among the fields?

How could the farmers be so stupid as to think the Rainsinger right?

But Rush understood, too, that his failure to fully restore the canals had created this opening for the priests. He had seen the desperation poorly hidden on the faces of too many people who had come to him during trade-day hearings. He had made promises and asked for more time. And they had given it.

But what choice did they have?

Now, evidently, the Rainsinger offered them one. If Earth Holder was any indication, at least some of the farmers were ready to give up on the Watermasters.

Rush shook his head and told himself he was worrying for no reason. The people standing in that plaza listening to Morning Green spout off were mostly believers already. Those who weren't inclined to worship the Ta'atchul wouldn't have come to hear the Rainsinger speak. There were a lot more farmers, and others in Crookstaff Village, than had stood in the crowd this morning.

There would be no outcry against the Watermasters, he reassured himself. His people had better sense than that.

He became aware that someone was watching him. He turned his head and saw Spadefoot—face shiny and free of paint.

Relaxed, as if he hadn't flown into a rage the night before, the young priest said, "You seem better this morning."

"What," Rush demanded, willing to adopt the same pretense, "does the Rainsinger's proclamation mean?"

"The visions of the Ta'atchul are not maps, to be followed from one point to the next."

"I don't ask for a map. But something so vague doesn't help at all."

Spadefoot shrugged. "Plans are useless against forces that are beyond our understanding. The Ta'atchul have not sent the rain. Start with that."

"Do they demand our belief, as the Rainsinger says, before they'll send the rains?"

"There are disbelievers among you."

"Of course there are! Your Ta'atchul are new; we've survived for ages without them."

Spadefoot pointed out, "There was the Long Thirst."

"Are your own devotions to the Ta'atchul not enough?" Rush stepped closer to the younger man, who put up a hand as though to ward him off. But Rush had no intention of brawling. "Does everyone have to pray to these beings in the sky—and only them? Are we to turn away from Mother Ge?"

"It doesn't seem like you Watermasters really pay her any mind when you go rummaging around in her bones, making the water go this way and that."

"We work for the sake of her people," Rush replied. "As we've done since time out of mind. We perform the ancient rituals, just as we've always done."

"But do you speak to her? Do you, Rush, truly believe in her, deep down in the inner recesses of your heart? Because if you don't, why not simply renounce her and accept the Ta'atchul, as Morning Green suggests?"

Rush had no answer for that question, beyond an unreasoning, impulsive *I can't.*

Spadefoot continued, "You Watermasters see no need to call on forces beyond this physical world, do you? Yet you proved unable to keep your own people safe. For that, when the Long Thirst came, you needed the Stormbringers. And now you turn away from the words that the Rainsinger speaks for your own redemption. Why is that?"

"Our people still need us," Rush muttered.

"Then I cannot persuade you to go through *these* rituals," said Spadefoot, lifting his right hand for emphasis, "rather than *those* rituals?" He raised his left hand as high as his right one. "To open your heart to the Ta'atchul and deny Mother Ge?"

"No."

"You should think about why not." With a gesture of farewell, the young priest left him there.

Rush watched him go. Why not deny the Allmother?

He thought about the goddess's bounty. With the crops short, most people had already gleaned mesquite pods and agave hearts from the desert and nearby foothills, cattail roots and bulrush tubers from along the canals. There were big fish in the river, abundant rabbits in the grassy meadows. He did believe she gave her people what they needed.

So why, in this time of hardship, didn't the Watermasters pray to Mother Ge for help? An obvious answer was that Watermaster words had no power. Mother Ge had given the Watermasters minds, hands, and strong backs to make and repair the canals. Adding prayers to their knowledge, skills, and labor would be useless. The Smokemothers were the ones who appealed to the Allmother.

He dropped his gaze to the path in front of him but didn't really see it as he wondered why, this turning, she had left them dry once again. Had she withdrawn from the world of her own making? And if so, could she have sent the Ta'atchul to act in her stead?

Maybe the Rainsinger was right. Maybe the life-giving rains would fall only after people accepted the Ta'atchul into their hearts. Maybe the canals would never run properly again—but no one would notice, because they were no longer needed.

If that came to pass, Rush thought unhappily, scuffing a sandal in the dirt, then he and the other Watermasters would become unnecessary, too. And yet he could not accept that.

People would have to prepare for a new way of living. They could build terraces, runnels, depressions to hold water, even rock circles to catch the morning dew. Those projects meant backbreaking labor for one man, but if many worked together, the tasks could be divided and reallocated to allow one man to rest while another carried the heavy load.

Watermasters and Wilders were builders. They were good to have on work crews. Even the most critical farmers had to admit that.

And Rush knew how to squeeze moisture from the air and from the earth. During the Long Thirst, the Watermasters had used that knowledge to give the People of Two Rivers a chance to survive. Others had forgotten; the heronfolk hadn't.

He could advise everyone to do as he had once suggested to Earth Holder: give up on the canals and raise different crops. Plant teparies instead of speckled beans, the tiny grains of ki'ak and khov and babkam instead of corn. Start fields of slow-growing hannam and nopal cactus. Clear the desert and grow agaves for their hearts and yuccas for their fruits. Forget cotton, that most thirsty of crops, and dress in skins—or garments of yucca fiber, coarse though they would be.

Would the people of Crookstaff Village accept such drastic changes? If the Rainsinger was right, they might have to. Those who accepted the Ta'atchul and became the faithful, perhaps they would be willing to turn into a desert people.

And the others, those who didn't accept the Ta'atchul, who clung to Mother Ge and the old ways? They might have to leave their clanlands and retreat closer to the river, where the canals still ran.

Rush didn't see any of that happening without conflict.

He sighed, shook his head, and walked toward the nearest canal. There was no time to worry about Starflower and her father, about the Canalmasters' exhortation to take a mate, about finding Deerchaser and demanding to know why she had betrayed him. He had to concentrate on getting water flowing so his people didn't feel they had to choose between rejecting Mother Ge and starving to death.

Rush heard the voices first. Then the ravens and buzzards showed up.

He had been staring down at the long, graceful lines, carved deeply into the ground and then plastered over into glistening smoothness. So simple. Misleadingly simple. The canal simply wasn't filling with water as it should, and he had come back to his quarters to figure out why.

After the Rainsinger's proclamation a few days earlier, he had spent every waking moment from sunup to sundown on the move. Coaxing farmers to join work crews away from their own fields. Making sure the ditch bosses knew exactly what they were supposed to do. Keeping the hotheads of the clans from fighting with the Wilders instead of working next to them.

He was so tired, he could hardly think. He could feel a solution to this specific headgate problem drifting just below the surface of his mind, but he couldn't get it to reveal itself.

And now the hunters showed up with their noise and commotion.

He couldn't focus, between the shouting of instructions and the wailing of tired children and the moving of ladders and loaded drags and the incessant barking of dogs unhappy about being left outside the wall of the hunters' butchering ground.

Granted, they probably had a lot of deer meat to distribute to the farmers. Judging from the number of voices he heard, every hunter from anywhere close to Crookstaff Village—and all their family—had to be there, just on the other side of his half wall. He didn't remember the noise ever before being so intense from the work area.

Sometimes laughter and upraised voices would make their way to him from the hunters' ward. Sometimes drumbeats and songs and flute playing would let him know they were conducting some ceremony or another. When they had meat in the smokehouse, the smell of it would make his mouth water. But never before had they interrupted something important.

His temper stirred as he became so focused on the sounds that he lost the idea that had been teasing at him. His pulse quickened further when he heard a voice he hadn't expected and couldn't at first credit as truly being there. Rush strode to the low wall and studied the scene below.

First he saw a throng of women around several of the dog-pulled drags outside the wall that enclosed the Masterholding. They were unwrapping hides to reveal stuffed carry sacks. A few men with sacks slung over their shoulders climbed ladders to the top of the hunters' mound, where others waited with sharp butchering knives. A few women carried strips of meat to drying racks erected along the wall.

He leaned against the half wall and cast his gaze toward the entry plaza. Several boys were sliding over the enclosure wall and jumping off rather than climbing down the ladder braced on the inside. Near them and along the wall, slipping a brownish fur quiver over her head, stood Deerchaser.

The boys crowded around her. "Finish the story!" one shouted.

"You know how it ends," she said. "It's time to get to work."

But they persisted, until a weary-faced woman standing nearby said, "They won't be any good to us until you finish the story, Deerchaser. Go on."

She picked up near the end of the tale of the boy who wouldn't kill a deer—a story detailing the mistakes of a boy who was sent out time after time but took the huntmaster's instructions too literally. Rush couldn't hear beyond her first few words, because the women who were hanging thin strips of meat on the drying racks began a song:

> *"Out of her bones the Mother she sends us;*
>
> *The mountains, their call do we hear.*
>
> *The winds blow us hither, lead us by our antlers;*
>
> *They gather around our ears."*

Deerchaser finished her story while the song continued, and the boys crowded around begging for another. She seemed tired to Rush.

Storytellers were usually those who had finished raising their children and their children's children. Was that how she saw herself, he wondered: done with her own family and surrounded by these boys for brief times, only as long as an ancient tale lasted? Did she feel the loss of her son less when she had these others around?

But more important, what was she doing here? His curiosity rose until it became all-consuming.

Deerchaser was a clan-daughter and as such would have the right to work Cloud-Leaf Clan's fields for her entire life. Very few ever gave up those use-rights. The ones Rush knew personally at Sky River had fallen in love with hunters or healers and were blood-mated—bound together for life and marked with matching tattoos. A tattoo Deerchaser didn't have.

He'd heard of some who took up basket making or pottery making or weaving or a similar craft that would allow them to trade for everything they needed—as Starflower might eventually do. Or they went to the Smokemothers as Cornmaidens, to bear fatherless children who were blessed by the goddess. Evidently Deerchaser hadn't done that either.

A dim memory rose of a long-ago conversation they'd had about her father being a hunter. She had been angry at her mother for taking her away from the hunters to live with her mother's clan after her father's death. Rush remembered the helplessness he had felt as she sobbed about losing her father.

Then he reminded himself that she didn't deserve his sympathy. She owed him an explanation. He pushed away from the wall and went to find her.

 Deerchaser

The Temple of the Mist I challenge, shadowed by light of day.
In righteous anger his hand I shall stay: today no blood will flow.

—FROM THE STORY-SONG OF DEERCHASER

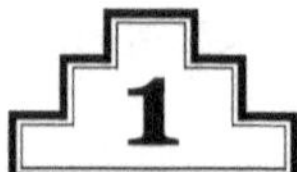

"Off with you," she told the boys when she finished the story. They had chores to do, now that the meat was unloaded and being sliced for jerky. Fondly she watched them race away, their shadows playing over the high wall of the hunters' ward.

"Deerchaser!"

She didn't have to look at Rush to know who had called her name. Though tempted to walk away and pretend she hadn't heard him, she braced herself to see that once-loved face again. She had thought about what she might say to him—if ever she spoke to him again.

The words she blurted out after turning toward him were not ones she had ever practiced: "You've been fighting again!"

Her urge to soothe his bruises with cool water surprised her, but not as much as the evidence that this man, the responsible, calm, well-respected Canalmaster, hadn't outgrown the need to settle disputes with his fists. She expected him to tell her to keep her opinions to herself as he once would have, long ago.

Instead he said, "More fought *with* than actually *fighting*."

"There's a difference?"

"When you're fighting, you get to hit back. In my case, the hitting was all one way—with me on the receiving end."

She struggled to keep from smiling; she had always enjoyed his easy humor. "So what you're saying is, you're just not a very good fighter?"

"Unlike you. You know all about getting back at the one who hurt you."

"I don't know what you mean." She feared, though, that she did.

Rush's answer confirmed it. "Would you have let me go to my grave never knowing of my son?"

Deerchaser kept her face still. The blank expression came readily now.

Although everyone had assured her that her loss would ease in time, she was still waiting for that to happen, after four turnings, nearly five. She swallowed hard. When she felt herself able to speak, she asked, in a low voice, "What would you have done differently, had you known? Would you have stayed? You were a ditchrunner. Too young to take a bondmate. No family to take me in—"

"You—and my son," he finished implacably.

Her throat burned, hot and tight. "And *our* son, yes."

Through all these turnings, she had assumed he knew of their son's existence but hadn't cared enough to inquire after either mother or baby. Only with that cross-purposed conversation after the chich'wipedho game had she realized the old Canalmaster hadn't sent him word of the birth. She was sorry for that. But it was none of her doing.

"You know I wouldn't have stayed," he said. "I couldn't. I had no choice in the matter. But why didn't you let me know back then, or tell me yourself once I returned? Was it to punish me?" Muscles twitched above a set jaw.

Deerchaser recalled the long moons after the birth when she had drifted between death and life. She had been brought back through Mother Ge's mercy. Brought back changed, blessed by the Allmother with a gift or under the shadow of a curse, depending on how one took her newfound abilities. She had paid a heavy price for her survival—and that was before her son had been taken from her.

She lifted her chin and crossed her arms. Let him think what he wanted, she told herself. But a pathetic voice in her head asked, not for the first time, whether he would have even cared had she given up and died. She whipped up her temper in defense against her own weakness.

"What did I know? That you hadn't deserted me?" She stepped forward and jabbed a shaking finger at him. "But that's exactly how it felt to me then. I didn't know about your parents' death and your . . . the burden of your family being dropped on your shoulders. Because you didn't tell me. Would you have wanted the responsibility of a baby, too?"

"What I might've wanted doesn't matter. You did what *you* wanted, with no thought for me."

Deerchaser recalled the doubts that had assailed her as she grew big with child. She passed a hand over her face. Her fingers felt cold. "I did what I had to."

"As did I. There wasn't time to say goodbye. The messenger came, told me my parents were dead and I was needed up at Sky River."

"You could have told me that night. You didn't leave until the next morning. There would've been time. Instead, you just disappeared."

"The old Canalmaster said it would be kinder . . ." He trailed off as if he realized how that must sound to her.

"Kinder!" she exclaimed. "I was the object of pity for a very long time. Everyone laughed at me! You made me into a joke, until . . ." *Until my son died, and then the pity turned to a smothering sympathy.* "For a very long time."

"I just wanted to explain why I left so suddenly."

"You call that an explanation?" She recrossed her arms. "And after, when your brother and sister were settled, when you could have returned here in a day but never did, what am I supposed to think about that?"

"I couldn't leave my post." His voice sharpened. "What I was doing up at Sky River was important."

She could understand that. Maybe not forgive it, because it meant she was less important than his duties, and that hurt. But doing what needed to be done even though it was not what you really wanted to do . . . Oh, yes, she understood that.

"Why are you so—" His gaze drifted up to the tattoo above her left eye, then the tear below. He tucked his hands behind him and rocked back on his heels. "I don't want things to be left unsaid between us. Let's sort this out somewhere quieter," he suggested.

She hesitated, then agreed. She would rather not have to deal with him at all, but he was obviously not going to drop the matter. He was right. There were too many prying eyes and ears here. And plenty of others to do the work. Unlike the other women of the deerfolk, she wasn't really essential after the end of the hunt.

They both remained silent while they made their way out into the desert, away from the village and its surrounding fields. Once they passed beyond earshot of unwanted witnesses, the air between them became heavy with strain again. He seemed as reluctant to break it as she was.

Her dog joined them for a bit, dancing around their feet and sniffing at Rush before racing up the path to find and re-mark where other dogs had been. Eventually Shadowdog glanced back with a toothy, tongue-lolling grin. Then he slipped into the brush and was gone from sight.

"Did your clan accept him?" Rush asked abruptly.

Deerchaser knew he spoke of their son.

Cruel memories seized her: her mother's bondmate refusing to let her live with them in the final moons of her pregnancy, the cold reception she had gotten from the old Canalmaster, the hunters treating her like an unwanted burden. Only the Smokemothers, those priestesses of the goddess who worked in darkness and light, in smoke and blood, had stood between her and starvation, for they took her in as they did any girl who came to them pregnant but not mated. Yet in the end, even they had cast her out when she refused to give up her child and become a plaything for the priests.

In Deerchaser's darkest days, Mother Ge had set her in motion on a new life-path, one that had taken her far from Cloud-Leaf Clan. Deerchaser had taken her infant son and gone back to the hunters, valuable to them in a way she hadn't been before, because she now could find their quarry through water-scrying. It only worked for deer, and it required that she go out with the men into the desert and the foothills, and it set her apart from the rest of the women of the deerfolk.

The other women didn't go out with the hunters. Instead they stayed near camp and performed sedentary tasks: butchering, tanning, cooking, reshaping blades. She had never quite been accepted by them, though they were her father's people and she had spent her childhood among them— they treated her only marginally better than her mother's clan had done as soon as she was known to be carrying the child of a Watermaster.

She told him none of this. "We did fine."

He nodded. "No one pushed you to take a man to stand as his father? Or they did, and you refused?"

His eyes heavy-lidded and unhappy, the nightspawn actually acted as though the matter were any of his concern. Though she had to admit it might have been, had she let some man into her life as her own mother had done—a man who might not have treated another man's child generously.

She realized that she and Rush would be forever bound, one to the other, by the son they had made together, even though their boy was no longer with them. More, she felt that same familiar tug toward Rush even though she knew how destructive it was. She had experienced that aching desire with no other man, either before him or after. She fought the compulsion to sway toward him, to give in, to surrender. *Remember how eager he was to leave,* she reminded herself, *how easily he managed without you, how many he found to replace you, and how soon.*

His bruised face and stiff movement served as warnings that he hadn't changed in that aspect. Whether he won Starflower's affections or not, the fact that he pursued the prettiest girl in the village told Deerchaser all she needed to know about him.

"Would you prefer to hear that I leaped straight from your bed into another man's?" she inquired with forced casualness. "But we've already decided that's none of your concern."

"I'm not asking as your lover. I'm asking as father to that boy-child you bore. Except I never was important enough as either, it seems, for you to—" He broke off.

She watched as his mouth worked and his nostrils flared. He had to exert considerable effort to control himself. This was a side to him she hadn't seen before. He wouldn't strike her, of that she felt certain, but she sensed he was tempted. She would never have expected to be able to produce such strong passions in the easygoing Watermaster.

"Why did no one else tell me?" he finished in a voice unexpectedly plaintive.

Deerchaser hesitated, uncertain what to answer.

The old Canalmaster hadn't approved of her, even before she was known to bear Rush's child. But she had never learned whether it was personal or whether no daughter of any clan would have been considered good enough for the old Canalmaster's favorite.

Cloud-Leaf Clan certainly hadn't wanted any involvement with the Watermasters. Her mother still felt that way.

She sighed. "I suppose they figured you already knew."

He shook his head and shifted his feet to angle away from her, taking his face out of her view as he gazed toward the low mountains where she had spent most of the past several days. "More likely that I knew and didn't care." He went on, "Everyone thought you must have sent word of our child's birth. But you never did."

"How could I have? I didn't know where you were. Not exactly. Because you never sent word back to me! You just left!" She had been in no condition for the journey to Sky River, not for many moons after giving birth. After that, she had needed to adjust to the changes in her own life.

By then too much time had passed. Too much water down the river, as the old saying went.

He shook his head. "How you must have despised me."

Jolted by the pain and sorrow roughening his voice, Deerchaser stared at him for a long, assessing moment. "For a time, I suppose I did."

"But no longer?"

She wasn't sure what to say or even what she felt. "Not so much."

If he wanted forgiveness from her, she felt incapable of giving it. That quality had been wrung out of her heart long ago. She couldn't even forgive herself. But she could make an effort to be kind. At least one of them should be. "You've done a good job as Canalmaster. They say you're fair. And . . ."

His shoulders hunched as she spoke. Did he hear nothing but pity, she wondered, in her attempt to be generous? She tried to find some higher praise. "And that your dealings with the farmers are helpful."

"Helpful."

The words limping off her tongue weren't what she wanted to say. And then they came to her. "Yes, in a way that was desperately needed in this hard summer. People felt they couldn't get the old Canalmaster to listen to them. He left everything to the ditch bosses, who proved useless. The farmers had to try to work together themselves—you know how well that usually goes. Then you came in, a steady hand. You reminded them that, by the Allmother's grace, we have endured flood and drought before. You gave them things to do so they didn't feel so helpless."

The quiet defeat in his posture eased slightly as she spoke, and he turned his head to look at her. "You call it the grace of the goddess." He shrugged. "I rely on preparedness and hard work. And a good bit of luck."

She bit her lip at this indication that he believed in luck more than in the Mother-of-All-Things, though that was hardly surprising: the Watermasters had never been devout servants of Mother Ge. They left that to the Smokemothers. The farmfolk these days weren't so different from the canalfolk in their relationship with Mother Ge.

Deerchaser reminded herself that if she didn't sense the Allmother seeing through her own eyes when she scried, she would have trouble believing in an active goddess too. For too many, Mother Ge may have created the world, but she had not walked in it since the First Days. Deerchaser had been one of the doubters until her son's birth. Balancing on the edge of death had converted her into a believer.

She said, "At least you're not encouraging the priests in their call— 'Turn from the goddess and bow down to the Ta'atchul instead.'"

"I'm not telling people to pray to the goddess, either."

"You don't need to believe, to have Mother Ge act on your behalf," Deerchaser argued, though she understood that her words would have no more impact than water breaking against a deep-set rock. People believed what they believed and no amount of argument would change their minds. "We all are her children, and she is the only divinity we need."

Rush looked down as he kicked one moccasined toe against the heavy earth. "So you know for a fact that the priests are wrong? Tell me, Deerchaser, would you find it in your heart to cut the people off from the Ta'atchul, just as you cut yourself off from me? Cut my son off from me?"

She stared at his profile and wondered how he would respond if she told him she did indeed know the priests to be wrong. But he didn't give her time to decide whether to share this other secret with him.

He turned to face her. Ruthlessly he continued, "Just as you tried to serve as both mother and father to our son?"

Blood rose in her cheeks. "I was here," she snapped. "Which is more than you can say!"

"I would have been, had you given me the chance."

She felt as brittle as frost on the grass. "As you were for your sister and brother? Or did you foster them out as soon as you could?" His expression gave her the answer.

He stepped closer. His work-hardened shoulders blocked out the weak light. "They belonged with a family," he told her. "A real family, with a mother and father together. That's what I found for them."

Deerchaser refused to be intimidated. "A mother alone can do just fine."

"I am *not* your father. Don't assume I would have done the same by my child."

She stared at him. Once, and only once, she had told him about her father having always been gone, more interested in the hunt than in his daughter. Scarcely more than a child in those days, she would have done anything for the first man in her life.

Rush had remembered her confession all this time? And dared to throw it back at her?

He reached for her. She slapped his hands away. "You left me without a single look!" As her father had done, time after time—until at last he never returned, giving her no chance to say goodbye or tell him how much she loved him.

"I am a Watermaster. We go where we're needed."

"I needed you!"

He looked as if she had struck him. "I had responsibilities."

"You never came back to see whether you left anything of yourself— more family—here! You had to have known there was a risk, but you didn't care, you didn't—"

"I'm back now."

The steady weight of his gaze made her press her hand to her mouth to stop the spate of words. She couldn't believe she had said she needed him. She tried to remember the anger that had sustained her through so many turnings of loneliness and desperation and misery.

"Won't you relent just a bit?" he urged. "Tell me about my—our—son. Trust me with those few scraps of his life that it's not too late for."

She shook her head and managed to whisper through her fingers, "You don't know what you ask of me."

"I'm asking you to let me know a small part of him."

Rush waited, but for several heartbeats Deerchaser couldn't speak. She felt as though something was melting inside.

Finally, she said, "His friends—the other boys—called him Littlereed." Saying aloud the name of a child who hadn't gone through the naming quest was viewed by most people as safe. Even so, Deerchaser felt a little anxious about it . . . and at the same time pleased that his name was being spoken again, as if he were still alive.

"After me?" Rush asked. He, too, was named for a plant that liked to have its roots in water.

"More because he was a scrawny little thing," she recalled with a shaky laugh. "But I called him . . ."

These days, she only thought of her son as Littlereed. She had almost forgotten his original name, which might tell Rush far too much. And her, too. She wasn't sure she could handle seeing Rush's response to this part of her secret. Yet she needed to know.

"What did you call him?"

"Pumpkinhead," she admitted after a long pause in which she went round and round trying to decide how much to say.

"Pumpkinhead?" He snorted. "What kind of name is that?"

"It didn't come from me, at first. The midwife gave him the nickname." She took a deep breath and cleared her throat. "It was a difficult birth. Others took care of him for a while, until I was on my feet again."

She watched his face go blank as he thought about it.

"You mean his head was so big, you nearly died?"

"It wasn't quite like that. Well, it was . . . but I lived."

He looked appalled. He started to say something, then strode away without another word to her.

She hoped that meant he would have been saddened if word had come to him, up at Sky River, that she had died. She feared it meant he would always be walking away rather than dealing with difficult truths.

But she had to admit, she often did the same thing. It was not a good trait to share.

That night, in the small hut she had built outside the village, at the edge of a wash, she nestled her feet against Shadowdog's warm back and considered whether she had done the right thing. Not in telling Rush the truth about how close she had come to dying or in concealing what had happened to her during her brush with death—and the blame she deserved in Littlereed's. But going back further, to when Littlereed was young, when it was just the two of them, mother and son.

She sighed and laced her fingers across her belly. Should she have found a man to father her son?

At the time she had been certain she was doing the right thing, that the men of the deerfolk would stand in for any fatherly acts that only men could do. All else, she had thought she would have to do herself.

Teaching archery was the least of it, though others—those who called her unwomanly—might disagree. She had taught Littlereed how a boy was to treat other boys and girls, clan-uncles and aunts, priests, remembrancers, traders, and the like; if he had lived, she believed that she could have taught him how a man ought to act.

But maybe he would have been better off with a father who had teased him and played with him and disciplined him and loved him. If she was honest, it really was her dark, scarred heart that had kept her from placing her reliance on any one man. Her father's inability to be the sort of father she wished for and then her mother's mating with a man who didn't want to be a father at all had led her to doubt that good, loving fathers existed.

In trying to protect her son from a father who might have ignored him, she had prevented him from having any father at all. And she had kept Rush from ever knowing the precious boy he had helped to create.

Her lips curved into a smile in the darkness as she remembered how very sweet and cute and funny and wicked and mischievous and stubborn and horrid Littlereed had been. All those moments . . .

She should tell Rush about them, she thought, as she waited for the pain in her heart that always struck when she thought about Littlereed. After a few moments she realized it wasn't coming.

She hoped that meant she was finally past her grief, the guilt of losing her young son to the canal. Maybe now she could make things right with Rush. Tell him he was forgiven. Ask for his forgiveness.

Her eyes sagged closed on the thought of parents without children, children without parents, back and forth.

The dream, when it came, started with Handsome Man and his begetting and begetting. The eyes, heavy with charm. A sensual mouth bracketed with laugh lines. It was Rush's face.

Deerchaser woke partway and then fell into sleep again, slipped into a different dream.

Skystone, the gambler, wants to take the beautiful virgin of Shining Water as his lifemate. He goes to her and offers her all his wealth of the blue stones, handfuls of it, enough to dress her in, but she refuses him, saying she has beauty aplenty of her own. He goes again, offering her the strength of his arms, all the protection she could ever need, but again she refuses him, saying none would ever think to harm her. A third time he goes, promising to build her a house so tall as to rival the very mountains, and filled with the most precious things, but a third time she spurns him, saying only a fool would expect a man like him to hold to his promises.

What can he do, he asks of the Sun, to win this beauty for his own? Sun, jealous of a human who outshines him, gives him a many-colored ball and tells him to hide in the bushes and kick it out for the girl to find.

She takes it up in her arms. When the boys come to her and ask whether she saw this wondrous thing, she hides it under her dress and says she has not.

It grows inside her until it emerges, a pale-skinned, hairy monster with long claws and sharp teeth: the wicked Ho'ok, eater of children.

The mother they drive away, calling her Enemy Maker. She must live in a cave, with no one to see her beauty in the darkness, nothing lovely around her any more, no one to defend her against her hungry child.

Deerchaser moaned. *No,* she said in her sleep as she fought to leave the terrible story world, to escape Enemy Maker's head.

Struggling to wake from the vision, Deerchaser dimly became herself again. She had her eyes open, or thought she did, but the curved roof-walls of the domed hut were covered with pointed stars and she had no power to close her lids against the light that stabbed at her through the dark.

All is brightness, a blinding brightness, no stars now. Only the sun in the sky, hanging balefully, a sickening heaviness to the air, and everything gone silent. Then a black shape—not something just black, but instead a dark made up of color so deep that it swallows the light. With great jagged teeth it eats into the sun, undoing the Allmother's birth of her son, the first of her children: Sun himself.

Unbirthing the sun? Deerchaser tried to move her hands over her face to block out the sight, but she discovered herself to have no hands now, no arms or legs. A snake, a worm? she wondered wildly. What form had Mother Ge put her in this time?

What tale of long-ago was this?

But it was no story she had ever heard. The story from the First Days was that the Allmother, the creatrix, gave birth to Sun and Moon and placed them in the sky to light the earth for the creatures of the day and the night: Sun to warm and make crops green and light the way, Moon to cool and reveal the beauty of the stars and the night-blooming flowers for those who dare to see. Every night Sun disappears, every day Moon disappears, in a dance as ancient as time. That was the story. That was what everyone knew.

Back in her own body, blinking eyes too dry to have been closed in sleep, she found Shadowdog cowering against the wall, as far from her as he could get. She forced her eyelids shut, covered them with cold hands, and wept at this vision Mother Ge had seen fit to inflict on her.

The weeping afterward didn't last long. It never did. There was no point to it. Besides, she had become accustomed to the fright that invariably followed being uprooted from this world and placed in another.

The story-world visions had come to her, along with the streak of white at her temple, right after the birth of Littlereed, during that time when she walked along the river of death but finally returned to the world. They didn't strike often; the merciful Allmother sent them only while she slept. Since Littlereed's passing, that meant they came less and less, for she regularly had trouble settling into sleep.

At first, Littlereed had shown the same fearful response as Shadowdog, the same desire to get as far from her as possible. But then he came to accept them. He would pat her on the shoulder, gently, and wake her. It was their own secret.

She made sure no one else knew it, then or since. No man since Rush had ever shared her bed; night always found her alone. At hunt camp, she slept well away from everyone else. She didn't stay at her clan's moontime hut during her bleeding. She had no reason to, because there was no man at her isolated hut who needed to be protected from Mother Ge's blessing—the gift that allowed women to bleed without taking harm, while men bled only when injured.

Her clan-sisters and aunties—Starflower and the rest of them—knew there was something not normal about her. They thought it was just that she had joined her father's people and was no longer one of them, that she hunted and killed like a man. And that she taught their sons how to take life, shooting arrows and setting snares.

The water-scrying that she did for the hunters, through which she discovered precisely where to find their prey, only a very few knew about. The ones who did were sworn to secrecy. She needed them to know, because someone had to watch over her when she drank the dizzyweed.

The story-world visions, the ones that came when she was sleeping rather than scrying, no living man . . . or woman . . . knew about. She had no idea what would happen if anyone ever did find out. How different could she be, and still be accepted as one of the People of Two Rivers?

But this particular vision had frightened even her. Most of her dream-visions were like the first ones from this night, the stories of Handsome Man and Enemy Maker: stories she had heard all her life, stories of how the world and everything in it began, stories in which she became someone else.

In this last one, Mother Ge had shown her the sun being destroyed. She was no one in this story, just an observer.

Was the swallowing of the sun something that would come to pass, or was it only a phantasm born of fear—whether of the changes Rush might bring or of the new rituals the priests were introducing or of the time of prophecy arriving, culminating in the final test of her people?

More questions she asked of herself, more and still more, weaving her chilled fingers together, before she came to the final one. Who could help her sort through the meaning of what she had seen?

No one, she realized, unless she spoke of this dream and thereby revealed herself as the Allmother's mouthpiece—a claim that might make people think she believed herself the equal of the senior priestesses, those who had dedicated their lives to the service of Mother Ge. How sympathetic would the priestesses be to hearing that the goddess spoke directly to someone outside their order?

And if they did somehow believe her—what then? Would they keep her secret or betray her, as a fitting punishment for lying to them all those turnings ago, for taking Mother Ge's gift out into the village and training herself to use it?

Trying not to panic, she drew her knees up to her chest and buried her face in her cupped hands. There had to be something else she could do.

"Look what I got." Longthrow trotted up to Deerchaser in their usual practice ground in the desert east of the village.

She took the arrow-shaft straightener the boy held out proudly.

"I traded my rock dove skins for it," he told her.

Deerchaser cleared a lump from her throat and told him the tool looked perfect. Longthrow had trapped the rock doves over the past few turnings and had tanned the skins himself. She could see that the trader had dealt fairly with the boy. And why not? A talented youth so near to having his first man's bow and needing a quiver full of sharp-tipped hunting arrows and frequent replacements could become a valuable trading partner.

She both grieved and rejoiced for the impending loss of this lovely boy. The grief came from how many in her life she had been forced to let go of: her father, Rush, her mother, Littlereed, and soon this boy.

Probably Shadowdog, too. He'd been scarce of late, since the dreams of the disappearing sun had started. She suspected he was keeping company with a she-bitch. Deerchaser understood that was the natural order of things. Still, it was hard to face.

"Can we go try it?" one of the other boys asked.

She looked around at their eager expressions. Earlier, as she had neared the practice area, they had cried out with delight on seeing her, which had lightened her low spirits. Quickly they had rushed to surround her with much shoving and throwing of good-humored insults.

Now they could hardly wait to get away.

"Of course." She summoned a smile. It came easily enough; she felt genuinely happy for Longthrow, whose naming quest would surely take place soon. Each of the other boys would go too, when his father deemed him ready.

Her smile faded as they ran off without a backward look. She wondered who would have decided for Littlereed—had he survived—that it was time to give him his man's name. As for her, if they didn't practice shooting, what would she do until the deerfolk once more went on the hunt?

It was a trade day, as Longthrow had reminded her. She supposed if she didn't have anything else to do, she could go watch the chich'wipedho game.

She hadn't been asked to play for the clan again; the previous game, the day Rush had first accosted her, she had only stood in for an ailing clan-sister. Even though Cloud-Leaf Clan had won with her assistance, they didn't need her today.

Today she could visit the trade ground, poke around the exotic goods the Far-Traders had arranged on mats, stacked in burden baskets, and hung from portable stalls in the old ballcourt. There would be stories and songs, dancing and drumming. And acrobatics, most likely. Plus she could go to her clan's section of the village and have some food, a meal more substantial than jerky and mesquite-pod journeycakes, the typical hunt-camp fare. Indecisive, she stood in the midst of the shegoi and saltbushes and watched the boys race away toward the village.

Slowly she followed them.

$\wedge\wedge$

At the trade ground, she looked for something interesting to do. Her foot, encased in an ankle-high moccasin, came up against something hard yet yielding. She looked down to find herself practically standing over an old man, his hair gone to white and his upturned face so caved in upon itself as to seem a skull barely skinned with flesh: the remembrancer.

"Oh! I'm sorry!" Appalled by her carelessness, she knelt beside him, this ancient man who bore the memories of the village. "I wasn't paying attention."

"No harm." As his clouded eyes turned toward her, he seemed cheery enough, even though she had kicked his thigh.

"Are you sure you're all right?"

"Yes, of course."

His fingers, lumpy and as skinny as the rest of him, remained in constant movement, playing across a flat stick covered with carved shapes that must once have been crisp and sharp edged but were now little more than softened hollows. She knew he could read them as surely as the best hunters did trail sign; he kept the past alive in his mind with the aid of those symbols, though to her they meant nothing.

He said, "I suppose you were paying attention to the story, not where you were going? She has a right fine way with words, that she does."

Deerchaser glanced at the woman nearby, one of the talespinners, surrounded by children and more than a few adults pretending not to be as captivated as their offspring. "She's your daughter, isn't she?"

His fingers stilled. He grinned toothlessly and nodded. "That she is, that she is."

"Did you teach her those stories?"

"No, not I. This is her talent, not mine. I remember what actually happened. She deals in imaginings of how things came to be. Women's tales, those are, and winter is women's time."

Deerchaser pursed her lips. She didn't believe stumbling upon the remembrancer was just a coincidence. Mother Ge had put him in her path for a reason. She pointed at the long, carved stick, though in his blindness he couldn't have seen the movement. "You hold many memories on that."

"It is the keeper of the past," he agreed. "More than I."

"Do you remember . . ." She considered how to ask her question without revealing too much. For a long moment she just stood there, gathering her courage. "Does it tell of the sun ever vanishing?"

"Vanishing?"

"Being swallowed up. By some . . . thing. Some shadow in the sky."

"The sky holds many shadows these days. So does this world we walk in." His toothless jaw moved as if chewing on what he had said, and his fingers played over his stick like a flute. After a while he nodded. "The darkening of the sun in a cloudless sky, yes, I saw such a thing when I was young, when the priests first came. But quickly the darkness passed and the sun became whole again, just like the moon as it waxes and wanes."

The past few nights, Deerchaser had woken drenched in sweat and shaking from a dream: a blackness that blocked out the sun. She had lived through desperate days at her father's death and again at Rush's departure, when Littlereed was born, and when he died. But those had been filled with only heartbreak and sorrow. Never before had she felt such terror—just thinking about the visions made the fear rise again.

She had tried shoving the memories deep, burying the fear along with them. That hadn't worked. "What I dreamed, it wasn't a brief darkness, like the passing of a cloud," she explained. "The swallowing of the sun in my dream is something else. Something bigger. Like a shadow-monster that sucks the sun into a huge mouth." Even trying to describe it unnerved her. She fought against the chill that held her mind frozen on that image.

He cocked his head to one side. "The memories I carry are from my father and his father and his before him. They go back to the time before the Long Thirst, all the way back to the Days of Cold. The sun was said to dim then, veiled by dust spewed from a fiery mountain in the north. But a monster made up of darkness? No. That seems more like a woman's tale, of the time when the Mother-of-All-Creation still walked the earth."

"So," she murmured, disappointed that he couldn't tell her more. Perhaps it was, after all, no more than a dream spawned by some story heard and forgotten.

She began to rise but halted when he asked, "Did you see whether the dark remained forever or the sun eventually returned?"

"No." No, the sun didn't come back. In its place there was only the dark monster, shapeless with a huge open maw like that of the beaded lizard, whose unrelenting poisoned bite means death.

She dragged her thoughts back to the present. "I was hoping you'd say this has happened before," she muttered. "That the sun returns stronger than ever, just as when the Allmother turns it back in the midwinter festival, to bring us longer days and warmth and the greening of spring."

"A vision of renewal, then?"

"Let's not call it a vision. Say, rather, a dream." Not a glimpse of the future. She prayed that was so.

"I have no answer for you here, in my hands." He lifted the stick slightly and displayed it to her. "Perhaps the Skywatchers could tell you. They know the sun best. They understand where it goes and what it does."

Though she knew the secretive Skywatchers were an essential part of the People of Two Rivers, to her they always seemed more like creatures out of the most ancient of tales. They lived far away, somewhere north of Sky River, and never left their cavern.

Even if she thought going to them was the only way to find out about her dream, she wouldn't know how. Rush was the only person she knew who had gone back and forth between the two rivers.

Then she remembered that wasn't entirely true. Her mother, in much younger days when she had traveled with the acrobats, had done so as well. Deerchaser could ask her mother how to get to the place where the Skywatchers lived. But she would have to explain why she wanted to know. She would rather wander alone in the desert for days than do that.

The remembrancer continued, "If you're seeing shadows in the sky, perhaps you're simply worried about the Rainsinger's pronouncement."

"What pronouncement?" Still occupied with the question of whether to ask her mother for help, Deerchaser didn't pay close attention to the first part of what the remembrancer said. Only his mention of the Rainsinger cut through.

"About the hard times coming. People are treating his words almost as a prophecy."

A prophecy, was it? She hauled in a deep breath and compressed her lips to keep from uttering a fiery response: *The Rainsinger comes out with a wave of his hands and some sing-song words, and everyone treats them as truth, while closing their ears to my warnings about him.*

"The death of your son, Deerchaser, didn't cause you to stop living in the actual world. But perhaps it made you look for something beyond what you can see with your waking eyes."

Deerchaser froze when she heard her name. Her resentment about the Rainsinger slipped from her mind. She couldn't recall ever speaking with the remembrancer before. "How do you know me?"

Was he not blind after all? she wondered. But no, those milky, sunken eyes marked him as sightless, at least in the physical world. What Mother Ge showed him within his own mind, Deerchaser couldn't tell.

"Use your visions wisely and well," was all he said in return. "For when dark days of prophecy fall upon us, such gifts will be sorely needed."

He seemed to fall asleep then, or at least she could get no answers, no explanations, nothing more out of him.

She walked for a little while, away from the traders' stalls, away from the remembrancer, away from people who might see too much on her face. Eventually she stood on the canal bank and looked up at the sun where it hung in the sky. Safe, alone, she allowed herself to remember.

The first occurrence of this dream-vision had been followed by others, all showing the sun being swallowed up by the huge dark monster—as she had come to think of it. She was afraid to fall asleep, for when she did doze off, the spectacle woke her, leaving her sweating and nauseated and terrified. There was no point in striving for sleep afterward.

The first sendings from Mother Ge, what the hunters called her gift, had likewise come with sleepless nights those many turnings ago. Once she had recovered from Littlereed's birth, she had been able to sleep only during the day, and what little she managed to eat, she could consume only at night.

The Smokemothers had told her back then that even if she was too weak to tend Littlereed herself, sending a baby out into the world was not a separation—mother and child remained forever bound, as was Mother Ge to all her creatures. They had been less sympathetic when she lost him to the canal and asked them whether Shadowdog's arrival immediately afterward might mean that Littlereed's spirit had been placed in her dog companion. Indeed, they had called her crazy, moon-addled. Secretly she had agreed. But she had accepted the comfort of the dog's affections nonetheless.

If she went to them now and claimed that Mother Ge had been speaking directly to her for all this time, they would demand to know why she hadn't told them about her visions while still under their care, while they could have taught her how to use the Allmother's gift properly, safely, for the protection of the entire village.

But describing her dream-visions as sendings by Mother Ge would have led them to insist that she join their order, which would have meant giving up Littlereed. To be a Smokemother, as the Cornmaidens became once they gave birth, meant being a mother to everyone in the village, not just the child who grew in a woman's belly. The younger Deerchaser had been unwilling to do that. So she had told the senior Smokemothers what she needed to in order to remain out of their clutches. She saw no way back from that.

What was she to do now?

Go to the Skywatchers, as the blind remembrancer had suggested?

But none of the memory-signs under his fingers told him about the sun being swallowed. There was no story, even those of the First Days, that talked of such a thing. So if tales failed to offer any example of a giant monster eating the sun, the People of Two Rivers would experience it as new and terrifying.

She realized it didn't matter what the Skywatchers had to tell her. They were too remote from the people of Crookstaff Village in distance and in deed. Even if they did claim to know of some monster so massive it could swallow up the sun, would she, or anyone, accept their word that the sun would return?

And who would communicate the Skywatchers' reassurances to her fellow villagers, other than Deerchaser herself? How well would that fare, when no one believed her warnings about the Rainsinger?

She supposed she could seek out one of the four high priestesses. Once before she had tried that, with the Truthspeaker, when the Rainsinger demanded deer hearts. The Truthspeaker had refused to interfere with the Rainsinger's way of conducting the priests' ceremonies. Deerchaser didn't expect going to the priestesses to be any more useful this time.

Or she could simply carry on with her life and pretend her dreams meant nothing. Find a man. Make a new family. Look for joy and happiness in each day and stop looking for disaster around every turn.

As if that would work, she thought sourly. As if she could find a man who would understand when she refused to sleep in his presence. Another child, a new family? She didn't want that. Littlereed could never be so easily replaced in her heart.

Before her, the canal bank tapered down and vanished into the desert floor. She stopped and studied it. The canal itself was only a long, curved depression, very much like a dry streambed leading out of the foothills. Washed out generations ago, it carried water no more. But its remains told a story.

Once, in its active days, it had split here, forming two canals that carried water to fields on either side, before the temple was built. Floodwaters had torn out the headgates and overtopped the banks. And the

Watermasters had never gotten those canals running again.

Would the people of Crookstaff Village be like that canal, she wondered: divided and easily destroyed? She could see the Rainsinger's introduction of this new rite cleaving her people, by offering blood where the Allmother asked only for gratitude.

She had thought Mother Ge had begun to send her the dream-visions of the disappearing sun to prod her into action, opposing the Rainsinger's introduction of a new blood-rite in the upcoming Sun-Turning ceremonies. But what if the visions instead concerned his proclamation?

She decided she needed to find out what it was the Rainsinger had said. The easiest place to do that would be at the trade ground, where the biggest crowd was.

Deerchaser looked toward the village. At this end, the compounds squatted at the foot of the Temple of the Mist. Between them and her lay the chich'wipedho field. In the distance she heard the clash of sticks and players yelling.

She considered which way to go, either back along the canal or forward, around the temple—west or east. This was the simplest of decisions, yet she struggled with it and despised herself for that indecisiveness. Deerchaser wished for her life-path to become clear, for once. She was willing to do as Mother Ge wanted. But what, exactly, was that?

Here at the end of the canal, the path atop the bank was a narrow one. Brush and small, twisted trees had gained a foothold. Broken pots and castoffs from the making of stone tools littered the ground where water had once flowed. She felt every pebble and shell and root through the soles of her moccasins as she wondered whether this was to be the fate of every canal: to lie open and empty under a darkened sun.

She sighed and turned her feet toward the Mountains of Sunrise. She would circle around the temple precinct and come to the trade ground from the east. Why that direction? Because that was where the sun came from.

With the cold walls of the temple at her left shoulder, though, Deerchaser wished she had gone the other way. She always had the sense that someone was watching her from one of the shadowed openings in its great height.

She hurried toward the wash that would partly screen her from the temple with the bushes and scrubby trees that grew along its low banks. That way was longer and slower but let her breathe more easily. She turned northward just before she reached the fields being reclaimed from the desert by Starflower's father. Past the dipping pool she strode, past the path that led to the Smokemothers' compound.

As she neared the first house compounds of the oldest part of the village, she saw a couple in a half-hidden nook. Fresh love, she enviously thought at first, taking in the way the man leaned toward the woman.

Then Deerchaser recognized the swirls of hair, the big-eyed, broad-cheeked face with a sharp chin and pouting mouth: Starflower. As for the man, she didn't need to see his face to discern that Starflower's lover was Spadefoot. It was the way he stood, his stance as unique as his sturdy form and the unfortunate birthmark, though that currently was blocked from her view. After barely a moment the girl shoved the young priest away.

Deerchaser recalled the morning, several days earlier, when she had seen Spadefoot headed toward the river and, that same afternoon, Starflower returning to the village. That odd encounter with her clan-sister at the moontime hut had come right after.

At the time, she had thought Starflower wanted to get Rush to do her father's bidding. But now she wondered whether Rush was only a distraction and her clan-sister was playing a more dangerous game. Or even whether Starflower had become a toy for someone else's amusement.

Deerchaser fought her conscience. If Spadefoot had designs on a woman forbidden to him, could she stand by and allow her clan-sister to be drawn into a doomed love affair? But stepping between two lovers was never a good idea.

In the end, she didn't have to do anything. Starflower walked away from Spadefoot. He stared after her—unhappily, Deerchaser presumed—but soon moved on as well. He strolled toward the temple precinct's wall as if it wouldn't have mattered had anyone seen him together with the girl.

It might not indeed have mattered . . . to him. Even though priests were not supposed to take their pleasure with any but the Cornmaidens, Deerchaser doubted that the Rainsinger's son would suffer any consequences if he broke with custom. Starflower was another matter. She could face public chastisement, if the Rainsinger deemed it necessary. Or something even more lasting, if Mother Ge sent her a child.

Deerchaser tried not to worry about her clan-sister's likely fate. Starflower, after all, was the one who had gotten herself wrapped up with the priests.

Are you so different? asked a voice in her head.

She didn't make it to the trade ground to ask about the Rainsinger's proclamation. Instead, a Cornmaiden caught up to her and told Deerchaser that the Seedkeeper had summoned her.

"Deerchaser, daughter of Cloud-Leaf Clan, sit."

The high priestess's harsh voice sent Deerchaser back many turnings, to a time when she hadn't figured out how she would survive in the world with a baby to take care of. She reminded herself she was no longer that shaky, long-ill new mother. "Yes, Revered Grandmother."

Deerchaser settled herself on a well-worn mat that let the cold of the ground seep up through her feet and legs. She hadn't seen this particular priestess up close since Littlereed's birth.

Gray-haired and ancient for as long as Deerchaser could remember, the high priestess stank of tobacco. Deerchaser found it hard to breathe in the cramped cavelike room. Flickering tallow lamps rested atop poles around the Seedkeeper, but they did little to break up the dark.

The priestess spoke again. "You sought advice recently from my vow-sister, the Truthspeaker."

"Yes, Revered Grandmother."

"You would have us intervene in matters you do not understand." The Seedkeeper coughed, then picked up a small jar resting beside her and spat into it. "You think to set us against the priests. But these are complicated matters you will never understand. You must not interfere."

"The Rainsinger is planning to use deer hearts—"

"What if he does? We feed hearts and livers to women to strengthen their blood, do we not? How is this different? He is not hunting down people and cutting out their hearts!"

Deerchaser shuddered; she could see him ordering that done. "Revered Grandmother, as you well know," she said, trying to be respectful, "the Mother-of-All-Creation didn't give us the deer to be abused so. They're brothers and sisters to the people and deserve to be honored in the old ways."

The Seedkeeper glared at her. "Now you claim to honor the old ways? Pah!" she exclaimed in disgust. "You turned your back on Mother Ge and the old ways long ago."

"What do you mean?"

"You scry for the hunters—everyone knows this. You admit to dreaming of where deer can be found. But the important visions, the ones that affect everyone in the Valley of Two Rivers, these you deny!"

Deerchaser's mouth went dry. "What?" she asked hoarsely.

"You dream of the sun being eaten by a monster."

Shock ripped through her body. She had spoken of it only to the remembrancer, only a brief time before. She shook her head. The motion caused her to nearly topple over on the mat. "How can you—"

"You think you kept this vision a secret?" The priestess lifted a clawlike hand to her head and tapped her temple with a crooked finger. "You may have fooled the old Seedkeeper, for she accepted your dreaming as the ravings of a fevered mind."

Deerchaser could make no sense of the priestess's words. The last time she had seen the previous Seedkeeper was after Littlereed's birth; that priestess was the one who had kept her alive, when the midwife, this terrible old priestess, would have let her die.

But this dream of the sun being swallowed was new. Wasn't it? Numbness spread through her body. She could only listen as the Seedkeeper kept after her relentlessly:

"I saw it for what it was—a sign that you belonged with the Smokemothers. The Seedkeeper in those days, she was too soft. Day after day, night after night she tended you," the priestess grated out. "She read the smoke as saying you needed to be sweated, so she squeezed into your mouth, drop by drop, a restorative herb. When that failed, she went against my advice and gave you a dizzyweed potion, a dosing that should be given only to those who are in the Allmother's service. For more than a moon, she had little sleep; she gave all she had to you. In return for her bringing you back from the edge of death, what did you do? You lied to her. You look for someone to blame for the death of your son? Look to yourself."

"What are you saying?" whispered Deerchaser.

"He would have been better off taken from you and raised in the clan." The high priestess leaned forward. "It was dizzyweed that killed him! Oh, yes, I saw his body—the staring eyes, the swollen tongue. Many a time have I seen the signs of dizzyweed poisoning. Drowned, he did, in seeking to quench that terrible thirst!"

The bony finger turned on Deerchaser. "You led him to that, you and your untrained scrying. I brought him into this world; you were the one who sent him out of it."

Deerchaser stumbled to her feet. She backed up until a cold wall kept her from going any farther. She shook her head. "It's not true," she whispered.

She hadn't been there; she had been out on a hunt. Littlereed had gotten away from his minders and somehow fell in the water. But it couldn't have been dizzyweed. She was always careful to keep the dangerous herb well hidden, always made up only as much of the potion as she would need.

"You feared the priests and rejected Mother Ge. All so you would not have to endure the occasional ritual joining."

Deerchaser pressed trembling fingers to her head as though she could push the terrible thoughts away.

"So you denied your dreaming. You went back to your small, pathetic world. But you took Mother Ge's gift with you, and it killed your son!"

She's wrong, she has to be. With her heart battering at her chest wall, Deerchaser fought back. "Maybe it was your fault! Maybe you didn't do the birth-blessing properly. Did you not appeal to Mother Ge on his behalf when he was born? Fail to present him to one of the seven directions?"

"You dare challenge me on this?" The high priestess's eyes narrowed behind their cloudy haze.

"Too many women died under your care. I was nearly one!"

"Women, pah!" The priestess waved a hand as though to say *Who cares about women?* "I was the Childcatcher. I was there to bring babies into the world. How many of my infants died? Can you remember even one?"

None came to mind, though Deerchaser imagined there had to have been at least a few. Her ragged breaths sounded loud in her ears.

"The children, they are our future. I never failed to do anything to preserve the babies. Your son, I bathed in a tea made of the leaves of vavish, to make up for his mother's weakness. If a mother is not strong enough to live after birthing a child, as countless women have done since time immemorial, it is better that she die."

Deerchaser would rather have died than endure her son's death. But she hadn't. She had been left in the world. There had to be a reason.

A reason for Mother Ge to send her the gift of foreseeing.

A reason for her to see, night after night, the sun being swallowed up. A reason for her to see the Rainsinger, a knife in his hands and, at his feet, a body covered in blood. Her other dreams had her stepping into story-songs known to everyone. The remembrancer recalled no instance of a monster eating the sun in the past, and certainly no Rainsinger had ever performed a blood ritual. Those weren't things she would have heard in stories or songs. They weren't like her other dreams.

They were more like her dizzyweed visions, showing things that were yet to come—until now, predictions of where the deer would be. She wasn't always right. That had to mean there was a chance of preventing those terrible visions from coming true. Or else Deerchaser thought she truly would go moon-mad.

Her hands clenched so tightly, her nails dug into her palms. She barely noticed.

The Seedkeeper wasn't done yet. "There are many who value what I have done during my turnings of service to the village, even if you do not." She pierced Deerchaser with a rheumy gaze. "Your mother is one. She told me of your yammering about the Rainsinger and blood sacrifice."

Deerchaser wanted to defend herself, but in her disorientation she had passed beyond speech.

"You interpret your dreaming too directly, if you think the sun will really vanish and the Rainsinger would actually dare to shed blood during a ceremony. These things will never come to pass. Have you nothing to say, girl?"

Her nails forced themselves even deeper, until the bones in her hands ached. She shook her head.

"Easier for you to stir up trouble than to defend yourself, is it?" the Seedkeeper sneered. "You turned your back on your clan and became a hunter. As such, you suffer little risk from either flood or drought, the very things prophesied by the Rainsinger."

Everyone but her seemed to know what was in this prophecy. But she would never ask this terrible old woman what he had said. Finally she managed to force her thick tongue into motion. "Animals die, too, in flood and drought. And the deerfolk go hungry just like everyone else."

"Don't speak to me of hunters! That kind take care of their own first. While we Smokemothers, we who give up our children to the village, we do not have that luxury. Think! We are mothers to all the village! To have your child die and be helpless to save him, that was a dreadful thing, wasn't it? Think! Would you have us doom all the children to death, all the mothers, all the fathers, the clan-sisters and brothers, uncles and aunties? Is that what you wish?"

Deerchaser closed her eyes, dropped her chin, shook her head again.

The Seedkeeper's tone changed. "You have gained strength, Deerchaser. That is good. Especially if you have gained wisdom and self-control along with it. I did not send for you in order to scold and bully you."

"Why, then?"

"A warning. Stop talking against the Rainsinger and his changes to rituals that are his to perform."

"He's involving the deerfolk. That makes it our concern."

"Your concern should be this: the priest's corpse showed signs of dizzy-weed poisoning. Who do you think would have been blamed, had the body been found so far from the temple with no reason to look to the Wilders?"

"Why would anyone be to blame?" Deerchaser wanted to silence herself, stop arguing with the old priestess, go back to being speechless, and most of all to leave and be done with all this, but she seemed to have no power over her own mouth. "Wouldn't his death have been deemed an accident?"

"The priests cannot have anyone thinking they are not all-powerful. They would have cast suspicion on someone."

"The Smokemothers, you mean?"

"We are not the ones who stand in open opposition to them. Think, girl!"

The priestess meant her.

Every time Deerchaser considered that, chills swept through her. Every step she made, every breath she took, every face she saw reminded her that someone could think her capable of killing the priest—and the Seedkeeper thought her son had died the same way. Through dizzyweed.

Could that be true?

When she left the Smokemothers' compound, she didn't turn toward the mud-plastered brush hut she had built a little way outside the village, along a narrow wash, where she normally found solitude and quiet under the green-trunked ko'okmatki trees. In spring, with the yellow flowers that covered the trees and rained down on her, it was like living in a sunrise. Right now, though, solitude and quiet—indeed, the very thought of being alone—made her skin crawl.

Her body, barely under her control, made her movements stiff and uneven. She tripped and pitched forward. She would have landed on her face if she hadn't gotten her hands under in time. She turned over and sat right where she was, in the middle of the path.

A few people hurried past from the trade ground. They threw curious glances at her. Wondering whether calling attention to herself was now dangerous, she rose and dusted off her tunic, front and back. She hoped nobody had actually witnessed her falling over her own feet.

Shadowdog came bounding up to her wearing his most joyous, toothy grin. She stroked his head. "What should I do?" she asked him.

His tail, black except for the white tip, gave two brief wags. He sat in front of her as though listening.

"No, I mean it. I have no idea. The Mother-of-All-Creation sent you to me, so evidently she thought I really needed a dog. But what good are you, if you can't tell me what she wants me to do?"

His patience evidently exhausted, he ran off again.

"Thank you ever so much," she called after him. Where else could she go besides back to her hut to await the coming of night—with its visions of the sun going dark and the Rainsinger with a bloody knife in his hand?

There was the hunters' ward at the Masterholding. But she had just spent several days with the deerfolk, mostly in the haze of dizzyweed. After what the Seedkeeper had just told her, she might want to distance herself from them.

She could go to the trade ground as she had originally planned, to find out exactly what the Rainsinger had said in his proclamation. But that would take her right into the shadow of the temple, which might not be a good idea, if the Seedkeeper was right. If the priests could have actually desecrated a body just to lay an accusation against her.

Ultimately, after wandering northward through the village, she wound up in front of a tidy woven-brush gate that closed off access to the work yard and low adobe buildings within: her mother's compound.

It was no larger than anyone else's but nevertheless stood out for its neatness. No green potherbs disturbed the perfection of its walls. The knee-high rabbitbrush had been beaten back to a respectable distance. The ground was smooth and level, nearly as polished as the walls, higher than a tall man.

Knobbyroot, her mother's new mate—as Deerchaser still thought of him despite the couple's many turnings together—made sure all was in order, always. She despised him; he felt much the same way about her. That was part of the reason she seldom came here.

But today . . . today, where else could she go?

She swung the gate open, observing with reluctant admiration that it did actually swing rather than sag and scrape. Like everything else belonging to her mother's bondmate it was impeccably maintained.

As she entered, she saw her mother backing out of the storage building with a few stalks of corn in her arms. Most of the farmers had taken to cutting off just the ears and storing them in large granary baskets on the roof, but Knobbyroot insisted that leaving the ears on the stalks was best, as that made the kernels less prone to mold. So he had built racks in the storage building for the cornstalks.

The racks looked oddly full in the building's shadows, given that everyone else had complained of a sparse crop this turning. But Knobbyroot, born into one of the oldest families in Cloud-Leaf Clan, had a great deal of influence in the clan and the village—and some of the best fields too.

Deerchaser called out to her mother.

The other woman turned and looked to see who had greeted her. "Why, Deerchaser! Such a pleasant surprise."

Quickly she pushed the reed door closed with her backside. She walked over to her cookfire under the vatto and piled the cornstalks beside it. Then she stretched from side to side and bowed backward in a graceful arch.

Deerchaser guessed her back was paining her again.

Once she had been an acrobat, one of those who performed at the village games. Not for her the chich'wipedho. No, that, according to the clan-aunties, had been too tame for her.

She had tumbled her way into the heart of Deerchaser's father. She would show off for the village, even other villages, on trade days like today, being propelled by one of her fellow acrobats high into the air to flip head over heels, or walking across a length of rivercane, suspended on the shoulders of two of her troupe and just thick enough to bear her weight.

And then she had taken a bad fall—not even while tumbling, just a misstep on rocks while out at hunt camp.

Where once she had been a daring swallow, mastering the currents of the air, now she was a little gray rock dove, scraping about for what could be gleaned on the ground. Even her appearance had gone from lean and graceful to a plumpness that seemed much more akin to . . . to Starflower, Deerchaser realized. Though her face was angular like Deerchaser's, it was softer and the angles fit together from forehead to cheekbones to chin, all balanced and perfect.

"You did invite me," Deerchaser reminded her. *Come and eat with us,* her mother had said. *You're getting so thin.*

But that had been several days ago. After a hunt, the deerfolk gave out whatever couldn't be fitted into the smokehouse or dried for jerky. Those who had relatives among the farmfolk were, by custom, the ones to deliver the packets of meat. But in recent generations, the hunters seldom took mates outside their own people. Deerchaser was one of the few who still claimed kinship in another clan. So it fell to her to deliver the partly dried strips and gobbets to several households (including her mother's) and to the clan's moontime hut.

"Am I still welcome?" she asked.

"Of course. I'm always glad to see you."

Deerchaser reminded herself of all the times the words were spoken but not borne out by her mother's actions. She shouldn't expect too much. Once her mother found out what she had come for, the pleasant mood might vanish quickly.

They seated themselves on deerskin-covered mats under the vatto. Her mother offered her a nice hot draft of atole, the sweet and filling drink made from mesquite flour.

Staring down at it, she thought about the hard work her mother had done to pound those bean pods into flour. Many people didn't bother. Some even cut down the mesquites that volunteered in their fields, saying the deep roots drank up the water that the crops needed, though others claimed the fields containing mesquites produced better, and they left the thirsty trees alone.

Deerchaser sipped her mother's atole. It tasted better than what she was able to make herself from what she gathered outside the clanlands, as if simply growing in the fields somehow tamed the wildness of the trees and sweetened their beans. Or maybe, she thought, her mother was just better at making the atole tasty. It took off the chill of fear.

She cradled the warm jar in her hands and looked down into the liquid as if it held the answers she wanted. "I've been to see the Seedkeeper."

"Whatever for? You detest that woman, you know you do." Her mother took up a cornstalk and wrenched off one ear, then started to peel back the dry husk.

"I do, yes. So you'll understand why I don't want you gossiping with her about me."

"What do you mean?" Her mother didn't look up from the ear she was husking.

"About the Rainsinger!"

"Oh, you mean your notions about some blood ritual? The Seedkeeper already knew." She glanced up. Upon catching a glimpse of Deerchaser's face, she added, "You haven't exactly kept it to yourself. Half the village knows, I'm sure. Anyway, she always asks about you."

"Always? You've talked with her before about me?" She heard her voice rise, and her cheeks felt hot.

Her mother nodded. She placed the bare ear on the nearby trough metate and pulled another off the stalk.

"How long has this been going on?"

"Since she saved your life and gave you back to me."

"She didn't save—"

"She understood how I felt then. And later, after you ran off to the hunters. Only a mother can understand what it means to lose a child."

Deerchaser's heart constricted. Littlereed's wide-eyed expression in death rose up in her mind again. Dizzyweed. Absent mothers. Guilt.

She swallowed and looked down into her atole again. In that moment she understood something about herself.

Deerchaser had a craving. A desperate need for someone to see her, know her, care for her. Where it had come from all of a sudden, she couldn't say. But it was part of what had brought her back to her mother this day.

Her hands began to shake. She put down the atole. *I killed him,* she wanted to confess. *It's my fault he died. He wouldn't have been curious about dizzyweed else.* She held those words tightly inside.

"Shell the corn, please." Her mother gestured toward the metate. "You wouldn't be making such a fuss if it was anyone but the Seedkeeper. I can't understand why you've taken such a dislike to her."

"Mother, she wanted me to die, way back all those turnings ago. She told me so, straight out." Deerchaser picked up the ear of corn as her mother handed her the second one. She began to rub them together to knock the dried kernels off the cob and into the metate.

"Oh, that can't be true. I'm sure you misunderstood." Her mother leaned forward and picked up a forked stick made of polished stonewood. She adjusted one of the rocks that ringed the firepit, pushing it back into alignment using the stick. "The Smokemothers did everything they could to save you."

"The one who was Seedkeeper back then, she did," Deerchaser corrected her. "The one who was midwife at the time wanted me to die. Because I was weak and couldn't be a strong enough mother to my boy."

"No, no, I remember those days very well. She was worried about you. You came down with birth-fever, and there was no milk for the babe. Poor thing had to be taken away from you and put to another new mother's breast. You can't remember, of course, because you were wandering in that fever dream, and no wonder. It brought on a dark cloud of unhappiness, blocking out the joy you should have gotten from being a new mother."

Deerchaser frowned. "What fever dream?"

"Darkness across the face of the sun or something." Her mother waved a half-stripped ear of corn. "You were raving about it, I recall."

As though a cold splash of rain had trickled down her spine, Deerchaser shivered. "The sun going dark? I had this dream back then—and you knew?" As she thought about it, a foolish sense of betrayal ran through her. Her mother had never mentioned such a dream to her, not in all these turnings. Was it just a dream, then, and not a vision sent by Mother Ge? She shoved that idea around and around in her mind, poking at it, unsure how to feel about it.

"Of course," her mother assured her. "The Smokemothers told me all about it. They wanted me to convince you to stay with them. But I knew you couldn't be having real visions. I was sure once you got better, you would come home and settle into your life again. Here with me, with my grandson. But then you went back to the hunters, which made no sense at all."

The familiar complaint pulled Deerchaser out of her thoughts. Irritated, she answered as she always did: "You made it impossible for me to stay. Nothing I did could please you. Much less Knobbyroot."

"You deserted me," her mother protested. "You ran away, just like your father did—always off hunting."

"Maybe he wouldn't have done, if you hadn't picked at him all the time," Deerchaser muttered. She gave the ears of corn in her hands a vicious twist.

Her father had been both brave and foolish, always willing to risk his neck. That thirst for danger had been something her parents shared—until her mother's accident. Then her father's courage gradually became something for them to argue about.

Deerchaser still remembered the day the hunt leader came to their brush hut. He told them her father had been kicked in the head by a deer after running it down and wrestling to the ground. He had been teaching some boys how to end the suffering of a wounded deer, the hunt leader had explained to the bereft woman and girl.

Deerchaser's mother, dry-eyed, had just looked at the body that had been her mate. Then she had packed up her possessions and moved back to her own people. Deerchaser, all of twelve turnings old, had been forced to go along, leaving behind all the playmates she had ever known.

Looking back, she understood that she could have tried harder to fit in, to be happy, to not resent her mother for that choice. Once she got older, she could have claimed use-right to one of the lesser clanholdings, offering it as a bribe to get some farmer as her bondmate. She could have made herself into a soft, yielding creature like her mother, someone Mother Ge wouldn't torture with visions.

Her mother pointed a stripped ear at her. "I was all alone! I hated living with the deerfolk. They made no effort to include me once he was—" She broke off. "You would've found the same thing if you'd gone to the Watermasters looking for them to take care of you. You ruined your life over a careless boy."

Deerchaser placed the empty cobs beside the metate. She stared at the scattering of corn within. "It didn't ruin my life. It gave me the love of my life: a child."

Her mother wouldn't have had to feel alone back then, when her mate died. She could have made Deerchaser into her whole world, as Deerchaser had done with Littlereed. Instead she had returned to Cloud-Leaf Clan and dragged Deerchaser with her. All too soon, Knobbyroot had shown up, with his fine fields and his preference for order and quiet.

Deerchaser recalled how lonely her young self had been when her mother had forced her to leave the deerfolk. But she had learned that being alone was not the worst thing; being with people who made you feel bad all the time was worse.

"Nothing would have sent me to the Watermasters," she told her mother. "Plenty of girls have babies without a mate. Their families and clans stand by them. Help them."

"But to give yourself to a ditchrunner!"

Heat rose in her cheeks. Rush had proven careless with her heart, but at least he was an honorable man. If he had known about his son, he would have made a good father. "Was it worse because Rush was only a ditchrunner back then?" she snapped. "Or would any Watermaster have been just as bad?"

Knobbyroot ducked under the vatto and shot her a sharp look. He was a smallish fussy man, vain about his appearance. She had to wonder why her mother had picked someone so unlike her father, whom she remembered as being tall, sharp-featured, bold, and willing to try anything. Everything Knobbyroot was not.

Pointing a finger at her, he ordered, "For your mother's sake, you need to stay away from the Canalmaster."

She tamped down the rebellious voice that wanted to tell him, *I'll do as I please.* "Why do you say that?"

"Support for them is dangerous now, since the Rainsinger has spoken against them."

"I thought," her mother said, picking at a lingering piece of husk, "that he was very careful to not speak against them. That he told everyone to not overreact and not listen to rumor."

"What do you mean, 'speak against them'? Against who?" asked Deerchaser.

Knobbyroot seated himself across the fire ring from her.

Her question unanswered, Deerchaser tried again. "I was out on a hunt and missed his proclamation. What did he say?"

Her mother murmured, "He spoke of the young rain priest's death. And what will befall any who dare harm a priest."

Knobbyroot added, "Not that it was a farmer. Who but the Wilders and Watermasters could he mean by 'Your enemy will lie with your woman; he'll eat your food and demand to be clothed and brag of wickedness'?"

"I imagine there are any number of idle young men in the clans who would match that description," Deerchaser said.

"You can scoff." Knobbyroot shook a chastising finger at her. "But know this—he foresaw punishment of those who follow the old ways instead of accepting the Ta'atchul in their hearts. 'The Ancestors bring the rain no more,' the Rainsinger said. He said, too, that the canals will lie empty in the coming days, scars on the land. We saw that happen this turning; it will only get worse. Your precious Canalmaster can do nothing to make it better."

Deerchaser thought of the full storage building. If all that corn had come from Knobbyroot's fields, those sections of the canals had been far from empty. "So if the Rainsinger makes people choose between the Watermasters and the priests, they should choose the priests?"

Knobbyroot said, "The priests bring the rain. They have the power now."

"Because farmfolk like you *give* it to them." She understood in her very bones that men such as the Rainsinger should never be given more control over other people.

That was why she had tried to convince the hunt council not to supply him with the deer hearts. They had pointed out that if they refused the priest's demand, he would acquire the hearts from somewhere else—and then the rites of gratitude to their four-legged brethren wouldn't be done properly, if at all. They had argued that would anger the Allmother.

Deerchaser had thought Mother Ge would be angrier about having a blood-rite added to the midwinter festival. How much worse would it be if people like Knobbyroot started to pray to the Ta'atchul instead of the Allmother?

Impatiently Knobbyroot said, "The Watermasters have no connection to the land. That makes them dangerous."

"What do you mean, no connection?" Deerchaser had never thought Knobbyroot especially clever, but his willingness to mouth the words of the Rainsinger dropped her opinion of him even lower. "They built the canals. Have kept them running since the First Days."

"No fields," he said. "No crops. They raise nothing with the labor of their back and the sweat of their brow."

"That's unfair. As if only farmfolk bring food into the village, all by themselves. Would you ignore hunting, fishing, gathering? We all are children of Mother Ge, all of us given the desert's bounty."

Her mother waved the same husked ear she had held all this time. "Wandering around, picking up whatever comes into life on its own, that's entirely different. Watermasters and Wilders, and hunters too, don't feel the seasons change around them, don't hold dirt in their fist to make sure it's ready to work, don't pray over seeds and treasure every green shoot."

"At least the Watermasters are a part of us," Deerchaser argued. "The priests keep to themselves. They don't walk in the fields or put their hands in the dirt or pray over the seeds. People holding onto the old ways get sneered at. And now the Rainsinger is calling for them to be punished."

"Why do you defend the Watermasters instead of your own family?" Knobbyroot's hands balled into fists as if he wanted to strike her. He thumped them down on his knees.

"I'm not! I just don't think they're the ones to worry about. Maybe Rush hurt me all those turnings ago—"

"You don't think it's all one? This Canalmaster, he betrayed you. The old Canalmaster, and others like him, they have betrayed all of us." He was practically spitting, he was so angry.

He went on, "Look at all the land they're fallowing, claiming the canals can't put water in them as in the old days. I've heard Earth Holder can't even get this new Canalmaster—your Canalmaster—to come by and look at the ditches he's been cleaning out, let alone muster a work party to connect his fields to the canal."

Deerchaser protested, "You can't believe a word Earth Holder says! The man is a snake."

"You shouldn't condemn a man based on rumor," her mother said in gentle reproof.

Knobbyroot glanced her way but didn't comment. His gaze returned to Deerchaser. "Since we have to do everything ourselves anyway, what do we need the Watermasters for?"

Deerchaser pointed out, "You don't do everything yourselves. The Wilders and ditchrunners do most of the labor, under the direction of the ditch bosses, following the Canalmaster's instructions. Just as they always have done."

"With the Wilders coming right into the clanlands and slaughtering a Stormbringer," Knobbyroot vowed, "they won't be stepping foot in my fields. Or anyone else's, if I have anything to say about it."

"You don't really think the Wilders had anything to do with that, do you?" Then she remembered what the Seedkeeper had said about his death being from dizzyweed. *Better to blame them than me,* she thought.

But how could anyone really believe that the Wilders had walked right into the clanlands and killed a young priest without being seen? There was always someone watching in the clanlands. She had never managed to get away with anything.

And in this instance, she had seen the priest, or one she assumed to have been him, heading up toward the river the day he must have died. If the body had been discovered by the river, blaming the Wilders would make more sense. In the clanlands? She shook her head.

In a smug, I-know-better voice, Knobbyroot declared, "The Wilders are the tools of the Watermasters. We have no more need for their kind."

"Certainly we do . . . *you* do," Deerchaser argued, "if the canals are to bring water to the fields, just as they always have done. You can't really believe the priests when they claim to call down the rains."

"We farmers know all we need to know to keep the water running in the canals," he told her.

Sarcastically she said, "But of course. Any two neighboring farmers squabble over exactly how long to let water run on the upstream fields, and that's with the ditch boss standing right there. You farmers will be able to work it out on your own—as soon as the canals freeze over in the middle of summer."

Knobbyroot looked down his nose at her. "You scoff. But everything has changed since the coming of the Stormbringers."

"Don't let's argue," her mother said.

For her sake, Deerchaser didn't tell Knobbyroot that he was a stupid, naive, arrogant man. She was grateful for the argument. It had proved a welcome distraction from one surprise after another: her son had died of dizzyweed, her mother shared Deerchaser's secrets with a woman who hated her, she was having a recurring bad dream rather than a vision, and her mother's mate really believed there was no more need for the Watermasters anymore, now that the priests could call down the rain.

She told her mother she had to go.

"Before supper?" her mother asked, lines of worry creasing her forehead.

"I came for the company instead of the food." Deerchaser gave her a hug and bade her as warm a farewell as she could manage.

Her feet took her toward the Masterholding, a familiar way. But she didn't climb the ladder that stood against the west wall, which would have let her climb down into the work yard of the hunters. Nor did she turn southward and take the path to her own hut.

She went around to the east side of the enclosing wall and climbed the other ladder, the one that took her up to the top of the Watermasters' mound. She found her way through a maze of buildings and soon stood in front of a woven-reed door.

Deerchaser lifted her hand to the braided cord that would slip the latch and let her in—but her heart misgave her. She and Rush had never been invited into each other's homes. She spread her fingers flat upon the ribbed surface of the door. As goosebumps lifted the fine hairs on her skin, she wondered whether she had enough courage to go through with this.

Only, she was tired of being angry with Rush. She wanted to make peace. She wanted . . . just that. She wanted.

"You shouldn't be here," said a young voice to her right, startling her.

She glanced over to see a pair of boys standing at the mouth of the narrow passageway she had just come through. They had shells and beads entwined in their many thin braids, Watermaster fashion, and were garbed in stained doeskin tunics and scuffed leggings, all slightly too small and decorated with light-colored ratty ribbons that she knew, despite the fading light, were the pale blue of the heronfolk.

Ditchrunners they were, only a little younger than Rush when he had first come to Crookstaff Village. The skinny one, Tumbler, was the one who had given her a welcome breathing space by taking Rush away from their initial encounter some days back. Tumbler had family in Cloud-Leaf Clan, she recalled. The other had chubby cheeks that reminded her of Littlereed during his first few turnings.

"What're you doing?" the second one demanded.

"Looking for the Canalmaster."

Tumbler said, "He'll be awhile. You could wait."

His friend elbowed him in the ribs.

"Hey!" He responded with a one-handed shove. "It's *her!* She's all right."

The blunt assessment made her smile. "What's your friend's name, Tumbler?"

"This here's Plastercrack. We call him Crack."

"Shut up!" Crack ordered his friend.

"What d'you want with our Canalmaster?" Tumbler asked.

Deerchaser said, "I thought the Canalmaster might want some stew."

"There aren't no pots. He don't cook," Tumbler said.

She blinked in surprise. "Not at all?"

"My gran's the one what cooks for the Canalmaster."

"Tonight I'll save her the trouble."

"She don't mind."

"Shut your whistler," Crack told him.

Using her I'm-an-adult-being-polite-but-it-will-pass-if-you-make-me-repeat-this-request voice, she said, "Would you ask your gran for a pot, please, Tumbler?"

"I'll go," Crack muttered before Tumbler had a chance to say anything. "But I'll be back."

As he jogged away, she figured he would be back shortly—though whether with a pot or with some fierce clan-auntie was another question.

Tumbler rocked back on his heels. "The Canalmaster don't much care for people poking through his stuff."

"Then I won't do that. Where is the meat the hunters delivered today?"

"They don't bring it here no more. They take it to my gran directly. She cooks for all of us: Canalmaster, ditchrunners, ditch bosses."

"Why don't you go after Crack and tell him we need the meat from your gran, along with some dried squash and potherbs? I'll cook for your Canalmaster tonight."

"I'm really not s'posed to leave someone alone up here." His face twisted with doubt.

"You said it yourself, I'm all right. I promise I won't steal anything or muck about with his stuff."

The boy shrugged but took himself off.

To open the door, she first had to untangle a complicated knot in the cord. She guessed this was where Rush slept; he'd always had a weakness for knots, and it made sense that he would use one to make it hard for anyone to intrude into his private place without his knowing.

She peered into the cramped room, lit only by the smokehole in the roof and the doorway in which she stood. A scattering of grit covered the polished floor. She wondered whether that meant Tumbler's clan-grannie cooked for Rush but didn't sweep out his quarters.

A small broom stood beside the door. She was tempted to use it but refrained.

A sleep pallet occupied one corner. Benches lined two of the walls. She guessed from the lack of wear on the deerhide covers that they probably saw more use as storage bins than places to sit.

In another corner, several tall poles made of cane were tied upright. These had markings along their length. Some diggers and shorter pieces of cane, cut in half and hollowed out, rose above the lip of a large burden basket that leaned against the wall. A net hung from the ceiling seemed to hold oddly shaped things—more tools, she guessed. A bulging carry sack rested on the floor next to the sleep pallet.

As she glanced around, she placed one hand on her hip and braced her chin on the thumb of the other hand while she tapped her forefinger against her lips. Other than where he slept, his surroundings spoke only of work.

There were no clothes, no weavings or paintings, no colorful ritual gear. Here, where Rush lived, there was no color. Just various dreary browns. So where was the beauty he appreciated—not just feminine faces and bodies but bright hues and graceful shapes?

She was tempted to go in and see what the bins held. But that would count as messing with his stuff. Instead she pulled the door shut behind her. She didn't bother to refasten the cord.

Along the other edges of the little plaza outside the Watermaster's sleeping quarters were small rooms accessed by what she presumed were roof hatches, since no doors were visible. A quick investigation of the few doorways nearby revealed several pallets of bedding in each room; these were closed off with hides rather than woven doors.

In one alcove she had just found a stack of wood and kindling when the boys came back, laden with pots and folded skin packets tied with cords. Tumbler told her that his gran had already cut up the roots and meat and squash for stew for the evening meal and that if Deerchaser wanted to cook for the whole gang she was welcome to. He seemed surprised when she said that was fine.

She supposed he (or his gran) thought she would refuse, that the prospect of cooking for several hungry young men and boys would scare her off, but hunt camp was good practice. When she had conceived this notion of preparing Rush's supper, she hadn't expected it would be on quite so large a scale. The prospect would let her see him surrounded by the people he spent the most time with.

Under the vatto, Tumbler and Crack built a small fire in the fire pit. While they did that, she arranged the flat rocks on which to sear the meat. The large pot that held the other stew ingredients, a coarse grayish vessel with thick walls, that one she filled with water and placed on a platform of rocks at the edge of the fire.

The rest of the meal came together without any setbacks. Although that seemed to irritate Crack, Tumbler visibly relaxed. Other boys and young men came to the plaza one and two at a time and seated themselves in the shelter of the vatto, though not without casting suspicious looks at Deerchaser. Their expressions eased as the tantalizing smell of stew began to waft through the vatto.

In a little while, Rush came into view at the mouth of the passageway. He paused there. His eyes skipped over the group of youths and homed in on Deerchaser. Then he strode in, planted his feet, and crossed his arms.

Nerves jangling, she rose.

"You don't wait for an invitation before making free of someone else's home?" he demanded.

"I made you supper." She gestured toward the fire, though he had to have smelled the stew already.

She could tell by the stormy expression on his handsome face that he wanted to lash out at her. He didn't—she supposed because of the wide-eyed young men watching.

He went to the door of his sleeping quarters, looked down at the undone knot, then gestured for her to join him.

Deerchaser obliged. She stood beside him in the doorway.

"You didn't go in?" he asked.

She looked at the floor, the grit scattered there. "No, obviously." A hunter knew better than to leave behind tracks.

His mouth twitched down at one corner. Then he crossed to one of the storage shelves on the short end of the room and took down a cloth, which he rubbed over his sweat-dampened hair. Unexpectedly, he peeled out of his shirt and leggings and stood almost naked before her, wearing only his breechcloth.

She tried not to think about how good he looked with his muscles sliding under his skin. A little too late, she turned her back. But she didn't leave or even draw the door closed.

She heard a rustling and some soft creaks and wondered whether he was taking off even his breechcloth. Her mouth went dry; she felt her heart beating faster.

"You can turn around now," he said. When she did, she found him once more fully clothed, wearing a woven cotton shirt and belted leggings. The leathers he had slipped out of hung from one of the support beams.

He watched her steadily. "Why did you come?"

"To cook for you. To offer you a long-overdue apology. To welcome you home, as I should have done several moons ago. To talk. As an old friend."

"I don't need anything from you."

"Not even to take comfort from one whose blood mingled with yours in the child we created?" She stepped into the room and laid a not-quite-steady hand on his arm. "You asked about him, before. I wasn't ready."

"And now you are? What changed since our last talk?"

After her son's death, she had been determined that no one would ever get close enough to cause her heartache. She had turned away other men, mostly of the deerfolk, who had tried to break through her shell. Anger and grief had been her companions, lurking in the background waiting to attack whenever someone reminded her of what she'd once had . . . and lost. She didn't want their cold company anymore.

Clamping her hands together, she said, before she could change her mind, "He used to like balancing tummy-down on my feet, lifted up into the air. He would spread out his arms and pretend to fly. It was the freedom, I think." As she expected it would, that got Rush's attention.

So she told him everything she could think of, talking in his sleeping quarters as he ate the stew she had prepared for him. She found as she did so that the pain eased with every word, as she remade Littlereed from memory, birthing him into existence in his father's world.

While she talked, Rush asked no questions, but he didn't toss her out, either.

They sat together in the dark until he stirred and went a small distance away. The soft, dusty smell of tinder wafted to her nose, then the rasp of a bow-drill flint lighter sounded. A moment later a spark winked into sight. He lit a couple of tallow candles, which drove the darkness back to the corners.

Still without saying anything, he drew her over to lean against him. She pillowed her head on his shoulder.

His head turned, bringing him closer, so that she could feel his breath upon her. His eyes lowered to her mouth, then met hers in wordless inquiry. She leaned in and offered him a kiss.

In the moments of sighs and groans and melting pleasure that followed, she knew once more what it was not to be alone. Grateful to

Mother Ge for having brought her here, no matter what it would cost her later, she finally slipped into blissful, exhausted oblivion.

Deerchaser awoke shaking, with clammy skin, to find a musky male body looming over her.

She balled her hands into fists and drew in a breath to shout, but a familiar mouth closed over hers. As she closed her eyes in relief, she heard Rush say, "Remember me now?"

Her eyelids flew open and she shoved his face away. "This is no time for jokes."

Then she bit her lip. It was her fault, not his, that she had fallen asleep and let the dream in. The Allmother's sending had ruined their brief reconciliation, just as she might have expected, had she been thinking straight.

It was foolish to have come to him at all, let alone to have opened the door to that intimacy they once had shared. What was done could not be undone; what was dead and gone could not be revived. Feeling vulnerable, she scooted away and sat up. She clutched at a thin hide and dragged it up to cover her breasts, not that he could see her in the dark anyway.

"You were crying out. Bad dreams?"

"You don't want to know," she muttered.

"Tell me anyway."

She considered making up some excuse, but what would be the point? He would turn away, of course—what sensible man wouldn't? Better to have it happen now, before she got all wrapped up in him. *Don't make the same mistake as your mother,* she warned herself. "A sending from Mother Ge, showing the end of the world."

He said nothing at first. Then, in a low voice, he asked, "You believe the goddess is speaking to you?"

"Speaking through me, rather." She made a useless gesture at the blackness that surrounded them.

Suddenly feeling him all too close, she pushed herself to the edge of the sleep pallet and sat up. "Believe me or not, I don't care." Sweat and disappointment chilled her through.

After a quick slithering of furs, warmth closed around one bare ankle. "Why wouldn't I believe you?" His hand slid upward.

She kicked at him and stood up. "No one does." With outstretched arms she moved toward the thin shadow she thought was the roof pole where she had hung her clothes. "But just because no one believes me doesn't mean I'm wrong."

"I do believe you," he said. A rustle, and his voice coming from somewhere around the height of her hips, told her that he had sat up. "Or I'll try to. Tell me about this sending. A dream?"

Her groping hands encountered her tunic and leggings. She began to pull them on. "A vision, rather. Night after night it wakes me from sleep. I shouldn't have let myself fall asleep."

"What is it you see?"

Pausing with the deerskin tube above her left knee, she said, "It doesn't matter. If it comes to pass, it will be too terrifying to bear. If not, then I'm just crazy, moon-addled."

"But you believe Mother Ge is really sending you this vision, dream, whatever? And not like the dreams one sees during a naming quest? You think whatever it is, it's actually going to happen?" He sounded doubtful.

She didn't blame him.

Deerchaser finished drawing the legging the rest of the way and tied it in place. "She sends me visions of deer: where they're going, where they'll be. She has for a very long time. It's why the deerfolk keep me around. I'm useful."

He didn't say anything to that.

After struggling into her tunic, she added, "I can come back another night."

"Is that what you want?"

Her eyes could barely discern an outline of gray slightly less dense than the darkness of the Canalmaster's sleeping quarters. "I don't know." *Yes.* "Would you want me to?" He didn't answer. She supposed he didn't know, any more than she did.

After pulling the pin out of the flap that held the door closed, she stepped into the night. The moon, nearly full, reflected off the lingering clouds, giving off a dim glow that would light her way home.

Only then did she allow herself to feel the embarrassment and humiliation of being awakened so abruptly from something that had felt so right. Get her hopes up only to have them dashed again? Not this time, she assured herself. This time, she wouldn't build a future with Rush out of wishes and a foolish girl's imagination.

Mother Ge had given her a twisting life-path, dangerous and solitary. Deerchaser considered asking Rush to help—as a Canalmaster, he would have far more influence than she could ever hope for.

But he needed to use his influence to repair the canals. With the farmers torn between the priests and the Watermasters, Rush was more important than any Canalmaster before him. Pulling him into her own fight against the Rainsinger would risk everything. And besides, what if she was wrong about Morning Green, about Mother Ge, about her visions, about everything?

The next day, Deerchaser emerged from the low-roofed entrance to her hut. Still tired and groggy, she lifted her face to the sky and stretched. Exhaustion had caught up with her as soon as her back hit the sleep pallet. She had fallen asleep—and hadn't, this time, been woken by dreaming of the sun being swallowed or the Rainsinger with his bloody knife.

That didn't mean she felt rested.

High overhead, a pale, weak sun glowed behind thin clouds. As a child she had sometimes wondered, if no one saw the Sun-Turning—because of a cloudy sky or rain pouring down—did it really happen? After all, people didn't actually know why the sun turned back in its journey along the horizon. They just trusted the winter sun-festival to make it happen. As long as the days became longer again and spring arrived, no one cared how these things came to be, whether brought about by the Skywatchers or the priests or the Allmother herself.

It seemed to her that Mother Ge could hide the swallowing of the sun behind rain or cloud. But would she? If it was her will that her people see the baleful omen, surely that would have to come soon, before the Rainsinger introduced blood to the ancient rituals.

Deerchaser's sleeping mind seemed to have woven together the two events: the vision the Allmother was sending her and the Rainsinger's introduction of blood sacrifice. Could it be a coincidence that she was in a position, being of the deerfolk, to learn about the Rainsinger's plans and was the one the goddess was choosing to speak to and the one who had a long-standing connection to the Watermasters as well? She was the only one in whom all those threads came together, a complex knot like the ones Rush made to keep people out of his private space.

But what was she to do? What *could* she do, when no one else seemed to trust that the Allmother still acted in the world and expected her people to . . . to what? What did Mother Ge want her people to do?

Confused, cotton-headed, overwhelmed by thoughts that had chased themselves around and around as she slept and now wouldn't leave her alone, Deerchaser rubbed the heels of both hands against her eyes, blocking the red of her eyelids with the black of her body. It reminded her too much of the dream of the dark-sun, and she shuddered.

"Deerchaser!" a woman called.

She looked around and saw Laughingbird striding toward her. Deerchaser greeted her clan-sister. "You're a long way from home."

Laughingbird twisted her hands together. Her face looked pinched. "I thought you should hear this from a friend."

"What is it?"

"Starflower—you remember her, from the moontime hut, asking questions about Rush. She says he . . ." Laughingbird took a deep breath. She unclasped her hands and with trembling fingers pulled a hair out of her eyes. In a shaky voice, she went on: "He forced himself on her."

Ice flooded Deerchaser as she tried to make sense of the words. Her heart pounded so hard, she staggered, off-balance. She struggled to breathe, but a weight lay on her chest.

Laughingbird rushed forward and grabbed her, holding her up.

Dimly she felt as if a feather had drifted down from the sky to land on one finger. It perched there, presenting a perilous choice. The slightest movement, the merest breath could send it spiraling downward—but on which side?

What did it matter? What did anything matter?

Gradually she took strength from her friend's embrace and stiffened her knees, her spine. She pressed against the other woman's shoulders to pull back, ease away.

Deerchaser knew she had to make a choice but couldn't see what it was: between Rush and . . . and what? She had to think.

Could he have done such a terrible thing? That, she couldn't believe. Rush was used to women offering themselves to him, as Starflower had evidently done. But if the girl had then rejected him in favor of Spadefoot, would he have sought revenge? Could he have hurt a woman, any woman? No. Impossible. Let alone Starflower, a child half his age.

"When? When was this?" she asked hoarsely.

"Last night. I came as soon as I heard. Better that you find out from a friend."

"Last night?" Deerchaser frowned. She hadn't stayed the entire night, but surely he wouldn't have wanted another woman after she left.

Even if Rush had energy enough to slake any lingering desires, only a monster could do such a thing. Even when she had hated Rush for deserting her, she had never thought him capable of harming anyone.

"Deerchaser?"

"She's lying." Deerchaser stared at Laughingbird, willing her friend's belief. "Starflower wasn't with him last night."

"How do you know?"

"Because I was."

Laughingbird placed a gentle hand on Deerchaser's shoulder and leaned closer. Quietly, wearing pity on her face, she said, "That can't be true. Someone saw him with her."

The morning sunlight, feeble as it was, seemed to dim even further. The previous night, with Rush, Deerchaser had experienced a glimmer of hope that this time might be different, that finally she could find affection, consolation, maybe even love. Now that ember of warmth and light was being extinguished.

Like before, when Rush had left Crookstaff Village the first time, she saw her chance at happiness disappearing, her own inner sun—the thing that she had finally realized lit her up and made her real—being swallowed by despair.

Last time, too young to know better, she had accepted that he was gone, and she had gone on without him, patching her broken heart back together. This time she would fight.

⋀⋀

Deerchaser sat with her mother under the vatto as she had done just the day before. "I have to speak with Knobbyroot."

Her mother looked up in surprise from the basket she was waterproofing with a coating of mesquite pitch. "Really? Whatever for?"

Deerchaser couldn't remember any other occasion when she had sought out his company; her mother had good reason for being curious. "I need his help."

One of the headmen of Cloud-Leaf Clan, he also served on the village council. If the clan believed Starflower rather than Deerchaser—taking the side of one clan-daughter over another—the entire village council would soon be sitting in judgment on Rush.

She wouldn't expect Knobbyroot to speak up for the Canalmaster. Their most recent discussion—just the previous day, she realized—had given her to understand that her mother's mate believed the Rainsinger, that he actually thought there was no more use for the Watermasters because the Ta'atchul would send rain to everyone who worshipped them, or pretended to.

Nor did she think she could exert any influence over Knobbyroot. But if she could sway her mother to her side . . .

She managed to relate what Laughingbird had told her and didn't break down in the telling. Hopeful, she waited for her mother to agree that this false accusation had to be stopped.

Instead, her mother set the basket aside and murmured, "This isn't a good time to take up with a Watermaster. Not with the canals still broken and everyone fearful of the Wilders."

"I'm not taking up with anyone," Deerchaser said. "It was just one night. Surely I can spend one night with a man and not have people supposing I'm his!"

"But you were his once before, weren't you?"

Deerchaser hesitated as she recalled feeling that her whole life had darkened when he left, all those turnings ago. "You said yesterday that one shouldn't condemn a man based on rumor. I would remind you of that. It hurts to be the target of gossip. Especially when the things being said about you are false."

"Why should I care that the man who hurt you is finally receiving justice?" Her mother, forehead furrowed, gazed at her. A flame tattooed above her left eyebrow stood out on the skin where it folded.

"Hardly justice, if it's founded on a lie."

"To protect you," her mother told her, "I would say anything. Especially a lie. Rumors that are untrue can be useful—if they're believable."

Deerchaser leaned closer. "Are you saying you started a rumor about Rush and Starflower?" If that's all it was, her mother could take back the rumor, admit to starting it out of motherly protectiveness.

"No, not that."

Disappointment struck like a fist in her stomach, driving out her rising hope. "What, then? What else have you done?" Her mother had talked about her with the Seedkeeper and with Knobbyroot. Who else?

"Don't worry, I said nothing about you. I just told people that I'd heard there was a caliche pick in that priest's body and shells in his hand."

"The rumor about the Wilders killing him came from you?"

"With you always criticizing the priesthood, I knew you'd get blamed for his death if I didn't do something," her mother explained. "Especially when the Seedkeeper said the man drowned from dizzyweed poisoning."

Deerchaser blinked. "But surely the priests take dizzyweed all the time. Why would I have anything to do with it?"

"He *drowned.*"

As Littlereed had done. But still it made no sense. "How would I even have given the dizzyweed to the priest?"

Her mother looked startled. "I don't know. People heard 'dizzyweed' and 'drowned' and asked me if you'd said anything."

"You didn't think they were just worried I might be upset?" Deerchaser shook her head. While she could understand her mother's protectiveness, the gossiping could have terrible consequences for the Wilders—and all who depended on them. "But that's all the more reason for defending Rush against this false accusation. Stirring up trouble with the Wilders is one thing. To let it affect the Watermasters is another matter. The farmers need the Watermasters, whatever Knobbyroot thinks."

"The Seedkeeper said the Watermasters can take care of themselves. You have only us, now that you've left the clan."

"Who is this 'us,' if you won't go to Knobbyroot and ask for his help?"

"I won't ask him to help the Canalmaster. Not after the Rainsinger's proclamation. Taking the side of the Wilders and Watermasters over the farmfolk would be too risky."

Deerchaser saw the determination in her mother's set jaw and un-blinking eyes. She wouldn't be easily persuaded. But Deerchaser had an arrow in her quiver she had hoped never to use. She took a deep breath and let it out again, slowly, steadying her heart, preparing a final shot. "If you get Knobbyroot to bring me as a witness against Starflower, and let the clan decide whose side to take—hers or mine—I'll return to Cloud-Leaf Clan."

Eagerly her mother said, "You'll stop going out with the hunters? And never take dizzyweed again?"

Deerchaser hesitated: she didn't know where she would live, what she would do all day, every day. She looked at her mother's partly waterproofed basket, at the immaculately swept courtyard. She wouldn't be needed for home tasks. Knobbyroot did what needed doing in the fields, and she could never work beside him. In the end, though, the choice was clear.

Without her on the hunt, the deerfolk could still find their prey—though it would take longer—and still help feed the village. Without Rush as Canalmaster, the heronfolk would be in disarray, under attack from the Rainsinger and with half the farmers hostile toward them. The canals would fail; the Rainsinger's desire for blood would doom her people.

Deerchaser felt the weight of the decision settle onto her shoulders. "I will," she said. "If you will also tell people these rumors about the Wilders killing the priest are false."

"Yes, of course."

Once they had sworn to the terms, they went to find Knobbyroot. Deerchaser followed her mother out of the compound and around the back to where he sat on a reed mat. He was shaping an animal figure out of willow twigs. He motioned for her to be seated on a second reed mat, conveniently placed as though he had expected her—or, more likely, some other visitor had already come and gone.

At the prompting of his raised eyebrow, her mother said softly, "She's come to talk about this accusation lodged against the Canalmaster."

"News spreads quickly." He looked back at the skeletal figure and bent a few more twigs into place.

"I have to be there, at the clan assembly," Deerchaser said.

"You know that's impossible." He didn't take his eyes off his project. "No one outside his family and hers can attend. Other than the clan elders."

His family? Who would that be? "I am a witness to his actions. My testimony can free him."

"A witness. You were there?" He stopped working on the little figurine. He leaned toward her, eyes glittering as he searched her face.

She swallowed. "I spent the night with him."

"The whole night through, until morning?"

She didn't allow herself to hesitate. "Yes."

"I see." Knobbyroot studied her, still with that piercing intensity.

She tried to shine with trustworthiness, even though her entire body felt closed off and dark, all her muscles drawn taut, even her skin too tight.

He asked, "You're certain of his innocence?"

"Absolutely."

He nodded slowly, then rolled the half-completed figurine over and over, absently. "There have been things said of you, as well, most especially in recent days. Are you prepared to stand against those who doubt you?"

Not doubt her word, but doubt her. She tried to unlock her clenched teeth to speak calmly. "If you mean my visions, they're genuine. The Allmother speaks to me. Where the hunt should go, what the spirit-song should be, which arrow will fly true."

Her mother's mouth tightened, and Deerchaser remembered what she had vowed only moments earlier.

"Your criticisms of the Stormbringers . . ." Knobbyroot said. "Do you also claim divine inspiration in that?"

"You know I do."

"To speak against the priesthood is a dangerous thing."

"Is it right for them to speak against Mother Ge, to offer blood to their false gods? They've already perverted the reasons for the Cornmaidens' very existence, taken the place of the Smokemothers in our oldest ceremonies, and now wish to replace the Watermasters. What more will you let them get away with?"

"Most would argue that what we have gained from them is greater than anything that may have been lost," he murmured.

"So where will it stop?" She flung out her arms in a wild, childish gesture. "What will happen when they place themselves above the will of the people?"

His fingers tightened on the split-twig figurine. She heard something crack. "Such a thing would never happen. Sensible people see that the Stormbringers are right. The rest will come around soon. The will of the people must be done."

Deerchaser quoted to him, "'She is the world, and the world lives in her. Her blood fills the rivers.' What about the will of the people who still hold to Mother Ge?"

"You come to me with these same tired complaints against the Stormbringers, exposing yourself as an unbeliever still." He shook his head. "Why should I have anything to do with you, let alone take the side of the Canalmaster? I've put up with you, Deerchaser, for your mother's sake—"

Her mother interrupted. "She has promised me that she'll return to Cloud-Leaf Clan and cut herself off from the deerfolk forever." She went to stand behind him. Her white-knuckled fingers closed around his shoulders. "Please! Do this for me, out of the love you have for me."

For several long heartbeats, Knobbyroot stared at Deerchaser with eyes hot and angry. At last he said, "You know I cannot disappoint your mother." He put down the twig animal, and his hands went up to cover his mate's. "Not for any other reason would I do this."

"I understand." Deerchaser nodded. She felt exhausted, as much by her success as their clash of wills. What would she do now? But she refused to give him the satisfaction of seeing her inward quaking. She sat still, as upright as her spine would make her.

"You are prepared to swear to the clan that you were with Rush of the heronfolk all night and that you know, for a certainty, he is innocent of the charge laid against him by Earth-Holder's daughter, Starflower of Cloud-Leaf Clan?"

"I swear it."

Knobbyroot's lip curled. "You have much confidence in this man."

"So we have a bargain?" Deerchaser wanted it said outright.

"We have a bargain."

Deerchaser sat quietly in the feasting plaza where the elders of Cloud-Leaf Clan were assembled to hear the claim against Rush. The satisfaction that had come over Knobbyroot when he agreed to bring her before the elders worried her. She had spent a considerable amount of time trying to figure out what cold calculation had settled his anger.

Maybe he wanted Deerchaser humiliated again, used and abandoned by a man who had left her once before. More likely he expected her to turn farmer and figured she would be embarrassed to betray her clan-sister, a bit of disloyalty that would be frowned on in the best of times.

Although she regretted what it might do to Starflower, speaking the truth was necessary. She knew that. A sharper regret arose from denying the deerfolk and swearing her loyalty only to Cloud-Leaf Clan. And then there was her suspicion about what had made Knobbyroot so smug.

She had a disturbing sense of being trapped, like a deer being driven into a blind arroyo with no way out.

At the other edge of the plaza, beyond the hooded and cloaked clan elders sitting in judgment, Rush walked around the corner of the nearest house-compound. His face was grim, his eyes dull. Two men of the clan flanked him.

She took in his defeated expression. He looked like a man who had grappled with death—and lost.

The next moment, Rush spotted her. She shivered at the intermingled rage and pain that came over his face, driving out the dullness from his eyes.

"Deerchaser! Tell them it isn't true!"

I will, she wanted to say, but she had been cautioned to silence until the interrogator invited her to speak.

The elders murmured. The masked interrogator, an elder chosen by lot, told them, "This clan-daughter has come forward as a witness."

Rush's gaze wavered from hers. Confusion spread across his face. "As witness? Then she isn't the accuser?"

He thought she could do something like that? Her throat went suddenly dry. A lump in it threatened to choke her.

The interrogator thumped a crook-headed staff against the ground. "The guilty man will be silent—of his own accord or otherwise," he ordered.

"He's not guilty!" Deerchaser exclaimed.

"This witness," said the interrogator, turning his head toward her, "will be offered the same arrangement as the accused—be silent or be silenced!"

Shocked by the hostility in his voice, Deerchaser shut her mouth. She had never been a party to a clan hearing before and had no idea whether adversarial treatment by the interrogator was normal.

"Who is—" Rush began.

At a gesture from the interrogator, one of the clansmen behind Rush slipped a gag between his teeth, wedging his mouth open. She gathered, from the awkward angle of his shoulders, that his hands were already bound behind him.

When Deerchaser started to protest again, the interrogator looked out of the narrow eyeholes of the molded leather mask with such wrath that she swallowed the words. The mask was a sign of his office, an indication that he was not to show favoritism or prejudice. It didn't seem to be working.

"You swear to speak truth?" he demanded of her.

One of the other elders said, "She bore a son to this man. Why should anything she says be believed?"

Under the interrogator's intimidating stare, Deerchaser said nothing while some of the elders argued among themselves about whether her testimony should be allowed. Knobbyroot, hooded like the others but recognizable by his voice, surprised her by pointing out that her certainty of innocence on Rush's behalf was all that mattered. The protests subsided.

"With that settled," the interrogator declared, "Deerchaser, daughter of Cloud-Leaf Clan, may speak."

Within the clan, decisions were made by consensus. Deerchaser had counted on that; all she had to do was convince a few of the elders that Starflower was lying, and there would not be enough support to take Rush before the village council.

She repeated her claim that she had been with Rush all night. Through his gag, he couldn't contradict her outright, but he grimaced and shook his head vehemently.

"Then what?" asked the interrogator.

"What you mean?"

"Did he accompany you through the village, walk you to your hut?"

Deerchaser couldn't say yes, she realized; someone might have seen her go. Someone always was watching. "No. I left alone," she admitted.

The interrogator raised his voice. "We have three different stories here, with no way to determine whose is the truth. But there is another witness." He made a motion with his hand.

Two more men of the clan escorted Spadefoot into the plaza. Except for his topknot of hair and his tattoos, he might have been mistaken for any man of the farmfolk in his simple kilt and shirt and sandals.

The interrogator looked at him. "As a representative of the Stormbringers, your independence could be questioned."

"Why is that?" he challenged. "I am vow-bound to serve this village. I have no allegiance to any of the parties."

Deerchaser bit down on her lower lip, hard. No one dared say, in public, that everyone knew the priests hated the Watermasters. Would anyone bring up her own dislike of the priests, which apparently was nearly as well-known?

Knobbyroot declared, "Standing as father to the one clan-daughter, I say let the Stormbringer speak. He has sworn vows to the Ta'atchul, and there can be no stronger testament to his worth." His reasoning convinced the holdouts to agree, although Deerchaser thought obedience to Mother Ge would be a more desirable indication of a man's character.

"You swear to speak truth?" the interrogator asked Spadefoot.

"I swear."

"Did you see this woman, Deerchaser of Cloud-Leaf Clan, leave the Canalmaster's quarters?"

Spadefoot didn't look at her. "I did, yes. I saw her slip from his sleeping quarters well before dawn."

She closed her eyes as her lie—under oath—was exposed.

"Was she alone?" came the question from the interrogator.

"Yes, though the Canalmaster came out a short time after. He was too late to catch her. She had passed out of sight once he got down to the path below the Masterholding. He looked for her, I think, but evidently didn't know where to find her."

"So she was not with the Canalmaster all night long?" the interrogator asked.

"No. But when she left, she didn't seem upset. She was walking as a satisfied woman does."

A look from the interrogator silenced the stir among the elders caused by Spadefoot's words—except one, who asked Spadefoot, in a crackly female voice, "Why were you watching?"

The interrogator chided her: "I am to ask the questions."

She turned toward him. "I remember when you used to put beans up your nose. Don't tell me to be quiet. If you were asking the right questions, I wouldn't have to interrupt." She addressed Spadefoot: "Go on, young Stormbringer. Tell me, why were you atop the temple, watching the goings-on below?"

He hesitated. "I thought I heard a woman scream some moments before and was curious where the sound came from. I waited for it to come again, but it was only the once."

"A scream," she repeated. "You heard this from the heights of the temple and through the walls of the Canalmaster's sleeping quarters?" She sounded doubtful.

"I was on top of the temple, yes."

"And this scream came before Deerchaser left the Canalmaster's quarters?"

Her gaze went to Deerchaser, who explained, "I was awoken by a dream. An unpleasant one. I might have cried out."

The interrogator stamped his staff a few times to silence the buzz of interest her statement stirred.

One of the elders commented, "A dream, you say. One of these visitations from the goddess we've heard so much about?"

"Too much dizzyweed," someone said. Laughter erupted.

The interrogator's staff pounded so many times, it stirred up a cloud of dust around him before the plaza became quiet.

"Deerchaser, clan-daughter," the interrogator said, "you swore before the wise elders assembled here that you would tell them the truth. But two others have contradicted your testimony. Do you deny Spadefoot's claim to have seen you leave before the night was over?"

"No." She cast an apologetic look at Rush, who met her gaze unhappily.

The interrogator declared, "Your guilt in forswearing yourself is proved, and your punishment prescribed by long custom. You are to be whipped, vow-breaker, until you bleed."

"What? No!" she protested.

Rush roared around his gag and rammed his shoulder into one of the men who served as his escort. More rushed in to subdue him even as Deer-chaser cried out for them not to hurt him. Others grabbed her to keep her from running to him.

The interrogator stabbed his staff at her. "Taking a woman against her will is an act unforgivable, and lying to protect a man who would so abuse another is the worst thing a woman can do! You think on that while you suffer the touch of the willow. For betraying your clan-sister, you deserve the pain that is coming to you!"

"He is innocent!" she shrieked, clawing and striking out against those who held her but unable to do anything as Rush collapsed to the ground under the weight of half a dozen men.

Spadefoot

As the sun goes down in the west, the songs of fire will bring it back.
Standing before me in the land, my brothers sing it home.

—FROM THE NEW FIRE CEREMONIES

Spadefoot watched Deerchaser attack the men keeping her away from Rush. She struck with hands and feet and spat foul threats at those who held her. Locks of hair twisted like snakes, torn loose from her fishtail plaits. That odd streak of white shone brilliantly in the sun.

Unlike her, Spadefoot kept still and deliberately quiet, his face impassive. He knew his birthmark and tattoos served nearly as well as the interrogator's mask to hide his emotions from others—if not from himself.

Guilt sat heavy on his shoulders. In exposing her untruth, he had grabbed the wrong end of the idea: tail rather than teeth, as they say. Until a few moments ago, he had felt certain she loathed the Canalmaster and was Rush's accuser. He had come forward as a rescuer to nobly defend Rush against an accusation he assumed to be false.

Now he saw Deerchaser had the same intention.

How to undo what he had done? "I did see the Canalmaster—" he started. *Go back to his quarters,* he would have finished.

The masked interrogator cut him off. "The punishment of our clan-daughter is purely a clan matter. We have no need of you anymore." He motioned with his staff for Spadefoot to go.

Spadefoot's blood heated at the dismissive gesture. He rocked forward onto the balls of his feet and opened his mouth to protest. But he forced himself to subside. In truth, it *was* a clan matter. If he interfered, if he claimed some privilege by virtue of being a Stormbringer, he would be no better than Morning Green, overturning tradition for his own purposes.

But whipping her for trying to protect another? That went too far.

A quick glance at the people filling the feast ground showed frowns and wrinkled brows suggesting that many of her clan agreed with him. Yet no one, not even her closest family, stepped forward to keep her from being dragged, struggling and protesting, toward a vatto at the end of the plaza.

The interrogator's choice of punishment would not be overruled, Spadefoot realized. There were too many witnesses, and so her half truth could not be ignored.

That was his fault. His testimony had contradicted hers, and who would dare challenge the son of the Rainsinger? Yet in this instance, some individuals had done just that.

The interrogator, for one, ordering him to leave the clan hearing. Spadefoot jammed his thumbs into his belt and tapped his forefingers together, the only movement he allowed himself as he pondered the unusual resistance to his priestly authority.

Knobbyroot, for another. When he had gone to the man earlier that morning to have Deerchaser withdraw her complaint, her mother's mate had deliberately withheld the information that she was not Rush's accuser. Knobbyroot had let Spadefoot reveal his knowledge that Deerchaser had left Rush's hut the previous night on her own, unharmed and seemingly happy.

Spadefoot's first mistake had been to assume something with no proof. His second had been to trust Knobbyroot. Those two errors in judgment had brought him here to the Cloud-Leaf assembly and condemned Deerchaser to a brutal punishment.

He would rather have left. Instead, he forced himself to stay and watch the results of his interference. Although the lesson would be more painful for Deerchaser than for himself, he figured that the very unfairness of that—when he was the one who had done wrong—would make it stick in his memory.

At another level, he had to admit that the attitudes of Knobbyroot and the interrogator were what he had been working toward: to be seen as just another priest, not the son of the Rainsinger and most certainly not the one of prophecy, the savior of his people. Still, it stung his pride.

Two of the young clansmen held a weeping Deerchaser upright while another stripped off her tunic and shirt, leaving her breasts bare. She tried to cover herself, but the one holding her clothes stopped her.

The clan-grannie who had questioned Spadefoot said, "For pity's sake, turn her around!"

They did, so that the crowd saw only her unprotected back. Then they took her hands and pulled them behind a thick upright post that held up one corner of the vatto's brush roof.

Keeping silent took every bit of will Spadefoot had. But he could remain here as witness only if he played rabbit and froze, reminding nobody of his presence. His hands slowly tightened into fists and his back teeth hurt, so tightly was his jaw clenched, as he battled the urge to demand her release.

Deerchaser's face was pressed against the pole. Her arms wrapped around it in an unwilling embrace, wrists tied together on the other side.

She pulled against her bindings, the muscles in her back straining visibly. She said not a word.

Spadefoot, chilled by guilt, could no longer bear the sight. He shifted his gaze to Rush, though what met his eyes there did nothing to ease his conscience.

Rush lay where he had fallen. His eyes were closed, but his chest still moved with his breathing.

The bruise on Rush's temple reminded Spadefoot of the task the Canalmaster had recently undertaken on his behalf. That was another bit of interference that had resulted in violence, all unintended on Spadefoot's part. Rush had done nothing to deserve such ill treatment.

True, Spadefoot had lost his temper and gotten into a shouting match with Rush a few days earlier, but he had regretted it almost immediately. And it was not really about whatever he had made it out to be, anyway.

As the midwinter festival drew near, he felt angry almost all the time, from rising in the morning to falling asleep at night. He had come so close to finding out his true parentage and thus escaping the prophecy—and then Nighthawk had died. After that, Rush seemed his only way of getting the information he needed from the Wilders. And evidently Rush had done so; at the very least, he knew enough to guess the identity of Spadefoot's blood father.

Foolishly, Spadefoot had lashed out instead of letting Rush reveal, in his own time, what he had learned. Spadefoot had offended the man who could help him prove that he was not the Rainsinger's son . . . not the one of prophecy . . . not the one born to be the savior of the People of Two Rivers.

Spadefoot wiped beads of sweat off his upper lip, then tasted salt on his tongue. He became aware of dampness on his forehead, on his neck, in the hollow of his breastbone as his heart thudded hard against his ribs. He was afraid, he realized. Of what, he could not be sure . . . yet he felt a darkness descending upon the plaza as surely as night followed the sinking sun. But the sun still shone upon the clanfolk assembled there in the place where they often ate together, laughed, listened to stories, sang and danced.

He looked again to where Deerchaser stood—naked above the waist, wrists and ankles tied to keep her in place. He could not recall ever hearing about, much less witnessing, a whipping. He had lived his first ten turnings in the village, fostered by a pair of elderly sisters who had protected him from such things, if they ever occurred. During the next seven or eight turnings, he had been so influenced by Morning Green that everyone outside the vow-brethren seemed unimportant. Others were to be used, as he had used Rush.

And then Nighthawk had told him the shocking news that Morning Green was not his father, and Spadefoot had tried to find out who was.

Everything had become twisted after that.

Rush stirred on the ground. The interrogator moved his hand sharply. He said something Spadefoot could not hear.

One of the hooded elders near the vatto picked up an olla from the ground and dumped its contents on the Watermaster, causing him to sputter and flounder like a hooked fish on a canal bank. Someone nearby pulled out the gag that had been shoved into his mouth. He gasped for air.

Deerchaser turned her head to watch. Tracks of tears streaked her cheeks. She pulled back, the muscles in her back and arms flexing; Spadefoot wondered whether the bonds would cut into her wrists with her valiant efforts to get free. And would she even notice?

"Leave him alone!" she shouted.

"Don't do this to her!" Rush pushed himself onto hands and knees, sat back on his heels. His dripping head wove back and forth as if he could not hold it still—or perhaps in an attempt to clear it. "Whip me instead. This was my doing, none of hers."

The interrogator pointed his staff toward Rush like a spear. "Do you confess, then, to forcing yourself on her clan-sister?"

"Who?" demanded Rush in a rough voice. "Who is my accuser? Let her stand forth!"

Spadefoot thought that was as clear a statement of innocence as there could be, if Rush did not know what woman had cause to accuse him.

"You tell us," the interrogator insisted. "Speak her name! Confess! Confess, and we'll let Deerchaser go free."

A few other men arrived at a trot. One bore a large olla, capped to keep the water from sloshing out. Another carried a handful of willow branches.

Spadefoot gathered that those were to whip her with. He hoped the water was intended to clean her up once the punishment was done and to soothe her whip-torn skin with its cool touch.

Vow-breaker she was and would be lashed for it until the blood ran. To his mind, this clan's punishment was a blood ritual far more inhuman than the one Morning Green planned, the one Deerchaser had been crying out against.

Spadefoot's stomach twisted as he thought about being a part of this terrible event. No, not just a part, he corrected himself—the cause. He had brought it about.

Hoping someone would step in and pardon her and relieve him of his guilt, he looked around the assembled clan. Standing at the front, watching Deerchaser, her own cheeks glinting with tears, was a woman he took for her mother, small in height but curvy. Next to her, with one arm placed around her slumped shoulders, was another slight female.

Heavily in argument were the interrogator and a cluster of clan elders.

From their passionate gestures of negation and uncomfortable glances at Deerchaser, Spadefoot guessed they were having trouble finding anyone willing to wield the lash.

But plenty seemed willing to see her get whipped; more people began to arrive, in ones and twos. Their avid expressions told him their motivation had little to do with justice. They would find satisfaction in her suffering and then go home without another thought to why she had been put through such misery. The reluctance to actually be the one to hold the whip just gave more time for everyone to hear about the gruesome spectacle and assemble to watch it.

So we are not such a gentle and peaceful people after all, he thought, recalling that Deerchaser had made that claim in her protest against the deer-heart ritual the Rainsinger planned. We are a bloody-minded, suspicious, fearful people.

He wondered what, after this day, her opinion of her own clan would be. Would she ever think of them as gentle and peaceful again? How could she ever go back among them with anything like trust?

Raised voices called Spadefoot's attention to the knot of clan elders.

One man protested, "You shouldn't use her punishment as a threat to make him speak!"

The interrogator argued, "She stood up before us and lied, trying to free a guilty man."

"Guilty? Or innocent?" the other man shot back. "We don't know that for certain yet. Not until the village council conducts an inquest. We are here," he reminded the others, "only to decide whether to take the side of the accuser, our clan-daughter, in that inquest. The council will determine whether he is guilty or innocent."

A hooded Knobbyroot, his voice now familiar to Spadefoot, waded into the argument. "There will be no time for an inquest until after the Sun-Turning. Will you let him walk free until then, like an innocent man? Would you risk having him do this to other daughters of other clans, perhaps even to your own child, your own mate?"

"Were *you* there," said the one who protested the clan's hasty judgment, "to see this alleged assault, to make you so certain of his guilt? If so, perhaps you could explain why you did nothing to stop him."

"*I* was there," came a young female voice, tremulous and halting, from behind Deerchaser's mother.

Spadefoot watched as the clan-daughter—he guessed from her words that this was the accuser—stepped around the two crying women. She unwrapped her headscarf and lifted the veil up off her face to reveal a bloodied nose and upper lip, every feature bruised and swollen.

Though beaten and frightened, she was still recognizable to Spadefoot as Starflower, beautiful just the day before.

Hot fury surged in him. His fists ached to inflict the same kind of abuse on Rush. A voice of reason in his head reminded him that he had believed Rush innocent before he knew the accuser's identity. That it was Starflower should make no difference to him.

And yet it did. Seeing her bruises, her dried blood, her poor face enraged him.

She said, "I beg of you, don't whip Deerchaser. She knew nothing of what was done to me."

But she was not looking at her clan-sister. Starflower had eyes for no one but Rush, lying on the ground, his gaze locked with hers.

Spadefoot tried to read her expression through the discolorations and deformities. The longer he studied her face, the more he thought she was apologetic, not fearful or distressed. If Rush was innocent . . .

Then his anger should not be wasted on the accused man. It should be turned on whoever had assaulted her.

Rush said something, a garbled, indistinguishable word. He spat to clear his throat. "*You* have done this? *Why?*"

In his own head, Spadefoot repeated the question. Why would any woman make such a claim if it were not so?

But the interrogator evidently had no doubt about her honesty. He moved forward and settled his big hands gently on Starflower's shoulders. "You needn't answer him, little clan-daughter. Turn away. You aren't obliged to be anywhere close to such a one as the Canalmaster."

"He has a right—" Deerchaser's words were muffled. She broke off with a strangled cough, then turned her face to the other side of the pole. "He has a right to face his accuser."

"She's little more than a child," the interrogator said. "She has a soft heart. She would even free *you,* when for all she knows, you plotted with the Canalmaster to assault her."

Deerchaser retorted, "Soft heart? You mean she has a pretty face, and that's all you care about."

Spadefoot realized he was hearing no defense from Rush, only Deerchaser. He turned his head and saw that Rush was once again gagged. Two large men with many-braided hair, their tunics flying the heron-feather-blue ribbons of the Watermasters, stood over him.

"It isn't fair that Deerchaser should be punished," he heard Starflower say. He went back to watching her as he tried to figure out what was going on in her mind.

"She lied," the interrogator told her.

"So did he." Starflower pointed a shaking finger at Knobbyroot and then spoke to him directly. "You promised me a hearing by the clan. You told me I would be the one to determine Rush's punishment. I didn't want *her* involved. Or all these people."

Still directing her plaint to Knobbyroot, she said, "It was supposed to be me and Rush and you and a few other elders. I could have endured that. But this? No." She slashed both hands sideways in emphasis. "If there's an inquest, everyone in the village will know what happened to me."

Spadefoot supposed that was true anyway; gossip put its sandals on early in Crookstaff Village. But sympathetic though he might be toward Starflower, her embarrassment would not be the worst in this.

There was Deerchaser, tied up, mostly naked, and waiting to be publicly whipped. How could the cruelty of her own family, her own clan, not mark her forever?

Beyond that, Rush's reputation would never recover, even if he could be proved innocent. There would always be some—particularly after Morning Green's recent proclamation—who would believe him guilty. The people of Crookstaff Village would be divided beyond all recovery.

Spadefoot's hands felt clammy as he thought of the other thing he had hoped Rush could do: prove the Wilders innocent of killing Nighthawk. He opened his fists to expose his sweaty palms to the cooling touch of the air.

Knobbyroot sighed. "I'm sorry, child, you must have misunderstood what I said. Such a serious offense has to go to the village, once the clan decides it is borne out."

"But—"

The interrogator said something to her that made her fall silent. He gestured for a clan-auntie to lead her away. She kept casting looks back over her shoulder at Rush.

Spadefoot watched until she was out of sight. As she walked haltingly away, he could hear the clan elders arguing over who would lash Deerchaser until she bled.

Despite all the power Deerchaser attributed to the Stormbringers—and rightly so—Spadefoot was powerless here, where her people held sway. He struggled to come up with a solution that would help any one of the three caught up in this mess, but he failed, as useless as a snake thrashing about after its head had been cut off.

In the end, the interrogator himself had to whip Deerchaser. His hands shook as he sorted through the willow branches and selected one of a middling length and thickness.

He stood behind Deerchaser and began to apply the lash, leaving welts on her back. Well-toned muscles shuddered at first in the triangle that led from her shoulders down toward her waist. After several strokes, her entire body began to jerk. Somehow she managed to remain silent.

The interrogator switched hands and moved to her other side, placing the lash in a set pattern with the strokes overlapping only in the center. It was carefully done, Spadefoot realized, to keep from laying down one blow atop another. The first trickle of blood finally appeared where the skin was struck twice in the same place. The interrogator threw down the willow branch as though it burned him.

The woman Spadefoot assumed was Deerchaser's mother had turned toward the other woman she had been standing with, whose arms encircled her now. The shoulders of both of them heaved. Most others in the crowd just looked stunned.

Spadefoot could not see Starflower anywhere. He hoped she had not been in Deerchaser's line of sight. He had found the spectacle deeply disturbing—all the more so because of Deerchaser's eerie quietness. And he was not a softhearted girl.

"What do we do with her now?" demanded Knobbyroot.

The interrogator said, "Her punishment is finished."

"Do we just take her home like nothing's happened?"

"Of course we do!" her mother cried.

In a thick voice Deerchaser said, "I won't go with you." On the other side of the post, someone squatted close and with a knife freed her ankles. The cords binding her hands had already been cut. She pulled them off with jerky movements as she turned to face everyone who had witnessed the blooding. She grabbed her shirt and held it across her breasts.

"You claimed Cloud-Leaf Clan as your own!" her mother argued.

"Yes, I did. And then your mate betrayed me. He led me into this trap and let it snap shut on me. Cloud-Leaf Clan I am by blood and vow, but I won't stay under the same roof as Knobbyroot. You're mated to a bully and a cheat—he is to blame for having me whipped."

Knobbyroot said, "You got what you deserved."

Wincing with every cautious step, Deerchaser walked toward Rush. She knelt beside him and with her free hand ran trembling fingers down his arm. The other two Watermasters stood nearby, their faces sour, but did not interfere.

"What will you do?" asked the hooded clan-grannie who had questioned Spadefoot earlier.

Deerchaser continued to stroke Rush, whose expression could not be made out through the dirt and blood as he looked at her. After a long silence, she said, "I have my own hut. I will stay there, as I have for these many moons."

"Alone?" the clan-grannie asked.

"Let Rush come with me. I will see that he—"

"No," said the interrogator.

"But—"

The woman who had been comforting Deerchaser's mother stepped forward. "I'll come home with you. You shouldn't be alone. And your back will need tending."

Deerchaser shook her head. "You don't have to worry about me, Laughingbird. Stay with your children."

"Don't be stubborn. They can do without me for a few days, just as they do when I go to the moontime hut."

Casting her a wan smile, Deerchaser accepted the offer.

"And I also," said an older woman in the green tunic of a bonemender. "There may be scarring, but with the right herbs you should heal quickly enough." She shot the interrogator an accusatory glare and helped Deerchaser to her feet.

Spadefoot winced at Deerchaser's gasps of pain as she straightened.

Once standing, she resisted being led away. "What about Rush?"

"Yes, what about Rush?" asked one of the clan elders. "There was no answer to Knobbyroot's question—are we to let him go free as though he were innocent? There will be no time to call together an inquest until after the Sun-Turning. And what of Starflower if we do so? Why should she walk in fear through the village? What agonies of the mind are we prepared to condemn her to, this clan-daughter who did nothing wrong?"

Knobbyroot crossed his arms over his chest. "We can't risk having him spend his rage on the next woman who crosses him. We all know he can't be trusted. He proved that many turnings ago, when he left Deerchaser with a child in her belly. I say we determine his punishment right now, and that it be more painful than Deerchaser's—a stoning, I say, followed by exile forever from the People of Two Rivers."

"No!" shouted Deerchaser.

Starflower, all eyes on her, pushed her way to the front of the group. "I will take him as my mate!" she exclaimed. "I will see to it that he never hurts any woman."

In surprise the interrogator asked, "You would be mated to the one who attacked you?"

Her gaze darted from one face to another.

The clan-grannie who had questioned Spadefoot said, "He isn't the one, is he?"

Starflower just stood there twisting her hands together.

To the interrogator, Deerchaser said, "If she won't answer, ask Spadefoot what he was talking with her about yesterday. Ask him why Rush is the one she chose to accuse."

Spadefoot wondered uneasily where Deerchaser was going to take this line of questioning.

Her eyes locked with his. "Ask him why he met Starflower and his own vow-brother up by the river the day before the priest was found dead."

Spadefoot's stomach clenched. *What do you know?* he wanted to demand. *What did you see?* Instead of revealing too much with such questions, he crossed his arms and pretended indifference.

"You brought him here to bear witness against me—now ask him!" she insisted.

The interrogator, frowning, glanced at him. Spadefoot curled his upper lip and shook his head, as though what she claimed was so ridiculous that it deserved no response. His shame grew. *Later,* he sent out to her, though of course she would not hear, *I will make things right.*

The interrogator said, "It's no good, Deerchaser. You can't cast your guilt onto someone else. And we all know how you feel about the priests. Don't ask us to believe you again."

Deerchaser stood for a moment, openly trembling, wadding up the cotton of her shirt. She sent a hot look around the plaza in which her clan eyed her with disapproval, their sympathy evidently all used up. "Cowards, the lot of you," she said.

That stirred them into protestations of how they were not the ones doing wrong.

Spadefoot noted that Starflower had disappeared again and Rush now stood, held up by the two other Watermasters. A cloth still covered his mouth. Evidently he was not to have any say in what happened to either himself or Deerchaser. Spadefoot saw his own seething anger reflected in Rush's eyes.

To quiet the murmuring crowd, the interrogator pounded his staff. He announced, "The Canalmaster will be turned over to the heronfolk. Under condition that they keep him away from the village until the inquest."

"Watermasters!" Knobbyroot's mouth worked, and he spat in the dirt. "We're to rely on the Watermasters? The same who allow our riverbanks to be infested by the Wilders? The same who stand by and wring their hands in the face of a prophesied doom? The same who have failed us over and over again, their only claim on us being their ability to keep the canals running—and now proving unable to do even that? What do you expect the Watermasters to do if he runs off again?"

"What do you care?" Deerchaser demanded. "So he goes back to Sky River. How is that any different from exile?"

The interrogator began, "His people can—"

One of the two Watermasters beside Rush interrupted. "I, Holdsbreath, am Canalmaster now. This man can no longer claim the protection of the heronfolk. We won't take him. He is yours to do with as you decide."

That caused many in the group to mutter among themselves and cast hostile glances toward Rush, as though the rejection by the Watermasters indicated his guilt. The same Watermasters, Spadefoot thought, who had provided water to the fields since time out of mind, who had built the canals, the great mounds, even the temple. The ones who had saved the People of Two Rivers since well before anyone had dreamed up this prophecy about the savior born of outlander and old blood. And now the farmfolk were turning on them, all because of some words Morning Green had stepped forth and proclaimed. Such a split would be disastrous.

Spadefoot found himself saying, "I will see to him."

Everyone stared at him.

The inquisitor shook his head. "There is no precedent for what you suggest. The heronfolk must be responsible for one of their own."

"But they have refused him," Spadefoot pointed out. "Surely no one can find fault with the Stormbringers taking responsibility for him."

"What will you do with him?" demanded Knobbyroot.

Spadefoot cast a contemptuous glance at the older man. "Do you question me, a Stormbringer of the highest rank?"

"No, of course not," Knobbyroot had sense enough to say. "Only, this is a decision on which you should ask your father—"

"The Rainsinger is busy preparing for the Sun-Turning." Spadefoot met the other's frown with granite calm. "Do not think my youth permits you to take liberties with my authority. What I said earlier, that was not a suggestion. Or a request. The Canalmaster will lodge with the Stormbringers until you declare him innocent or the inquest convenes, at which point the village council will decide his fate. Not Cloud-Leaf Clan."

Spadefoot turned away. He knew he needed to explain himself to Morning Green before anyone else carried the tale to the Rainsinger. "Clean him up and bring him to me at the temple," he ordered over his shoulder.

"Wait!" the interrogator called out.

Knobbyroot hurried to intercept him. "You can't—"

Spadefoot brushed past. He had learned much from observing the Rainsinger. Only a weak man let himself get caught in an argument.

"Spadefoot!"

Startled by the female voice, Spadefoot dropped his pace to a walk and lifted his head, expecting for one absent-minded moment to see Starflower.

For Starflower it was that he had been thinking of, as he jogged back to the temple precinct from the Cloud-Leaf clanlands. Thinking of her accusation and who could have assaulted her, if not Rush. Thinking of the last time he had seen her, just the previous day, after she sought him out to assure him she had told their secret to no one. Thinking about how he had teased her by pretending to think she was the source of the rumor about the Wilders killing Nighthawk.

Had his teasing driven her to commit a desperate act? Backed into a corner, could she perhaps have inflicted the injuries on herself? Was the accusation of Rush—the entire incident he had just observed—his fault?

"Spadefoot!"

The repetition of his name pulled him out of those disturbing thoughts again, focused him on the well-trodden path and the wintry sunshine bright on the plastered walls of house compounds. He looked down the path and found the source of the call: a group of giggling girls drifting toward him. Cornmaidens, obviously. Veiled as required when outside the Smokemothers' compound, they wore long red skirts topped by simple, unadorned cotton tunics nipped in at the waist with matching sashes.

This was a favorite place for Cornmaidens to waylay priests for light flirtation: the nearby wall gave them a place to lean on and a welcome bit of shade, close to the temple gateway and just off the path from the Smokemothers' compound in the old village. Normally Spadefoot would pause and indulge them.

Today there was no time for indulgence.

He glanced at the guard tower above and to the left side of the temple gate. Rainedge, the warder who looked down at him and the Cornmaidens, was more of a rival than a friend. Spadefoot knew Morning Green would hear about this encounter, no matter what was said. But not until after he had made his plea.

"Spadefoot, what happened with the Canalmaster?" asked the first of the four girls as they drew near. "Did he really do something terrible?"

The sweet scent of earthflower indicated that this one was Moonbright, who wore the aromatic love-herb between her breasts in a small pouch suspended from a necklace: a bold effort to capture his heart. Spadefoot knew his evenhanded appreciation of all the Cornmaidens pricked at Moonbright's conceit, though it could never shake her high opinion of herself.

They pressed close to hear his answer. The brush of familiar hands, the fragrance of soaproot in smooth black braids, the remembered taste of salt and a woman's hidden garden upon his tongue stirred him more than Moonbright's earthflower ever could.

"You know I can't stop to talk." He smiled at them all and tried to ease past. "My vow-brothers would be jealous, if here I lingered surrounded by the most beautiful girls in the village, instead of discharging my duties."

Moonbright stayed him with a firm hand on his arm. "Nonsense! We heard you were called as a witness. So, what did you see?"

"Nothing half as interesting as you, my dear Moonbright. Now, I must be away. The Rainsinger is expecting me."

"Of course, of course." She pressed his arm and leaned close to murmur, "It's my night in the rooms again."

One of the other girls, her belly round from a child within, hushed her. "You can't say that."

Spadefoot's mouth quirked in a smile that he quickly hid. Of course Hummingbird would be the one to advise caution; she had more sense than most of her fellow Cornmaidens. And, too, a kinder heart. She was the only Cornmaiden to express her sympathy for his loss after Nighthawk's passing.

Moonbright lifted her chin. "It's only Spadefoot. He wouldn't tell." She pressed his arm. "Would you?"

Spadefoot placed a hand over hers. "She's right, though," he said. "You never know when someone might be listening. Or watching. I wouldn't want you, my dear Moonbright, to get in trouble." He lifted her hand away and pressed a kiss to her fingers before releasing her.

Stormbringers were never supposed to know who awaited them in the sacramental rooms. Cornmaidens and Smokemothers alike disguised their face and form behind veils and cloaks as they walked at night from their compound to the dark rooms in the temple precinct. The rota was made up by the Smokemothers based on arcane rules supposedly handed down by Mother Ge.

A woman was not supposed to know the identity of the Stormbringer who lay with her, either. With his pale skin that gleamed in the dark, Morning Green was the exception. Spadefoot's mother had used that distinctiveness to claim that she had lain with only one priest—Morning Green.

And from that one fact, Spadefoot's entire life-path had been laid out for him. There could be no deviation, so long as he was thought to be the son of the outlander Morning Green.

"What's wrong?" asked Hummingbird.

Spadefoot shook his head and assumed a morose expression—not difficult, given the turn of his thoughts. "Only that I must leave you all, though it breaks my heart." He sighed loudly. "Farewell, my lovelies."

As he left them, their giggles and light chatter resumed.

Again he met the eyes of the gate warder. Feeling time slide by like a flooding river, Spadefoot debated whether to climb up and give instructions to Rainedge to let Rush into the temple precinct. Spadefoot was still known as the son of the Rainsinger, after all. His instructions should be followed here, if nowhere else.

Yet such pridefulness had gotten Deerchaser whipped, Rush beaten while delivering Nighthawk's ashes, and perhaps even Nighthawk killed. Spadefoot dropped his chin as guilt surged through him again, making his footsteps heavy.

He entered the gate but turned away from the ladder that would have let him ascend to the tower and order about his vow-brother. Instead he strode to the right, toward Morning Green's workshop, where he would have to abase himself.

It was no more than he deserved for the much-regretted result of his efforts this day.

As Spadefoot passed from the sun of the temple precinct to the shade of Morning Green's cell, he shivered at the abrupt change. The stench of rot and sweat and urine made his eyes water and his stomach roll.

He swung back toward the doorway and moved his hand in a punctuated arc from head to chest to belly to privates, the required gesture of obeisance to the Ta'atchul. The brilliance outside hammered at his eyes, blinding him to the symbols of the Ta'atchul painted on the walls surrounding the entrance. The voices of fellow vow-brothers and the *who-will-cry-for-me* call of a rock dove seemed muffled, as though that world could not enter the place where the high priest held sway.

From behind, he heard a foot shift.

Spadefoot spun about. His eyes strained to adjust to the dimness as he looked for Morning Green, normally a slash of paleness in the dark. The first thing he saw was a heart lying in a grayish stone basin set on the adobe altar. Only after did he espy the Rainsinger, leaning forward over the basin.

Morning Green cupped the heart in his hands and lifted it above his face. "I will drink the life-water of mine enemies and clothe myself in it." Blood streamed out of the severed vessels and coursed over his skin.

Inhaling sharply, Spadefoot stepped back. His nose burned from the smell of salt and something else, something coppery.

Morning Green frowned and placed the heart back in the basin. Now Spadefoot understood why he was not as easily seen as usual: his face, arms, and bare chest were splashed with blood, darkening his skin so he looked like anyone else.

He studied the organ for a moment, then shifted his gaze to Spadefoot. His eyes seemed lit by a fire within as he held as still as death, his breath imperceptible, red oozing down his cheeks the sole movement until he spoke: "What favor have you come to beg of me?"

Spadefoot tried to shake off his unease at being alone in the small room with the dangerous and unpredictable high priest. He supposed some tale-bearer had already told Morning Green what had happened with Rush. If he repeated what Morning Green already knew, he would be chided for wasting precious time. If he offered different information, it would be treated with suspicion. And if he answered Morning Green directly, his request would likely be denied out of hand.

A man—or priest—underestimated the head of the temple at his own risk. Spadefoot had long ago vowed not to forget that.

"Do not let yourself be preyed on by false emotions," the high priest warned. "There are those who would sway you through some pretext or another. Remember where your loyalties lie."

Spadefoot chose words he hoped they could agree on. "We are sworn to serve the village, oathbound to speak the truth and protect the people."

"Truth, you say. Protection." Morning Green gazed at him with pale, cold eyes burning in a dark-streaked face. "What happens when one man's truth brings harm upon another man, a family, a clan, a village, an entire people?" His voice became louder with each word until he thundered, "Who do you protect, when protecting one means the doom of many others?"

He slammed his open hands down upon the altar. His right hand struck a small bowl, the kind used to store ground pigment. It tipped, spilling out a red powder: cinnabar, Spadefoot noted in a corner of his mind.

Who do you *protect?* he might have asked in return. But the question was unnecessary. Morning Green had shown many times over that he would protect himself above all.

Spadefoot had even come to suspect that he had done something to Nighthawk, though perhaps not intending it to result in the young vow-brother's death. Poison was Morning Green's favorite tool. Not only dizzyweed, as had carried off Nighthawk, but also lies, prophecies, and false magic.

How could anyone hope to combat such dark tactics in the service of such an unfettered thirst for power? Yet Spadefoot had to believe the Rainsinger could be beaten. If he lost that faith, he might as well give up his plan to be free of the prophecy and follow his own life-path.

He had to admit to himself, though, as he stared at the cunning old priest leaning on the altar, that his was not a very well formed plan, shapeless and shifting and only dimly perceived. It was more the ghost of a plan, no more solid than smoke and as difficult to hold on to. So far, it had caused only suffering to those who had been involved, however tenuously: Nighthawk, Rush, Deerchaser, Starflower.

Yet the alternative was too awful to be borne. If Spadefoot failed,

Morning Green would be free to inflict his truth on everyone in the valley—this short-sighted notion that the Watermasters were unnecessary.

Morning Green's eyes narrowed. "Speak," he ordered in an ominously quiet tone.

Spadefoot obeyed but was careful to keep his answer ambiguous once again. "One can regret the harm and try to limit it to those who deserve to be punished. Perhaps the doom need not fall on those who are merely hesitant to change."

His vagueness evidently satisfied the Rainsinger, whose shoulders seemed to relax. "People cling to the old ways not out of belief," Morning Green declared, "but out of selfishness."

He grasped the heart, brought it close to his eyes, and poked at it. The wall gave under his finger but sprang back. Liquid trickled out. This time it looked thin and watery.

Spadefoot told himself it was just a red-dyed liquid rather than blood, but his stomach churned anyway. He closed his eyes until he could breathe steadily. This clench of the guts was what the audience for the Rainsinger's blood ritual would feel. That was the main reason why he wanted no part of it: there could be no return from such a dark path.

Morning Green glanced at him. "You have come today as a defender of the Watermaster, I hear. But this I tell you true: there is no need for heron-folk now that the Stormbringers are here and the rains come as bidden."

"Not always," Spadefoot pointed out. "This past summer—"

"The rains came to those who placed the Ta'atchul first in their heart, who turned from the old ways and revered us, not the goddess." The strange light came back into Morning Green's eyes as he smiled at Spadefoot, revealing a cluster of stained and crooked teeth in his upper jaw.

Us. That small word rang in Spadefoot's head.

"What wickedness we shall see punished when at last the righteous prevail," Morning Green went on. "Perhaps sooner rather than later. Perhaps I shall see to the punishment of your Watermaster myself."

That threat jolted Spadefoot out of his puzzlement about what Morning Green could have meant by *us*. "No!"

"No? You dare tell me no?"

"It is not I who would stop you," Spadefoot made haste to say. "Let me point out, punishing him would be unwise. As I am sure you know already, the clan elders have given him into my keeping for a few days. They will expect him delivered to the village inquest unharmed." Or, rather, no worse harmed than the men of Cloud-Leaf Clan had already done.

Morning Green glowered. "An inquest." Gesturing wildly, he went into a familiar rant: "If a man is incapable of making a decision without relying on the opinion of others, that is a sign that there is no divinity within him.

A true leader commands, while others discuss."

"The Watermasters also have a single leader. Would you say there is divinity within the Canalmaster?" After the words had escaped his mouth, Spadefoot could have kicked himself for feeding the flame of argument.

Predictably the Rainsinger snapped, "He too has a whole council to whom he must answer. The heronfolk are no different from the clans. Or the Smokemothers. Only the Stormbringers truly understand the natural order of things: greatness rises to the top."

A fleck of spittle clung to the corner of his withered lips. Spadefoot watched it tremble there.

"Tell me, my son, what will you do in return for this request to allow an unbeliever within these walls—and at such a time?"

The trap, laid so carefully, waited for Spadefoot to step into it. He wished he were rash enough to declare open rebellion, to insist that he would not reveal when it was time for the New Fire ceremony unless Rush was welcomed into the temple. Instead he numbed himself to the inevitable and bowed his head. "You want me to be a liturgist for your blood ritual. This will I do."

"Not enough," Morning Green answered. "You were always going to obey me in that!"

Spadefoot kept his head down, closed his eyes, and said nothing. Nighthawk was to have performed in the ritual. Upon his death, Morning Green had made Spadefoot and others learn the part. But Spadefoot had said outright, rashly, that he would not do it.

"No, you must choose between protecting your Watermaster and that clan-daughter you desire."

"Starflower?" He straightened abruptly, and his eyes almost hurt, so fast and wide did they open.

Morning Green waved a hand as though to say her name was unimportant. "The one who drew you into clan matters."

"I didn't come forward because I desire her—"

Morning Green's arms whipped out, knocking the heart onto the floor, as he roared, "Do not lie to me! I see your thoughts! I am master here, not you! It will never be you!"

To Spadefoot's ears, his next words sounded like nonsense tied together with strange gasps and pauses. The young priest struggled to put them together but soon realized they must be in Morning Green's outlander tongue.

Then, clearly, he heard, "You are a servant to the Ta'atchul, while I—"

The Rainsinger broke off. He stood there breathing heavily, glaring, eyes wild.

To hide the dread he thought had to be visible on his face, Spadefoot stooped and picked up the heart. It felt heavy and cold in his hand. What claim had been trembling on Morning Green's tongue that he had stopped himself from saying? *We. Us. I.*

Carefully Spadefoot placed the lump of flesh in the basin.

The Rainsinger's hand shot out and grasped his arm with surprising strength, and he flinched. The leathery touch made his skin crawl. Morning Green's grip tightened, bony fingers barely padded with flesh digging into Spadefoot's arm.

The high priest spoke: "Imagine the valley mantled in green, covered by crops with which to fill our bellies. Rich with cotton bolls bursting full, for mantles with which to cover our backs. Imagine the expanse from the Mountains of Sunrise to the Old Man Mountains, all unmarred by cuts and channels that tie the People of Two Rivers to just this plot of land, and this one and this—always just so far from one bug-ridden, slime-filled canal or another, and no farther. It lies within my power to lift these people out of that precarious existence. Would you refuse that? Turn your back on your destiny?"

"I refuse you nothing." Spadefoot quelled the voice inside that clamored for him to run from this place and find somewhere that had never heard of the Ta'atchul, never seen a man such as Morning Green. "What do you want from me in return for this one favor: to keep the Watermaster here until the village council can judge him guilty or set him free?"

Morning Green searched his face. At last the Rainsinger said, "This is my demand." He released Spadefoot's arm. "Swear by the Ta'atchul that you did not bring the Watermaster here to wreak violence upon him."

Spadefoot kept very still as he absorbed what Morning Green thought his motive was: revenge for the attack on Starflower. *Unharmed,* he was sure he had said . . . had the Rainsinger not heard him, or simply disbelieved him? And how many others would suspect Spadefoot of having the same thirst for vengeance, fueled by desire for a girl he could never have? After a speechless moment he ran his tongue over his lips and said, "I swear, the Watermaster has nothing to fear from me."

"Very well. Bring him. He can go in the Seekers' complex."

Relieved and worried at the same time, wondering why the Rainsinger had given in after exacting so little from him, Spadefoot strode out of the small plaza of Morning Green's compound. He was brought up short by the sight of Rush, even more battered than before, swaying on his feet at the gate to the temple precinct.

Rush had not been cleaned up: dirt stained his tunic, and his kilt hung crooked. He looked as if he had been dragged all the way from the Cloud-Leaf clanlands.

Rainedge, though not as tall as Rush, blocked his entrance.

"Step back," Spadefoot told the other priest. "By the Rainsinger's orders, this man is welcome here."

Though clearly reluctant, Rainedge moved out of the way. Spadefoot walked over to stand next to the Watermaster.

"Have you come to gloat?" Rush peered at Spadefoot through puffy lids mottled with every color from pink to red to purple. His lips were swollen. A cut on the lower one released a fresh trickle of blood down his chin as he spoke.

"No gloating. I plan to help you—assuming you are innocent, as you claim to be."

Rush's eyes narrowed and he winced. "Why would you think I am?"

"The way you look at Deerchaser makes me believe you're a man well and truly caught by a woman."

"Yet you had her punished for speaking up for me."

"It was an unfortunate result. One I hadn't intended." Spadefoot motioned for Rainedge to return to the gate tower. "Go!" he said when his vow-brother was slow to comply.

Spadefoot moved closer to Rush and took his elbow. Step by step he helped the Watermaster through the gate and into the temple precinct, which suddenly seemed too open, exposed, too big . . . and the two men slowly moving across it too small. "You need another witness," he said for Rush's ears only. "Someone who saw you return to your quarters and stay there."

"Who?"

"It doesn't matter." Morning Green's rationalization would be true enough in this case: *All that matters is what people believe to be so.* "So long as you're innocent."

"I've done nothing to be ashamed of."

"Nothing ever?" Thinking of Rush's desertion of Deerchaser all those turnings ago, Spadefoot arched one brow. The challenge was not out of meanness but because he wanted to put some backbone into the Watermaster, who struck him as dangerously subdued in spirit. The older man did not respond as Spadefoot had hoped.

"Why did you agree to stand up for me?" Rush knuckled away the blood from his chin. "Do you enjoy the sight of me brought low?"

"No." Spadefoot shook his head. "Any injustice is painful to see. And that's what this is, I'm certain."

"Lofty sentiments coming from a priest."

Spadefoot accepted the sarcasm. He supposed he would feel the same, were they two to switch places. "I want to see you freed, your name cleared."

"Everything to go back as it was before?" Rush's forward movement stopped. He swayed a little. "Even if I believed you, it's too late for that."

"You would prefer to give up? You're tired of the responsibilities of a Canalmaster? You want to be clanless, purposeless, exiled?"

They passed a wall, and the Seekers' complex came into view at the southern end of the temple precinct. A large building with rooms of different sizes, it was currently empty. The boys who had been lodged there since midsummer had been split into two groups: the few who stayed to be initiated into the priesthood, and the many who, for one reason or another, returned to their own clans. The initiates now stayed with the other priests.

"No," Rush snarled.

"Then fight for what you do want."

They lurched along, one step after another.

"Tell me true," Spadefoot said after they had covered a third of the distance to the Seekers' quarters. "Is there anyone who saw you after Deerchaser left who could vouch for you? If so, I promise to find them. I'll convince them to come forward and tell the inquisitors what they know."

Rush turned his head toward Spadefoot. His eyes held a dull gleam of hope. "Why should I trust you?"

With heartfelt sincerity, Spadefoot told him, "It would be a terrible thing if the Watermasters were separated from the clans across a divide that could not be bridged. 'If the Canalmaster could do this to one of the clan-daughters,' they'll say, 'then no Watermaster is to be trusted.' Such a thing can't be allowed to happen."

Rush grunted and faced forward again. "The farmers will see through this scheme of yours."

Not mine. Spadefoot understood Rush's stubbornness, could even sympathize with his distrust. But he had to be persuaded to let Spadefoot help, or he would not have a chance in the village inquest. "People will believe anything, if it's presented convincingly enough."

The Rainsinger's proclamation the other day—about dark dreaming and white and black fire and the faithful and the ungrateful and hidden enemies—had been well rehearsed to sound convincing. Though people were supposed to believe that the Ta'atchul had sent it in a pure vision to the Rainsinger, in truth it was made up one word at a time in Morning Green's head. Spadefoot had heard bits and pieces over and over again in the days leading up to the dramatic moment.

If left to work its poison on the minds of the listeners, the proclamation could split the people in two: those who supported the Watermasters and those who supported the Stormbringers. How many would have sense enough to see that both canals and rain were necessary, that the choice Morning Green had laid out would lead to the destruction he claimed to want to prevent?

To break what he realized had become a rather long silence, Spadefoot said, "We have to be convincing."

"We?"

Spadefoot scrubbed his free hand over his face. "You have to convince them they haven't heard the whole truth. Believe me, I'm not your enemy."

"Hard to believe," Rush replied. "The entire village heard that we argued a few days back and thinks we were fighting over Starflower. Where did that come from, if not you?"

"You have a suspicious turn of mind." They were nearly at the Seekers' quarters. Rush was weakening, his steps becoming more uneven. Spadefoot wondered if they would make it the rest of the way without mishap.

Rush pulled his arm free. He stopped and turned on Spadefoot. "With good reason. You priests are a vicious lot—even your own kind aren't safe." He sagged to one knee.

Spadefoot grabbed him and pulled him up as he said, "Was it what he knew about you that got your half brother killed?"

Nowhere in the temple precinct could that be safely discussed. To shut up the Watermaster before he said too much, Spadefoot answered coldly, "That's a matter for Stormbringers and no one else."

He felt Rush's walls go up—so sudden was the Watermaster's internal retreat, it felt like a slap across the face.

"We're through here." Rush stared straight ahead. "Take me to whatever hole you're planning to let me die in."

He sounded like Morning Green, Spadefoot thought in mounting frustration. "Here it is." He gestured toward the door that stood open in front of them. "Sorry if this 'hole' isn't as bad as you expected."

The Seekers' complex had one building with a narrow door that led into an antechamber. Beyond that and to the side was a larger opening into a spacious room, one of the largest in the temple precinct. That room, where all the new Seekers slept, had light coming through the doorway of the antechamber.

Once Spadefoot closed the door behind him, the room would be dark. He wondered whether the Watermaster would even notice, so swollen were his eyes.

He urged Rush inside and moved him toward the north wall of the room, behind which was an area for storage, with access only through the roof. "Wait here," he instructed.

Sleep pallets were stored in the nearby corner. He found one that looked long enough to accommodate Rush's height and whacked it a few times to drive out any spiders or scorpions that might have taken up residence. Remembering the uncomfortable moons he had spent in this room as a Seeker, many turnings ago, he put the sleep pallet down near the wall that got some morning sun and warmed a little during the day. On it he placed several layers of deerhide covers to ease Rush's battered body.

Then he helped Rush walk over to the prepared sleep pallet. The tall man sagged onto it with what looked like the last of his strength.

"I'll go find you some water," Spadefoot told him. There was no answer, not even a grunt or a moan.

He checked to make sure Rush was still breathing, then left the room and pushed the door shut. With a bone pin he fastened the leather door loop so Rush could not open it from within. That precaution was taken to keep the Seekers from wandering the temple precinct at night—particularly when the Cornmaidens were being escorted to the fertility rooms. He supposed a determined man at full strength could break out of the room, but not Rush in his present condition.

First he went to find a couple of priests who did not seem to be busy. To one he said, "You, go find the Watermaster some food." To the other he said, "And you—" Initially he intended to send the other priest for a healer, but then he thought maybe he should do that himself, if he wanted it done quickly. "You stay here and guard the Watermaster."

The two looked at each other but did not protest their instructions. Spadefoot was relieved when they did as he had told them without saying they would have to check with Morning Green. He still had an uneasy feeling that the Rainsinger's agreeableness did not bode well for Rush.

But why should it matter? he asked himself as he exited the gate and waved his acknowledgment of Rainedge's greeting. It was only Spadefoot's guilt over the outcome of the clan's hearing, after all, that had made him step in on Rush's behalf. He hardly knew the Watermaster. They were not friends.

As he walked unseeing along the path toward the village, he wondered why he had felt so compelled to go against Morning Green's wishes to slip the Watermaster into the temple precinct. Rush had lost his importance to the village if he was no longer the Canalmaster; another now claimed to hold that office. Spadefoot could see that as long as the Watermasters were content with a new leader, their internal conflicts and rivalries were none of his concern—or Morning Green's, either.

Rush himself had become insignificant. A few days ago everything had been different. Nighthawk had claimed to trust Rush, and Spadefoot had trusted Nighthawk, and that somehow made Rush more valuable than this Holdsbreath.

A nagging suspicion began to insinuate itself into Spadefoot's mind: What if that trust was misplaced right from the beginning?

What if Nighthawk was not really Spadefoot's half brother but had lied about that to separate Spadefoot from Morning Green? What if Nighthawk had been sent to the Stormbringers by the Watermasters, or even the Wilders, to gain knowledge of the priesthood's secret rites and ceremonies or even to report on the Rainsinger's plans?

Spadefoot tested his response to that idea, like poking at a loose tooth with his tongue. What if Nighthawk had been given a killing dose of dizzyweed because Morning Green found out he was a spy? What if everything was part of a plot to bring down the Stormbringers?

What if Spadefoot really was the son of Morning Green, the one whose coming was prophesied, and Nighthawk had lied?

Appalled by that thought, Spadefoot stopped on the path. Someone bumped into him and apologized—rather fearfully, he perceived. "My fault," he assured the older woman.

He recognized her as the one who had kept a close eye on him when he had gone to the Watermasters' quarters the first time. "Wait," he said when she would have gone on. Torn between old suspicions and new, he hesitated, thinking hard.

Rush had been far away, up at Sun River, when Nighthawk had come to the priests, several turnings ago. If there was a long-lived Watermaster plot, it could not have been Rush's doing. But he might have learned about it after returning to Crookstaff Village. Was he an enemy of the Stormbringers? If so, Morning Green would be right in saying Spadefoot should have no more to do with him than absolutely necessary.

One thing had to top the list of what was necessary, though: get the Watermaster patched up. Even Morning Green could not want anything to happen to Rush while he stayed with the Stormbringers.

"What is it, young Spadefoot?"

He tilted his head as a mark of respect. "Auntie." The form of address was more familiar than a young man not of her clan should use, but he hoped it would reassure her that he meant no harm. "I would ask something of you, on the Canalmaster's behalf."

She listened, at least. After he explained what was needed, she agreed to summon a bonemender—though she seemed upset when he told her the healer would have to go to the temple precinct, as that was where Rush was being held.

He returned to the gate and called up to Rainedge, instructing him to let the healer through without him.

"A Watermaster. Now a bonemender." The gate warder shook his head. "You're wasting your time with that lot. You'd be better off in the temple fussing with your little paintings."

"Glad to know you consider 'my little paintings' so important." Spadefoot smiled with satisfaction as his vow-brother's cheeks reddened.

For the past few turnings, on Morning Green's orders, Spadefoot had charted the sun's path in the sky and tested his readings against the Skywatchers' timing of the sun-festivals. The Temple of the Mist had been built with holes oriented toward the rising and setting sun in its upper rooms, but in themselves they were no more accurate than watching where the sun rose or set along the horizon.

Most of Spadefoot's vow-brothers made fun of his efforts to track the sun and meticulously paint a calendar-spiral to show where its rays struck the interior of the temple at dawn, midday, and sunset. Out of the Rainsinger's earshot they asked why anyone would need to know exactly when to declare the start of a sun-festival, when the Skywatchers did it for everyone across the valley.

They did not do it where Morning Green could hear, though. He did not like having his orders disrespected.

Spadefoot sorted through the stack of emptied water ollas near the gate to find one of a reasonable size. A lone man would not need much water to drink, but he would need his wounds cleaned and might want washing up. Once Spadefoot found a jar he thought would work, he started for the gate.

Rainedge gestured at the olla. "You heading for the dipping-pool to get some water for the Watermaster? You should send a Seeker instead."

"A Seeker? You mean an initiate," Spadefoot reminded him. "And have to explain to the Rainsinger why I think myself more important than a new initiate? I'll just go."

His vow-brother shrugged one shoulder. "Do as you please. Wouldn't want to keep the Canalmaster waiting."

"I'll be sure to hurry back, then, since you're so worried about him." Spadefoot took satisfaction from the answering snarl on Rainedge's face.

Once again Spadefoot left the temple precinct. He usually felt about five turnings younger and almost happy the moment he escaped the stifling wall. Today, though, he could find little reason for happiness. There were too many worries and accusations and suspicions. Too much that could go wrong. Had gone wrong already.

Carrying the olla under one arm, he headed east, for the dipping-pool—and Earth Holder's new farmstead.

He would straight out ask Starflower for the truth about who had beaten her. Surely there would be some way to force that man into a confession without revealing Starflower's testimony to be a lie, without forcing the clan to punish her too, like Deerchaser.

But he did not have to go all the way to the farmstead to find her. On the embankment of the dipping-pool, Spadefoot saw Starflower and her father on the other side, in what he at first mistook for a comforting embrace.

She clutched at her father's wrists as he grabbed her by the back of her neck and pressed her toward the brink. "No, no!" She resisted, but so precarious was her footing that Spadefoot feared she would topple over.

"Get down there and wash yourself." Her father pushed her onward. His hand slipped off her nape when she stumbled. "Thought to betray me, did you?"

As the older man lifted his face, Spadefoot saw four evenly spaced scratches raking down his left cheek. They were not fresh, as though Starflower had just now defended herself from him; the blood had been cleaned off.

Spadefoot heard the olla shatter on the hard desert soil. He slid down the bank of the dipping-pool, charged across the half log that spanned it, and climbed up the other side. As he emerged into the sunlight, he felt the cold shadow of hatred still wrapped around him.

He grasped Starflower's hand and spun her away from the pool. When her cloak billowed out, more bruises on her neck and wrist became visible.

"No! What are you doing?" She tried to pry off his grip.

Their first meeting had started in a similar way, with her struggling to get free of him. But there was no panic in her eyes now when she looked at him—that came when she saw Earth Holder. With one hand Spadefoot drew her behind him and squared his stance.

"Stop!" she said in a choked voice. "Don't."

He released her just as Earth Holder roared "Take your hands off my daughter!" and shoved at his shoulder.

Spadefoot, well braced, did not budge. He lifted his hands away from his sides, trusting Starflower to have sense enough to stay put. "I'm not going to hurt her," he said. "But she is coming with me."

"I will never let you take her!"

"And just how will you stop me?" Spadefoot hoped the other would shove him again, maybe even throw a fist. He would prefer not to get out of this without a fight, something to rid him of the awful suffocating sensation that had crawled into his chest upon seeing Starflower being manhandled.

"Your father won't like this," Earth Holder muttered.

"Too bad he isn't here! It's between you and me, one man to . . . Well, something that should be a man."

Starflower wept behind him. Her sobs tore at him.

"Come here, girl!" Earth Holder stepped forward and to the side. He gestured for Starflower to take his hand.

Spadefoot put out his arm to block the older man. "You don't need to go with him," he reassured her without glancing back. "Your life is not his to determine."

Earth Holder only smiled, a sly, nasty quirk of his mouth. "Starflower, my dear daughter, do you want to leave me?"

"No." The word came out as a whisper.

"You see?" the older man flung at Spadefoot.

"She's afraid to say other-wise. How small a man are you?" Spadefoot taunted. "Did you beat her because she wouldn't do your bidding otherwise? Those are your bruises on her face, her neck, her arms." When her father would have argued, he stated flatly, "Those are her scratches on your face. Don't bother to deny it."

Earth Holder grabbed Spadefoot's forearm. Spadefoot slammed his other hand down on top of the older man's and squeezed until the farmer's lips went white and drawn. "She's terrified of you. Makes me wonder why."

Stubbornly, her father grated out, "Release her."

Instead, Spadefoot lifted Earth Holder's hand off his arm. Then he muscled the older man out of the way and, ignoring him, turned to look full-on at Starflower. He deliberately gentled his voice and held her gaze with his own. "Trust me. I told you before that I would help you—and I did then. You remember. I can do it again now. Let me take you away from him. Say the word, and I'll make sure he never hurts you again."

She made no answer, just cast him a troubled glance upward through long lashes as her breasts heaved with deep, panting breaths. Her shirt had come unlaced and hung partway open, exposing the top of the gently rounded mounds, an expanse of smooth skin the color of polished stone-wood. Above that, dark bruises and misshapen lumps and clotted blood made his anger flash into a blistering rage.

"Don't listen to him—he can't do anything for you. Now come!" Her father snatched at her hand.

Spadefoot struck Earth Holder's arm away. The farmer stood half a head taller than himself and had a greater reach, as well as being older and hardened by labor. Spadefoot punched him hard and fast.

Earth Holder's nose flattened and spurted blood. He put up a hand and touched the wetness. His fingertips came away red. He snarled and charged forward.

Mindful of the shrieking girl behind him, Spadefoot did not sidestep the attack. Instead he grabbed the oncoming fist and pulled it, twisting as his opponent fell so they hit the ground together, Spadefoot atop the older farmer. He placed an arm across Earth Holder's neck to cut off any attempt to draw breath. With his other hand, Spadefoot covered the mouth of Starflower's father.

He waited until the awareness of death came into Earth Holder's bulging, panicked eyes, as the man's thrashing attempts to throw Spadefoot off came to naught. Then he leaned forward and murmured, "Now it looks like you fought a man, rather than your own daughter."

Spadefoot released his hold, got his feet under him, and stood up. He turned to Starflower. Her mouth hung open midscream—distorting her cheeks, her chin, even her temples. Her frightened gaze shifted from her father to him. Her mouth snapped shut and her arms extended, shakily, palms out and fingers spread.

Ignoring her feeble attempt to ward him off, Spadefoot threw his arm around her shoulders. He tucked her close and drew her along with him.

They were several strides away before she spoke. "You're wrong!" she said through rattling sobs. "The bruises . . . It wasn't . . . my father!"

Now that he had her away, he was not quite sure what to do with her. Absently, mulling over the problem, he asked, "Who laid rough hands on you, then, if not him?"

"It was Rush!"

He snorted. "Those are never the marks of Rush's hands on your wrists."

They were too broad and heavy, obviously from the farmer's tree-stump fingers, not the Canalmaster's long, slender ones. But a beating, even by her father, was less awful than the other part of her claim. Protectiveness surged in him again.

"Did anyone actually force himself on you, Starflower—put himself in you, and you not wanting him? Tell me his name. I'll make him suffer so he never dreams of doing such ever again."

"Just take me home," she pleaded.

He frowned. "To your mother's clanholdings, you mean?" *Where your accusation against Rush just got your own clan-sister whipped.*

Her eyes flashed to his as though she would actually consider that possibility. Instead she said, "To my father!"

"No. Just—no."

"You're going to make him even more angry with me! You don't understand what he can be like!"

"I can see what he's like. I can't believe you such a fool as to actually go back to him."

She shook her head. Spadefoot felt the movement against the side wall of his chest.

"He'll come and get me if I go to the clan," she argued. "He'll take me away again."

Though Spadefoot could see one big reason for being reluctant to go to Cloud-Leaf Clan, it had nothing to do with her father. And it made more sense than returning to someone who treated her so roughly. "Surely the clan elders would protect you. You aren't something he owns; you aren't a tool or clothes or bedding. You're a clan-daughter. You're old enough now to make up your own mind."

"You don't know what he's capable of!"

Spadefoot thought about a man who could beat his own daughter and blame it on another, frighten her so much that she would stand up in front of her people and lie, risking the same punishment as Deerchaser. "If you really won't go to your clan—"

Again she shook her head.

"—then I'll take you to the Smokemothers."

It was the obvious solution. The Smokemothers would be the best protection imaginable for a girl who needed to get away from her father. No one would dare enter their compound without first gaining permission.

Girls, and women too, often went to the Smokemothers when they needed a safe place. Usually it was when they found themselves with child but did not know or would not admit who the father was—just as Spadefoot's own mother had done all those turnings ago, according to Nighthawk. But sometimes it was to escape a mate or a man who would not listen to a simple no. When a clan needed to intervene between a clan-son and a clan-daughter, the Smokemothers could give them some breathing space.

"No!" Starflower tried to dig in her heels as he tugged her along but soon gave up and trotted beside him, her battered face upturned piteously, her voice desperate. "You promised this would be my choice! Already you go back on your word?"

"I can't leave you with him. He hurt you, Starflower."

"He—"

Spadefoot stopped and with both hands turned her toward him. Through her cloak he squeezed her shoulders. He hoped there were no bruises under the cloth. "Don't say he didn't. It's too late for excuses."

Her eyes filled again, but at least she gave up trying to defend her father. "I can't be a Cornmaiden—I won't!"

The intermingled panic and anger that roughened her voice puzzled him. "Being a Cornmaiden isn't so bad. Good food, pleasant company—"

"I would kill myself rather than lie with one of the priests!"

He tried not to feel insulted. He shook her gently to bring her gaze back to his face. Softly, persuasively, he said, "You don't have to do that if you don't want to. The Smokemothers' duty is to protect women from harm, not add to your fears."

He did not add what he might have, just a little while ago: *No one would be so cruel as to take a girl who had been violated and force her to lie with a man.* The people he had grown up among were acting strangely these days. But no girl could be forced to become a servant of Mother Ge. The Smokemothers' order had no room for the unwilling.

Her wide eyes, the whites showing around the dark centers, stared almost sightlessly at him. He wondered if she heard anything he said.

"You can't stay with him any longer." He deepened his voice, imbued it with the richness normally reserved for ceremonies, and gave her another careful shake. "That part of your life is over. Even if he hadn't forfeited any right to your love and loyalty, you are no longer a child, to remain under your father's roof."

A father who beat her.

His heart pounded against his ribs as he remembered the perfection of her face the day before. The most perfect small but well-shaped nose, the most perfect kissable lips, the most perfect angle to her cheeks and tiny cleft in her chin, the most perfect crescent-moon forehead. Her hair drifting down from its coils above her ears, charmingly disheveled. And he had seen from the first that she was bright and clever, too.

She would be the most popular of all the Cornmaidens if she decided to take the vows—and wouldn't that set off Moonbright! He thrust away that whimsical notion, recognizing it as unworthy of himself and Starflower too.

What would it take to convince a girl to change her mind after that declaration *I would rather kill myself?* Impulsively he asked, "If we could promise ourselves to each other like any other man and woman, Starflower, would you have me?"

"No."

"If I made it so I was the only one of the brethren you lay with, what would you say then to becoming a Cornmaiden?"

"No! I can't!" She covered her face with both hands. "Stop it, just stop! Let me think!"

Spadefoot found his fingers tightening and forcibly relaxed them. It was natural that she would not want any man, after what had happened to her. He did not think Rush had forced himself on her—but someone must have, to make her so fear the idea of bedplay.

He reminded himself that he could not take her as his mate, anyway, even if she did want him. He was a Stormbringer, bound by vows, rules, tradition.

The Stormbringers had to beget children upon the Cornmaidens and the Smokemothers. That quickening, the mixture of priest's moisture and woman's seed in the dark of the womb, was necessary for the survival of all the People of Two Rivers. *Before the coming of the priests, it was different.* He silenced the small voice of protest, telling it, *We no longer live in those times.*

"All right." Spadefoot turned her to face north again. He released his grip on her shoulders but grasped her hand without giving her a chance to think. He headed toward the Smokemothers' compound in the old village, for that was the best alternative for her.

He would take her there, see that she was admitted to their protection, and go on about his business: make sure Rush had food and water and see that the bonemender had come to treat him. Then Spadefoot needed to climb to the top of the Temple of the Mist to track the sun and prepare to announce the advent of the New Fire ceremony.

She went with him obediently enough. Far from protesting, she said nothing as she walked along, head bowed, stumbling every now and then. He wondered if her eyes were so filled with tears that she could not see the path. Her hand trembled in his.

He felt an aching pity toward her but could think of nothing to say to make her forget her misery. He recalled that day up by the river when he had found her lost and sobbing, scratched and bruised, crouched at the base of a mesquite tree. Before he found her missing sandal and she became so charmingly flustered. Before he pulled Nighthawk's body from the backwater and she returned to being terrified.

Then, he had soothed her using his voice and the skills Morning Green had taught him. Fears of disembodied spirits and imaginary killers were easy to overcome—phantoms, both. Now, his anger toward Earth Holder had robbed him of that ability to comfort and rally her. He felt helpless, awkwardly so, in the face of the pain, physical and otherwise, that she had to be suffering.

He wanted to go back and use his fists on Earth Holder in a well-deserved beating. But . . . he was a Stormbringer, and Stormbringers did not harm the people they vowed to protect.

At least not openly. Spadefoot would have to find another way to exact revenge on Earth Holder. And there would be a way. Morning Green had taught him that there always was a way to inflict a righteous punishment on the deserving.

Once at the Smokemothers' compound, Starflower's panicky face and clutching fingers kept Spadefoot from leaving her in the anteroom of their main house. She was in no state to explain why she came seeking shelter.

The protectiveness he felt toward her was different from the way he felt toward the Cornmaidens, he realized—some of whom stood nearby in the small, three-walled room and directed curious glances at him and Starflower. They called forth gentleness, sweet words, admiration, even sympathy and comfort when feelings were hurt or personal tragedy struck.

But they had chosen to be here. They were pursuing a life that held good things.

Starflower was escaping a miserable existence. She was wounded in a way he did not understand. She needed to heal.

He tried to explain that to one of the older priestesses, a stout woman who, despite her matronly appearance, folded her arms and seemed unmoved by Starflower's plight. Distant and silent, Starflower was doing little to persuade her.

"We select only certain plants to continue their line," the priestess said after he finished.

"Yes?" he prompted, not seeing what that had to do with giving Starflower a place to stay for a while. The girl burrowed closer to him.

"Vigorous leaves and shoots. Fast growing. Best yield. Strong, to outcompete the weeds." The priestess's expression suggested she believed Starflower was a weed rather than a crop plant.

"There are some among the order," she continued, "who wonder if it makes sense to work so hard to keep the babies of weak women alive. A woman who cannot survive the birthing of the child, perhaps her bloodline should be cut off."

Spadefoot stiffened. His own mother was one that this priestess would deem weak. Beside him, Starflower uttered a small, undefinable noise. "You have no call to make that judgment," he said tightly.

"Enough!" The low, rough voice came from beyond the offending priestess, from a shadowy corner of the room. An elderly woman, wren-thin and wrinkled, stood there, leaning on a staff. She was watching him, not Starflower.

She crooked one spindly finger and said, "Come."

Though he half thought she meant for only him to join her, he separated himself from Starflower as much as he could, took her hand again, and kept her with him. The other priestess drew back to give them room to approach the old woman, eldest of the high priestesses: the Seedkeeper.

The Smokemother in charge of the Cornmaidens, she—not the one who dared to imply that Spadefoot and Starflower were defective—was the one who would determine whether Starflower would find sanctuary among the Smokemothers.

"Don't leave me with her," Starflower said under her breath in a quavering voice. She clutched his arm and hung back like a child to place his body between her and the Seedkeeper.

Spadefoot felt sorry for her, to be so wracked with uncertainty and alarm, but—"It's here or back to your father," he told her. "Or Cloud-Leaf Clan. You choose."

She bit her lip and allowed him to draw her along, following the Seedkeeper into the depths of the main house. The way was lit by sputtering rushlights carried by Cornmaidens, one before and one after their little party.

As Spadefoot walked with Starflower into the inner rooms, scented with tobacco smoke and herbal concoctions, he felt her hand shaking, more even than when they had been on the path leading to the Smokemothers. He wondered what could be frightening her so.

She seemed very young compared to the other Cornmaidens, though she had to be about the same age. Sheltered, he thought.

Or the opposite of sheltered—she had already suffered so much. The Cornmaidens had each other, despite their squabbles and rivalries, but Starflower was terribly alone.

No mother, a sister who had passed away, that strange little brother who hung around the temple precinct instead of playing with friends, and a father . . . Spadefoot's jaw clenched at the mere thought of Earth Holder. She squeaked a protest. He muttered an apology and loosened his grasp.

After passing through a few rooms, they entered a low-ceilinged chamber. Its walls were plastered not with the pale caliche-based wash favored by the Stormbringers but with what appeared to be mud from the bottom of the canals, likely mixed with something to make it stick. It had a heavy, earthy odor that made his head swim. The darkness seemed to absorb the tiny flames cast by the rushlights, making the room seem larger than it was.

Starflower cast him a beseeching glance. He ignored it and reminded himself that this was the best place for her.

The Cornmaidens settled the rushlights into stands on either side of a bench at the back of the room. They helped the Seedkeeper up onto the bench and pulled a rabbitskin robe over her legs. At a motion of her hand, they left the room.

From her perch, her glittering gaze seemed to reach deep within him and pull out all that he had done that was careless or unkind or petty, beginning with the earliest memory—that of a playmate he had made cry by pushing the boy down while playing take-the-hill—and ending with the most recent: his testimony against Deerchaser.

At last the priestess released him from her testing stare. He had to look away. A sidelong glance at Starflower showed big fat tears rolling down her cheeks. He wondered if this was what she had feared in coming here. What faults, what personal failings, had the Seedkeeper pulled out of her?

"An interesting pair." The Seedkeeper sounded as though she spoke through gravel. She rasped in a breath, and the cords stood out in her neck.

Covering her hair was a cloth dyed deep red-brown with a few wisps of white escaping it. Her face was as deeply seamed as a thirsty cactus. Her eyebrows were so thin as to be almost nonexistent. Where they should have been, six flame emblems of motherhood were tattooed, three on each side, winging up toward her hairline. Six children she had borne, and six she had given up to the village: that was what the tattoos meant. There were no tears under her eyes marking any deaths.

One brow lifted. She expected an answer.

He explained his purpose in bringing Starflower to her. Gravely, without interrupting—without so much as blinking, as far as he could tell— she listened to what he had to say. Then she turned to Starflower, against his side, still dripping tears like a cracked water olla.

"I gather this is not your idea, girl. Do you want to become a Cornmaiden?" asked the Seedkeeper in her harsh, raspy voice.

"No, Revered Grandmother," she breathed.

"That would seem to settle the matter." The high priestess looked at him. "Why are you pushing her to do this, young priest of the Ta'atchul?"

"She needs protection from her father, who beat her."

Starflower denied it with a shake of her head.

"You can see the bruises all over." He shifted his feet into an easy stance indicating his willingness to remain in this one place all day if necessary. It was a bluff, of course.

He had to get up to the observation tower and make sure his calculations were correct before the sun got to the highest point in the sky. The spiral painted on the wall of the calendar-room was not quite complete. Without today's observation, he would be unable to give Morning Green the certainty about the New Fire ceremony that the Rainsinger demanded.

And there was Rush to worry about too.

The high priestess sighed. "Let me look at her more closely." She beckoned for Starflower to approach.

Again the girl shook her head—though Spadefoot did not know how, with her face buried against him, she saw the Seedkeeper's gesture.

"Go on, now," he told her. He turned and slid his hands to her shoulders to separate her from himself.

He missed the warmth of her as soon as she was gone. But that, he knew, was a sensation he had best get used to. His chest constricted, as though a too-tight band were wrapped around it.

Was he falling in love with her? He rejected the idea almost as soon as it came to him. No, pity and protectiveness, that was all he felt toward Starflower. He would not allow an infatuation to distract him from his plan to counter Morning Green's dangerous ambitions.

With her head bowed, she took one step forward, then another, toward the Seedkeeper's small figure. As Starflower neared the priestess who was to become her protector, Spadefoot had the eerie notion that a hazy glow enveloped them both. He fought the urge to rub his eyes to clear them.

The nimbus of light slowly faded. Some pressure in his ears seemed to pop right before that weird haze vanished entirely.

The Seedkeeper raised one hand toward Starflower, let it hover for a moment, then pulled it back. "You were tested in the winter of your first bleeding."

Although it was a statement rather than a question, Starflower answered. "Yes, Revered Grandmother," she whispered, her chin tucked almost to her chest.

"Why did you not come to us then?"

"I was not chosen."

"Not—?" The priestess sounded surprised. She cocked her head to one side. "I think you misremember what happened during the testing. You were indeed chosen, asked to join the Cornmaidens. It was Mother Ge's gift to you."

Starflower raised her head. Fiercely she swore, "I'll never lie with any man, never to the end of my days!"

The high priestess eyed her. "I believe it must be too late for such a vow, girl. Did you not claim to have lain with the Canalmaster, against your will or no?"

Starflower jerked as if slapped. Spadefoot could not remain silent any longer.

"Revered Grandmother," he said, offering the respect due her office in the hope that it might ease her mood, "Starflower has suffered enough. I brought her here for shelter and a place to regain her health, not to make things worse."

The cloth-shrouded head moved with the slowness of a cloud forming as it swung toward him. "You are young, Spadefoot, but not so much, surely, that you think to tell me what to do."

"I expect you to do what is right, Revered Grandmother. And I will not remain silent as you bully this girl."

The priestess's brows rose, creasing the flame tattoos. For a moment she sat unspeaking, her breath still rasping in and out.

With each noisy wheeze, Starflower's face grew more pale and her trembling worsened.

Finally the priestess asked him, "Why did you bring her here, to the house of the Allmother's servants?"

"I told you, her father beat her."

"No. It's a lie." But Starflower's defense lacked sincerity. "My father loves me."

"And I thought she should be away from men for a while," Spadefoot said. "Here she can be safe."

The Smokemother's gaze swept over Starflower from head to foot. Spadefoot had the unsettling thought that the priestess's glance, though brief, could discover every wound, even those hidden deep inside. A moment later, the priestess returned her attention to him.

"I meant," she said to him, "why are *you* the one who brought her here? What are you to her? A lover?"

"No," he and Starflower said together.

The dark stare bore through him now. He felt as though he stood naked before the priestess, that she saw through to a truth he was trying to conceal even from himself. Then she seemed to turn inward as though in a trance.

When she emerged from wherever she had gone in her head, she dismissed him without a word or gesture; she simply withdrew her attention from him as though he were no more than a clod of earth on the floor. "You are determined to never accept a man into your body?" she asked Starflower. "Is this a thing you swear?"

"Yes."

Spadefoot pressed the Seedkeeper: "What do you say? Will you offer her sanctuary?"

Another few breaths grated along his nerves. Then the Seedkeeper told him, "If she agrees, yes. But only so."

Holding up a spindly hand to cut off Starflower's response, the priestess said to her, "Before you answer, you must know this." Again came the harsh breath, once, then again. "You bear a child in your belly already."

Spadefoot did not think, at first, that he had heard her right. He stared at Starflower, whose mouth hung slack in shock, then back at the priestess. "How can you tell?" he asked.

"The signs are unmistakable," the Seedkeeper declared.

"But so early?" he persisted.

"Not as early as all that. A moon, I would guess. Two." She held up two crooked, stick-like fingers.

"No!" Starflower exclaimed. "That's impossible."

The Smokemother's mouth twitched.

Spadefoot struggled to draw air into lungs that had seized tight. *A baby. But then who was the father?*

The Seedkeeper gestured for Starflower to approach. The girl left his side and slowly walked toward the priestess, perhaps unwilling but incapable of refusing. Her hands were locked together by white-knuckled fingers over her belly.

The old woman lifted a clawlike hand and brushed back a lock of Starflower's hair that hung loose from her temple. Gently she said, "A man's seed is tricky. Just bedplay, when it's your time and he is potent, can make a child. Did you not realize? Like Yucca Woman, a drop on your belly is all it takes."

Bedplay. Spadefoot imagined Starflower's lush form writhing with pleasure under another man's hands.

But with whom? Rush? Had he lain with her and then cast her aside for Deerchaser, so that Starflower, as a woman scorned, had accused him of forcing himself on her? Or was it one of the many youths who adored the beautiful Starflower, would do anything for her? Had Earth Holder beaten her because she would not tell—or did not know, among so many—who was the father?

The pressure on Spadefoot's chest grew heavier. Spots danced before his eyes.

After a moment, the priestess went on, "No, I can see you didn't understood the dangers in what you did." She let her hand settle onto Starflower's shoulder, but Spadefoot felt she was talking to him when she said, "The father is not always who everyone believes, even when the woman swears it to be so. Only the Allmother really knows."

To Starflower she said, "Will you stay with us, where we can tend to your hurts and give you peace?"

Starflower slapped at her belly. "Peace!" she cried. "I'll have no peace from this . . . this thing inside me! Get it out!" She collapsed to the ground, wailing and tearing at her clothes.

The high priestess looked at Spadefoot. "There's a storm coming . . . I can feel it in my old bones. You feel it too. There can be no holding it back. What matters is what side you take after it comes. But do not wait too long, for the day of reckoning will be upon us soon. Go now. Go now, and remember that the Rainsinger is not the only one who sees what is coming."

Unnerved, Spadefoot turned and left them all—woman, girl, and unborn—in the flickering dark of the room.

Spadefoot was nearly to the temple precinct when two youths accosted him. The pale blue ribbons on their clothing would have told him they were ditchrunners, even if he had not recognized them: they had challenged him that first time he went to the Watermasters' quarters.

"What've you done with our Canalmaster?" asked the first.

His moon-round face was pugnacious, his bare feet crusted with dirt. His hair seemed already thin on top, with scalp showing through between many narrow braids wrapped together at the back with another ribbon.

The other said, "Your lot took him to the temple."

"Yes, he's here," Spadefoot acknowledged.

"We won't let you torture him," declared the first one.

"He's safe. No one will hurt him." Spadefoot started past them, but the thinner boy grasped his arm.

"He needs tended," the boy said, evidently more practically minded than his fellow. "And a bonemender. And some water, I s'pose," he added.

"Aw, give over, Tumbler. This 'un don't care. He's the one what testified against our Canalmaster."

Spadefoot stared at Tumbler until the boy released him. "The healer has been sent for," he told the ditchrunners. "Food and water will be provided. What Rush really needs is proof of his innocence. Can you give him that? Either of you? Do you have certain knowledge of where he went when he left his sleeping-quarters before dawn?"

They flushed. The first one mumbled, "We was sleeping."

But Tumbler said, "That Starflower, she come looking for him earlier yesterday."

"What? You didn't tell me that," said the other boy.

"'Course not, Crack. It di'n't make sense he would've gone after *her*. Not when Deerchaser's the one he's been looking for."

"What did Starflower say she wanted with him?" Spadefoot asked.

Tumbler shrugged. "Nothing. She di'n't say nothing." He shifted from one bare foot to the other, then burst out, "It's not right for him to be locked up for doing nothing wrong."

"I agree," Spadefoot said.

After a sidelong look at him, Tumbler said, "My gran, she says she wouldn't be s'prised if you poisoned him with your priest food."

Spadefoot shook his head. "No poison. He's probably as safe as he would be back at his quarters. More, maybe," he suggested, "with that Holdsbreath in charge. He doesn't seem to care much for your master."

"That 'un!" Tumbler scoffed. "He's mad 'cause he got passed over when Rush got himself assigned as Canalmaster. Di'n't much like being left a ditch boss."

"*Is* the one called Holdsbreath the new Canalmaster, as he claims to be?" Spadefoot asked.

The one called Crack snarled, "No!" just as Tumbler said, "Prob'ly. Holdsbreath's the one Twistedtrack wanted in there all along." At Spadefoot's look of inquiry, he explained, "Twistedtrack's the Canalmaster upcanal, at Coyote-Willow. He don't much care for Rush."

Crack muttered, "Always mucking about with stuff he oughta keep his nose out of. Like *you* people do," he added, shifting his scorn from Twistedtrack to Spadefoot.

"Your people *are* my people," Spadefoot pointed out.

"Outlanders!" The word was an insult in Crack's mouth.

"I was born in the valley, just like you. I even have old blood in me. I'm hardly an outlander."

"You would rid us of the Allmother and set up false gods in her place."

"That's a large assumption," Spadefoot told the stocky boy. "You know nothing of what I believe, what I would do."

"Don't you believe your own father's prophecy?"

"I don't place a great deal of trust in visions," Spadefoot said truthfully enough. "The drying up of the land comes every Dry-Grass Moon and lasts until the winter rains. The sun vanishes behind the leading edge of heavy cloud with nearly every storm. Sometimes the canals get washed out by floods and need fixing, sometimes the crops are poor. These are not events to cause fear and uncertainty, no matter what Morning Green has to say."

Seeing that the boys obviously still doubted him, he ordered, "Go on, now. I'll see to your Canalmaster."

Not really having any alternative, they obeyed, though they cast backward looks over their shoulders. He assumed they would go back to their duties. They were ditchrunners still, even if their master was no longer in charge.

Relieved to have that taken care of, Spadefoot gazed up at the sky. The sun drew near its highest point, marking midday, when the shadow cast by the post he used to measure its path would be the shortest. Depending on where the sun's midday shadow fell along the curves he had drawn atop the observation tower, he could determine whether the New Fire ceremony would start at sunset today or tomorrow.

The lines, originally marked with rocks and then drawn in charcoal and now permanently etched in plaster, had taken him three turnings to complete. He only needed this one last set of observations to confirm what to tell Morning Green—whether to light the fire at sunset tonight or tomorrow. And then mark the end of the calendar-spiral on the inner wall of the temple's highest west-facing room.

Morning Green had encouraged Spadefoot to pursue this idea. In the

Rainsinger's way of thinking, the Stormbringers should be able to do what until now been exclusive to the Skywatchers. Because the Skywatchers were dwindling in number, and because of his own hunger to learn all there was to know about the world, Spadefoot had readily agreed.

Until the past few moons, he had thought he was doing the right thing in pursuing the things he was curious about. That was what had led to the dipping-pool, after all. But of late he had started to wonder whether helping Morning Green achieve his ambitions would do more harm than good. And then Nighthawk had sought him out.

Nighthawk, who was now dead.

Spadefoot shoved that distracting thought away. He looked up at the sun, though he did not stare at it directly. The quick glance he allowed himself showed that he still had time enough to check on Rush.

An unreasoning sense of betrayal coursed through Spadefoot as he stood before the open door. He assumed at first that Rush had broken free, that he had misjudged the Watermaster's honor. Then he saw that the door's leather hinges remained intact. The bone pin and the loop it slipped into were also undamaged.

He went into the building to make sure Rush was indeed no longer in the Seekers' quarters. There was nowhere to hide in the room, and a quick look around yielded no sign of the injured Watermaster. The bedding Spadefoot had arranged for Rush appeared to have been piled up with the rest. Someone had let Rush out—maybe on the Rainsinger's direct order. So where would they have put him?

Spadefoot went again into the little plaza and looked around in vain for an indication of where Rush could have been taken. Frustrated, he struck the wall with the heel of his hand.

That was when he saw the ladder. It had not been there, leaning up against the wall, when he had left the Seekers' quarters not long before.

He strode over to it but halted with both hands on the rails as he struggled with himself about whether finding Rush could wait. A glance at the sun showed that he was almost out of time if he was to make this final observation.

But he could not ignore his earlier doubt about Morning Green's agreement to allow Rush into the temple precinct. It seemed significant, in hindsight, that Morning Green had gotten Spadefoot's promise to leave the Watermaster unharmed . . . but had made no such promise himself.

Spadefoot scaled the ladder as rapidly as he could.

He found no body on the roof. That was a good thing, he told himself. But it did not answer the question of where Rush had been taken.

He looked around, then down as he remembered that the storage room tucked away behind the sleeping area could be accessed only from the roof where he stood. The trapdoor that led down into it had been very recently mudded over with a thick layer of adobe, its dark coppery red color indicating that it was still wet and very heavy.

He was unpleasantly reminded of an old stoppered jar he had once seen. When he had removed the stopper and looked inside, he had discovered the bones of a mouse that had crawled in and died, unable to breathe or get out.

Spadefoot crossed the intervening space, knelt by the blocked trapdoor, and called out, "Are you down there?"

When he heard no reply, he bent closer and called again, louder this time.

"Let me out!" It was the Watermaster's voice.

Spadefoot sat back on his heels. "You're sealed in."

"Yes, I know. There's mud in my hair from it."

"Are you all right?"

A brief quiet ensued. Then, "Your warders very generously let me use the ladder to climb in here instead of tossing me down like they did the jerky and journeycakes. They were a little more gentle with the water olla and a nightsoil jar. But the air is getting close in here."

Spadefoot closed his eyes for a moment. He felt the sun shining down on his head from high in the sky and knew he did not really have time to free Rush. Still, he could not leave the Watermaster to die like that mouse. No matter what Morning Green might, in his pride or hatred, believe, the death of the Watermaster while in their care would be disastrous for the Stormbringers as well as the farmfolk of the village.

He said, "I'll see what I can do. I'll be back."

"You told me that before." Rush sounded bitter. "Anyway, what do you care if I live or die? You're the one who had me sealed in here."

"That was none of my doing. Trust me on that."

"Trust you? Trusting you is what got me hit on the head a few days ago. It's what landed me here!"

"I have to go, but I'll return as soon as I get some tools. You'll hardly know I'm gone. I *will* help you."

Rush went silent again. Spadefoot could not blame him. "I will," he repeated. "Trust me."

"I don't have much choice, do I?"

Spadefoot turned away. He pulled up the ladder, then lowered it into a narrow space on the other side of the storage room, where the Seekers' tools used to be kept. When he dropped down into the small enclosure, he was relieved to see some plastering trowels and mixing paddles. He selected one of each, tossed them up on the roof, and climbed the ladder again.

He returned to the trapdoor and began to pry at the adobe with a paddle. A large chunk came free, but the material underneath was softer. It had been laid down as deep as his hand from heel to fingertips. Such a layer would be too heavy for any man to shift, even after it dried and became rock hard; whoever had mudded Rush in had not wanted him to escape.

The material had to have been intended for some other purpose than sealing the room, Spadefoot realized as he worked. The clay for the adobe had to have been collected, combined with water and dry grass on a mixing pad, and hauled here still wet to be applied. Unless Morning Green had planned all along to get Rush into his clutches, there would not have been time to prepare the mud for this purpose.

Spadefoot dug and tossed, dug and tossed, not caring where the adobe chunks flew; someone could clear it off later. He needed to be careful, though, to go down just to the level of the trapdoor without breaking through the reeds and sending a whole layer of adobe onto the head of the man below.

The quiet disturbed him. "Rush?"

"I'm here."

"Keep talking." *So I know you're still alive.* Spadefoot struck the woven reed matting and began to work the wet adobe loose along one side.

"Talk about what?"

"Tell me . . ." He cast about for something they might both be interested in, something other than Starflower, which would likely be a sore topic. A man was easier to deal with once he saw what you had in common—or better yet, how he was superior. "Tell me about the Skywatchers and the Belly of the Mother. You're from up that way. You must've seen them."

"What about them?"

"What does the Belly of the Mother look like?" Spadefoot had three sides of the trapdoor free now, visible all the way down to the saguaro-rib frame. "Far-Traders just say it's a big red rock with holes through it. So how do the Skywatchers track the sun with it?"

"I don't know that, exactly. But the cliff, the whole thing, is called Mother Sleeping. When you're on the flats looking up at it, it looks just like a giant woman lying down: Mother Ge herself."

Pleasant memories rang in Rush's voice, a bit of awe. Spadefoot was glad to hear it. Then the Watermaster's tone flattened, as if he remembered his situation.

"In the middle—that's where the name Belly of the Mother comes from—there's a double cavern. From below, you can see straight through it to the sky. There's a big cavern to the south. It narrows down on the back side, in the north. The south side is where they light the fires for the New Fire ceremony."

"Have you ever seen the fires blazing?"

"A few times."

"It sounds grand. I've never been anyplace beyond right around here."

Spadefoot had never minded before. He was not sure he did even now. Although his only taste of freedom came when he stood atop the temple with no one else near, his whole world lay spread before him in those moments: northward were Crookstaff Village, the canals, fields and desert, Earth River and beyond it the buttes; when he turned around to face south and west, there were the gentle curves of dry washes and in the farther distance the line of hills known as the Tipped Basket, behind which the sun set in the summer.

With the adobe cleared away from all four sides of the trapdoor, he paused. A glance at the sky showed that the sun had begun to descend in its daily journey. There was no point in going up to the observation tower now.

With a sigh of resignation, he began to scrape the mud out of the crevices where the reeds crossed over the saguaro-rib framework of the trapdoor. He wielded the trowel carefully and at a slower pace. There was no longer a need for hurry.

"You never went on the salt journey, to the Wide Water?" Rush asked.

Spadefoot admitted, "I've never even been north of the river or gone into the mountains where the sun sets."

That statement met with silence from below. Eventually Rush said, "I don't suppose I ever will again, either."

For a moment Spadefoot did not know what he meant. Then he understood that the Watermaster did not expect to survive this incident. Spadefoot's hands stilled. He promised himself he would do all that he could to make sure Rush was proven wrong.

"Look up. Do you see daylight through the trapdoor?" he asked. Something slid across the floor of the storage room, followed by a groan.

He remembered Rush's injuries and guessed the bonemender had not been allowed to tend him. Spadefoot resolved to take that up with Rainedge, though it was unlikely that Rainedge and the warders had done this without the Rainsinger's explicit instructions countermanding his own.

"Yes, some," Rush answered.

"I'm not sure how much more I can get loose." Spadefoot stood. "I have to go." This time he did not promise to come back. He would have to deal with Morning Green first.

Reddish clay staining his hands began to tighten on his skin as it dried. He brushed them against each other to knock off the adobe.

Rush asked, "Can you look in on Deerchaser, make sure she's all right?"

"I'll do what I can." Spadefoot walked to the edge of the storage room, pulled up the ladder again, and descended to the Seekers' plaza.

For some reason he did not want to explore too closely, Rush's request made him think about Starflower and her lies as he walked across the temple precinct. Spadefoot wondered whether he himself, like the interrogator, had been fooled by her pretty face. Had anything she told him been the truth?

Then he recalled her terror, first up by the river and again with her father and finally with the Seedkeeper. He felt certain *that* emotion, at least, was honest. And he had the idea that maybe she was on the edge of fear all the time, the same way he was on the edge of anger.

He had gotten only halfway to Morning Green's quarters when a strange sensation made him stop. He looked down at his hands. The tightening he had earlier felt in them seemed to have moved up his arms and become more intense, like the pricks of a tattooing needle. The prickling quickly flowed across his skin, all the way from head to heels.

The sensation was not all that different from what he experienced while dowsing, as he had done to locate the dipping-pool. Yet it filled him with foreboding, the same way he had felt a few turnings ago when he had experienced a lightning storm on top of the temple. Perhaps the overdue winter rains were coming, though his weather sense said no.

He gazed at the sky but saw nothing amiss there.

In his distraction, he had forgotten about Morning Green. He started when he heard the Rainsinger call to him.

On each side of Morning Green and a step behind stalked a broad-shouldered man, face like stone, hands and bare arms scarred from sparring—two warders who often accompanied him when he went into the village. Their hands showed the same staining of red as Spadefoot's.

He looked away from them and focused his attention on the Rainsinger. The dark bluish tattoos normally stood out against Morning Green's light skin. Today his color was higher, signaling a dangerous mood.

Spadefoot walked forward to join him.

One clawlike hand closed around his shoulder. "So." Morning Green's voice cut, knife sharp. "This has been a busy morning for you. First you defile our sacred space with an unbeliever, then you steal a girl from her father, a man to whom she owes her loyalty—nay, her very existence. And now, the sun is descending toward the horizon and you have not told me whether tonight is the night we have long awaited."

Spadefoot crossed his arms and at the same time shifted to pull his shoulder out of Morning Green's grasp. "You know somebody moved the Watermaster into a storage room and covered the trapdoor with adobe. It could have killed him."

"As the Ta'atchul will," said Morning Green.

"Evidently the Ta'atchul did not will it so," Spadefoot argued. "They sent me to free him."

"You swore an oath to follow me, to accept what I say as the truth: the only truth that exists for you."

"I swore to follow the Ta'atchul. Not you."

The muscles in the jaws of the two hard-faced warders jumped, and the tendons tightened in their necks. Spadefoot knew they could do nothing to him here, not during daylight hours, when his vow-brothers might see. Rush was lucky he had come along when he did. *And Nighthawk?*

Morning Green's eyes narrowed. "Is this what it has come to? Would you steal the office of Rainsinger from me? Do you think yourself so powerful? Pride can lead to a long fall."

"That is not what I want," Spadefoot answered honestly.

"We do not get what we want always. I, for one, wanted a son who would use his gifts to their fullest. A man who would carry out his duties for the benefit of all." Morning Green turned his pale face up to the sunlight, which he usually avoided lest he turn a fiery red. "Yet you are not making those final observations you told me were so important. Are we lighting the fires at sunset today, or are we not?"

Although Spadefoot had missed the midday observation of the sun's shadow path, he realized it did not matter. The New Fire ceremony would not begin tonight. Of that he was certain, all the way to his marrow.

But should he tell Morning Green the truth—or let the fires be lit a day too early? Neither would reduce Morning Green's influence: being wrong would just make Spadefoot look foolish in the eyes of his vow-brothers and the people of the village, while being right would let Morning Green argue that the Skywatchers were no longer needed.

"Well? Is it tonight?" The Rainsinger had an avid look in his cold eyes.

"The Sun-Turning comes tomorrow," said Spadefoot, not yet ready to defy the head of the temple. Not while Rush was here. "At the coming of night tomorrow, the Skywatchers will light the ceremonial fires in the Belly of the Mother."

"You had better not be wrong."

The next day, in the same plaza where Morning Green had accused him of neglecting his duties, Spadefoot waited to be proved right.

Earlier, in the morning, he had sent to the Smokemothers asking about Starflower and to the healers about Deerchaser; he had gone to see Rush in the storage room and told him that Deerchaser's wounds were healing; he had ordered that more water and food be taken to Rush; and he had made one final observation of the sun when it reached its peak in the sky. Despite everything going as well as could be expected, he had felt there was something terribly wrong.

Spadefoot obediently chanted the liturgy for this new blood ritual in counterpoint to the Rainsinger's exhortations. Three of his brethren stood with him, all four in a line and wearing identical headdresses: turkey feathers mounted at the top of an oval mask of cottonwood painted black above and white below; long hanks of gray hair representing rain hung down from the bottom half. Each young Stormbringer wore a shell net hanging from a hip belt, with only a thin cotton breechcloth to shield his flute and rattles from the sharp-edged shells. Their voices were tuned with his as each in turn delivered the responses.

He did not much care about the words, repetitive as they were and having much to do with obedience to the will of the Ta'atchul; he could have said the lines in his sleep, so often had the Rainsinger forced them to rehearse. Obedience was his theme—though he had trouble feeling it— while good heart, the courage to accept change, and the sustenance of life were the messages spoken by each of the others.

The call and responses centered on one crucial element: blood. The beat of it. The ebb and flow. The warmth.

Spadefoot had difficulty focusing his attention on the ritual. It was brilliant, of course . . . Morning Green's doing. With the Temple of the Mist rising behind them and a dark, pitted stone altar before, the Stormbringers were on display for all the people to observe.

This was not a ritual reserved for those few of sufficient rank to receive an invitation to enter the temple precinct. No, through what Spadefoot assumed was carefully planted rumor, helped along by the curiosity stirred up by Deerchaser, news of the Rainsinger's blood magic had spread throughout the village. A huge crowd gathered here to witness the ritual.

Not even the spring ceremonies, when the Smokemothers gave out blessed seeds and the Watermasters danced to harness the river-serpents, were so well attended. Spadefoot figured Morning Green was pleased by that. Yet a glance cast in that direction through the eyeholes of the mask showed no trace of emotion, no pleasure or pride, upon that face.

Morning Green was dressed in the long gray robes he wore nearly all the time, even in the heat of summer. The robes exposed only his hands and his face, painted now with black clouds and gray rain-drizzle. Long strings of small white twisted shells, like elongated raindrops, hung from a rabbit-fur mantle on his shoulders, with turkey feathers fanning out around his neck. His arms were painted with black stripes that spiraled down from his shoulders. On his brow was a mirror that reflected the light of the lowering sun into the eyes of those in the crowd who looked directly at him.

Spadefoot did not think any of the avid audience could see the deer hearts that lay in the trough atop the altar. They certainly could not see the red-tinged liquid pooled in the narrow channel cut into the trough. Nor would they realize that the pillar on which the trough rested was hollow—or, more precisely, consisted of several parts cut and fitted together as neatly as Morning Green's homily. Within lay a firestarting kit.

After a beat of expectant silence and a glare from Morning Green, Spadefoot realized he had missed his cue. "Then all must submit to the lords of the sky," he said quickly. "For theirs is the only will."

From Spadefoot's perspective, the Ta'atchul should not need human devotion. Obedience, yes. The focusing of people's attention on them, and them alone, that could be important, for such all-powerful beings were likely to be prideful.

But surely they cared nothing for whatever else was thought to rest in the human heart. The exhortations calling for courage, for morality—those were to benefit the Stormbringers, not the Ta'atchul. To explain why an ever-greater part of the ceremonial round should be given over to the Stormbringers. To weed out any who disagreed.

Spadefoot watched Morning Green's back tense as it became his turn in the liturgy again. Maliciously he let one too many beats go by before he delivered his line. It was a petty vengeance, he knew, and he cautioned himself against doing it a second time.

What the Ta'atchul wanted with blood was unclear to Spadefoot. The truly divine could have no use for that which was vital to mortal creatures. But if the rapt looks on the faces of all the mortals gathered here were any indication, he figured he was the only one to whom such doubts had occurred.

The back of his neck prickled. Without thinking, he began to lift a hand to smooth the hair there. A warning hiss and elbow to the ribs from his right-side companion aborted the gesture. He normally had no difficulty in following the instructed form: eyes front, arms at sides, keep feet still, no words other than those of the liturgy.

Today, though, this new ritual seemed to be going on too long. Another glance at the crowd convinced him that he was the only one to feel that way. They listened intently, drinking in every word.

Spadefoot shifted his weight. Again came the undervoice remonstrance, but he could not stay still. Something felt wrong.

The light was fading, he realized. With the Temple of the Mist blocking his view of the sun, he could not see why. He told himself a drift of cloud had blown over, although when the rite had begun, the sky had been clear—as it had been for too many moons now, with the winter rains late in coming.

The Rainsinger came to the dramatic part of his discourse. He strode to the altar, where his hands became busy with the firestarter. To Spadefoot, watching from behind, he seemed to never look down to see what he was doing, yet a wisp of smoke soon curled up from the dry duff.

He lifted a deer heart in one hand and raised it above his head. The blood-red stuff within gushed out, cascading down his arm and off his elbow, to splash upon the altar and the liquid there. The onlookers gasped with shock. Some near the front recoiled. Spadefoot knew that what they took for magic was the result of much effort on Morning Green's part, both to preserve the heart and to find the right mix of ground minerals and dyes to fake the color and flow of fresh blood.

But he gaped along with them when Morning Green lifted a flame-tipped reed and lit the blood-tinged liquid on the altar. With a flicker and then a whoosh, fire burst into existence, flashed up over the Rainsinger's head, and then . . . consumed itself and vanished.

The consternation of those who had witnessed the impossible was released in loud exclamations and shrill chatter, except among the four Stormbringers who formed an arc between the Rainsinger and the wall. Their covert, shaken glances told Spadefoot he was not the only one who had been kept in the dark about that little detail of the ritual. By comparison, the lighting of the New Fire would seem a letdown.

He felt a chilly breeze. More than a breeze: the air around him simply cooled. The fine hairs on his nape lifted, and he found it hard to breathe. The air began to take on the quality of twilight, though a look at the sky showed no clouds that would block the sun. Yet the light dimmed.

Spadefoot took off his mask and pushed his way past his vow-brethren, ignoring their hissed warnings. Once beyond the shadow of the temple, he peered sidelong at the sun, experience having taught him not to stare directly at it.

A darkness built on the horizon. It seemed like one of the towering gray-bellied clouds of summer, though it grew in the west rather than the east, whence the summer storms came.

It was not a cloud, he realized—the darkness was dirt, not rain. It rose from the ground upward. The twisting, shifting column thickened and deepened and broadened until what had likely started as a small whirlwind became a wall. This was not the season for dust storms. Nor had he ever seen one so large and mounting so fast.

Though odd and disturbing, that was not what was swallowing up the light. The dust storm had not risen high enough to cover the sun.

Spadefoot heard murmurs from behind and spared a glance over his shoulder. People had turned from Morning Green's ritual and were pointing toward the sun.

"Don't look! Don't look at it!" Spadefoot's voice rang out even louder than the Rainsinger's had done earlier. Unfortunately, only a few people left off their absorption with the fading sun to watch him. Too few, he realized; the others risked being blinded by their curiosity.

"Get back to your place," snapped Morning Green, who moved up beside him. Only then did the Rainsinger turn to see what spectacle had replaced his ritual in holding the crowd's attention. Off-balance, he swayed dangerously for a moment.

Spadefoot grabbed at Morning Green to keep him from falling, but his hand slipped off the greasy, fake red blood still dripping from Morning Green's arm. As the Rainsinger lurched toward him, the mica mirror opened to Spadefoot like an eye. He saw himself, small and distorted in the reflection.

With a quick upward twist he snatched the mirror off the Rainsinger's head and strode toward the temple's smooth plastered wall. He had used a piece of mica before to cast the reflection of the sun onto a wall to trace its orb, but he could not remember exactly how he had made it work.

A shaft of light caught on the mica and bounced upward. Spadefoot dropped to his knees and changed the angle.

And there it was. The image at first resembled the moon, but it diminished from half full to a crescent as he watched. It seemed like a bite taken out of the sun's brilliance. He stared at the shadow on the wall in mounting horror.

As he knelt there, unable to shift his gaze from the sight, he wondered whether this could be Mother Ge's response to Morning Green's blood ritual. A sign to turn from the Ta'atchul, or she would take the sun from them forever.

He became dizzy, and his hands began to shake. Then he saw that the darkness itself was changing, turning into wavy lines like snakes or ripples on moving water. But it seemed to be slowly receding too; with each breath he thought he saw a larger arc of the sun shining through.

"It passes," he said with relief. "It passes!"

"Blood will bring back the sun!" he heard Morning Green proclaim.

Morning Green took him by the chin, raised his face to the sky, and made a slashing movement across his forehead. There was no pain at first. Spadefoot stared at the obsidian blade in the Rainsinger's hand. A piece of his hair was caught on it.

He reached for the hair, but his aim was off. Something warm trickled down his forehead. His eyes stung, first the right and then the left. He put out his tongue and tasted the salty heat of his own blood. "You *cut* me." A throb began in the track of the knife.

Above him, Morning Green roared, "Behold as I deliver the people from the malice of the mother-goddess! She sent her shadow, in the time of woman, to deprive us of the light. She grieves, jealous that you are turning from her, giving yourselves over—heart and heart's-blood and body entire—to the mighty Ta'atchul. Do not be afraid, for by my own blood, drawn from the son of my loins, I call upon the Ta'atchul to drive her shadow away. But to defeat her for always, to conquer this evil entirely, they require a like sacrifice from you."

Spadefoot sagged on his heels and put up a hand. It found his skin gaping open, a strange sensation. "You're mad," he tried to whisper. His unvoiced words barely bubbled through the sticky fluid on his lips.

"The Ta'atchul shall turn back the blackness from the sun, but the power to overcome the goddess's power lies in your hands!" the Rainsinger howled. "Take your knives and draw the blood of all the enemies of the Ta'atchul, and the sun will be thereby restored!"

"Blood! Blood! Blood!" came the chant, quietly at first. Then the rest of the gathering picked it up, raggedly, in little pockets here and there at first but strengthening into a thunderous rumble.

"They understand at last," Morning Green said.

Spadefoot heard immense satisfaction in those four words.

A hand grasped his elbow. "Rise up," the Rainsinger told him. "The one of prophecy shall not grovel before the goddess."

He blinked up through a red haze of his own blood. He had never loved the man he had once thought of as his father, though a much younger Spadefoot had felt admiration, which had faded to respect, which had slowly become resentment and resistance and suspicion.

Now—

Now he tasted something unfamiliar, something bitter, something that lay cold and thick in his mouth along with the blood that dripped down from the wound of Morning Green's making. For the first time, he knew dread. This man could not be allowed to turn the people against each other . . . and against Mother Ge.

"I am the sun made new! I am the sun made new again!"
Hurling it high from the east to the west, from shade to shadow I throw it.

—FROM THE SONG OF CREATION

One of the Cornmaidens rushed into the workroom where Starflower sat struggling to keep herself from cracking apart like an eggshell. The girl's fishlike eyes bulged with excitement.

Starflower wanted to be interested, but she couldn't escape her misery. Every shift on the reed mat, every turn of her head made her ache. But worse, she despaired of ever forgetting the smell of her father's skin, his hot breath on her cheek, his hands pawing at her, the feel of his fists on her face, his voice spewing threats and insults and lies. *I'm your father—I'll tell you what you can and can't do . . . You're too stupid to make your own choices . . . Don't you dare tell me no . . . There'll be no quickening if the skin flute doesn't go in.*

If she was indeed with child, then the Seedkeeper and her father both had lied: him about how making babies happened and the Seedkeeper about when the child was put in her belly, because her father hadn't started to put his hands on her that way—*This is a gift for you, so you aren't frightened by what takes place between a man and a woman*—until after deciding she was to seduce Rush.

Maybe Deerchaser was right in saying that everyone lied. The only difference was what they chose to lie about.

Figuring out the lies didn't matter if she indeed had a baby growing inside her. There was no reason to figure anything out. Her life was over.

But if the Seedkeeper had lied, and there was no baby . . . But if her father had lied about how babies were made . . . But then the baby wouldn't be a few moons old, and that would again mean the Seedkeeper had lied.

Around and around and around her thoughts and memories chased each other.

The fish-faced girl twisted her hands together. "Something's *happening* outside!" she announced. "Come see!"

Most of the other Cornmaidens rose from their tasks and ran out. Starflower remained seated, but a faint stirring of curiosity made her look out the nearest opening of the workroom. The wall ended about knee-high. Above were woven-reed panels that folded to let in the light. It was shadowy out there, dim.

It seemed too early for twilight, but since her arrival in the Smokemothers' compound, time seemed to have crystallized, like the dark sap that seeped out of the mesquite trees in the fields. She thought she'd spent only one day in this place but couldn't swear to it. She might never swear to anything again, after what she'd done to Rush the day before.

Her father had beaten her for not being willing to claim Rush had forced himself on her, and then he had taken her to Knobbyroot and made the complaint himself. Under his threatening glare, what was she to do but agree? Only after he left did she tell Knobbyroot that the punishment she wanted for Rush was that he be made to take her as his mate. It was the only way she could think of to save them both. And it had failed.

She sat there contemplating the gathering darkness outside. It was nothing compared to the darkness in her heart as she thought about the many lies she had told and the ones that had been told to her.

A Cornmaiden pulling threads from a woven cotton shirt to make a design around the neck suggested, "Let's go see if they're lighting the fires."

"It's too early in the day for that," said a soft-looking girl, her belly as big and round as a water olla, who deftly plied a needle as she attached shells to a doeskin dress.

The thread-puller set aside the shirt. "It's obviously later than that! I can hardly see what I'm doing." She rose and held a hand down to the pregnant Cornmaiden, who shook her head.

"It's too much work to get up," she told her friend. Then she spoke to Starflower, startling her: "You go."

Starflower would have refused, but she saw that they three were the only ones left in the workroom. If she stayed, the one about to give birth to a baby would undoubtedly talk to her. She couldn't bear that. What if the girl was nice—and then died while bringing forth that new life?

She rose and walked to the door, which opened onto the Smokemothers' large central plaza. The sky had yellowed almost to the putrid hue that heralded one of the late-summer windstorms. But there was no dust blowing about; in fact, the whole village seemed to have gone eerily quiet. And cold.

Starflower shivered and hugged herself.

The other Cornmaidens stood in the plaza. They all looked in the same direction. Starflower followed their gazes and saw the sun glowing balefully in a faded, hazy sky.

One turned away, the heels of her hands pressed to her eyes. "I can't see!" she cried. "I've been struck blind! Something is eating the sun . . . We're all going to—"

A Smokemother, her face drawn and anxious, came bustling from the other direction. "Hush now!" She hurried the hysterical girl back into the workroom. "Sit down and face the wall. Keep your eyes closed," she said from the doorway. She turned, set her hands on her hips, and ordered the other girls, "Don't look right at the sun! Doesn't anyone have any sense?"

"But it's dark!" protested one of the Cornmaidens.

"Not dark enough," the Smokemother told her. "Even during a storm, the sun can still shine bright enough through the clouds to blind you."

Starflower drifted farther into the plaza. She lifted her face and stared right at the sun. Blindness would be welcome. To never again see her father's face . . .

"Stop that!" The Smokemother grabbed her by the shoulders and turned her away.

Starflower fought her but got a slap across the face for it. When she opened her eyes, she was rewarded by the sight of nothing but flashes of light and shadow. She almost smiled.

"You're here in our care," the Smokemother warned. "That means we'll take care of you even if you don't want it. Inside!"

Starflower couldn't tell where the workroom was, couldn't see her hands as she held them out before her. Before she could say as much, someone smacked into her. They both grunted from the impact.

She staggered back, flailing her arms for balance. There were no more flickering lights now, only darkness—a terrible, frightening sensation, as for a moment she couldn't tell whether she was upright or falling. What madness had come over her? she wondered, as her desire to be blind vanished and she stood there blinking.

"Get out!" she heard the Smokemother say.

Then came a boy's voice; it reminded her of Vineslayer. Through the dampness brought on by her fluttering eyelids, she began to regain her sight, doubled and spotty though it was.

The boy brushed off his tunic with abrupt, angry gestures and declared, "The Rainsinger needs whoever here has the steadiest nerves." His officious manner fell away then. Shakily he announced, "Spadefoot's head is sliced wide open! Somebody's gotta keep him from bleeding to death, and the Childcatcher isn't around to do it! Hurry, one of you lot!"

Starflower's stomach heaved as she recalled the blood trickling down Deerchaser's back, Spadefoot's cold face as he watched. She turned away and found herself weeping.

"What did he say about Spadefoot?" someone asked. "He's been hurt," another answered. Several of the Cornmaidens began to speak over each other. Their voices echoed off the adobe walls of nearby buildings. The cacophony made Starflower's ears hurt; she placed her hands over them.

The Smokemother silenced the girls with a few sharp words. Starflower took her hands from her ears in time to hear the Smokemother say, "No reason to worry about Spadefoot. Mother Ge has him in her keeping. Where's Hummingbird?"

"Here."

Through her tears, Starflower couldn't see very well. But she thought the Cornmaiden with the swollen belly was the one who had spoken.

The Smokemother said to whichever one was Hummingbird, "You go. And take some cloth for bandages. Head wounds bleed a lot. Remember to wash it off first with lots of water."

"Yes, all right."

"Sharptongue, you've worked with the Childcatcher. Package up whatever herbs she uses for cleansing and healing, if she can't be found. You lot—go find the high priestess."

Several of the Cornmaidens began to bustle around. Starflower stood uselessly out of the way.

"Starflower, what are you crying about?" The Smokemother sounded exasperated. "Spadefoot will be fine."

"I wasn't worried about him." She was, a little, but then she reminded herself how much she loathed Spadefoot for bringing her here. "That boy, he came looking for the Childcatcher. What can she do for an injured man?"

"A woman's body sometimes tears when the baby comes out too fast. It takes someone with a steady hand to sew her up."

"Oh." Starflower's hand flew to her belly.

"It won't happen to you. Not with your first. They come slowly, in their own time."

She supposed that was intended to be reassuring. But she wondered whether that was what had taken her mother's life.

"That's not where babies come out anyway," one of the Cornmaidens said, pointing at Starflower's hand where it rested on her skirt.

The heat of embarrassment rose in her damp cheeks. At the moontime hut, the more experienced women had likewise made fun of her.

She wasn't stupid, it was just that she'd relied on her father to teach her about women's things. As awful as living with him had become, never before had she believed that he wanted to see her come to a bad end. Now she had no reason to think he cared about her at all.

The Seedkeeper had tried asking her questions that first day. She only vaguely remembered what had been asked, before the Seedkeeper had sent her to the workroom, perhaps unsatisfied because she hadn't been able to answer anything in a way that made sense.

Most of the questions were about Spadefoot, she recalled: how she knew him, why he took an interest in her, what she thought of him. Then the Seedkeeper asked about her accusation of Rush, about whether she'd conspired with Deerchaser in accusing him.

When she'd walked into the workroom that first day—as a newcomer and brought there under mysterious circumstances—ten or twelve Cornmaidens had turned their heads to watch her. Now, in the plaza just outside the workroom, she found herself the object of their gazes again and almost wished for the blindness back.

"Most of us are quite fond of Spadefoot," one of them told her, hostility clear in her voice.

Starflower drew her bottom lip between her teeth. "It's not that I don't care about him—" she began.

"You said you weren't worried about him," another Cornmaiden said. "He's been attacked!"

"We don't know that," the Smokemother pointed out.

"The Seeker said he'd been sliced open," the girl argued. "What else would it be?"

Starflower saw in her memory Spadefoot heaving that corpse up onto his shoulder, the vision of the owl-spirit pursuing . . . *her,* she'd thought then. But maybe *he* had become its target, by shifting his vow-brother's body. But he couldn't die from that. Could he? Could a priest's soul seek vengeance on one of its own?

Or would that untethered spirit be more likely to come after her, the one that had disturbed it? Could it have entered her body and quickened a new life within?

She felt hot and dizzy, overwhelmed by an urge to get away from all these prying eyes. The sun had brightened. It beat down on her head.

She'd forgotten, in the excitement of the past little while, about the dark veil that had seemed to draw across the face of the sun. It might have been a forewarning of Spadefoot's doom, she thought. But it was gone now.

There was no reason for her to still be upset. Unless . . . her hands dropped to her belly again. Unless the Seedkeeper was right that she somehow had gotten a child planted there. Maybe the Seedkeeper and her father had both told her the truth after all. If she was indeed carrying a child, its creation might not have happened in the usual way.

On the last day of the midwinter festival, the light of the setting sun angled through the open panel and shone on Starflower's hands. Her fingers were bloody from tearing beargrass lengthwise into strips. She hadn't worked much with beargrass before, but that was what was available in the workroom, because it could be made into durable sleeping-mats. She didn't care about the blood. Nor did she mind the pain as she worked; it blended in with her older cuts and bruises.

One of the girls had given her a knife to cut the narrow leaves with to save her fingers from the rough edges. She'd put the knife down after she imagined stabbing it into her belly over and over. She knew that was crazy. And more often than the Seedkeeper saying she was carrying a baby, she heard Deerchaser saying that everyone lied.

There was no way to know what to do. So she just sat there and tried to work and not worry.

A sandal-clad foot nudged her and brought her out of her dark thoughts.

"What?" she said sharply to the girl who stood over her.

"The Dreamwalker wants you."

"Why?"

The girl shrugged. "You'll learn not to ask questions when summoned by one of the Revered Grandmothers."

Starflower felt like saying she wouldn't be here long enough to learn anything, but that would likely start an argument that she didn't have the strength for. Anyway, who knew how long she would be with the Smokemothers? Maybe forever, until she died. "I'm going, I'm going."

Slowly she walked across the flat, hard-packed ground toward the long building where the high priestesses lived and worked. The sun felt warm on her skin. If she had any desire to heal, she might have taken her mat outside to work. As it was, all she wanted was for this day to pass into the next.

A Smokemother led her through the passages to the Dreamwalker's cell.

The order's seer gave her no greeting, no pleasantries of *How are you?* or *Have you settled in?* "The Rainsinger must be stopped," she said. Her hair stuck out distractingly from the cloth that covered her head, and her eyes burned into Starflower's. The whites were tinged with red, and the pupils were so large that the brown color surrounding them was only a thin ring, thinner than the last crescent of a new moon. "You understand what he is claiming?"

Starflower had no idea what the priestess was talking about. "No, Revered Grandmother."

The Dreamwalker frowned. "After his sacrifice of Spadefoot, the Rainsinger changed the words for the New Fire rituals. Drawing his son's blood seems to have driven him to madness. You have heard none of this from the Cornmaidens?"

She shook her head.

"He claims the Ta'atchul have chosen him to bring peace back to the People of Two Rivers."

Starflower said nothing in response.

"Well? How do you suppose he proposes to do so?"

"I don't know, Revered Grandmother."

The Smokemother's eyes narrowed on her. "He wants to be rid of the Watermasters. We will have no more need of the canals in the new world he wants to inflict on us. 'When all the green ribbons have dwindled to dust,' as the rainbow knife prophecy says, only then will he be happy."

As a farmer's daughter, Starflower had long heard complaints about giving up a goodly portion of the crop to the Watermasters. And not just them. Farmers blustered about having to share their harvest with the Stormbringers and Smokemothers too. But no one actually thought it possible. Except, now, the Rainsinger.

"Tell me, girl, what would happen if there were no more canals, if the green ribbons held only dust instead of water? What of the crops so precious to the farmers then? Hmm?"

"If what you say is so, the Rainsinger says we must trust in the rains. Place our faith in the Ta'atchul."

The sudden fury evident in every line of the priestess's frail seated form made Starflower take a step back, uncertain whether that rage was directed at her or the Rainsinger. "Revered Grandmother?"

"We do not lay our faith in the Ta'atchul, nor does the Rainsinger speak for anyone who bides in this house." The Smokemother glared at her. "We serve Mother Ge, the one who made us . . . and everything in our world."

"Yes," Starflower ventured in an attempt to pacify the angry priestess. She was no Cornmaiden, and she didn't serve the goddess.

A sudden thought struck her: what then was she? She might never be able to return to her clan, her mother's people, once they knew she'd lied about Rush. She knew of no way to remain here, safe from her father, without becoming a Cornmaiden, and if she did that, she would be at the mercy of the priests, no matter what Spadefoot promised.

If the Seedkeeper was right, anyway, she carried a baby already and would soon start to puff up like a toad. Then she would know that her time in the world was nearly done. But the Seedkeeper couldn't be right.

The Dreamwalker said, "The highest service is to bring forth new life."

"So we've been taught, Revered Grandmother."

"The Seedkeeper admitted you to this precinct claiming you were with child. And not just any child, but that of the Rainsinger's son." The Dreamwalker's mouth twisted in contempt. "That would make you a very important young woman. Exceptional, even. And do you know why?"

Starflower shook her head.

"Because if you have indeed captured Spadefoot's heart and caused him to break his vow to the Ta'atchul, the Seedkeeper believes you will be able to separate him from the Stormbringers, even from his father, and bring him to Mother Ge. It could shake the Temple of Mist to its foundations!"

The priestess went on, "Do you know what the problem with that is?"

Again Starflower shook her head.

"Do you not?"

"No."

"The babe's father is your own father, not Spadefoot! You are a disgusting creature, engaging in carnal relations with your own blood kin and passing off the issue as that of the Rainsinger's son!"

"That's not true!"

"I have seen it in my visions," the Dreamwalker told her coldly. "Your wickedness is what brought the desolation of the sun, as Mother Ge's warning. You deserve to be expelled from this house, or worse!"

"I never have lain with any man! I'm still untouched!"

Starflower, frustrated by the priestess's refusal to believe her, fell silent, fuming. What more could she say? She'd told the Seedkeeper, had told her clan-sisters at the moontime hut. And it was the truth. Her father had never put himself inside her.

If there was a baby, it was forming in her as in one of the stories of the First Days—made from a knot of cholla thorns or from a ball or from moonlight, the father not human. Or human once but no longer alive?

"The inquest for the Canalmaster begins tomorrow," the Dreamwalker told her. In a softer voice, she added, "If you indeed have never lain with a man, you will tell the truth to the inquisitors and see the Canalmaster, an innocent man, set free."

Anger heated her blood as she understood what the priestess was doing. "You just now accused me of being with my father in a way that is forbidden," she retorted. "Was that a lie, a test to see if I would confess?"

"A test, yes, but not of your guilt. Of your backbone. To find out whether you have the courage to admit the truth."

"And risk a whipping, like Deerchaser?" She didn't see herself as a coward, but she also didn't think these priestesses were to be trusted.

"We will protect you. But in answer to your question, you will tell the truth about the Canalmaster because you must. The Watermasters cannot afford to be at odds with the farmers. We cannot afford for them to be so. These are critical days, what with the dark-sun and so much stirring of prophecy and vision."

"I don't see what that has to do with me."

"It has to do with everyone, if the Allmother is walking among us."

"Why isn't that a good thing?" Starflower asked. "She's the giver of life, bringer of water, enricher of spirit—"

"Do not think of her as only those loving aspects spoken of in song and prayer. Remember that what she gives, she also has the power to take away. That is why we have midwives to sing the spirit into the world and soul-cutters to sing it out. Life and death, water and thirst, beauty and horror. Life in balance. Never be so foolish as to believe that she brings only goodness and hope. After all—" The priestess leaned forward and beckoned Starflower closer.

When she drew near enough to smell the tobacco smoke and the dizzyweed on the seer's breath, she heard, "She made your father." Recoiling, Starflower was caught by the Smokemother's harsh stare. "If you do not want to end up in his grasp again, you will do this."

Starflower felt herself being backed into a corner. The room was so small, there was no space to shield her from the other woman's will, battering away at her resistance. "You promise you can protect me from punishment?"

"While you are with the Smokemothers, neither your father nor the interrogators have any authority over you. Sanctuary, remember."

Yes, sanctuary from her father. But not from the priests, not if she became a Cornmaiden and eventually joined the Smokemothers' order. Starflower's hands formed into little impotent fists against her sides.

The priestess's face twisted into something like a smile, nearly drowning her eyes in a ripple of wrinkles. "Testify to the Canalmaster's innocence—whether it is the truth or not—and I will give you what you want most."

"Anything?"

"Anything in my power to give."

Such slyness there was in the seer's voice, Starflower wondered if she was expected to ask to be rid of the baby. Instead, she said, "I want to go home. I want Cloud-Leaf Clan to take me in."

She had gained the seer's promise, though she wasn't sure she could count on it. And so the next day she found herself once again cloaked and veiled and watching the inquisitors assemble to decide Rush's future. The inquest was held in the trade ground, where she had walked with Rush not so long before. On one end of the plaza was the Temple of the Mist; on the other, the Masterholding. She could hardly bear the waiting.

Although she couldn't see Rush, she knew he had to be there, listening to the rumble of conversation and even occasional laughter, just as she was doing. Some people sounded as carefree as if this was just another day.

Others spoke of the darkening of the sun. They argued about why it had happened: some called it a punishment by the Ta'atchul for the people's lack of faith; a few said it was a warning sent by the Allmother to stop the Rainsinger's blood-rite. No one really understood what had made the sun come back, either, though many argued that it had to be the blood pouring from Spadefoot's head.

No one knew whether this weird occurrence would ever happen again. But everyone had an opinion.

Something similar was true for this inquest: although no one but she and Rush knew what had happened between them, everyone had an opinion. For many, it was something to gossip about, to laugh about, while for others, it was something to ruin lives over.

Starflower shook her head and twisted her hands together.

When she briefly heard her father's voice somewhere in the crowd, she flinched. Not being a member of Cloud-Leaf Clan, he hadn't been permitted at the clan hearing. But there was no way even the Smokemothers could keep him from this inquest. Or so they'd explained when she suggested it.

Finally one of the masked men among the inquisitors stepped forward and said, "We are gathered here today to determine the just and appropriate punishment for this man—"

One of the other inquisitors interrupted. "You get ahead of yourself. His guilt hasn't been proved."

"The woman who declared him innocent perjured herself in the clan hearing. No others have stepped forward to proclaim his innocence. That is sufficient to mark him guilty."

"There is one here who would speak to free him," the Dreamwalker stated coolly.

Starflower couldn't see the priestess, but she recognized the voice. Her stomach fell as she understood that the moment of reckoning was upon her. Her mouth went dry, and she licked her lips.

"What trick is this?" demanded the man who wanted Rush punished.

"No trick. Come forward, clan-daughter. Speak truth this time."

A dead silence fell as Starflower advanced to the edge of the crowd and hovered there, unable to take that last step into the space where Rush stood waiting, his face marked with angry bruises and his clothes torn and dirty. A hand between her shoulder blades shoved her forward.

She heard some muttering about bringing in a new witness without warning. It turned into a roar of protest as she pushed back her netted veil to reveal her face. She clamped her hands over her ears to block out the din echoing off the walls.

The hubbub settled gradually as the first inquisitor bellowed for quiet.

She lowered her hands as he spoke to her, his white-painted mask glinting in the sunlight. "If you say now that this Watermaster is innocent, then you lied to your clan before. Do you know the punishment—"

A strong-voiced woman spoke up to say she'd taken sanctuary among the Smokemothers and thus would receive no punishment. Starflower hoped that proved to be so. She didn't think she was strong enough to endure such a whipping as Deerchaser had suffered.

The first inquisitor spoke to Starflower, but his voice was loud enough for all to hear. "You swear, by the Allmother's mercy, to tell us the truth?"

"I . . . I do so swear." She took a deep breath. "This man—" Although the Dreamwalker had told her what to say, getting it out was harder than she'd expected. "He's—"

She took another breath and plunged ahead. "The Canalmaster never violated me. My father beat me to make me say so. That's where I got these marks on my face." Defiantly she added a few words of her own: "But I've never lain with any man." She faltered at the possibility that the Seedkeeper would contradict her, but when the old priestess's raspy voice didn't sound, she gathered her courage and went on with the prepared speech. "Rush never laid a hand on me. This is all a conspiracy against the Canalmaster. My father—Earth Holder, that is—and Knobbyroot desired to ruin him and put Holdsbreath in his place. I heard them planning to do just that."

"She lies!" she heard as a protest from another of the inquisitors.

"Silence!" The main inquisitor spun toward the woman who'd said Starflower was under the protection of the Smokemothers. "You! Do you countenance this ridiculous claim? A conspiracy! You would make a fool of me so?"

Again voices rose, as people raged at each other, at Rush, at the inquisitor, at her. Starflower found herself in the midst of a turbulent anger that surged and built like a flash flood. Uneasily she reminded herself that she was still under the protection of the Smokemothers and none would dare harm her. But as people shifted and the crowd tightened and moved in around her and she was jostled from one side and then the other, she became less sure of her safety.

There was hatred all around, some of it directed at her. Her eyes met those of Knobbyroot, whose dark and angry face promised retribution. What her father's response would be, she didn't even dare imagine. He might even be close to her now, in the buffeting crowd. But, strangely, his reaction wasn't the one that most concerned her. What did the man she had wronged think about her confession?

She stared at Rush, willing him to look at her, give her any indication that he could forgive what she'd done. She'd been forced into it by her father; she bore the marks of his anger on her face. She'd come here today to make things right, as much as she could.

Out of the corner of her eye, Starflower saw the Dreamwalker, a straight-backed, wild-haired figure unafraid of the massed people and undeterred by the commotion, which diminished as she moved through it. The priestess positioned herself next to Rush, who looked forward and didn't speak.

To the main inquisitor the seer said, "The Allmother has given to me the gift of in-seeing. Do you doubt this?"

He glanced around the other inquisitors. If he wanted to call her gift into question, he decided against it: "No, Revered Grandmother. I will grant that is true."

"Do you grant also that the Allmother has given to me the ability to scry, using blood?"

"Yes, Revered Grandmother."

"Then listen to what I have to say. The Watermaster who stands before us today has never entered her body. I have done a blood-working on her, and this I swear, as an avowed servant of Mother Ge."

Starflower was startled. Such a look into a person's past required blood still fresh and red. It wasn't done lightly, for it was said to sap the scryer's strength. How could the seer have done a blood-working on her, without her knowing?

She remembered one of the Cornmaidens cleaning off her cuts and bruises after the Seedkeeper had sent her to the workroom. She hadn't thought to ask what would be done with the bloodied cloths after.

People began to murmur.

"This clan-daughter claims she has never lain with a man," said a masked woman in the group of inquisitors. "Why, then, is she with the Smokemothers? Is this yet another tradition we're overturning in these dark days?"

"She claims to be an innocent, yes," the Dreamwalker said, "but the Seedkeeper has seen that this isn't so. She bears a child. And it belongs to the priest Spadefoot."

"No! No!" shouted Starflower. "That's a lie!" There was a stabbing pain in her belly, just like moontime cramps. *There's no babe in me. It's impossible!* But the pain was so intense, she couldn't get the words out.

The Smokemothers had turned on her, just as she'd feared. What was she to do now? There was nowhere else to go. She was all alone.

Clutching her belly, she dropped to her knees with the wild, almost pleasurable thought that maybe there was a monster inside her, like the witch Ho'ok, formed from cholla branches and a priest's angry spirit, and it would burst her open from the inside and she would die and all of this despair would leak out of her and the agony would all be over.

Ringing in Rush's ears and the echoes of voices off the plastered walls had made him miss much of what had been said in the past few moments. But he gathered that Starflower had recanted her accusation.

So. Was he a free man?

His mouth was dry, and his throat felt like it was lined with cotton. When he coughed, his chest hurt. The priests hadn't fed him or provided water since the second day of his imprisonment. Nor had Spadefoot come to see him again.

Rush swayed. He'd managed to climb the ladder out of the storage room when the priests had released him this morning, then walked on his own while being escorted from the temple precinct to the trade ground. He felt a flush of pride for remaining on his feet this long. He was determined not to fall on his face in front of these people who despised him.

In his time in the storage room, he'd had plenty of time to think. What he had concluded, bitterly, was that he had done everything in his power to restore the canals so that next summer the farmfolk would have water for their fields. If they were too foolish to realize that and to understand how utterly untrustworthy the rain priests were, they deserved what was coming to them.

His bitterness carried over to Deerchaser, perhaps unfairly. He couldn't help but wonder whether she had turned against him too, since she didn't seem to be in the plaza. He almost hoped the whip cuts on her back were worse than the bonemender had led him to believe, because otherwise it meant she didn't care what happened to him. Four days he'd worried about her, and now as he looked around there was no sign that she had given him a single thought.

He was finished with this place, he realized. In their readiness to believe Starflower's accusation, the people of Crookstaff Village had exiled him as surely as if he had done the evil deed she'd accused him of. They had believed the worst of the Wilders on the basis of a false rumor; they had likewise condemned him, because of what this girl had said, even though she had now taken it back. The fact that they believed him capable of harming her . . . such a judgment he couldn't forgive.

He glanced at her, the one who had ruined all his plans and ambitions. She knelt, sobbing, a stricken look on her face. Reluctantly he felt pity for her. Someone had beaten her, after all, and perhaps done worse than that.

The Dreamwalker made an impatient gesture to someone in the crowd. Another Smokemother came forward. She coaxed the overwrought girl up and led her away.

"You can go," the main inquisitor said.

Go where? Rush wanted to ask, but he doubted he could get the words out. Then he realized the order wasn't directed at him. The man looked instead at the high priestess.

She held her ground. "You would condemn the girl for falling for a man's blandishments, yet what of Spadefoot? Is he to go unpunished for breaking his vows? He should be cast out of the priesthood!"

"That is for the rain priests to decide," the inquisitor answered. "Or perhaps it has already been done. You must ask the Rainsinger whether his son's oathbreaking is the reason he bloodied Spadefoot to bring back the sun from its vanishment."

None of what he said made sense to Rush. Though he listened, the next exchanges between the Smokemother and the main inquisitor didn't clarify what the man meant by Spadefoot being bloodied or the sun vanishing.

"It was the Rainsinger's introduction of a blood-rite that made the sun go dark," she argued.

"You cannot know that," the inquisitor said. "Blood-working and in-seeing you and your kind may perform on clan-daughters like Starflower, but there is no scrying to be done on Mother Ge."

"No blood-working is needed to see that the Rainsinger's defiling of time-honored ceremonies made the Mother-of-All-Things withdraw the sun's light from us, as a reminder of all that she provides."

"The Ta'atchul—"

"Ah, yes, the priests' imaginary beings in the sky," the high priestess sneered. "But even the boldest of the rain priests dare not claim the Ta'atchul are gods, only magical. How, exactly, are they different from the Ancestors or even the Cloud People of the old religion? The priests never say. These Ta'atchul are not mentioned in the tales of the First Days, which describe the creation of the world and everything in it. For Mother Ge we all are her children, even the Ta'atchul. Challenge that truth—deny her—and you risk losing everything."

Some in the audience nodded and murmured to each other. But Rush didn't see the passion in their eyes that had followed the Rainsinger's proclamation a few days earlier. This high priestess, with her tufts of hair sticking out and her smoke-roughened voice, didn't compel her listeners to believe, not like the pale-skinned orator did.

"This is a battle between male and female," she continued, her voice rising as though she realized she was losing people's attention and was desperate to get it back. "Between the destruction that the priests would bring upon you and the granting of life that Mother Ge has always . . ."

Rush, with little interest in the priestess's condemnation of the priests, decided that since no one stood in his way, he was free to go.

He turned his back on the temple and started toward the Masterholding. In his present state of hunger, exhaustion, and dizziness, it seemed to recede even as he plodded in that direction, one step after another, heading for the northeast corner, the one farthest from the plaza but closest to his quarters. He would have to climb a ladder higher than the one in the storage room. Surely he could manage that.

A group of men pushed past him. He lost his footing and dropped to his knees. Laboriously he rose.

One of them turned back and spat on him. "Watermasters!" the man growled. ". . . come after your women . . ."

Rush couldn't make out everything the man said. The hearing in his left ear was diminished, as if that side of his head were underwater. It had been for a few days, since the beating he'd taken during the clan hearing. He ignored the provocation, just stood there with his head bowed and waited for his tormentor to run out of abuse.

It didn't take long. When the man got bored and left, he supposed that was a testament to how pathetic he looked; abusing him must have been like beating up on a child. He leaned against a house wall and placed his hands on the cool adobe for support.

Crack and Tumbler ran up to him. "Are you all right?" Tumbler asked.

"It's not as bad as it looks," he tried to say. His tongue stuck to the roof of his mouth.

In the storage room, he'd found a small nodule of heavy dark-gray stone, hard yet yielding. Some of the Far-Traders up at Sky River had talked of such things. He'd placed it in his mouth once the drinking water was gone, and he'd chewed on it to produce saliva to moisten his dry mouth. He had taken it out to sleep last night. When the priests had come for him this morning, he hadn't taken the time to grope for it. He wished he had it now.

"Water," he croaked.

"You want water?" Tumbler asked.

He nodded. The movement nearly made him pitch over. A headache that had been gathering force ever since he'd emerged from the darkness of the storage room into the light struck hard. He put his left hand up, felt around, and found some dried blood in his braids, even in his ear, the one that felt plugged. But his head hurt on the inside too, tight and hot behind his eyes and forehead.

With a worried look, Tumbler waved Crack off to get him some water.

Rush remembered that he wouldn't be welcome at the Masterholding, since Holdsbreath believed *he* was now the Canalmaster. Rush fixed his gaze on the house compound in front of him and headed for it. Strength fading fast, he skirted its wall. As soon as he got to the other side, out of view of the mound, the temple, and the trade plaza alike, he slid down the smooth plastered surface and sat hunched in the shade, arms slung over his knees. He dropped his head onto his arms.

Never before had he felt this weak—not even during his naming quest, which he'd weathered easily enough by imagining himself resting on the bottom of the river, breathing air through a hollow rush stalk just like Coyote in one of the tales of the First Days. He couldn't remember which story now.

The Namers said they thought he'd sped up time in his mind so the days of the ordeal passed without affecting him much. He'd tried doing the same in the storage room, but it hadn't worked. There was no peace to be found, no distancing himself from his worries: mainly Deerchaser and Starflower, his defender and his accuser.

Now, Starflower had become his defender, Deerchaser was nowhere to be found, and the farmers he'd dedicated his life to had turned on him.

He tried to work some saliva into his mouth. "Deerchaser," he mumbled, seeing Tumbler's dusty feet beside him.

"No one's seen her. Or Spadefoot. Not since the day of the dark-sun. The day they took you."

Rush recalled hearing a disturbance that first day. He lifted his head and looked questioningly at Tumbler.

The boy eagerly told him about the sun's disappearance and the duststorm that blew up out of nowhere. Once the storm had blown itself out, the sun had reappeared. Rush recalled Deerchaser's vision, the one that had woken her, screaming, from sleep. In all that had happened since then, he'd forgotten. *The end of the world,* she'd called it. *Too terrifying to bear.* Was this unnatural darkness what she'd seen?

But Tumbler wasn't finished. He explained that some people said the goddess made the sun go dark as a punishment for turning away from her; others believed the storm was sent by the Ta'atchul, for failing to worship them; and still others claimed both strange happenings were warnings from the Ancestors of some horrible fate that was coming, when the one of prophecy would come and save them.

"Spadefoot," Rush said, only half in question. His raspy, thick voice sounded as though it belonged to someone else.

"The Rainsinger cut him!" Tumbler exclaimed, slashing his hand to show how. "Sliced his head wide open! With darkness eating the sun, the Rainsinger gave up the blood of his own son t' bring it back! And it worked!" He waved wildly around at the sunshine. "It worked! The sun came back!"

Rush could understand why many of those who witnessed the darkening of the sun credited the Rainsinger with restoring it. Magic was funny that way.

Claiming the ability to do magic was a powerful thing—just look at the high priestesses, to whose magical gifts he at least partly owed his freedom. A few generations back, the priests had taken credit for ending the Long Thirst, in a bargain that allowed them, outlanders all, to become an essential part of the People of Two Rivers.

So his people wanted to rely on magic now, not the knowledge that the Watermasters had employed on their behalf since time began. He felt he should be angry at that. But he could muster only sadness.

Crack came around the corner with a small jar of water. Rush reached up, took it from him, and drank a few swallows greedily. His stomach spasmed as the water flowed in. He had to struggle to keep from gagging.

Anxiously, Tumbler said, "Where you gonna go?"

Rush shrugged. Speaking was still too difficult. He wet his lips and again filled his mouth with water, letting it ease down his dry throat.

Crack looked unhappy. The boys exchanged glances.

Tumbler said, "Holdsbreath moved in—"

"He burned and broke your stuff," Crack finished.

"Everything. Clothes, maps, tools, everything. Grading stones broken. Plumb bobs shattered." There was sympathy in Tumbler's eyes.

Rush swigged down more of the cool water.

It didn't much matter that the maps were destroyed. He had them in his head. He knew where the base of a headgate needed shoring up, when water needed to be moved through and when it needed to be held back, how much water would fill a field and how much would be too much. He knew every detail of every canal, no matter how small, from The Wing all the way to Earth Holder's attempt to wrest fields back from the desert.

He had studied it all since the moment of his return to Crookstaff Village. The main canal, all seven major branches. Every channel and ditch, every gate and weir, every field. He could walk it in his head—could imagine it greening up in spring, just a few moons away.

That only made him feel more sorry for himself. He had the knowledge still, and only that. He could never again use it anywhere along Earth River. The tools could be replaced. His reputation? Never.

Feeling somewhat refreshed, he became aware that Crack and Tumbler were looking at him, expecting him to . . . to do what? he wondered.

They were a little older than he calculated his and Deerchaser's son would have been. For some moons now they had been listening to him go on about responsibility, duty, doing what had to be done. But what, exactly, had to be—or even could be—done?

If he contested Holdsbreath's claim and the rest of the Earth River Canalmasters supported him, defying Twistedtrack to restore Rush to the position Holdsbreath claimed, that could destroy what little credibility remained for the Watermasters along Earth River. Starflower's accusation had ruined any chance for him to accomplish what the River Council had wanted; the farmers who believed Starflower's accusation but not her recanting of it would make Rush's continued service along Earth River impossible.

There was no going back to being what he had been. *He* was what divided the farmers from the Watermasters now.

What else could he do but go? He could seek out Deerchaser, but that would surely be a mistake too, even if she wanted to see him—the disgust and distrust directed at him would wash over onto her. He couldn't bring that upon her.

What did that leave him? One thing, and one thing only. He could return to Sky River—and be judged a failure.

He gathered his strength and pushed to his feet. "Go on." He waved Crack and Tumbler away. "Go to Holdsbreath. You have your duties."

"No," Tumbler said. The two boys stared at him defiantly.

"Leave me!"

And then it was too late.

Several men armed with digging sticks flooded into the space between the compound walls where Rush and the boys stood. One of them back-handed Crack, who staggered, then steadied himself and ran off. Tumbler placed himself between the grim-faced men and Rush.

"We caught ourselves a Watermaster," said a man distinctive only in not being very tall. He was a clan-sib of Fog-Thread Clan, whose fields had suffered over the summer. He smacked the broad, flat end of his digging stick against his hand. "Hiding behind a boy, are you?"

Rush felt a surge of energy. His focus sharpened as it had always done at the prospect of a fight. He moved Tumbler out of the way and stepped forward. "Go to your gran," he told the boy over his shoulder.

The angry faces were familiar. They had recently appeared in hearings before him. As he recalled, his decisions had gone against them.

". . . shamed her into recanting . . ." he heard, unable to make out more than snippets. ". . . probably carrying his child—just like that other, long time back . . ." ". . . ruined now, of course. What man wants to dip his line where one of *them* has been?" " . . . a seducer who turned mean when he was turned down." The group's mood darkened with every comment.

"And how is that any different from the rest of them?" The one who asked this question was a farmer whose field lay on the edge of Cloud-Leaf Clan's smallholdings. With his massive arms clenched over his chest, he growled out, "They see what they want, and take it! Isn't that what you're all about, Watermaster?"

Rush eyed the man and judged him to be a bully. "If you knew me, you wouldn't be asking."

The big man laughed. "Smart-mouthed just like all your kind. Parasites, the lot of you. Sucking us dry."

Rush recalled having heard of some incident involving the man's bondmate and one of the Wilders during the previous spring's reconstruction work. *At least we know how to please a woman,* he felt like saying—but had sense enough to refrain.

Another man, narrow of face and rabbity, taunted, "Hanging on all of us as surely as those useless baubles you have draped all over you." He darted in and flicked one of Rush's shell-hung plaits before scuttling out of reach. The man's field, one of the outliers for Water-Corn Clan, lay well down the Upper Branch canal. Another clan-sib, he'd been given use-right for a field that yielded less and less each turning. Rush had recommended it be retired.

"Sucking the life out of hard-working folks while you canalfolk play in the water, twelve moons out of thirteen. Happy as children and just as feckless," the short man said. His empty fist opened and closed; the knuckles on his other hand were white from gripping the digging stick.

"I was here working right beside you all summer long and through these past moons," Rush reminded them. "Listening to you when you aired your grievances against one another."

"Listening?" The big farmer laughed tightly. "Telling, more often. Does it make you feel like more of a man to tell a farmer what to do with his own kin's fields? And claiming a share of our crops on top of it."

Rush watched color rise in the man's face and a muscle leap in his cheek. "The priests promise much," he said, trying to be persuasive. "But even they don't claim you can do without the canals entirely."

"Canals, yes. Watermasters, no. We have no need of your kind anymore." The words produced a stir among those who surrounded Rush, but no one contradicted the heavily built farmer, who went on, "The canals are all built now. All we have to do is keep them in repair. Any simpleton can do that."

The group tightened around him, and his nerves twitched.

A deep voice came from behind him. "The water in the canals falls as rain upriver, where all are believers. We will have steady flows and generous crops only when we rid ourselves of unbelievers."

Most of the others seemed to find this reasonable, for there was much nodding of heads. Rush hoped there were a few who hadn't decided to throw away, on wishes and ignorant promises, the very strength that had always sustained their people. He said, "If those upriver believers were so successful, why did so many—including those who became our rain priests—come to our valley as refugees during the Long Thirst?"

"None of that!" The big farmer stepped forward and slapped his meaty palm against Rush's chest, shoving him back. "The Ta'atchul will hear."

Another hissed, "Just the kind of thing the prophecies were aimed at!"

"I say we cleanse ourselves of unbelievers, starting with him!" said the rabbity man.

The powerfully built farmer pulled a hafted chert knife from his sash. Two fingers wide and as deep as a man's palm, it could do a lot of damage. "When we're done here," the big man declared, "we'll go burn out that whole nest of Wilders."

Rush glanced at the rest of the group. If they condemned the big man, as tradition said they must, for wielding a knife with the intent to harm another, he might yet escape with his skin whole. But no one said a thing.

With a laugh, the farmer said, "Too much of a coward to defend yourself, are you?"

Rush's hands were empty, cold, and, he discovered, trembling. "I'm not the one so weak as to resort to violence."

The big man's face twisted. He charged Rush, knife outstretched.

Even as Rush twisted out of the way, Tumbler stepped in front of him. The boy took the blade in his shoulder. Everyone froze in shock, even the big farmer, who dropped the knife in the dirt.

Tumbler grabbed at his shoulder, then glanced at the farmer in bewilderment. A red stain appeared under his hand. It spread quickly on his tunic. Blood welled up between his fingers. He took his hand away and paled as he looked at it.

"Go!" Rush shoved him.

Wide-eyed, the boy stared at him. Then he ran off awkwardly with the bloody hand clutching the opposite shoulder.

"You could have killed him!" Rush exclaimed.

The big man muttered, "Wish I had. Watermaster brat."

"He's one of your own clan-children!"

"That makes it all the worse." Spittle collected at the side of the big man's mouth. "You Watermasters!" He spat. "It's not only our women you steal, but our children too." He stepped forward and clouted Rush on the side of the head with a granite-hard fist.

The blow set off ball lightning in his eye sockets. It was all he could do to keep from toppling over. From the side, the shorter man's digging stick smashed flat-on into his gut just below his ribcage. Rush found himself face-down with a mouth full of dust.

But he kept rolling and managed to struggle back to his feet. The knife attack had been intended to confuse and distract him, he guessed.

Were his dead body to show slashes and deep cuts, there would be trouble. This entire pack would have to deny that the big man had intentionally wielded a blade against him. He didn't think they trusted each other enough to risk false testimony at an inquest, not with Deerchaser's punishment still fresh in their minds.

But bruises? On top of the ones he already had, no one could identify new ones. They could beat him all they wanted.

He sensed the movement of an incoming fist rather than saw it, and he flinched away just in time. As the hard-muscled shoulder went past on the follow-through, Rush jabbed at the unguarded belly of the big farmer.

When his hand met a wall of muscle, he knew he'd miscalculated. In the winter leathers his attackers wore, it was easy to mistake solidity for fat. The farmer was barely rocked. Those arms began to move. Both of them.

Rush brought his knee up sharply into his opponent's crotch.

That felled him.

Not that it did Rush any good. His adversaries laid into him as a group. They pummeled him while he still stood, then kicked him after he fell and curled protectively around himself.

Only a few managed to get in a decent kick before a woman called out, "Stop this right now!"

The men backed off a little, looking from one to another as though waiting for someone to take over from the still-moaning big man as the leader.

"There will be no death to unbelievers here today," she declared with authority.

Rush tried to rise but couldn't get any part of his abused body to move as Deerchaser came to stand over him. He would yell at her later, he thought, if by some chance they both made it out. For now, he would work on breathing.

"Who'll stop us? You?" The deep voice from before was contemptuous.

She said without hesitation, "The Mother-of-All-Things works through me. I saw the swallowing of the sun in visions, before it ever happened. Just ask the remembrancer."

After several heartbeats, the deep voice said, "The Rainsinger was the one who sent away the storm and brought back the sun."

"It was Mother Ge who brought back the sun," Deerchaser stated with unshakable certainty. "After taking it away when the Rainsinger conducted that abomination of a ritual. Blood sacrifice—that's not our way!"

"He used the blood of his son to drive back the dark."

"It was the Allmother's love for us that ended the storm and gave us light again, just as she did in the First Days."

The rabbity man spoke from behind her. "We have only your word that you saw this vision."

"You can ask the remembrancer. Or if you dare, ask the Seedkeeper. Or my mother or Knobbyroot. There are many who know of my visions."

Struggling to his feet, Rush dragged air into his protesting lungs. "This is madness," he croaked out. Or thought he did. No one seemed to hear.

"But Spadefoot—" the deep-voiced man started.

Deerchaser interrupted. "Have you seen him since the dark-sun, seen whether he truly bears a wound on his forehead? Or was it all a trick, like shaking water from dry reeds or producing a full-grown seedling from a grain of pollen, as we've seen in rituals before?"

The men looked uncertain. "I saw the Rainsinger pour blood from a beating heart," one said. "That heart was alive."

"Did he? Or was it some other red liquid he poured," asked Deerchaser, "out of cold, dead flesh? We brought him that deer heart days ago!"

"It was Spadefoot's blood that brought back the sun," the deep-voiced man insisted.

She said, "The Rainsinger wants you to believe that. But if these Ta'atchul demand blood, they're monsters. The People of Two Rivers have never done such terrible things."

"It proves that the Ta'atchul are far more powerful than your goddess, just as the Rainsinger says."

The speaker with the deep voice became visible as his companions edged away. Rush finally was able to put a face to the voice, but it wasn't one he recalled having seen before. The fellow was likely not a farmer, or at least hadn't come before Rush at a hearing. Why was he with the others?

"Then where's the rain?" asked Deerchaser. "If the Ta'atchul are so powerful, where is the rain they're supposed to bring? It didn't come over the summer, not enough. And certainly not this fall."

"They're holding it back to punish unbelievers like you!"

She extended her arms upward, spread wide and fingers outstretched, and turned in a circle to rake her gaze over the men who surrounded her and Rush. "Then strike me down," she dared them. "Go on. Start the cleansing with me."

Rush couldn't believe her foolhardiness.

Lowering her arms but keeping them away from her sides, she arched her back in a grotesque parody of womanly invitation and lifted her face toward the sun. "If you truly believe these unseen sky-beings are more potent than the Mother-of-All-Creation, the one who made us and made the world around us, then strip my soul from my body and let it wander while you pray to the Ta'atchul to keep you safe. Go ahead. I won't even resist. Kill me."

The men stared uneasily at each other as she stood there exposed. Finally, the big farmer said, "You're not an unbeliever. You believe in Mother Ge. These Watermasters, they have no room in their hearts for anything greater than themselves."

She stretched her arms toward the group as though she would embrace them all. In a voice as weighted with significance as Morning Green's, she intoned, "It only starts with the Watermasters . . . do you think the Rainsinger will let it end there? Light one spark here, and soon fires will rage all through the valley. That's the prophecy: 'The land is burning.' Start the burning now, if you truly believe. It will happen anyway, if you follow the path of hatred and discord the Rainsinger has started down. Go on. Prove your faith in these false spirits of the sky. Start with me, for I refuse to turn against Mother Ge. I do not believe in the Ta'atchul: I deny their existence, their power. I call the Rainsinger a fraud, as I have done so many times before. Strike me down, right here, right now, as an unbeliever."

Her presence seemed more than just Deerchaser now, greater and more powerful, as though the goddess actually worked through her body. The men muttered among themselves, but even the deep-voiced stranger refrained from taking her up on her challenge.

"Now go!" she ordered. "Before I call down lightning upon your heads!"

As though ashamed to have their reluctance to act witnessed by the group, first one and then another drifted away.

Once they were gone, Rush leaned against the wall again. His head pounded, his vision grayed around the edges, and his heart hammered in his chest. Feeling as though his knees were about to give out, he eased to the ground.

He watched her walk toward the knife. She knelt to retrieve it. As she picked it up, the wet blood changed from red to a whole rainbow of colors, reflecting the sun like water. Tumbler's blood!

Rush swallowed the bile that rose in his throat as he thought about what had just happened. He wiped a shaking hand over his mouth. He wanted to go after the farmers, one by one, and kill them for what they had done to a boy whose only offense had been defending him.

"Tumbler?" he muttered. "Will he . . . ?"

"I saw him. He'll be all right. It wasn't deep." Deerchaser tucked the knife in her belt pouch and put her hand on Rush's shoulder. "His clan-grannie will see justice done."

Wearily Rush closed his eyes and told himself it wasn't his place to make that happen. The boys weren't his ditchrunners anymore. And Tumbler did have his clan to stand behind him. But letting go was difficult. After only a few moons, he had become attached to Tumbler and Crack.

Justice, she called it. That was what the clan had meted out to her, and she had accepted it. He opened his eyes and started to ask her why. He stopped when he saw the stiffness in the way she stood, her face pale and forehead beaded with sweat. "Are you all right?"

"Better than you, I guess."

"You shouldn't even be up, let alone here with me."

She squeezed his shoulder lightly, then dropped her hand away. "I'm all right, really. The cuts are all scabbed over, healing fine. Starting to itch. The bonemender gave me some salve to put on, but I can't reach. Maybe you could do it for me."

Rush was tempted . . . but he couldn't allow her to be coupled with him in people's minds any longer. As strongly as he could manage, he said, "You speak as if we'll be together."

"Why can't we?" She eyed him. "You blame yourself for my whipping, don't you! Well, stop it! It was my choice to lie, trying to save you—"

"As you chose to rise from your pallet early and risk yourself a second time? I don't thank you for it. They'll only be back, them and more like them. The Rainsinger has turned the farmfolk against me." The outburst exhausted him. His eyes drifted closed again, and his head began to spin. As the smell of stew from a nearby compound tickled his nose, he thought he might be sick.

"So you're going to sit there and feel sorry for yourself until they come back and beat you some more?"

The scorn in her voice roused him enough to look at her.

"You're going to let them win?" she added.

Which them? he wondered vaguely. Those farmers who attacked him weren't his real enemy. They wouldn't have dared do anything without Morning Green stirring them up. And there would be no punishment for the Rainsinger, Twistedtrack, Holdsbreath, anyone. He had no clan to seek justice. But maybe Morning Green would be punished after all; maybe Spadefoot would die, another man's son he claimed as his own.

A dead son. Rush's son, dead. Rush's son that he'd never known. His attempt to stoke his former righteous indignation didn't work. He didn't feel angry with Deerchaser anymore. He didn't feel anything. Just tired.

"Come on. Get up!" she urged.

"Go away," he told her. She didn't listen. Instead she prodded and pulled at him, fussing all the while. She hissed in pain a few times but kept nagging him to move. The more he tried to push her hands away, the more insistent she became—even to the point of grabbing him by the shoulders and trying to haul him upright with her own slight body.

Finally he gave in and rose unsteadily. She hurried to his side—his right side, where he could hear her better. He wasn't sure that was a good thing. She slipped his arm across her shoulders.

They started along the path, neither of them able to walk a straight line. He didn't know where they were going. He doubted they could get there anyway.

"What about Starflower?" Deerchaser asked. "What happened there?"

"I didn't harm her—"

"I know. I never thought it of you. But what did she say to set you free? And why did she make the accusation? Why you?"

"She's with child."

"Her father's?" Deerchaser lurched to a halt.

Appalled, Rush pulled away from her so he could see her face. "No—Spadefoot's. According to the Smokemothers."

Deerchaser pursed her lips and considered that for a moment. She shook her head. "I don't think so. I think he's just another who was caught up in her craziness."

"I wasn't," Rush said—but even as he made his denial, he knew it was only pride talking. He'd been locked in a dark hole for four days because of the girl.

His head felt like it had cotton packed into it. "Do you have any food?" he asked abruptly. He had gone without for too long. The water from the boys—Tumbler!—hadn't filled his belly.

Wordlessly she pulled some wrapped journeycakes from the pouch at her waist. She peeled one open and gave it to him.

Rush held it for a moment before he could make himself start. He bit off a small piece and chewed it. The burst of saliva hurt, and his stomach clenched in warning. He swallowed carefully, took another cautious nibble, then sat down again, off the path. "What happened to Spadefoot?" he asked. "I heard the Rainsinger cut him during a ritual." He continued to eat, slowly, letting each little bit moisten before he forced it down.

"Another horrible father," Deerchaser muttered as she toed at the dirt beside him.

Rush didn't tell her that Morning Green was not, in reality, Spadefoot's father; that secret wasn't his to share with anyone. Besides, her statement held true for Twistedtrack, too.

She said, "I heard Spadefoot's wound got infected. Injuries to the face always bleed so much, though, I would've expected it to clean itself out."

"You have much experience with injuries?"

"Boys," she told him. "They're always getting hurt."

He would have liked to find out more about the boys—Were they friends of Littlereed's? How had she collected them around herself?—but this didn't seem the time. This could be only a brief juncture for them, all too soon to end, almost before it started.

His throat dry, he swallowed carefully lest he choke on the crumbs. "Why weren't you at the inquest?" He didn't know he was going to ask the question until it was out.

"A friend of mine was supposed to come and get me."

"A man?"

She cast him an unreadable look. "No, as it happens. She must have forgotten."

"Or she was smart enough to know you shouldn't be there."

Deerchaser's face tightened, and she crossed her arms. "Make up your mind. Did you want me there or not?"

"Yes," he admitted after a pause. It didn't matter now if she knew. He reached for her hand. "Help me up."

They walked along the path awhile, hand in hand, before he knew where his feet were taking him—to the nearest canal. "I can't stay here," he told her.

"I know."

"I have to go back to Sky River."

"At least this time you told me," she said gravely. Then she smiled, and he realized she was teasing him. "But not yet," she added. "In your condition you wouldn't be able to make it from one waystation to another."

Rush found words building up inside him that he needed to get out before he left again. "All those turnings ago, the old Canalmaster . . . he said I had to go straightway. I was too—I don't know—embarrassed, I suppose, to say there was a woman more important to me than my own family."

"Was I?"

"I was stupid back then." Maybe he still was, for making such an admission: a smart man would drive her away for her own protection.

Just as he thought that, she proved it by saying "There's nothing for me here. Let me come with you."

"No." He stopped, halted her with the hand joined to hers, and turned her to face him before pulling his hand away. "It's too dangerous, being with a Watermaster. Haven't you seen that already? You said yourself the Stormbringers want us gone."

"I'm not safe from them here," she pointed out. "Morning Green will come after me."

"Your clan will protect you from him."

"Not now. Remember? I'm no longer of Cloud-Leaf Clan. After their betrayal, how could I ever trust them again?" Worry lines between her eyebrows and beside her mouth deepened, as though desperation was a familiar companion.

When she had come to his quarters and cooked supper, the lines on her face hadn't shown. For those few days, she'd seemed almost happy. Perhaps that was because of him.

He shoved away the thought, gratifying though it was. He couldn't allow her to give up everything for him. She might not value her clan now, but he was sure she would regret leaving if she made such a weighty decision right now, while still angry and hurt and physically weak.

Rush said, "If you don't think you can count on your mother's people, what about the deerfolk?"

Her shoulders sagged. "I've tried. No one will do anything. No one believes me."

Her sadness told Rush how to get her to drop this idea of going with him. He ran his tongue over his teeth and prepared himself to watch her walk away. "That night you woke me, you said you had a vision of the end of the world. Now you claim what you saw was the sun being swallowed up by darkness?"

Her eyes narrowed. "Ye-es," she agreed warily.

"But you didn't describe it to me at the time. I think what happened was, you had a dream of something bad and when it actually came to pass, you overlaid it on your dream."

"What do you mean?"

"I don't believe you, either," he lied. "We Watermasters spend our lives making things happen in the world without any help from unseen beings, whether Mother Ge or the Ta'atchul. So to me these visions and prophesies and things seem useless. Or worse. Just look at all the trouble they've brought you."

She surprised him by listening instead of turning on her heel and storming off. She cocked her head to one side, as though seeing deep into his soul. "You know how to read the flow of water, yes?" she asked. The question took him off guard.

He nodded.

"Can you explain to me, simply and clearly, how you do this? Even in a dry canal, you can tell where the water will go. Can you explain this to me so I could do the same?"

"It's more complicated than that," he replied stiffly. "Not just anyone has the skills and experience. It can't be explained."

"Isn't such experience impossible to see, to measure? I just have to accept on faith that you can do this?"

"It's not the same as visions!"

She seemed frustrated. "I know you're trying to drive me away. Would having me with you be so awful?"

He couldn't open his mouth and say yes. He tried to remember how angry and hurt he had been when he'd found out she had kept their son a secret from him.

All he could think was that he didn't have to try to tell her how it felt when everything went wrong. She already knew.

All he could feel was the earnestness of her gaze, the honesty and courage of her.

They could leave, the two of them. He would never have to worry about the Earth River canals again. He would never have to think about Starflower or Spadefoot or Twistedtrack again. And if the Dreamwalker was right, that the village would be divided—man against woman, priest against priestess, the Ta'atchul against Mother Ge? When that day came, he and Deerchaser could be far away, safe. Together.

It was a painfully appealing dream.

He shook his head. "You can't come with me. There's nothing for you at Sky River."

3

Deerchaser could tell that he had wrestled with himself and had almost given in. He did want her. But he was determined to protect her despite his own unsteadiness. She was confident now of persuading him that leaving Crookstaff Village together was the best plan. But bringing him around to her way of thinking would have to wait until they were both able to travel.

"Never mind. Come on." She took his hand again, practically the only uninjured part of him, and drew him onward.

This part of the village seemed deserted, oddly so. She wondered if everyone had retreated to their homes in confusion after the unexpected ending to Starflower's drama. It was good for her and for Rush: for once, there seemed to be no one to watch where they went.

"Where are we going?"

"Someplace safe, with water and food and herbs for the poultices you need." She didn't tell him it was her hut, because she was pretty sure he would argue: *It isn't safe. What if the farmers come back?*

She didn't look for any more trouble from them. It was their deep shame that had driven them off, not her threats. All she had done was bring them to a realization that they were in the wrong. With cooler heads, they would understand just how unforgivable their attack really was.

That those men, including at least one of her own clan, had been prepared to take actions entirely forbidden had frightened her. How close they had come to a killing madness!

Even now the memory of the incident made her shudder. A quick glance at Tumbler's cut while on her way to defend Rush had shown her how dangerous the group might be. By some great stroke of fortune, the knife had sliced only the meat of Tumbler's skinny arm, not a vein or artery. Light pressure would stop the bleeding—of that, Deerchaser was certain. The wound would start to heal quickly with the attentions of a bonemender, assuming the new Canalmaster wasn't an utter fool and would send the boy to the healers right away. If not, she expected that Tumbler's clan-grannie would see it done.

She had seen the boy's flesh wound, and despite the danger to herself, she had charged in, prepared to throw herself between Rush and the angry farmers. She hadn't felt so real, so sharp, so connected to anyone since Littlereed's death. Now that the fit of protectiveness had worn off, her knees felt weak, making it hard to walk.

But walk she did, though at such an uneven pace that the scabs on her back pulled against the surrounding skin in a rhythmless series of jolts. The discomfort as she and Rush lurched toward the canal bank reminded her of her earlier journey, when she had limped from her hut to the inquest to speak on Rush's behalf. Upon finding out he had gone already, she had thought she would have to search the village for him—or even pursue him northward on the main trail to Sky River.

Then the stouter of his two ditchrunners had come running out from a cluster of house compounds. "They have him surrounded," the frightened boy had told her. "We have to do something!"

She hadn't needed to ask who he meant. "How many?"

The boy had shaken his head. "I don't know. Six, ten, maybe? We have to get help!" He had clutched at her arm.

"Will the Watermasters come to his aid?"

"Not with Holdsbreath as Canalmaster. He hates him. But Rush needs help. And he sent me away!" The ditchrunner had looked hurt by this—though his fear must have been stronger than his desire to defend his master, or he wouldn't have left, she had thought at the time. She had sent the boy to the Watermasters' ward, just in case they would come to their senses and defend one of their own.

Upon seeing what had happened to the other ditchrunner, she might have more wisely given in to cowardice. But she hadn't even thought of her own safety. Even so, her need to protect Rush was a selfish one, she realized as she walked along, clinging to his hand. She was tired of being alone.

Hurrying to his defense had caused pain to radiate throughout her back—an ache not just physical but born of heartsickness as well. A disquieting sense of being cut loose from home and family and purpose had emboldened her. She quaked now at having dared the farmers to strike her down, but she didn't regret it. She had saved Rush. And had learned something about herself in the process.

For the first time, she had appreciated Rush's ability to handle himself in a fight, which had given her time to step in before they killed him. But now he didn't want to fight. He wanted to run.

That was what she wanted, too.

She knew herself to be unable to stand against the Rainsinger any longer. After all, what could one woman do to defeat the head of the priesthood—a man who had proven himself so cold-hearted and ambitious as to offer up the blood of his own son?

And why should she bother? she asked herself, as she and Rush unsteadily climbed the canal bank, relying on each other for balance. Once at the top, she guided him southward, toward her hut beyond the edge of the village.

As they walked along the canal path, she reminded herself that if some of the farmers had begun to turn their backs on Mother Ge, that was for the Smokemothers to deal with, not Deerchaser. After all, the high priestesses had told her so.

She didn't care whether she lived among these people anymore. They didn't feel like her people, and the village no longer felt like her home. It hadn't for a long time now.

If Rush didn't agree to take her with him, she would go on her own, she vowed. But the practical side of her pointed out that they both needed to recover first, because it was already time for a rest.

∧⌃

The next morning, Deerchaser stood before the waist-high entrance tunnel of her stick-and-mud hut and lifted her head toward the sun. She welcomed its warmth on her face. The day promised to be cool and clear, with the sky pitiless in its blueness, empty of any sign of rain.

A few spotty leaves still clung to the stonewood trees, which would in a few moons bear a pink haze of blooms on their branches. She would miss the spectacle, which always gladdened her with its beauty. And puzzled her, too. The trees were so large, but the flowers they made were the same size and nearly the same form and color as those of the tiny tepary bush.

Deerchaser had come to think there was significance in big things and little things being so much the same. She was one of the little things, had always been so. Yet for some reason Mother Ge had chosen her to foretell one of the biggest moments in the entire story of the People of Two Rivers. The Allmother had given her the dream-vision but no way to stop it—and then through a strange course of events had shielded her from seeing the sun actually vanish. Even stranger was that Morning Green was credited with bringing the sun back. Using the blood of his own son.

Deerchaser heard the crunching of feet in the dry gravel of the wash, coming from the direction of the village. Her first thought was that she had been wrong yesterday and the farmers were coming for Rush. The second was that her bow and quiver were near to hand; she could dive through the doorway and in an instant nock an arrow and let it fly. Despite a strong impulse to do just that, she remained where she was. There weren't enough footsteps for more than one or two people. And she wasn't sure she could bring herself to injure or possibly kill someone, even to protect Rush.

As quietly as possible, she closed the woven-reed door.

Rush had not done much besides eat, slake a ferocious thirst, and sleep since he had arrived. Deerchaser had been envious of his heavy breathing. Though exhausted, she hadn't managed to fall asleep. She had kept waiting for the dream of the dark-sun to return—or for Mother Ge to visit some other terrible dream-vision on her. But there had been nothing through the long night.

In the darkness, Shadowdog had come to the door and barked once, in his usual way. After she let him in, he padded over to the sleep pallet where Rush lay. He sniffed at the insensible man. then whined to be let out. She hadn't seen him since.

In the pale light of false dawn, she had thought about what she could pack on a drag, if Shadowdog could be coaxed to come with her and haul it. She had Starflower's basket and a few carry sacks. During the night she had considered what she would need for her new life with Rush. Clothes, food and water for the northward journey, tools for building and hunting and preparing meals . . . the list had grown until it seemed unmanageable.

As the footsteps came closer, she tensed. But when her visitor proved to be a woman, Deerchaser felt a little foolish. The face was familiar, recognizable for its wide, toothy smile that radiated happiness. The woman had been a Cornmaiden during those moons that Deerchaser stayed with the Smokemothers for Littlereed's birth. After a moment's thought, the name came to her.

"Redshoulders," she said with a nod, in answer to the other woman's hail.

After a few more casual words passed between them, Redshoulders told Deerchaser what she had come for: "The Truthspeaker wishes to see you."

"I was there some days ago. She didn't care to listen to what I had to say then." Deerchaser tried to keep her voice level; it wasn't Redshoulders' fault that no one in her order had paid attention to Deerchaser's warnings.

"It was awful, what happened to you."

Redshoulders' unexpected expression of sympathy threatened to undo Deerchaser. She hardened her heart against it. "Is that what the Truthspeaker wants to tell me?"

"No, that comes from me," Redshoulders admitted. "The Revered Grandmothers are disgusted by everything that's been going on, though. And I know they respect what you tried to do with the Rainsinger."

"They do, do they? How odd—since they told me to be quiet and refrain from criticizing him. And to stop claiming to have visions sent by Mother Ge."

The broad smile faded, and the Smokemother seemed a little nervous.

"Given that," Deerchaser pressed on, ignoring her visitor's discomfort, "what could the Truthspeaker possibly have to say to me?"

Lacing her fingers together, Redshoulders cleared her throat and said, "She needs your help to strip the Rainsinger of his power and cast him out friendless into the world."

The audacity of it nearly took Deerchaser's breath away. How, exactly, did the head of the priestesses think such a thing could be done, with or without her assistance?

Intrigued by the prospect of defeating Morning Green, Deerchaser knew she wouldn't refuse the summons.

Still, she hesitated. She glanced back toward the hut as she wondered whether she dared leave Rush unguarded. She could ask Redshoulders to stay with him—but he would be safer if no one knew where he was.

It occurred to her that he might recover enough to leave for Sky River before she got back. After all, he had departed Crookstaff Village before without bidding her goodbye.

A quiet, reasonable voice in her head suggested that if Morning Green was brought down, she wouldn't need to go with Rush. She could stay here in the hut she had built, and to the end of her days she could live much as she had done before her people, her clan, and her mother turned on her.

That idea didn't appeal. What she had told Rush was what she felt in her heart: she was done with this life. Regardless of whether the Smokemothers' mad plan succeeded or failed, she could always follow Rush and head northward on her own.

Redshoulders' questioning gaze nudged Deerchaser out of her thoughts. "I would be a fool to say no before learning more," she replied. After all, they couldn't force her to agree to anything.

Unlike the other Smokemothers, the Truthspeaker preferred to be outside rather than in, under the sky that Mother Ge had made rather than a roof built by the hands of men. Her face, reputed to be strikingly beautiful in her youth, still was handsome in age, set off by an intricate net of braids bound with fine cords. Her lips curved faintly as she watched Deerchaser approach.

"Revered Grandmother." Deerchaser bowed her head in respect.

"Clan-daughter. Did my messenger explain why I sent for you?"

"She did, Revered Grandmother. But I'm curious. Last time we spoke, you didn't want to hear what I had to say."

The Truthspeaker didn't lose her placid expression. "I had no indication, then, of whether you were a deceiver or a genuine servant of Mother Ge."

"You might have asked her," Deerchaser retorted. "You could have prepared people for the sun to go dark. It wouldn't have opened a gate of terror for the Rainsinger to fill with prophecy and blood-sacrifice."

The priestess's eyebrows lifted in reproof. Her tattoos showed that she had given many children to the village. "As I recall," she said, "you came to me over Morning Green's demand for deer hearts to be used in a ritual. It was not me you told of the sun being swallowed."

Deerchaser tried to remember whether that was true. She rather feared it was.

"But you are right, clan-daughter, my response proved shortsighted. It would have been better to stand with you in opposing the Rainsinger." The priestess spread her hands. "Unfortunately, I am bound by the rules of my order, as well as the traditions that constrain all of our people—even you."

Deerchaser wished Morning Green felt similarly bound by his vows.

The Truthspeaker continued, "Fortunately, the remembrancer has reminded us of a tradition we can turn to our advantage. But it relies on the wits and courage of someone outside the order who walks in the darkness with Mother Ge."

The compliment warmed Deerchaser, though she reminded herself that one shouldn't be too trusting of this priestess, who had achieved her high position by knowing exactly what to say.

With hardly a pause, the Truthspeaker continued, "You showed a stout heart in defending the Canalmaster and quick wits in driving off his attackers." She leaned forward and said, with quiet intensity, "Yes, clan-daughter, I know about that. And I vow they will be punished. All those who break from Mother Ge's law and harm another will suffer for it."

Her dark eyes caught and held Deerchaser's gaze. "For these and many more reasons, it's you we need." Her voice, rich and resonant, seemed to reach deep inside Deerchaser to wind around her heart and tug at it as she went on: "The woman who dared to stand against the Rainsinger once before. The woman who showed a willingness to lie for her man and take the punishment for it. What we wish to ask of you will be far more difficult, the risk much greater."

Unable to break free of the Truthspeaker's compelling eyes or the grip on her heart, Deerchaser fought to draw air into her lungs through a chest gone suddenly tight.

The high priestess, having baited her trap, sprung it: "Are you bold enough to bring about the Rainsinger's destruction—whatever it takes?"

Even knowing that she had been led down this path, one step after another, by a skilled speaker, Deerchaser had to struggle against the urge to agree, to simply nod her head and accept what Mother Ge's servants had in mind for her. She closed her eyes and breathed deeply before answering. "What, exactly, are you asking of me? What is this 'Whatever it takes'?"

The priestess blinked. Deerchaser felt grim pride at having taken the Truthspeaker off guard.

"A trial," the high priestess answered. "A magical trial."

It was indeed a traditional way of settling disputes between groups of people, but Deerchaser had never heard of an actual trial being conducted at Crookstaff Village, where testimony was what swung the verdict one way or another—not something so unpredictable as magic. And yet, hadn't her clan's hearing, with false testimony on all sides, failed to get at the truth? She knew there was a challenge involved in a trial, followed by a series of contests.

She frowned. "So am I to be the challenger, then? And Morning Green the one I need to face?"

The Truthspeaker settled back on her bench. "You will be challenger and combatant both, if you agree to it."

"I don't know magic!" she blurted out.

"All that you need to know, you will be able to learn. Mother Ge has given you a gift. You have not even begun to explore it."

Deerchaser opened her mouth and closed it again. She moistened her lips. *I can't!* was her first thought. Bold, courageous, quick-thinking—all those virtues seemed out of her reach at the moment. "What makes you think the Rainsinger will accept the challenge?" she asked.

"The outlander priests, of whom Morning Green is the last surviving one, had to undergo this same magical trial when they first entered the valley and promised to bring back the rains. This was how they established their power. The Rainsinger won't refuse, for to do so would make him seem weak, fearful of the Allmother's magic. Never fear; we will tell you exactly what to say to persuade him."

Never fear! Deerchaser could have laughed out loud if the Truthspeaker hadn't been completely serious in her reassurance.

"Why not one of the Smokemothers?" she asked, though what she really wanted to know was *Why me?*

"Bound by Mother Ge's rules, the Smokemothers must remain neutral." The priestess seemed distressed. "We could not violate that stricture in the days following the Long Thirst. No more can we do so now."

Deerchaser reminded herself that she had not yet committed herself. She could walk away from this mad plan . . . but the Truthspeaker was right: no one stood in a better position to undertake it than she did.

/\/\

And so it happened, after some back and forth over the details, that she found herself agreeing to work each day on learning the Smokemothers' magic until she was deemed ready—and then to challenge the Rainsinger to a trial of magic. She felt a little dazed as she quietly bade farewell to the high priestess.

On her way out of the compound, she walked past the work area where she had once sat, big with child. There, surrounded by knives and scrapers and awls and bundles of switches and strips from plants Deerchaser didn't recognize, was Starflower. The swelling of the girl's face had gone down, but bruises still marred it.

As had happened often since the clan hearing (only a few days ago, Deerchaser reminded herself, startled by the realization that her life had been overturned so quickly), she felt a mixture of pity and anger toward her abused clan-sister and wondered whether Earth Holder would be one of those punished by Mother Ge.

She walked over to say . . . something—though she didn't know what it would be.

The girl didn't lift her head to meet Deerchaser's gaze, didn't even seem to know she was there. One trembling hand reached out to the side to touch a sharp awl. Then it drew back into her lap and folded into the other one.

Unnerved, Deerchaser left the Smokemothers' compound without speaking to anyone else. She headed for her own hut and tried not to think further about the girl. Instead she concentrated on what she had agreed to do and how to explain it to Rush—assuming he was still there.

He wasn't.

She knew it as soon as she opened the door. She didn't even have to call out his name, though she swallowed the lump in her throat and did.

A worrying thought struck: what if the gang of farmers had taken him? The hut's interior was undisturbed, and the ground outside showed no sign of drag marks or a scuffle. Wherever he had gone, it was by his own will.

Her first impulse upon realizing he had left was to sink back into the resentment she had felt toward him for so long. But the next moment, she began to grasp how Rush might have felt all those turnings ago, torn between duty and a desire to be with her.

For she had no choice but to stay here in Crookstaff Village. She had committed herself to the most important venture she would ever undertake. She couldn't go after him—not until the trial was done.

/\/\

Under a pitiless clear sky, Deerchaser stood in the trade ground so close to the thunderstruck Rainsinger that she could have reached out and touched him. During the preceding days, while undergoing training at her hut by one Smokemother after another, she had prayed to Mother Ge for strength and skill, but the goddess had sent her not so much as a dream. And that had to be concealed from everyone around her.

Armed with no more than trumpery and fancy words, she was to be Mother Ge's champion against a man who had been performing ritual magic his entire life. Everyone knew, now, of her claim to have been touched by the goddess. They also knew she had been proven a liar.

She gathered her courage and repeated, "A trial by magic, Rainsinger—as prescribed by custom."

"This is an insult, not a challenge!" His normally pallid face had deepened to a red that obscured his tattoos. "You are not even a Smokemother. You are nobody!"

"I am a loyal servant of Mother Ge." Deerchaser's palms felt sweaty. Through a dry throat, she added, "If I were a Smokemother, I could not issue the challenge. According to the remembrancer, Smokemothers must refrain from choosing sides in a trial, since all are their children. Even you."

Although she delivered the words in a calm tone, inside she fought off an unexpected temptation. She was frighteningly aware of the chert knife in her belt sheath and the pulse beating in Morning Green's neck.

Her father had brought down deer by leaping onto them and severing the artery that led from heart to head. He had lost his life that way when one tore loose and trampled him. But before that happened, he had shown his young daughter how to deal death with a blade.

She wanted to press her blade deep and twist it hard. But dead, the Rainsinger would still have power; his followers would want to avenge him. Defeated, he would be vulnerable.

Still, the thought of the likely consequences was not what stayed her hand. That was the mere fact that she could imagine herself killing Morning Green—harming anyone. Who would she be, if she did such an evil thing?

She would be exactly what he had made of her, through his blooding of Spadefoot, his prophecies of hardship, his references to witchcraft, his casting of the Watermasters as enemies. He had split the people asunder. She hoped Mother Ge was strong enough to bring them back together.

With unblinking eyes as colorless as mist, he stared at her. "I serve the Ta'atchul, not your goddess."

"But they are beings of her making," she argued. "Would you dare say otherwise?"

The people around them, drawn away from the traders' stalls and blankets by the confrontation, murmured to each other. For moments that seemed to Deerchaser to last a lifetime, Morning Green held still and silent.

She wondered if he had been a witness to that trial all those turnings ago. Had he watched the Stormbringers' champion promise that the outlanders would renounce their loyalty to all other gods and swear obedience to Mother Ge? Had Morning Green made that same vow—and broken it?

Deerchaser found herself holding her breath, not wanting to disturb Morning Green's thoughts with so much as a puff of air. *Mother, let him choose right,* she prayed.

"Before agreeing to this magical combat," he said at last, "we need to determine what we Stormbringers will gain in our inevitable victory. After all, your defeat will mean that the Ta'atchul are superior to the goddess."

Many in the crowd frowned and muttered. They began to chant, only a few voices at first and then more. Deerchaser recognized the birth-blessing: "O giver of life, send now the sun to light this heart with love . . ."

The confrontation had been timed to occur on a trade day, when Morning Green would leave the temple and inspect the tools and cloth and robes on offer. If he wanted something there, he pointed at it, and it was his, without needing to give anything in return; his side of the bargain was bringing the rains during the growing season. But this past summer, the rains hadn't come. The Smokemothers were counting on the farmfolk remembering that.

The Rainsinger seemed startled as most of the onlookers raised their voices in unison. Wisely he let them finish: ". . . send now a life where the rainbow always comes." After that, the crowd quieted as though unsure of what to do next.

Contempt dripped from his voice as he asked, "How long are you prepared to wait for your goddess to send you the winter rains and the rainbows that follow?"

To pull his attention back to her, Deerchaser proceeded with the argument the Smokemothers had prepared. "The Ta'atchul are of her making just as we are. Look for their names in your own temples: Wind, Thunder, Lightning. These are what bring the rain."

His own temple, the Temple of Mist, was not included in her list—only the ones along Sky River. His scowl showed that he had noted the omission.

She continued, "All these are provided by Mother Ge for the benefit of her people. Your Ta'atchul are her gift to us, her sacred children who saved us from the Long Thirst. It is you, Morning Green, who is their enemy—not the Allmother as you have claimed. Through your prophecies and offerings of blood, you have corrupted the Ta'atchul—and your fellow Stormbringers. That is why the rains have not come."

The aged priest puffed out his chest. "Don't be foolish. I am only doing as the Ta'atchul require!"

"Prove it through this trial," she declared. "If you lose, there will be no more bloody rituals. And you must agree that the Ta'atchul, as Mother Ge's children, are less than she."

"Through the shedding of blood, I brought back the sun!"

Some approving shouts followed his claim.

Deerchaser said, "We would not discourage all those who believe in the Ta'atchul, nor those of your order who know the prayers and rituals. For there need be no conflict between the Ta'atchul and Mother Ge. If you cannot accept this, Morning Green, you must give over your power to another, end your time as Rainsinger, leave the village and never return."

"I suppose you would put Spadefoot in my place."

"That would be for the priesthood to decide."

With his color still high, he spoke to those who stood around them: "The Ta'atchul have proven their power by ending the Long Thirst and driving back the shadow from the sun. What did the goddess do?"

"She gave us life!" Deerchaser countered. That brought on a round of cheering. Once it subsided, she added, "If you're confident that you can beat me in a magical trial, you should have no hesitation over accepting this challenge."

The Rainsinger lifted his chin. "And when you lose? You have no position to give up. So you and your Watermaster lover must be banished— and with him, all of his people! Let the decent folk have their village back."

Many in Deerchaser's line of sight looked uneasy. They muttered to each other. From behind her, she heard the Truthspeaker say, "You go too far, Rainsinger! The stakes if you win cannot be banishment for so many."

"As the challenged, I am within my rights to demand what I deserve," Morning Green stated.

Again Deerchaser thought about the knife in her belt, but she didn't reach for it. Instead, she spoke words that came to her, not from the Smokemothers but—she hoped—from Mother Ge. "As the challenger, I speak only for myself. Not for the Watermasters. Not for the Wilders. Their lives are not clay in your hands or mine, to be shaped as you will. We do not ask for all the Stormbringers to be exiled," she pointed out.

The Rainsinger replied, "That is true. So what would you say, you who listen?" He swept one hand toward the crowd. "Would be enough if she and her Watermaster lover leave Crookstaff Village when she loses?"

Several people shouted "No!"

With a sly smile, Morning Green looked at Deerchaser. "You were whipped until you bled, for lying. I will have your blood again when you lose this trial."

A chill ran up Deerchaser's spine.

He went on, "Not as a punishment but as proof that the goddess, like the Ta'atchul, thirsts for blood. After all, isn't a baby brought into the world bathed in the mother's blood?"

"No," she breathed.

"Not enough to kill you," he said. "No more than you lose during your moontime. Or when you birthed your son. Just enough to offer as a prayer."

"What are you going to do with it?" she blurted.

His smile broadened. Before he could answer, a ripple started in the crowd. People moved aside as a tall man, cloaked and hooded, limped from the direction of the Masterholding. As he approached Deerchaser, he pushed back the hood, revealing a dear face mottled by yellowing bruises but looking much better than the last time she had seen it.

Turning from Morning Green, she extended her hands to Rush, glad that he was alive and even more happy that he hadn't left her alone again.

He grasped her fingers and squeezed gently, then released her. "You said you wished I could believe in what I cannot see, hear, or touch," he said under his breath. "I do. I must." He turned toward the old ballcourt and raised his voice: "I believe in Mother Ge!"

"So do I!" someone shouted back. "Yes! Yes!" others said.

He nodded in satisfaction. But not everyone agreed. Those who remained silent, including the Rainsinger, looked defiant.

Rush knelt before Deerchaser. "The Allmother will not want us blooded," he declared, loudly enough for those in the front to hear. "Yet know this. If this trial should go against you, gladly will I give up my heart's blood for your sake and walk into exile at your side."

Her heart leaped in her chest before settling back into a warm, comforting place she had not encountered in herself for a long time. Wishing she could explain that her failure was almost a certainty, she tugged him up to stand beside her. "Then it's agreed," she told Morning Green. "Exile for both of us, and a blooding if Mother Ge wills it so."

After a look around as if to judge the mood of the crowd, Morning Green agreed. "Challenge offered and accepted. Now for my terms as to the conduct of the trial. I am an old man." He shook his head as though not sure how that had come about. "No longer have I the strength of youth for such an unequal contest. I propose that someone as young as my challenger shall serve in my place."

He turned to Deerchaser, his mouth crooked into a malicious smile. "Spadefoot is who you shall face, not me. And the trial is to be held immediately!"

$\wedge\!\wedge$

The sun blazed down on Deerchaser's head as she stood in the sunken ballcourt. A few paces away was Spadefoot, feet planted well apart and hands behind his back. The set of his jaw made the lines of suffering beside his mouth all the more obvious. A reddened wound, still swollen and scabbed over, cut across his forehead at the base of the cloud-mountain tattoo. So weak and pale was he that she thought she might win the trial after all.

Above, on the bank of the oval ballcourt, sat the elders of the clans on one side, and on the other, a mixture of traders, hunters, healers, and Watermasters, along with Smokemothers, Cornmaidens, Stormbringers, and Seekers—packed closely together like kernels in an ear of corn. In the middle of the Smokemothers was the remembrancer, his blind eyes drifting disconcertingly across Deerchaser and Spadefoot.

Beside him, the Truthspeaker had gotten to her feet. The Rainsinger was seated on the remembrancer's other side. Viewed so close together, the leaders of the two orders could hardly have been more different. The priestess's skin was as dark as polished stonewood, while the priest's was as pale as frog-foam. Her hair, nearly black, was tamed into a cluster of braids, while his was white and messy, escaping the ribbons intended to hold it in a topknot. Her robes were the red-brown of blood, his the gray of rain. She was tall and straight, while he was shrunken with age.

Yet Morning Green was more to be feared. *Mother Ge,* she sent winging into the air, *your people need you desperately. I need you. Won't you come to me?*

"The remembrancer, not having the strength he once did—" began the Truthspeaker.

The old man nodded and raised his carved stick in acknowledgment.

"—has asked me to tell you why we are here and what is to happen . . ." The priestess spoke of the Long Thirst and the coming of the rain priests to the valley—although many of the elders were older than her and needed no reminder of those events. She spoke of that long-ago trial, held at a huge village along Sky River, through which the priests had become part of the People of Two Rivers.

As the Truthspeaker went on to describe how the trial would be conducted, Deerchaser noticed the onlookers starting to fidget. Even Rush, seated in a cluster of men flying the blue ribbons of the heronfolk, seemed bored, as though what happened here today didn't really matter. Deerchaser realized that the priestess's voice, loud and forced, had no power to captivate as it did when pitched more intimately.

She found herself distracted, too, wondering whether Mother Ge had left not just her but also the Truthspeaker, or perhaps had departed the valley, leaving her people behind. Could that be why the rains had not come? Could the swallowing of the sun have been a warning that the Mother-of-All-Creation would no longer take care of them?

Deerchaser swallowed hard. Could it be that Morning Green was right, that only those who turned from the goddess and worshipped the Ta'atchul would survive?

She cut a sidelong glance toward Spadefoot, beside her. He seemed intent on what the Truthspeaker was saying. Deerchaser thought he might be the only person in the ballcourt to be paying attention.

Then the priestess began the birth-blessing: "O giver of life . . ." The rest of the words drifted past, with Deerchaser only half hearing the familiar verse as she considered the unthinkable: that Mother Ge, praised as the giver of life, bringer of water, maker of wisdom, shaper of earth, enricher of spirit, contriver of dreams, and creator of beauty, might exist in the world no more.

"The trial begins," she heard the Truthspeaker say at last. "Go forth, my children. May Mother Ge smile upon you both."

As Deerchaser turned away to prepare for the first contest, Spadefoot began to speak in tones that carried without being loud. "When the fathers of my order first came here, they had been wandering, uprooted and uncertain, for much of the Long Thirst."

His voice felt like the cool caress of water on a dry throat. Deerchaser found herself unwillingly captivated.

"Their prayers to the Ta'atchul had nowhere yielded rain, and so they were cast out of one place after another. Only here, where Mother Ge holds sway, after they were tested in a trial just like this, did they find a home."

He seemed to grow larger, and his voice strengthened. "Here, where water and earth together have created life since the First Days, we Stormbringers found a home. We were accepted as one with the People of Two Rivers. Stormbringers and Smokemothers—as man and woman, priest and priestess—joined together, and that is the proper way of things. The woman who stands here as my opponent . . ."

Gesturing toward her, he said, "She has agreed to sacrifice herself for you and all those you love. No matter how this trial ends, she deserves your respect and gratitude, as does the man who will be at her side out of love. Never forget that the purpose of this trial, like the one that came before it, is to bring us all closer together, not to break us apart."

The listeners seemed struck to silence by his words, as if they turned inward to listen to their own thoughts. Deerchaser struggled to pull back from the seductive idea that the village could be a place where all were welcome. Where she could stay and live, with Rush beside her—so long as she won.

Spadefoot might actually believe that. Morning Green certainly didn't.

Neither did those farmers who had attacked Rush.

She picked up her waterskin and took a long drink. Lost in her distraction, she didn't notice the bitterness in the liquid until she had already swallowed it. Dizzyweed!

With Rush's help she had quickly gathered everything needed for the trial, but there hadn't been time to prepare a dizzyweed potion. Her gaze turned toward the Dreamwalker, seated in front of Rush: *A draught to make your spirit soar,* the Smokemother had told her a few days earlier, and she thought, *Oh, yes, that one might have dosed me.*

Although she distrusted dizzyweed prepared by someone else, it was done now. And it might help her hear Mother Ge's voice. Of course, that would only work if the Allmother actually spoke to her when appealed to.

She pulled her scrying-bowl, the rounded part of a deer's skull, from the burden basket that lay a third of the way in from the end of the ballcourt. Then she sat on the reed mat beside the basket and took up an old jar decorated with row after row of tiny waterbirds. After taking out the plug, she whispered a prayer to Mother Ge and poured the water from the jar into the scrying-bowl. She let the water settle and made herself oblivious to the sights and sounds and smells and sensations of the world around her. Then she linked her hands, bent over the container, and tried to open herself to Mother Ge, who had placed the skull in her path many turnings ago and had given her the ability to find things.

But no sign of magic came to her. She rose and patted down the back of her skirt. As her hand came around past her waist pouch, she palmed the sprout that lay within.

Stepping through the familiar Corn Dance, she sang the words that went along with it: "The Mother now draws nigh, she breathes upon the waiting seeds. The Mother now draws nigh, she spreads her cloak of green. The Mother now draws nigh, she gives us harvest out of season."

After completing the song, she walked over to the judges and showed them a small corn plant growing in the gentle curve of a potsherd. "Mother Ge says the land is not dead, merely sleeping." She stroked the thin leaves of the baby plant to show that they were pliable, not dried. "I give you life."

She heard a faint scratching and looked over to see that a few of the judges held mudballs in which were tiny spadefoot toads. She sighed and looked down at her one little green shoot, which seemed pathetic next to the young toads striving to escape captivity.

Certain that Spadefoot had won this contest, she didn't wait to see the judges cast their verdicts. Each one who thought she had the superior manifestation would toss a black-and-white kamas stick into the ballcourt; those who preferred Spadefoot's would instead throw down a green-and-blue kintsu stick. She went back to her mat and knelt there. She lowered her head, closed her eyes as though in prayer, and hoped to make a better showing in the next contest.

A protest from Morning Green caught her attention. She opened her eyes and watched him climb like a grasshopper down into the ballcourt, his robes hiking up over knobby knees.

"This is not a fair judgment," he declared.

Deerchaser looked at the ground in front of the elders: there were at least as many of the kamas sticks as there were of the kintsu. She marvelled at that.

The Rainsinger went on: "You dare to play favorites? Spadefoot's manifestation is ten times better. Everyone can see that you are biased against us."

A woman among the elders said, "For myself, I see that she brought forth a thing that will itself grow to make food."

"I also," another woman agreed, and some of the others, male and female, nodded.

Morning Green stared at them as though he could pierce them with his gaze. Then he called Spadefoot over to him and spoke quietly, their two heads close together.

One of the male elders called out, "It is not permitted to interfere with the conduct of the trial."

Turning from his son, the Rainsinger said, "Daily the Smokemothers went to her hut"—he pointed his staff toward Deerchaser—"to give her instruction before she issued her challenge. And it is me you would chastise for interference?"

"Did you not train Spadefoot in magic already?" the Truthspeaker asked with poisonous sweetness.

The male elder who had spoken up said, "Everyone be quiet. This trial is not to become an argument."

A breeze whipped up dust swirls that licked into crevices in the plastered walls and slithered over the ground. Deerchaser shivered.

Spadefoot looked up and studied the slice of sky that could be seen there. Deerchaser, following his lead, thought it had faded to a hazy blue, and she wondered if the sun would be taken from them again, perhaps this time not to return.

Then the young priest walked to the center of the ballcourt and prayed aloud to the overarching emptiness: "O wielder of justice, send now the storm to cleanse this land of corruption."

It was a prayer to Mother Ge, not to the Ta'atchul, Deerchaser realized. She heard thunder in the distance.

The people standing atop the embankment, behind the seated judges and other onlookers, craned their necks in the direction of the temple. Thin dark clouds began to sweep across the face of the sun.

A flash of light cleaved the air. A heartbeat later, thunder—much closer—crashed. Deerchaser smelled the sizzle of lightning and felt the hairs on her arms lift.

The roll of thunder continued after the spots cleared from Spadefoot's eyes. Not thunder, he realized, but blood coursing through his veins hard enough to shake his body.

He had not called down the lightning. That had been someone else: Mother Ge working through him, or perhaps the Ta'atchul. Spadefoot did not really care which. It was enough that the winter rains would soon begin.

The Rainsinger stared up at the place in the swiftly building clouds where lightning had emerged before snaking to the ground.

That made twice in less than a moon that he had been confounded, thought Spadefoot with a twinge of satisfaction; the same slackjawed astonishment had twisted Morning Green's face as darkness moved across the face of the sun during his ritual. Then the Rainsinger had snapped out of his immobility to slash a knife across Spadefoot's forehead.

Spadefoot's hand drifted up toward the still-tender line. It divided the tattoo that marked him as a full priest holding all the secrets of the Stormbringers. It had cut him free of the last bit of loyalty he felt toward Morning Green.

Unfortunately, the lightning strike jeopardized his plan to lose the trial and thereby gain his vengeance on the old priest. He glanced at Deerchaser, who gazed up at the sky from her mat. She looked utterly defeated.

Movement at the entrance to the ballcourt drew his attention. He turned his head for a better look. A veiled Cornmaiden stood on the top step. She glanced first to the left and then to the right, where the high priestesses sat. She waved to get the Truthspeaker's attention, but the priestess was oblivious. The observers seated on the bank of the ballcourt huddled together and looked in amazement at the sky.

After a moment, the Cornmaiden descended the steps and motioned Spadefoot over. He ignored her. Insistently she gestured again, then minced toward him, the short steps and the sway of her hips all he needed to identify her: Moonbright.

As she came up to him, she leaned in so that her left hand settled on his waist. "Hello, Spadefoot." Her breath felt warm on his neck.

"What are you doing here?" He eased back a step, and her hand dropped away. Up close, he could see her hurt expression through the veil.

"I brought news. For the Truthspeaker."

"Enough to interrupt the trial for?"

Moonbright shrugged. "That Starflower girl ran away."

He frowned. "She left the Smokemothers? Where did she go?" *Back to her father?*

"How should I know?"

He took her by the shoulders and shook her, not gently. "Where?" he demanded.

She lifted her chin. "She didn't say."

His hands tightened until Moonbright made a squeak of protest. "Did you at least see which way she started out?"

"East. Toward the desert." The girl's face settled into a pout.

Spadefoot looked southeast to where a column of smoke boiled upward. The same old-blood certainty he called on in dowsing told him what was burning. Only one structure out there would provide enough fuel for such a fast and hot fire. It had to be the fieldhouse where Starflower's father had carved out a farmstead from the desert.

Perhaps, he thought, he could beg the Ta'atchul to open the belly of the clouds and douse the fire with rain. No sooner had the notion come to him than a spear of pain struck at his head, along with a light so bright it would have outshone lightning. Smoke, stifling and hot, swirled in his throat. He clutched at his neck and would have cried out, but no sound came forth. He managed to fight off the piercing light and the choking smoke, which he knew did not really exist.

It's the effects of dizzyweed, he tried to convince himself as he forced his hands to his sides and willed the sensations to stop. *The dose Morning Green gave me for the trial was too strong.* But never before had he experienced anything of the sort from dizzyweed. He reeled from the stabbing agony, while the stench of burning flesh filled his nose—yet his eyes saw only the bowl-like ballcourt, whose banks curved into an ordinary sky. *Nighthawk. Was this what he had felt like at the end?*

Deerchaser rose to her feet and ran toward the Truthspeaker. "Starflower!" she cried. "Is Starflower still in your keeping?"

Spadefoot tried to say she was gone, but he could only feel . . . and knew in his bones that what he suffered was actually happening to Starflower.

"Yes, of course," the Smokemother said.

As the pain and smoke receded for him, he staggered toward the narrow steps.

Morning Green hobbled into his path and jabbed out his staff to block the way. "Where are you going?"

His throat raw, Spadefoot had to force the words out: "The lightning . . . Starflower!"

"Don't be a fool!"

Spadefoot pushed away the staff, but Morning Green still blocked him.

"You would jeopardize our destiny over a passing fancy?" the Rainsinger sneered.

Destiny. Fancy. The words scraped at a hollow place inside Spadefoot, like a tree exploded from within by a lightning strike, its innards shredded. He gestured at the spreading cloud of smoke. "The fieldhouse is burning, with people inside and you—you speak of them like they are nothing!"

Morning Green stabbed his staff toward Deerchaser, who had turned from the Smokemother and watched the confrontation between the two priests. "Leave, and you forfeit this trial to the Smokemothers. To her!" He gave the last word a bitter twist.

Deerchaser hurried toward Spadefoot. "What do you know?" She grabbed his arm.

Moonbright laid both hands on Deerchaser's and tried to pry it off. The older woman glared and shoved with her free hand, breaking Moonbright's grip and causing her to stagger. The Cornmaiden turned a wounded look on Spadefoot, but he did not come to her defense, only pulled away from the other woman.

Deerchaser urged, "We need to check. The rest of the contests can wait until we return."

Morning Green's scowl encompassed Spadefoot along with Deerchaser. "We?" he asked Spadefoot. "We? Are you taking up with these unbelievers now?"

"I'm doing what needs to be done!" Spadefoot shoved past Morning Green and scrambled out of the ballcourt.

The crowd of onlookers on the embankment separated for him. There was no thunder now, no blood moving in his veins, no brilliant light, only a deep, cold silence as of the grave.

Barely aware of the Temple of the Mist as he passed its high wall, he did not permit himself to hear anything, think anything. He simply ran onward, as fast as he could. Not feeling, not allowing his feet to waver from his chosen path.

Someone passed him with long, even strides. Spadefoot recognized Rush from behind and tried to keep up, but there was no catching the Watermaster, trained as a runner, who vanished from sight down into the old canal just upstream from the dipping-pool and clambered up the other side with hardly a break in his stride.

The climb down and back up took Spadefoot longer, and he was sorely winded by the time he gained the top of the canal bank and with his eyes traced the column of smoke down to its source.

Near it, Rush stood over a small form crumpled on the ground. As Spadefoot's quick strides carried him closer he could see it was not Starflower. There was no sign of her. But he knew where she was.

Spadefoot lurched onward, into the cloud of sparks. Yellow tongues of flame licked outward from the brush wall of the fieldhouse. The heat baked his skin and singed his hair. The smell called up a childhood memory of coming too near the blaze when one of his foster mothers was firing pots.

His steps faltered. A heavy body crashed into him. He slammed to the ground.

He could not breathe. Twisting about, struggling to get loose, he rammed an elbow into his attacker's stomach, then dragged himself onto his knees and pushed upright.

Windborne bits of thatch on his arms glowed sullenly where the fire had burned them loose. He slapped at them, scraped them off with the side of his hands. Charred sticks cracked under his stumbling feet. Only the hiss and roar of fire came to his ears—no screams or cries of distress.

As he staggered forward, the remaining section of roof fell in. A part of the wall around the door collapsed, exposing thicker branches fastened to the upright mesquite posts. The fire momentarily died back before bursting upward again.

Rush caught Spadefoot's ankle, yanked, and brought him down. With a snarl of rage, Spadefoot leapt on him. Both hands around the Watermaster's neck, he began to choke the life out of the enemy who would not let him . . . let him . . .

His hold was already beginning to slacken when Deerchaser kicked him in the side.

Spadefoot collapsed onto the blackened ground. Within the fieldhouse was only silence, except for the fire's hungry murmur. He pushed himself over to lie on his back, pressing the pain into the ground. Dazed, he stared upward.

Light rain drifted onto his face. The truth could no longer be denied—silence meant the flames were consuming no one alive. He was too late.

The fieldhouse was Starflower's funeral pyre.

"I'm sorry," he heard from Deerchaser. "So sorry."

"Not . . . your . . . fault," Rush gasped.

"She came back thinking our father would be at the trial," said a young voice, thin and desperate. "She said she needed her tools and her mother's beads. Her moontime blood was flowing. There never was a baby—it was only a lie the priestesses told her."

Spadefoot turned his head away from the funereal sky and looked at the boy, whose body it must have been that Rush had come upon. The boy trembled from his head down. His hands looked red and blistered, or perhaps it was just raindrops beading on them.

"Where's your father?" Deerchaser knelt by the boy and put an arm around him.

The boy's face was bleak. He pointed with a shaking finger. "In there. With her."

Gently Deerchaser said, "Vineslayer. That's how you're called, isn't it?"

He nodded.

Sitting up, Spadefoot felt hot and cold warring within him. Fire and rain. "You tried to save her? Is that how you burned your hands?"

The boy stared wide-eyed at Spadefoot. "She put a torch to the tool room. We saw it. Father ran back to stop her. She . . ." He gulped and fell silent.

"What happened then?" Deerchaser prompted. "Why did they go into the fieldhouse?"

"He shouted at her." The boy covered his eyes with both hands. "Bad names. Threats. 'You'll never be free of me—I'll kill you first!'"

Again Deerchaser spoke. "And then?"

The boy seemed to withdraw into himself. His voice became quieter, a hard whisper that Spadefoot had to concentrate on to hear, intermixed as it was with the patter of rain. "She *stabbed* him!" The boy jabbed a fist into his belly.

Spadefoot flinched from the suddenness of it.

"He pushed her inside. The walls were burning. I yelled, but . . ." His shoulders hunched, and he shook his head. "I heard her screaming, and they were knocking things over. Then . . ."

No one pressed the boy this time when he trailed off. He stirred and swallowed hard. Deerchaser wrapped her other arm around him and let him speak into her shoulder: "Then she stopped."

"Was that when you fastened the door?" Rush asked.

Spadefoot's gorge rose as he understood what the question meant. He had not noticed that the door was pinned from the outside.

The boy shuddered. "I heard him crawling across the floor . . . I knew it wasn't her. He killed her. He *killed* her." His sobs shook him so that Deerchaser lost her grasp and one arm fell free.

Or perhaps, Spadefoot thought, the boy's admission shocked her as much as it did him. Old stories told of fastening someone out in the summer sun or the cold of winter until they were near death, if they had been proven guilty of a heinous act. Perhaps an abuser of his own children deserved to be burned alive. But to pass such a judgment on Earth Holder without knowing that Starflower had already passed beyond all help . . .

In his memory, he clearly heard Earth Holder's threats to Starflower at the dipping-pool. Her father might very well have died rather than let her escape him, as her brother claimed. Could such a thing justify the taking of another man's life? Could anything?

Spadefoot recalled the hatred that had surged through him when Morning Green sliced him open. What might he have done, had he been capable at that moment or in the days that followed, rather than lying abed, weak and feverish?

"Hush now," Deerchaser crooned. "There's nothing you could have done. Never blame yourself for being the one who lives."

"Did the lightning strike the hut?" Rush asked.

"Lightning?" Only then did the boy seem to become aware of the raindrops. He pulled away from Deerchaser and rubbed one shaking hand over the other, then his face, leaving behind dark streaks and smudges. He stared at his hands, at the blackness on them. "I don't think so."

Spadefoot turned back toward the fieldhouse. Chased by rain, the red edge of fire retreated down the blackened walls. A few flames still crackled and heaved over unrecognizable humps within. One was a girl charred into ashes before her soul could be sung from her body. Another a man so wicked that he was killed by his own son—a terrible act that in this instance seemed fitting.

It was all so unnecessary. Spadefoot's hand knuckled grit into an already-stinging eye. He did not mind the discomfort. It was no more than he deserved. If he had not taken Starflower to the Smokemothers, if he had left her with Earth Holder, she would still be alive. She might have found a way to walk a different life-path than her father intended for her. Now that was impossible.

There was only one thing he could think to do. "Owl he flies within his gray mist." He began the death song, singing only for Starflower, not Earth Holder. As far as he was concerned, that evil man's spirit could walk these fields forever. "He bites through her flesh and her sinews. Leaving behind all the bones of her body, that which endures, Owl releases."

Deerchaser joined her voice with his. "This smoke that I see, it bears her upward in promise of new days to come. This smoke that I smell, it carries her essence in search of a new life to join. Ever and always the sun will rise, and another will bear her name . . ."

In a flash of memory, Spadefoot saw his vow-brothers around him as he and they all together sang Nighthawk's spirit to rest with this same song. He feared he might drown from sorrow before he ran out of words, but somehow he kept going.

When he and Deerchaser finished, and after a long silence, Rush asked, almost apologetically, "Do you suppose Morning Green and the Truth-speaker finished the trial?"

Spadefoot stared at Deerchaser. Her expression conveyed the same dismay he felt. In his fear for Starflower, he had forgotten the trial. Evidently Deerchaser had too.

"We have to go back," she said.

Before Spadefoot could agree, Rush asked, "What's going to become of Vineslayer?"

The three of them—Deerchaser, Rush, and Vineslayer—all looked at each other. To Spadefoot, they seemed already a family. Deerchaser and Rush had lost their son, and here was a boy not much younger than theirs would have been.

For a moment Spadefoot envied them: they would have something he never could.

The moment passed as Deerchaser said, "Cloud-Leaf Clan will take him in. He belongs with his mother's people."

The boy pushed away from her and scrambled to his feet. Spadefoot expected him to beg Rush and Deerchaser to keep him. Instead Vineslayer protested, "I don't want to be a farmer. I want to become a priest, like Morning Green!"

After the boy's declaration, the rain started to come down heavily, in great sweeps. Lightning flickered from clouds to the ground all along the eastern horizon, while in the west the sun hung low.

Spadefoot led the way back to the village as fast as he was able. He had not fully recovered from his injury and the fever that had followed, and the full-out run to the farmstead had exhausted him, leaving his knees weak and wobbly. His clothes were soaked through. So chilled was he by rain and grief that he feared he might never feel warm again.

The boy, despite losing his sister and killing his father, had no trouble keeping up. He scurried alongside and began to chatter once they passed beyond the downpour and into a light drizzle.

"I'm going to be a Seeker."

"You're too young," Spadefoot told him.

"I'm not."

"The Seekers have to go through their naming quest."

"You didn't," the boy pointed out. "You have the name your father gave you at birth. And you were younger than me when you joined the Seekers."

Yes, that was true, and he had resented it. He'd had no friends, no one his age, no one who would talk to him, until Nighthawk had come along, a mere Seeker when Spadefoot was already a full priest. A sense of loss hit him, as hard as when he saw his brother lying dead at the edge of the river.

He ignored the rest of what the boy said until he heard, "It's because my father was a witch, isn't it?"

Head spinning, Spadefoot stopped and turned his face up to the long-delayed gift from the sky. *No witch, just a bad man,* he wanted to say. *The world is full of them.*

He stood that way for a moment in the twilight that cloaked the valley. Thickening clouds covered the flashes of lightning and cracks of thunder overhead, while beyond the western mountains the setting sun lit the belly of the cloud bank with the colors of fire. Rush and Deerchaser caught up with them, and all four looked toward the west.

An idea briefly nudged at him, a way to defeat Morning Green. Before he could grasp it, the boy started yammering again, and Spadefoot's half-formed thought drifted away.

Irritated, he asked the boy, "Why do you want this? Why would you choose to bind yourself to a lifetime of service before you even know what your life could be?"

"Why wouldn't I want to serve the Rainsinger? Your father knows everything."

"He's not my father."

The boy's brows drew together. "Everyone knows . . ."

Spadefoot turned to Rush. "You know who my real father is. Tell him."

The Watermaster shook his head. "A guess, nothing more." Deerchaser stared at him.

With growing frustration, Spadefoot told the boy, "Some people believe your father is a witch. That doesn't make it so. Everyone believes Morning Green is my father. Again, that doesn't make it so."

"I don't understand," the boy wailed.

Spadefoot's forehead throbbed where he had been cut. He put a hand up to it. He waited for Deerchaser to demand the name from Rush. Surely her influence was powerful enough to make the Watermaster speak. But once again she failed to do what he expected.

"Are you all right?" Deerchaser asked him.

Her lack of curiosity made him feel more weary and discouraged than ever before. "Yes. Time to go." He motioned for the others to precede him on the path. Though it was wide enough for two to walk abreast, they all walked single file without speaking.

Their silence lasted until they arrived at the ballcourt and found it emptied of people.

"They must have postponed the trial for fear of lightning. Come to the Smokemothers with me," Spadefoot urged Deerchaser. She and Rush would not be admitted to the temple precinct but might not be safe elsewhere in the village. "We'll find out what happened while we were gone."

She gazed at him with a smile. "No, our life-paths split here. I lost the trial the moment I left the ballcourt. Maybe even earlier, when you called down the lightning. I'm no longer the Smokemothers' champion, only Deerchaser, clanless and unbound, who goes with the Watermaster away from this place." She sounded happy.

"This is what you were after, all along?" Spadefoot asked in disbelief.

"Yes. Freedom. A new life."

"Love," Rush put in. He grinned at her.

Deerchaser beamed back. "Exile," she breathed, as though it was a reward rather than a punishment. "But don't worry," she said to Spadefoot. "We'll take Vineslayer to the clan before leaving the village."

"So it's goodbye," he told Deerchaser and Rush, who stood side by side, a pair now, even if their mating had not yet been formalized with public affirmation and tattoos and a single home known as theirs. He figured they would find their own place somewhere along Sky River and never think of him or Starflower again. It shouldn't matter to him, but somehow it did.

As Spadefoot turned for the temple, the boy cried, "I don't want to go."

Spinning on his heel, Spadefoot shouted, "Just shut up and do as you're told!" His hands fisted and he kept yelling despite a sick feeling inside that told him his fit of temper was only going to make things worse. "You should be grateful you've escaped your father alive—that makes you luckier than your sister! Don't you dare throw that away!" Though certain that the boy would not listen, he finished, "Morning Green is a worse monster than you can ever imagine."

He headed for the temple to find out exactly what Morning Green had done to turn this, like everything else, to his advantage.

The slow-moving storm caught up with Spadefoot as he reached the guard tower and found that his luck had not improved; once again, Rainedge was the vow-brother stationed there. Spadefoot expected he would get thoroughly drenched before being allowed in. His fellow priest, sheltered by the brush roof, would see to that.

"You come by yourself?" Rainedge challenged.

"Who else should be here?" Spadefoot wondered if he was supposed to have Starflower with him—or Rush and Deerchaser. "The gather ground was empty. What happened?"

"The Rainsinger defeated the Smokemother, of course. Though you and the huntress both left, it made no difference, for he stepped up with true magic. Beside him, the Smokemother's efforts seemed no more than trickery."

"So he won, then?" Spadefoot's mouth pulled down. He wished he could believe that Morning Green's victory was not his fault. Yes, there was the lightning, but that would have been insufficient to cast the trial in Morning Green's direction, if Spadefoot's concern for Starflower had not driven him from the ballcourt. If Spadefoot had stayed and done what he was prepared to do, Morning Green would have been forced to acknowledge the goddess's power. Instead he had gained more of his own.

With heavy mockery Rainedge asked, "Did you imagine he needed you? Always you think you're smarter than anyone else, that you have the answer. That you're blessed by the goddess and yours is the only right way. Do you ever doubt what you believe to be so?" He broke off, then added, "I promise you, the Rainsinger will be remembered forever for what he did this day."

Spadefoot wished he could see the other's eyes, his face, to figure out why his voice sounded so strange. Or maybe that was just the drumming of rain on the tower roof. "What did he do? 'True magic,' you say."

"Above all else, he brought the rain."

"*He* did that? I told you this morning it would rain," Spadefoot reminded him. "Why not say it was Mother Ge who made it so? These are the women's rains, after all."

"'With lightning and thunder the clouds they open,'" the other quoted. He did not need to finish the familiar line: *the Ta'atchul have answered our prayers.* "Those of us who are faithful will not offer thanks to the goddess."

"Ah, but is it Morning Green or the Ta'atchul you're faithful to?"

Rainedge refused to be baited. "If you're as smart as you think, you'll mind your tongue when you next stand before him. And that will be as soon as you're done trading words with me—he ordered that you come to his workshop as soon as you get back. I guess with the old prophecy out of the way, you've become just like the rest of us."

"The old prophecy," Spadefoot repeated.

"About you saving everyone. With that done, you served your purpose. It was your blood the Rainsinger used to turn back the dark. Our brother's blood wouldn't have done after all."

Spadefoot had half his mind on what to say to Morning Green, when the last few words hit him. "What are you talking about?"

"The one who is gone—"

"Nighthawk. Use his name," Spadefoot demanded. "His spirit has been sung home. Or do you have reason to fear he'll come after you for revenge?"

"No, no. I mean, I have nothing to fear," Rainedge said hastily. "The Rainsinger told us to dose him with dizzyweed until he agreed to be the one blooded. He got away from us, that day he disappeared. Though it was odd." He sounded puzzled. "We searched the canals closely, figuring that was where his thirst would take him, and found no sign of him."

Spadefoot blinked. Did that mean Morning Green had not, after all, ordered the death of Nighthawk? And perhaps that he did not know Spadefoot was the son of another man?

For the first time, Spadefoot considered that his opposition to Morning Green might be a mistake.

He wondered how many of his vow-brothers saw him as thinking he was right all the time, smarter than everyone else, blessed by Mother Ge. He'd had a growing sense of unease about the Rainsinger and a certainty that the old priest could not be trusted with power. That there was a madness roiling Morning Green's mind. That Deerchaser's departure meant he was losing an ally. That Nighthawk had told him true in saying he was not Morning Green's son. That Rush could be trusted because Nighthawk had said so.

What if he was wrong about all of it?

He remembered standing atop the temple on a clear night not so long ago: a woman screamed, and Deerchaser left Rush's quarters. Everything that had happened since then seemed like a flash flood, tearing out head-gates and rumbling through canals and ditches, leaving nothing behind as the flood scoured everything clean.

He felt like one of those canals. Everything was gone. He had no idea who or what he was. With the rain running down his face, in the lowering darkness of the winter storm, he could have wept.

Rainedge started to speak again. "Your huntress and her Watermaster will find themselves at the hard end of a stonewood staff if they try to come back to the village. The Rainsinger posted guards at the mound."

Whatever his vow-brother intended with the warning, Spadefoot could not bring himself to care. *I don't want to go with them,* the boy had said. *She told lies about the Rainsinger. And Morning Green teaches that Watermasters can't be trusted.* What if Starflower's brother had the truth of it? "No matter." Spadefoot's lips and tongue felt numb. "They won't be back."

He started through the gate but stayed his steps when the other priest asked: "Is the girl all right?"

Spadefoot closed his eyes. "Dead. By fire." He opened them again and added, "She and her father."

"I'm sorry."

"There are worse things than being dead." Like being alive and alone.

Cold rain slashed Spadefoot's face as he hurried across the temple's central plaza. He hunched his shoulders against the slithering wetness and wished for an oiled cloak—but that would require going to his vow-brothers' sleeping quarters and opening himself to more conversations of the sort he had just endured.

Ahead, the brightness of Morning Green's open doorway glimmered, guiding his steps. He looked forward to escaping the dark of his mood and his thoughts, more even than the rain pouring down on him.

The Rainsinger would be angry, he supposed from what Rainedge had said. And with good reason, for the elder priest did not like having his plans overturned at the best of times and could not have been pleased to have to step in to end the trial. But Spadefoot was prepared to accept a well-deserved humiliation.

When only a stride separated him from the workroom, he paused and drew a deep breath. The wet-rock scent of damp plaster sank into his lungs, but it could not replace the stench of burning and death. He wondered if anything ever would. Giving a shake of his head, he went in.

He stamped his feet in the entryway to drop moisture on the reed mat placed for that purpose within the sheltering wall. As he stepped into the candle-lit room, he stroked off the water from his face and arms. He turned and started the usual obeisance to the Ta'atchul.

Before he finished, Morning Green started speaking. "The surprising thing about spadefoot toads . . ."

Spadefoot whipped around, startled by the Rainsinger's interruption of the gesture of respect.

". . . some do not die. They disappear for a time and emerge when most needed, as a sign of renewal. That is why I insisted your man's-name be Spadefoot."

Shattered mudballs and splayed-out toads covered the floor around the altar. While Spadefoot took that in, Morning Green went on: "Alas, like these withered carcasses here, you have only a brief space of time to walk—or hop—"

A joke from the Rainsinger? Spadefoot did not know how to respond to it. His face refused to smile.

". . . this earth, because you have proven yourself weak. Weak like these your namesakes, which did not revive for the trial. No more did you." The Rainsinger seemed sorrowful, perhaps even pitying, rather than angry. "I had thought you would succeed me as Rainsinger, when at last I did go."

Spadefoot said, "I know I failed you—"

The corners of Morning Green's mouth turned up. "No matter. Your weakness allows me to reveal my true nature." He straightened his shoulders, his spine, drawing himself taller so that he seemed more youthful. "Ta'atchul am I," he declared in a clear, resonant voice, "lord of the mist."

He brought one fist to his chest. "Born in the drylands, I bore the rain within me to this place, and here I remained, believing myself no more than a man. Now my eyes have been opened—" His eyes did indeed widen, and they gleamed hungrily, with the beating of his heart visible in the thready veins of his temples "—and I see what I must do."

Spadefoot listened in dawning horror. He had been wrong about Morning Green, indeed—but by underestimating the danger he posed.

"Much blood will need to be shed upon the fields to make them once again fill with life," said Morning Green with a terrible anticipation. "The Watermasters, their time is over, their sowing of fear and false hopes. The goddess too must fade as her children grow up and follow a new truth."

Morning Green came out from behind the altar, his right hand extended toward Spadefoot. In it was a black blade that reflected the flickering flames of the tallow candles. "Your blood gave power to the sun so that it threw off the evil shadowing it . . . and blazed anew. As do I, in my triumph over those who doubt me."

Spadefoot found himself unable to move. Did the Rainsinger know he had planned to lose the trial? Would Spadefoot, as a doubter, be the next to die? Or was his blood so valuable that all of it was to be drained from him now?

He braced himself for a killing blow. Instead the curved wooden haft of the knife was offered to him.

"Go forth, my son," Morning Green intoned. "As a beginning, lead the farmfolk against the Wilders. Slaughter them—man, woman, child—as vengeance for the death of Nighthawk, your vow-brother."

Shoving both hands out like an eagle-wing fan, Spadefoot refused the knife. He would go to the Wilders and warn them of Morning Green's plans, he thought numbly. But would they listen? Rush had said his father was a Wilder. Wasn't that right? Or was that Nighthawk?

Morning Green frowned and shifted the knife into his other hand, holding it as he had done right before slicing Spadefoot's forehead. "You must not refuse this! I am of the Ta'atchul, and my will shall triumph!" The Rainsinger plunged forward, perhaps a stumble on old legs: frozen there, watching time unfold, Spadefoot saw the knife pass over his own fingers toward his heart.

Just as when he had called down the lightning earlier, he felt himself being taken over by some force outside himself. He watched his hand seize the gnarled fist below the glistening black blade, turn it, and thrust it very slowly toward the man he had once called Father.

The knife ripped open the surprised old man from belly to breastbone, slicing through his skin with only a little more effort than the cotton of his tunic. Blood did not pour out but instead welled up, as the water of the dipping pool had done when Spadefoot had dug deep into the bed of the canal where his dowsing sticks had led him.

Morning Green's flesh split open like an overripe gourd. A few loops of thick, ropy intestines spilled out. He looked down and clutched at his belly, pressing his guts back in. Then his head lifted. "You cannot have killed me!"

Spadefoot stared into the Rainsinger's eyes. The pain must not have struck yet, he thought numbly; that was the only reason the old man was still standing. Spadefoot could not accept a world where Morning Green truly was one of the Ta'atchul. Mother Ge was a goddess, and her children were likewise sacred beings, but a man did not become divine. He became old and then died.

Especially with his innards falling out. Spadefoot backed up one step, then another.

Before he knew it, he was outside, with Morning Green's threats following him. "Run, yes, run, but you shall never get away! I will have you hunted down . . ."

A slight figure grabbed his shirt. For a moment he saw Starflower's face. Then he realized it was her brother, who looked at the black knife and exclaimed, "What have you done!"

The shirt tore at the shoulder and Spadefoot ducked out of it, leaving the cloth to dangle uselessly from the boy's hand. His hair spilled down over his shoulders. As he shoved it out of his eyes, he heard the boy cry out, "He's killed the Rainsinger!"

Spadefoot hesitated. The rain would drown out the boy's warning, and maybe he could be made to understand . . .

"Hei-ya! Hei-ya!" the boy shouted as he sprinted toward the gate.

In a few moments, Rain Edge would blow the ram's-horn trumpet and set up an alarm that had not been winded in Spadefoot's lifetime.

Spadefoot charged across the small plaza outside Morning Green's workroom. He leaped onto the food storage rooms and ran along their length, avoiding the roof hatches by luck more than care. Up again he jumped, this time onto the narrow corn bins that lined the old turkey pen.

Over the wall he went, so quickly that he could not hang onto the top. He plunged down two man-heights and landed heavily, jarring his knees and ankles. That put him free of the temple precinct.

Mountains rose up to the sky out there, and great rivers carved deep into the earth. Paths used by the Far-Traders led to all the corners of the world. North, south, east, west.

He did not need to head into the desert, of course. He could let himself be caught and punished for what he had done. And then what—force the village elders to decide whether his crime warranted death or only exile?

Lead the farmfolk against the Wilders, Morning Green had said. Whether they welcomed Spadefoot or drove him out, he had to warn them of Morning Green's intentions. The Rainsinger, after all, claimed to be one of the Ta'atchul, a being who could never die. *I will have you hunted . . .*

Spadefoot glanced at the knife. A man could not survive such a wound as Spadefoot had dealt. Not for long, anyway. But perhaps long enough to set some of the fiercer vow-brothers on the trail of vengeance.

And was Morning Green more than just a man? Was such a thing possible? With a trembling hand, he thrust the obsidian blade into the sash of his tunic and stood there a moment.

Then, limping a little on a tender ankle, Spadefoot crossed the chich'wipedho field and headed toward the old canal. He figured it was too dark to make directly for the Wilders' island across the unfamiliar desert, so he decided to follow the canal path—and quickly. The crossings would become increasingly risky as the heavy rain filled the canals with water.

As he went, his mind became more and more clouded with doubt. There was no point trying to explain to his vow-brothers or the people of Crookstaff Village what had happened. He was unsure, himself.

He both hoped and feared that his hand had killed the Rainsinger. Whether that would save his people or doom them, he did not know. Was he the one of prophecy after all, saving them from the bloodshed that Morning Green was about to inflict on them all? He believed so, for to think otherwise would be too terrible.

But he could not find courage enough in his heart to stay and find out.

Epilogue

Forth I go and feel
for future, for past, for what might have been
but the ribbons of green now lie empty.

—FROM THE SONG OF THE LONG THIRST

The music of drum, flute, hand rattle, and basket rasp brought Deerchaser across the desert flats to the dance. Young men moved in an outer circle, young women in an inner. They side-stepped in one direction with one partner, then spun apart like eddies in the river to pair with another.

"Why, it's the same as in the village," she observed to Rush. Her hand rested in the crook of his arm, close to his side. She liked the way that felt: comfortable, reassuring, more connected than just holding hands.

He smiled. "Did you expect something wild?"

"I suppose I did." She patted his arm with her other hand. The tattooed line of teardrops encircling her wrist matched the one on his, a visible declaration of their life-mating. She would never have believed it possible several moons ago.

Her gaze returned to the dance ground and drifted beyond, toward the mantle of spring flowers in all the colors of sunrise that covered the desert. The normalcy of the dance and the staggering beauty of this place between the rivers seemed impossible, given the grim deliberations of the River Council not far away. She shivered and tried to put that last thought out of her mind.

Standing apart and watching just as they were, a stocky, muscular young man caught her eye. "Look, it's Spadefoot!" she said. They hadn't seen him since the day of the trial—and the deaths of Starflower and

Morning Green. Nearly everyone accepted that he had killed his father, but Deerchaser knew from experience that rumors were often wrong. She didn't want to think Spadefoot capable of a cold-blooded killing.

Several youths left the dance. The drumming faltered first, then the haunting melody of the flute. As the music stopped and the circles broke apart, women sought their partners. Those left alone slowly came together in what had been the middle of the circles. All seemed purposeless, confused.

Except the deserters, who stalked toward Spadefoot. Their slow, stiff-legged movement reminded Deerchaser of the way hunters moved. She didn't realize she had taken a step forward until she felt Rush's free hand tighten on hers.

"Don't mix yourself up in this one," he warned. "He won't thank you for it—Spadefoot is a man grown and needs to win this on his own."

Rush's sister, Ripple, stood with them. Ripple, though only a little older than Spadefoot, had two children of her own and had been thinking of getting handfast with another man to try for a third. Up at Sky River, she had told Deerchaser that the uncertainty of where they would end up had changed her mind. Most of the heronfolk gathered here seemed to be in a similar condition of waiting.

"Is that really Spadefoot?" Ripple asked. "The one who killed the Rainsinger?" Her youngest, bouncing on her hip, babbled and clapped his hands. "Yes, Spadefoot!" she repeated in a high voice for her baby. Then she looked at her brother and wrinkled her nose. "I can't believe such a nice-looking fellow would do that. You know him, right, Rush?"

A big Wilder walking by stopped near their little group. Rush acknowledged him with a nod, as though he knew the man, but didn't introduce him.

"You shouldn't admit to it, not here," the Wilder told Rush.

The big man stood a little too close to Rush's sister for Deerchaser's liking, as he cast an admiring glance over the lovely young woman. "Who are you?" Deerchaser asked. "To him, I mean?"

"Nothing. Not any more."

Rush seemed surprised. "But you watched over him while he was in the village. Why draw away now?"

"The killing of the Rainsinger brought trouble on all of us."

The Wilder's condemnation irritated Deerchaser. "Are you so sure he did it? Or that it wasn't an accident?"

The big man looked down. "He won't say what happened. But that farmer boy saw 't done, an' he don't deny 't."

Deerchaser wasn't sure why she felt compelled to defend Spadefoot, who had caused so much trouble for her and Rush. But something made her argue, "We accept Mother Ge taking the lives of children in flash flood and fire. Should we also accept her sending the lightning down to punish a father who beats his children—or worse?"

The big man pressed his lips together and rocked back on his heels as he placed his hands behind him. "Yes," he admitted after a few moments.

That his reply seemed to be directed to Ripple rather than herself provoked Deerchaser even more. "Why, then, would you see Spadefoot as anything other than a knife in her hand? She used him before, after all, at the trial. He was the one who called down the lightning."

The man snapped, "He broke Mother Ge's highest law."

"Or she acted through him to destroy the Rainsinger." Deerchaser's heart began to beat harder, thudding against her ribs. The tips of her ears tingled, and her cheeks heated. She drew her hand away from Rush but then didn't know where to put it. She felt as if something precious to her was under attack.

"Even a knife is broken after its final use," the Wilder muttered.

She lost her temper then. "Are you saying Mother Ge is dead? For that is when we break someone's tools: after they pass from the world of the living." Deerchaser glanced toward Spadefoot, surrounded now by hostile youths. She pointed at the unfolding confrontation. "Should he be broken?"

She didn't have any loyalty to Spadefoot, she told herself. It was the unfairness of condemning him for something that seemed Mother Ge's doing and thus beyond any man's—or woman's—capacity to judge.

"People said . . ." She stopped because she ran out of air. She took a breath and tried again. "People said he was the one of prophecy. The one born of outlander and old blood, sent to save us all. But then Mother Ge gave me dreams of darkness and gave him the ability to wake the sun. Do you think the prophecy is over now, so it's time to cast him off like a shattered pot?"

"The outlander weren't his kin," the Wilder told her.

"So I've heard. What does it matter? The prophecy doesn't say 'a baby will be born to an outlander father.'" She heard her voice rise, but she couldn't manage to soften her tone. "Was he made only by his blood parents—or also by those who had the raising of him?" She found herself gesturing, drawing big circles in the air. "Mother Ge worked through him to bring the lightning. And also, maybe, to purify the priesthood, reconcile the Ta'atchul with Mother Ge, even undo the clans' opposition to the Watermasters. He could become a Rainsinger of one of the temples himself. He could change everything!"

Dead silence met her final words.

Ripple shot her a sympathetic glance. Quietly the young mother said, "Maybe he wanted a life-path he'd never thought could be his, free of prophecy and vows. A life-path that would take him somewhere he could be just himself."

Spadefoot glanced from one to another of the angry faces surrounding him. They blamed him for the recent attack on the Wilders' island, even though he had told them to expect it: enough time had elapsed between his warning and the attack that they had relaxed their vigilance. That was their own fault. Everything else was his.

One of the older boys, who seemed to consider himself the leader, poked a finger into Spadefoot's breastbone. "How can we trust you? You turned on the last ones what did!" Most of the others nodded.

Spadefoot tucked his thumbs into the belt of his kilt to keep from striking back. "There's no need for trust—you never have to see me again. I won't force my company on anyone. My feet itch to go." He let them think about that for a few moments. Then he added, "You may wish to stay behind and turn farmer."

"We'll hold our island!" The boy puffed up his chest. "We ain't cowards, ready to run off at the first sign of trouble."

With a sneer that was only half make-believe, half truly felt contempt, Spadefoot scoffed, "What—do you imagine the clans will let you live in peace on your little sandbank? Let you play and fish in the river and come into the village to beg food off them whenever you crave the taste of corn, beans, squash?"

"You cry peace 'cause you're still loyal to the priests," the boy shot back. "Let the old fools talk about where we oughta run to. We ain't going nowhere."

"When you feel your world getting smaller around you . . ." The bleak future came all too clearly into Spadefoot's mind, a memory of how stifled he had felt in the priesthood, set against the mix of freedom and loneliness he had experienced in his wanderings these past few moons, after being cast out from the Wilders. "When your womenfolk—assuming any stay—are unwelcome in the village, when they get assaulted by strangers . . . when your children—if you have any—get spat on and yelled at . . . will you be so eager to remain here then?"

"It won't be that way. They'll need us—"

"How are you going to make them need you again? Going forward, the priests will proclaim that anyone who doesn't get enough rain isn't faithful to the Ta'atchul."

"You can't be sure of that!"

"Who is it that calls down the rains?" Spadefoot deliberately reminded them that he was one of those who could accomplish that. "Another summer of no rain, or spotty rain, and come harvest time there'll be no crops. The farmfolk know this. They're convinced they have to keep the priests happy. Why else would they listen to the Rainsinger when he told them to attack you?"

"The Rainsinger is dead," the boy protested. "The attack came later."

"His poison isn't." Spadefoot let them consider that for a moment, then added a reminder that he had killed for their sake: "I thought silencing him would be enough. But his words live on."

"As do you—his son."

The accusation was nothing new. Usually it was not said openly but instead whispered behind his back. Hearing it outright stung more. He straightened his spine and lifted his chin. "I am heronfolk, by my true father's blood. And of The Wing, by my mother."

"What's your proof of that?" asked a scrawny youth, suspicion twisting his thin face.

"There are those who know my lineage."

The leader, as though he felt his control slipping away, blustered, "I say we fight the farmers! We take their food if we need it!"

"Who among you agree?" Spadefoot asked the others. He turned all the way around as he spoke, to look into each one's eyes so they could see his face, the pain he knew he bore on it, the still-pink scar on his forehead that told of the sacrifice he had already made on their behalf. "Who wants to turn axe and digging-stick and knife on your own people? You condemn me for doing the same, and rightly so. But I did it only the once, when I had to. You're talking of building an entire life on thievery and violence."

A fraught silence met his words. He suspected they had not thought of what they would do, just felt the unfairness of being turned out of their homes and wanted vengeance for it.

Threats had been uttered first, in most places, and then rocks thrown and women set upon and houses invaded. As the danger spread northward like wildfire in dead grass, most of the attackers had used the Rainsinger's death as their excuse. They battered down doors and tore apart huts all over the valley, claiming to be rightfully seeking vengeance on Spadefoot, killer of the Rainsinger.

In a fair world, they would have found him. But after warning the Wilders, he had gone into the desert as a self-imposed exile, a suitable punishment. Then Mother Ge had sent him to one of the outermost villages of Sky River, and there he had learned about what had happened in his absence. And that the Watermasters were gathering here.

He said, "Things will never go back to what they were." He had made the same argument to several groups of young Watermasters in the past few days. Older and wiser heads might be discussing other options, but Spadefoot did not think everyone should have to go along with whatever they decided to do. After what happened to himself and Starflower, he knew what terrible lengths people might go to, if they felt trapped into a course of action they did not want.

The face of the scrawny boy became even more pinched. "You know the canals could be saved. There ain't no reason for farmfolk and canalfolk to be at odds."

"Shut up!" one of the boys behind the scrawny boy hissed.

"What do you mean?" Spadefoot asked the scrawny boy.

He stared at the ground. "I seen priests go out at night and tear down the work we just done that day."

Spadefoot had trouble believing it. Surely his vow-brethren could have done no such thing. Or if they had, he would have known. But he never had really been considered one of them. The Rainsinger's son, he was. Not quite the same as the others. "Why didn't you tell anyone?"

The scrawny boy shrugged. "We figured going without the canals longer would show 'em how much they needed us." Some of the other boys nodded their agreement.

Though Spadefoot tried to muster outrage at the boys' silence, he had to admit it was a sensible plan. The farmers might not realize it, but the day would come when the Watermasters would be needed. The madness fostered by the Rainsinger would wear off. Perhaps then Mother Ge's people would once again be united: priest and priestess, canalfolk and farmfolk, hunter and healer and artisan.

He shook his head, more at the fantasy his mind created than at the scrawny boy. "It's gone too far for that now."

Over the scrawny boy's shoulder he saw three people he needed to see before it was too late. "Everything has changed," he told all the youths within earshot. "All you can do is make your own choice . . . and hope it's something you can live with."

Rush watched the striplings around Spadefoot peel away in ones and twos. "So they didn't come to blows after all." He felt oddly pleased by that.

The big Wilder—Rush still didn't know his name—said, "They never do. He's good at talking his way out."

Rush placed Deerchaser's hand back on his forearm in what had become their usual way of walking together. "So you still watch him."

The big man said nothing.

The music started again. Most of the youths who had confronted

Spadefoot found partners to start the dance with, and the circles began to slowly take shape.

Spadefoot started toward Rush and the others. Rush felt Deerchaser's hand tighten on his arm. As the former priest came near, Rush saw that his face looked older than his actual age, thinner and drawn. Ripple didn't seem to mind, though. She smiled at Spadefoot—rather foolishly, Rush thought.

But Spadefoot paid no attention to her. "Uncle," he said to the big Wilder, almost pleadingly.

"Uncle?" Deerchaser looked between the Wilder and Spadefoot as though seeking a family resemblance.

The big man shook his head. "Not any more." His voice fractured like ice. "And not by blood, ever." He turned his shoulder to Spadefoot.

Rush had thought Deerchaser was upset before, for the man's earlier condemnation of Nighthawk. That was nothing compared to the hot color in her face and the stony, slitted eyes she turned on the Wilder as she pulled away from Rush.

Instinctively he took a step toward her. With his own blood rising, he wanted to grab her and set her behind him. Compared to the big man, she seemed hardly more than a child, fragile and outmatched.

But her intensity gave him pause. This was the passion of a mother bear, of a goddess. He found that he couldn't interfere.

With quick steps she circled the Wilder and stood in front of him. Her fists lifted to her chest as though she would punch him in the face. "How dare you deny him!" she raged.

Instead of attacking the big man physically, though, she stuck up one finger. "He restored the sun."

The Wilder flinched and averted his head.

But she kept on. Another finger. "Called down the lightning. Called up the storm." A third finger, and a fourth. "Brought forth water so his people could drink when the canals were empty." She grabbed the big man's chin and turned his face toward herself. "He's been touched by the Allmother. You would betray him? Then you betray her!"

She let loose of the big Wilder, who jerked his head back and got a stubborn look on his face. Whatever the man might have said in return caught in his throat as Spadefoot pulled an obsidian blade from his belt pouch. Before Rush had time to do any more than draw a quick breath and step forward, Spadefoot reversed the glittering black knife and offered it to her, hilt first.

She backed away, her brow furrowed in confusion. "What am I supposed to do with this?"

"What is the punishment for taking a life?" He went down on one knee but kept his gaze on her and the knife raised in both hands.

She made no reply, just listened as he went on.

"I must leave my people forever. There will be no hearing, for I am clanless and without kin." Spadefoot glanced at the big Wilder, who didn't gainsay him. "The priests became my family when I took my vows." He extended the knife toward her. "Perhaps death rather than banishment should be my fate. It would be no more than I deserved. Yet neither Mother Ge nor the Ta'atchul took me while I was wandering in the desert. You, Deerchaser, chosen by the Allmother herself, punished because of my mistake, clan-sister to the one I let down the most . . . you shall be the one to decide whether I live or die."

She reached out and took the knife then, almost absently, as she stared down at him. "Mother Ge may have a further use for you."

"I cannot think what it would be. The prophecy is over." He sounded exhausted, defeated.

"Perhaps. But the people are divided, and desperate times are upon us. Such a one as you cannot be lost."

"I have broken my vows. I belong nowhere."

She glanced at the big Wilder, whose set shoulders made Rush think he was listening to every word. "You have kin among the heronfolk."

The big man made a noise like an injured dog.

"You! Turn around!" Deerchaser ordered him. He obeyed but wouldn't meet her eyes—or Spadefoot's. "What would it take for your people to accept him?"

When Spadefoot started to protest, Deerchaser shushed him. She repeated her question to the Wilder.

"A killer he is," the big man exclaimed, his mouth twisting as though the words pained him to say. "Oathbreaker! None dare trust him."

Deerchaser retorted, "Unless you're as wicked as the Rainsinger, you shouldn't fear Mother Ge will order him to do the same to you."

She took a step toward Rush, put her empty hand on his chest, and waved the knife at him. He didn't think she even realized it was in her other hand. "I would promise his good conduct," she said, "but I am not one of the heronfolk."

Rush realized what she was suggesting. "He still bears the marks of the priesthood," he pointed out as his mind raced. What would happen to him, not to mention Deerchaser and Ripple, if he vouched for Spadefoot and the former priest killed again? To his mind, the risk was too great. But he feared she wouldn't let this go. For whatever reason, she had become Spadefoot's protector.

Deerchaser looked down at the knife, then at Spadefoot's face. Her hands trembled. She moved toward him, bent over, and whispered something in his ear. He nodded, one short jerk of his head. His face went blank. Lowering his other knee, he sank back on his heels.

She closed her eyes briefly, as though praying. She opened them again and slowly drew the knife across his cheek, the one that bore the birthmark. Spadefoot flinched but then held himself still.

At first Rush didn't think the blade went in deeply enough to score the skin, but after a moment, a narrow band of red appeared. She made another two strokes on the same cheek, each above the other so that the welling blood from one didn't interfere with the next.

With each touch of the knife, Spadefoot winced, and Deerchaser waited for him to . . . either protest or prepare for the next cut, Rush supposed. Spadefoot bore the pain with a silent courage that reminded Rush of Deerchaser during her whipping. His face tightened until it became almost skeletal.

The first three gashes obliterated Spadefoot's lightning tattoo. She made another three lines of blood on the other cheek, through the spiral tattooed there. Her hand visibly shook as she finished with two more cuts on his forehead, one below and one above the scar left there by the Rainsinger.

She rested her free hand on his shoulder. Rush wondered whether that was to steady herself or Spadefoot. He thought it could have been either, for they both breathed hard as though they had been in a race.

Then Deerchaser squeezed gently and got Spadefoot to look up at her. "Your vows are from a former life. It's time to choose a new name for yourself. A man's name, not the one the Rainsinger gave you when you were born. With that, no one will be able to call you an oathbreaker or a killer."

The big Wilder jerked his head around. His eyes went round, whites showing around the dark centers, as though he saw something wonderful.

Spadefoot didn't hesitate. "Nighthawk," he said firmly. "I will be called Nighthawk."

Deerchaser smiled at him. She gave the knife back to him, straightened as she took her hand off his shoulder, and turned toward Rush. "Nighthawk has paid his penance in blood. Just as I did, when my kin demanded it. What say you, Rush?"

Rush knew she wouldn't actually demand that he vouch for Spadefoot—no, he reminded himself, Nighthawk. This decision had to be Rush's entirely. He glanced at his sister, who wore her sympathy for Nighthawk openly on her face. Even the big Wilder seemed concerned about the younger man, who remained on his knees as blood trickled down his face.

There were many reasons to stand up for Nighthawk, some that Deerchaser had mentioned and more besides. Mother Ge using him as a tool to destroy the Rainsinger. His skills, whether learned from the priests or given him by the goddess, at bringing rain and tracing water under the ground, at determining the movements of the sun and moon, at talking his way out of trouble, even at charming women young and old. His willingness to accept responsibility for his mistakes—and possibly wisdom enough to learn from them.

Such a man could be a good friend or a dangerous enemy.

"I will—" Rush began, ready for a reckless throw of the kintsu sticks, let them fall as they may.

A young woman carrying a bundled infant rushed forward. She dropped down in front of Nighthawk and gave a strangled laugh. "Didn't we just do this?" she scolded the startled young man. She handed her baby up to Deerchaser and began to wipe Nighthawk's face with her sash.

He grabbed her hand to stop her, but his face bore a spark of warmth and pleasure that Rush had never seen on it. "Hummingbird!" he exclaimed. "What are you doing here?"

"I followed you." She stroked his hair.

"You couldn't have. . . I've been many places since last we saw each other. And you were . . ." He took the hand she had on his head but then looked baffled, as though he couldn't figure out what to do with it. On his knees, he was at a disadvantage.

"Let's say, then, this is where I expected to find you."

"Why? I'm no Watermaster."

"It just makes sense."

"Go back where you came from," he told her, "before anyone notices."

"There's no going back," the girl said in exasperation. "Not for any of us."

Deerchaser, Ripple and her baby, and the Wilder—all stood silent, seemingly as gripped as Rush was by her fervent outpouring of speech.

"The Watermasters will never again be welcome in the Valley of Two Rivers," declared Hummingbird. "The priests and the Smokemothers, they'll never allow it. They're greedy for power, and they'll fight over it for turning after turning once the Watermasters are gone. They'll do anything to come out on top, even if it means condemning everyone else to a slow, lingering death." Her voice was low but certain. "They've already convinced the farmers they don't need the Watermasters—as well say up is down, east is west, dark is light. But that's something they all agree on, priests and priestesses, and they'll get their way."

She shook her head. "I can't watch it happen. I'm . . ." She trailed off and shrugged, then took a deep breath and swiped a hand across one eye and down her cheek. She pulled it away and looked at it as though amazed to find herself crying. "Whether you leave with the Watermasters or not, Spadefoot, wherever you go, I am going with you!"

"But you're a Cornmaiden!" He plainly saw that as an insurmountable condition.

"No more than you are a Stormbringer—now." She rose and pulled the edges of her tunic aside to fumble with the ties of her red skirt. "I can choose to be free!"

Nighthawk ordered, a little desperately, "Keep that on . . ." His voice faltered to a halt as she dropped the skirt and shrugged out of her tunic.

Her naked form, all feminine curves and mystery, was revealed there in the sunlight. Rush swallowed hard and pulled his gaze away. Others stared with plain desire. As if a wind blew the intoxicating scent of her to the musicians, the drum and flute halted once again, and then everyone seemed caught up in watching the bloody former priest and his Cornmaiden. Most of the young men—and women, too, Rush noted—appeared to be envious.

He pictured his own slender Deerchaser wearing the lushness of this girl and swallowed again as his loins tightened.

"I birthed your baby," the girl told Nighthawk. Her hands clasped her belly. "And he'll be ours! He won't be sent out for fostering to a family who may come to resent him . . . and he will never grow up without knowing the name of his father!" She was practically shouting at the end.

"Should we tell her it's no longer Spadefoot?" Rush whispered to Deerchaser. She laughed and hugged the sleeping baby close, nuzzling the infant's fuzzy head.

Hummingbird looked around. Proudly, unflinchingly bare, she challenged the many gawkers: "Have none of you ever seen a naked woman before?"

Scrambling to his feet, Nighthawk grabbed up her discarded tunic and tried to put it around her shoulders.

"You're bleeding all over it," she protested.

Deerchaser grinned. She said to Rush, "Come on." She gestured to Ripple, too, and the Wilder. She tucked the baby in the crook of one elbow and laid her other hand on Rush's arm.

"Where?" Rush asked.

"Anywhere but here." She nodded toward the young couple, curved around each other and oblivious to the rest of the world. "I don't think he's going to care overmuch about whether he's accepted as one of the heronfolk. He's no longer alone."

"You're walking away with her baby," Rush observed.

"She knows he's safe with me. When they've worked things out, they'll come find us."

⋀⋀

Glossary

atole: Beverage made from parched corn or mesquite flour

blood-bound: A man and woman sworn to each other for life, wearing matching tattoos around their wrists; they are called lifemates

blood-scrying: A way of seeing the past actions of the individual whose blood is being used in this magical rite; frequently used by *mamakai* to determine the cause of an illness

bondmating: The joining of a man and woman, either temporarily (signified by a cord braided of their commingled hair and tied around their wrists) or permanently (signified by a line tattooed around their wrists); they are called bondmates

bonemender: One of the healers, called in to tend injuries

caliche: Hard calcium-based layer in soil; often mixed with other components to make a water-resistant plaster

Canalmaster: The Watermaster in charge of a village's canal, or section of canal; he allots water to individual farmers and reconciles disputes concerning irrigation water between neighbors

chich'wipedho: Game played by two teams of women in a field in which a pair of round stones held together with leather is moved down the field with curved sticks

clanlands: Use-rights to these fields are passed down from mother to daughter, reverting to the clan when no daughter inherits; a man can continue to farm the land after the death of his bondmate

clan-sister, clan-sib, clan-grannie, clan-daughter: A person within the same clan but not in the immediate family

comal: Flat pottery griddle for cooking directly on a fire or balanced on hot rocks

Cornmaidens: Handmaids to the goddess, Mother Ge; after being impregnated by the Stormbringers in fertility rites, some few are selected to become Smokemothers, while the others return to their clans to raise their children

digging stick: Heavy farming implement made of stonewood, with a large, flat blade at one end for digging and hoeing and the other end tapering to make a hole in the soil for planting

Far-Traders: Traders who connected the People of Two Rivers with groups outside the valley, bringing in goods such as copper bells, bright feathers, and tanned hides of exotic beasts

handfast: Temporary partnership of man and woman, generally intended for the bearing of a child; marked by a braided cord worn by both around their wrists

heartfast: Long-term partnership of man and woman; marked by a matching tattoo on each lifemate's wrist

inquest: Convocation of village elders, called inquisitors, to determine the guilt or innocence of a person accused of harming another; the head inquisitor, or interrogator, asks the questions

jacal: Type of fence consisting of vertical branches or posts set close together and interwoven with branches sometimes chinked with mud

kintsu, kamas: Short sticks made from saguaro ribs divided in half lengthwise (thus rounded on one side and flat on the other) and used for gambling: *kintsu* by men and *kamas* by women

kuhtpul: Locusts whose buzzing indicates the start of the summer rains, called the male rains because of their violence and short duration

Long Thirst: The devastating drought ended by the Stormbringers

makai: A magic-wielder (pl., *mamakai*), found among the healers as well as those chosen to be priests or priestesses

mesquite: Deep-rooted tree of the legume family; leaves drop during dry spells and help fertilize the soil, while the beans can be pounded in a stone crusher to produce a protein-rich flour

moontime: The days of women's regular bleeding, tied to the cycles of the moon; women during their moontime go to the clan's hut to avoid contaminating those in their family who may need to hunt or harvest food or perform healing ceremonies

Mother Ge: The Mother-of-All-Creation; the goddess of fertility served by the Smokemothers and formerly worshiped by all the People of Two Rivers, before the coming of the Stormbringers and their introduction of a new religion

Namers: Elders who give adolescent boys and girls their adult names upon completion of a naming quest; before the quest, young people may have one or more child names, often based on appearance, and afterward, they may be better known by nicknames or may have their names changed by some significant event

obsidian: Black volcanic stone that breaks along fracture lines to create a sharp but brittle knife

ocotillo: Thorny shrub that puts out small green leaves and, at the tip, a stalk of scarlet flowers after the winter rains; when planted close together in a row, ocotillos make a fearsome living fence

old blood: Those who trace their ancestry to the days before goddess-worship; one born of the old blood and outlander was long ago prophesied as bringing times of plenty or, alternatively, as saving his people from a cataclysm

olla: Large fired-clay jar with a wide mouth and narrower neck used for storage, especially of water

orders: Cross-clan groups, especially religious based, who draw members from nearby villages because of skills rather than kinship; these include the Stormbringers and Smokemothers

outlanders: Those who are not born of the People of Two Rivers

piki bread: A thin batter of ground corn drizzled onto a hot comal to cook; typically eaten for breakfast

Rainsinger: Head of the Stormbringers for each temple

River Council: Joint council of elder Canalmasters for both Earth River and Sky River

saguaro: Giant cactus, the fruit of which ripens at the start of the summer rainy season and provides the base for a celebratory alcoholic beverage

shegoi: Desert bush whose resinous leaves are most strongly scented during the summer rains

sivanyi: Stormbringers whose magical displays make them the most feared of the priesthood

Skywatchers: Group responsible for tracking the sun through the seasons, dictating the timing of the four sun-festivals, particularly the Sun-Turning

Smokemothers: Priestesses of Mother Ge; the four high priestesses give up their names and are referred to by their position (Childcatcher, Truthspeaker, Seedkeeper, Dreamwalker)

stonewood: Desert ironwood, *Olneya tesota;* the wood of this long-lived tree is dense and hard, making it useful for digging and chopping tools

Stormbringers: The priests who worship the Ta'atchul; they came from beyond the Mountains of Sunrise and ended the Long Thirst, and now are responsible for singing the summer rains into being as well as conducting essential ceremonies during the sun-festivals

Temple of the Mist: Southernmost temple of the Stormbringers, headed by Morning Green as the Rainsinger

trial: Magical challenge to determine the rightness of the cause of one group of people as opposed to another; judged by representatives from all the clans

turning: Marker of time consisting of a full year; at the Sun-Turning ceremony of midwinter, the sun reverses its path along the horizon, and the days start to become longer

vatto: Shade structure made of branches woven into a flat roof supported by mesquite posts

Watermasters: Ancient sect that keeps the canals in operation and distributes the water among the many canal branches and feeder ditches

water-scrying: A way of seeing into the near future, generally used by hunters to locate their prey

wattle: Type of hut construction having fine branches woven horizontally through upright posts; often covered with mud

Wilders: Those of the Watermasters who choose to live in isolation along the rivers; their self-imposed exile from the rest of the People of Two Rivers makes them feared and despised

In the modern-day state of Arizona, where the Salt and Gila Rivers meet, the aptly named city of Phoenix rose from the ruins of an ancient civilization. Long before Europeans gazed on this blistering desert valley ringed with mountains, a proud people called the land home.

Here they lived, creating beautiful things, some of which linger in the painted pottery, jewelry, and rock art passed down to the valley's present inhabitants. Here they built vast systems of irrigation canals, astronomical observatories, cities containing walled family compounds and multistory buildings, and immense platform mounds that may have served as artificial mountains, bringing them closer to sacred beings in the sky who sent life-giving rains in answer to their prayers.

Then they vanished.

Perhaps they died, most of them, leaving a pitiful few to be absorbed into the O'odham people said to come from the south soon afterward. Perhaps they left, joining the better-known Hopis on the mesas to the north. Perhaps they stayed and changed with the coming of the Apaches and, soon after, Spanish explorers and missionaries, becoming a new people quite different from their ancestors. Whatever became of them, the Akimel O'odham, who inherited their land, named them the Hohokam, "those who are gone."

Was it an environmental cataclysm that brought about their downfall? Or the creeping weariness of a civilization past its time and torn apart by internal strife? Or invasion by another desperate people? Or were many factors mixed in a terrible conjunction—not of stars, but of individuals whose lives were driven by ambition, despair, envy, fear, love, courage, pride, and honor?

This is a story of what might have been.

Water—sometimes too much, usually not enough—established the timeline for this chronicle of the collapse of the Hohokam. A generation-long drought parched the American Southwest in the late thirteenth century AD, leading to unprecedented migration across the region. Once the drought was over and the summer and winter rains returned, these people did not enjoy a cultural blossoming. They merely hung on.

Then something happened. Droughts, floods, eclipses, dust storms, volcanic eruptions, tornadoes and microbursts, and other calamities had occurred before, yet the farmers of the Valley of Two Rivers had persevered. What transpired after more than a thousand years of irrigation farming to cause their disappearance?

Decades of research and personal experiences in the central Arizona desert inspired me to create a world in which the canals run like green ribbons through a quilt of adjacent fields. Villages of neat adobe compounds, punctuated with platform mounds, ballcourts, and greathouses, stand straight and tall, statements of these inventive people's mastery of their homeland.

Desert washes shine with pink-blooming ancient ironwoods, sunshine-yellow clouds of paloverde blossoms, and the graceful pink to purple flowers of desert willow. Rivers carry water through groves of cottonwoods and willows and past bosques of mesquite trees filled with an unimaginable variety of birds, singing and calling out a warning when people intrude. Beyond lie grasslands populated by rabbits and other small animals. In the desert flats, the immense saguaros tower over creosotebush, barrel cactus, flame-tipped ocotillo, and, in the spring, a multicolored carpet of flowers that pop up and as quickly fade.

This is a landscape of richness and contrast, fraught with hazards yet achingly beautiful.

In this world the worst dangers come from human actors: the ones most trusted by the People of Two Rivers.

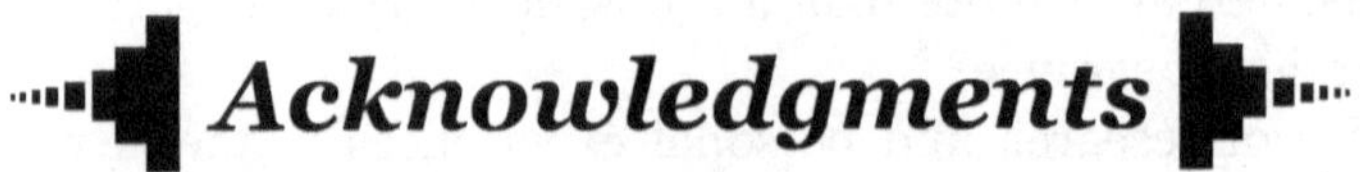

Acknowledgments

I am immensely grateful

To the beta readers who gave me valuable comments and support: Agnes Bennett, Matthew Boyington, Sara Drane, Delores Everts, Marcia Finfer, Sharon Gerkin, Angela Godel, Ann Graf, Rosalie Kerl, Dave King, Mark Murray, Mark Sliwoski, Adam Vukelich

To my writing critique partners: Alison Valentine and James Zarubin

To those without whose diligence, patience, and professionalism this book would have suffered greatly: copy editor Nancy Basmajian and designer Kara Hudgens

To all my wonderful friends, family, and additional readers of earlier drafts who have given me support and helped me get through the darkest times

And to the many archaeologists, anthropologists, ethnologists, museum curators, biologists, historians, astronomers, and others whose dedicated research and sharing of knowledge gave me a foundation for creating the world of the Watermasters

Any errors, omissions, and obscurities are entirely my responsibility (though some typos may have originated with the cat who helped me with the manuscript)

Sally Bennett Boyington fell in love with the Southwest during a childhood vacation in Flagstaff, Arizona. Later visits to ruins and a memorable kachina coloring book spurred a lifelong fascination with the history and people of the Southwest.

During the twenty years she lived in one Arizona city or another as an adult, she witnessed devastatingly beautiful sunrises and sunsets, experienced spine-tingling moments of awe, and came to understand the fragility of human existence.

Brought up in a family of readers, at four years old she demanded that her mother teach her to read. Three years later, she had a Halloween poem published in the newspaper. Creative writing had sunk its teeth into her and never quite let go.

For a long time (300 books' worth), making a living with copy editing took priority over writing, but personal changes and recent developments in the publishing industry convinced Sally to share her imagined worlds with readers. She hopes they stimulate thoughts, conversations, and a new perspective on the real world in which we live.

** (Author photo by Kara Hudgens Photography Co.)*